A FAIRFIELD ROMANCE: BOOKS 1-4

LYDIA REEVES

MAYBE IT'S YOU

CHAPTER 1

ELLEN

y mother named me Sparrow. She claims it was because the trilling birdsong was the first sound she heard after I was born, but I maintain it was more likely that she'd been high as a kite on whatever magical drugs the hospital had given her, and never stopped to consider that her choice of name might traumatize a small child. My father, however, had had the foresight to sneak an extra middle name in on my birth certificate—just in case. And so, it was this name—his mother's name, the somewhat more functional Ellen—that my friend Dana used when I called from the car to tell her I was about six hours away from her house in eastern Ohio, and probably wouldn't get there until well after midnight.

"Ellen, it's fine," she said, seeming to understand that I needed to be reassured I wasn't putting her out. "I'll just leave the door unlocked and the porch light on. Come in and make yourself at home."

It was true that I felt awful for keeping her waiting—after all, I'd originally planned to be there the day before, but time got away from me, as it so often did. But Dana just laughed and assured me that she knew me well enough to know I'd be there whenever I got there, and she was excited to see me whenever that might be. I blew her a kiss and hung up.

It had grown darker in the time I'd been on the phone, the clouds gathering to block out the setting sun, and the first drops of rain hit my windshield as my headlights lit up a sign for the next exit, just five miles down the highway. I realized I was starting to feel sleepy. After a day and a half on the road, I'd exhausted my music collection and was more than ready to get out of the car and into a real bed. I hated to make the trip last a second longer than necessary, but if I was going to make it through in one piece, I was going to need caffeine.

The exit appeared out of the darkness to my right and at the last second I took the ramp, glancing at the sign as I went. Fairfield, Indiana. Another sleepy midwestern town surrounded by cornfields.

Well, as long as they had coffee.

The rain was coming down harder as I made my way into town, searching for a gas station. It didn't take long to find one, and I pulled in, figuring I'd go ahead and fill up my dented Honda Civic while I was there. Two donuts and a steaming paper cup of coffee later and I was waiting for my car to fill up, eager to get back on the road for the last leg of the journey.

I hadn't seen Dana more than a handful of times in the nearly eight years since we'd lived together. She'd been my roommate in college, at the illustrious Savannah College of Art and Design. Or at least, she had been for the two years I'd been there, before I decided college wasn't for me and moved across the country to try to make it as a freelance illustrator in San Francisco. But we'd kept in touch over the years, as she'd graduated and found a job in Ohio, then gotten married, had a baby, and settled down.

I, on the other hand, had quickly grown tired of the bustle of San Francisco and relocated to a tiny town near the border in southern Texas. Another year and I made my way overseas to Paris, then found myself bouncing around Europe for a couple of years. Back in the States, I tried my hand as a starving artist in New York City for about six months before I was offered something I'd never considered before—a job with a fixed location. So, with much trepidation—and much encouragement from Dana (less so from my mother)—I accepted the job and moved again, this time to sunny San Diego. And there I stayed, settling in the same place for three years—the longest stretch of my life.

It probably shouldn't have been a surprise when *that* didn't work out.

So, off I went again, to Phoenix this time. Six months there before the restlessness got the better of me once again, and here I was, back to the comforting familiarity of being on the road, driving through the middle of nowhere.

The pump clicked off and I replaced the nozzle, climbing back into my car and heading back out onto the road.

To be fair, this part of the middle of nowhere was pretty cute. It was hard to see through the sheeting downpour, but the little road ran right through what appeared to be the center of town on its winding way back to the interstate. Tall brick storefronts rose on either side, bright streetlights illuminating their colored awnings. I'd already forgotten the name of the town, but it seemed warm and cheerful, even in the pouring rain.

There was no one else out on the road tonight, and I slowed for a stoplight, looking around the intersection with interest as I waited for the light to change. The coffee was kicking into my system, and I felt a little more alert as I squinted through the darkness, reading the signs on the illuminated storefronts. An antique shop on one corner, a used bookstore across the street, and what appeared to be a barber shop next door, complete with old fashioned striped pole. Amazing. I didn't know they still made towns like this.

After a long moment the light changed, and I stepped on the gas. My car, my sturdy little Honda Civic that had taken me across the country multiple times without complaint, chose that exact moment to give a mighty shudder, then stall out in the middle of the intersection.

Blinking in surprise, I turned the key in the ignition, shutting the car off, then back on. Nothing happened. The headlights flickered once, twice, then went out. I tried the key again. Nothing. In the darkness, the pouring rain was loud against the windshield as I sat, dumbfounded in my unresponsive car.

It only took a moment for my wits to kick in. Sitting in a car with no lights in the middle of an intersection during a storm at night wasn't ideal. I tried the hazard lights, and again, nothing, so I grabbed my purse from the passenger's seat and ducked out of the car.

I was drenched in a matter of seconds. The rain plastered my hair to my head and soaked through my clothes as I hurried through the rain and tried to figure out what to do.

It was late enough that all the stores were closed, and I was miles away from anyone I knew. I hugged my purse to my chest, hoping my phone was safe and dry inside. Okay. First step—get out of this downpour and figure out who to call for help.

The antique shop was closest, with an awning stretching over the sidewalk, so I headed toward the dry spot there, glancing nervously over my shoulder at my car, sitting dark and lonely in the road, just waiting for someone to come along and hit it. Everything I owned filled the trunk of that car, and I really didn't want to deal with being rear-ended right now.

Under the relative safety of the awning, I huddled against the glass storefront and dug my phone from my purse, dialing the number for roadside assistance. That was one thing I'd learned from years of traveling, and I felt a pang of gratitude toward my parents for drilling its importance into my head. I could still hear my dad's voice. *Always have someone to call for help, and always make sure someone knows where you are.*

"Hello," a friendly female voice answered.

"Hi, I'm—" I broke off when the voice continued to speak, and I chuckled when I realized it was obviously automated. "Your call is very important to us. Please hold for the next available representative."

Ten minutes later I was still on hold. I fidgeted, pulling my damp shirt away from my torso. I turned, looking worriedly back toward where my car sat, dark and lonely in the middle of the road, and only then did I notice a dim light coming from inside the bookstore across the street. The store was clearly closed for the night, but the light came from deep within the store, shining faintly through the rain-spattered windows. Was someone in there? Someone who could help me?

Praying for luck, I ended the call and dashed back out into the rain. I hurried across the street and pounded on the door.

I'd knocked three times and was on the verge of turning away when the door swung open and my breath caught in my throat.

The man in the doorway was tall—a foot taller than me easily, and I wasn't exactly short—and not just tall, but big and solid. Backlit in the entryway, all I could see was that his hair was dark and his eyes were dark, and he had a *presence* about him that for a brief moment made me forget why I was there in the first place.

It was only when he wordlessly stepped aside and gestured for me to enter that I remembered my car and managed to form a coherent thought.

"I'm sorry," I said, feeling grateful as I stepped into the dry warmth of the store. "I know you're closed, but my car broke down in the middle of the road," I gestured back with one hand, "and I don't know anyone here; I barely know where I *am*, I was just passing through—I needed coffee—and now I need to. Um. Call someone. About my car. And I'm dripping water everywhere. I'm so sorry."

The man still hadn't said a word, but the side of his mouth quirked up almost imperceptibly at my rambling. Embarrassed, I grimaced, and his grin grew slightly wider.

He watched me for a moment longer with those dark eyes, no doubt waiting to see if I would keep going if left to my own devices, before finally taking pity on me. "Wait here. I'll call a tow truck for your car, and I'll get you a towel to dry off."

His voice was low and gravelly, like he didn't use it a lot, and I could feel it reverberate all the way through me. It took a second for his words to sink in.

"I called roadside assistance," I told him, "but I was on hold forever. I can try to call again." But he was already turning away.

"It's okay. My friend Tony does auto repair just down the road; he can be here in five minutes."

I nodded, half my brain processing his words, the other half watching as he walked a few steps away into the store. His back was a broad expanse under a dark green sweater, and I was mesmerized by the way his muscles shifted beneath the fabric as he reached into his pocket and pulled out a cell phone. I let my eyes drift south, then pulled them guiltily back up when he turned, covering the phone with his free hand to ask me, "What kind of car?"

"It's a Honda. Um, Honda Civic. Red. I stopped at the light and it just died. I thought…" But he had already gone back to his phone call, though his eyes lingered on me as he spoke with his friend, humor lurking in their depths.

"Great. Thanks, man. See you soon."

He ended the call and slid his phone back into his pocket.

"Tony's on his way," he told me, and I gave him a grateful smile.

He smiled back, a full smile this time, and I felt my entire body heat. The expression looked warm and easy on his face, well-worn smile lines creasing by his eyes and mouth, suggesting that while his gravelly voice may not get a lot of use, his smile definitely did.

The space between us felt charged, like an electric wire connected us, and I opened my mouth to speak, but before I got a chance, I saw his gaze drop to my hands.

"You're shivering," he observed. "Let me get you that towel."

He was gone before I had a chance to question why he kept towels in a bookstore. He was right though. It wasn't exactly cold outside, and though it was already September, the heat of summer was still clinging fiercely. But the rain had soaked me through to my bones, and in the chill of the air-conditioner, I found myself shaking with cold.

Wrapping my arms around my sodden torso, I turned to take in the interior of the shop. It was small and cute, with a little area near the door set up as a cafe. Wrought iron chairs framed sturdy tables, and a display case showcased a variety of pastries. Beyond that, the store stretched out, tall heavy wooden shelves filled with all variety of books. A staircase to one side led up to a thin balcony that wrapped around three sides of the room, with more shelves climbing to the ceiling. At the back, a large brick wall stretched from the floor up to the two-story ceiling.

The wide expanse of brick was only broken by a single door, through which the mystery man had disappeared, but he reappeared not long after, carrying two fluffy dark blue towels. I stayed where I was, not wanting to track water through the store, and he crossed the room and handed them both to me.

"One for your hair," he said at my confused look, and I accepted them gratefully. "Thank you...?" I trailed off, and he dutifully filled in the blank.

"Sam. Like on the sign."

I hadn't noticed the name of the store as I'd run through the rain, but I saw it now, the logo emblazoned across the floor mat I was currently dripping water onto. *Sam's Books.*

I grinned and offered my hand. "It's nice to meet you, Sam. I like your bookstore. I'm Ellen."

The hand that enveloped my cold, clammy one was huge and dry and blissfully warm, and I found that I didn't want to let go. I wanted to grab his other hand too and let more of that warmth seep into me.

Fortunately, I was saved from what might have been an awkward situation by the sound of the bell over the door, and the well-timed entrance of a man wearing a rain jacket over a plaid shirt and worn jeans, a pair of jumper cables gripped in one hand.

CHAPTER 2

SAM

*T*ony's well-timed entrance broke me from the trance of the shivering stranger's sparkling eyes and the feel of her hand, small and cold in mine. When the door opened, I dropped her hand and she turned to him, smiling a wide grin that seemed to light up her whole face.

She was gorgeous, small and petite with dark hair—currently a wet curtain dripping down her back—and a smattering of freckles across the bridge of her nose. Her eyes were a bright, clear green, wide set, with droplets of water beading on her lashes. She looked like the kind of girl my brother, Jeremy, usually went for. The thought was sobering.

"That you in the middle of the road?" Tony asked, gesturing back with one thumb.

She nodded. "Tony, right? Am I glad to see you! Yes, it just died. It was fine all day; it's never given me any trouble before now." She eyed the cables he was holding. "Are you going to jump it? Will I be able to keep going?"

Tony shook his head. "I was gonna try, but the rain's getting worse out there. I think I should get it back to the garage. My place is just down the road. Are you in a hurry? I can take a look at it in the morning and figure out what's wrong."

Ellen shook her head. "It's fine. I was supposed to be in Ohio tonight, but I'm already late. I can wait an extra day."

"Where you coming from?" Tony asked.

"Arizona. Phoenix."

He gave a whistle. "Just you? That's a lot of driving."

I blinked. That *was* a lot of driving, especially for one person. I wondered what her story was.

She gave him a shrug and another smile, but this one didn't quite reach her eyes. "I'm used to it."

She had wrapped one of the towels around her shoulders, but she was still visibly shivering. I repressed the urge to reach out and pull the towel tighter around her. Her gaze turned to me and I looked away before I got lost in those bottomless eyes.

"Come on, Tony," I said quickly. "I'll help you hitch up the car. Ellen, you can stay here and dry off."

She nodded as I grabbed my own jacket from the small office behind the checkout counter. "I'm going to call around and look for a hotel room," she said, pulling out her phone. "Anywhere you recommend?"

I thought for a second. "There are a few places closer to the interstate, and a couple of bed and breakfasts here in town. Let me know where you find a room and I'll drive you over when I get back."

She nodded again, already thumbing through her phone as I headed out the door.

Outside, the rain was coming down in sheets, and we worked quickly together in silence, pulling Tony's truck into place and hooking up the little red Honda. The fresh air and cool rain on my face was invigorating, and it felt good to get out of the bookstore. I loved the place, but I'd been shelving books and balancing receipts since before the sun came up this morning and I was beginning to feel a little stir-crazy.

I only had one thing left that needed to get done today, but I'd been unintentionally putting it off all day. That was the main reason I was working so late, long after the time I'd usually have locked up the shop and gone upstairs to my little apartment above the store. Every time I walked past the boxes stacked behind the counter and thought about setting up the display, I somehow found something else that needed to be done. My latest distraction came in the intriguing form of a soaking wet stranger, and was certainly the best distraction yet, but I really did need to get that display set up. I would have to make time for it later.

Fortunately, the road was deserted, and we were able to make quick work of Ellen's car.

"Tell her I'll call in the morning once I know what's going on with the car," Tony said, practically shouting over the rain.

I nodded and waved as he ducked into the cab of the tow truck, and then he was off down the street, taillights bright in the darkness.

Ellen glanced up when the door chimed as I let myself back in, shaking water off my jacket. She was perusing the shelves toward the back of the store and I headed back to join her.

"Your store is lovely," she said, running her fingertips lightly over the row of book spines on a shelf.

"Thank you. Tony said he'll call you in the morning when he knows what the problem is. Did you find somewhere to stay?"

She shook her head and her brow creased. "Is there something going on in town this week?" she asked. "I called seven different places and they're all booked up."

I looked at her in surprise. "No, it's...oh, wait." It was

September; I tried to remember the exact date. "Yeah, it's the fall festival. I didn't think of that."

She raised a questioning eyebrow.

"We're only a few miles from the state park," I explained, "and every year they throw a big festival when the leaves start to change. It's pretty popular, and it can get pretty busy here in town."

Her eyebrows furrowed. She looked small, dwarfed by the blue towels she had wrapped around herself. "Well, one place said they had a room open tomorrow, but that doesn't help me right now. I guess if you took me over to Tony's I could sleep in my car." Her voice was doubtful and her nose wrinkled at the thought.

Sleeping in a broken-down car in the rain sounded like a terrible idea to me as well. I had a spare room. I opened my mouth to offer it to her, then hesitated. A young woman traveling alone in the rain. Car breaks down. Moody shopkeeper takes her in. It was the setup for a million true crime TV shows. And she looked smart enough to know that. Still, I wasn't sure what other options there were. "You can stay with me."

She looked confused, but at least she wasn't screaming or calling the police. She glanced around. "In...the bookstore?"

Her expression was adorably befuddled, and it startled a laugh out of me. "I live upstairs. I've got a spare room; you're welcome to it."

Her confusion cleared, but she raised an eyebrow at me. "You know we just met, right? But you expect me to stay in a stranger's home? A strange *man's* home?"

My mind started racing for a solution. Of course I didn't expect her to stay with me. She could take the apartment, and maybe I could sleep downstairs. I could put a sleeping bag in the stacks. Or I could call Tony or Geoff and crash on one of their couches. Hell, my truck was big enough—I could probably fit across the bench seat.

Before I could voice any of my thoughts, a smile broke across her face and she shrugged. "Sam, I accept your offer. Honestly, I really don't want to sleep in my car so I guess I don't have much choice. But just so you know, I've taken self defense. And you have to promise you won't murder me in my sleep."

She raised her hands in a mock-threatening pose, and I couldn't help but laugh. But instead of joining in, her expression turned to worry. "What is it?"

She looked down at her purse. "My car's gone...I wasn't even thinking. All my stuff is in there."

That's right. She'd said she was coming from Phoenix. "Are you moving?"

She nodded.

"Is there a moving truck following behind? Do you need to call someone?"

She shook her head. "No, everything I own is in the car." She laughed when she saw my expression. "I move a lot. I don't need much. But it's all still in the car. I don't even have pajamas or a toothbrush."

"I can lend you those. Or I can give you a lift to your car if there's anything you need tonight."

She paused, then shook her head. "I guess it'll be fine 'til tomorrow. This isn't the first time my plans have taken a surprise turn. Thank you, Sam." She smiled up at me, the wide, bright smile of a person that had never known a stranger. It lit her face and I felt an answering warmth deep inside me.

"Well, come on up and I'll show you around and get you settled. Then I have to come back down and finish up a display."

"Okay. Let me call my friend Dana first and let her know what's going on. She was expecting me tonight."

I gave her space while she made her call, then when she was done I led her toward the back of the store and through the door set into the brick wall. The narrow staircase there led up two flights and dead-ended at my apartment. I unlocked the door and let her go ahead of me. The space was small—two tiny bedrooms attached to a main living room and kitchen, but I'd moved in when I'd bought the building just over a year ago, and it was more than enough space for just me.

She stopped in the middle of the living room to look around and I stepped up behind her. "Wow," she tilted her head back to slant a glance at me. "It's very...manly. Just like the bookstore. I can tell you own both."

I tipped my head questioningly at her, and she gestured around with a vague motion. "All the leather, and dark wood, and exposed brick. And the books. It reminds me of, well, like pictures of an old eighteenth-century study in a manor house. All you need is a deer head mounted on the wall."

I'm not sure what expression she read on my face, but she laughed and patted my arm. "It's a good thing. I like it."

Raising an eyebrow, I stepped around her and made my way down the short hallway. "Here's the bathroom, if you'd like to take a shower to warm up while I finish up down-stairs. Next door here is the spare bedroom. There's a lock on the door."

She poked her head in and looked around while I went into my own room and grabbed some clothes from my dresser. Returning to the hallway, I handed her the pile. "You can sleep in these if you like, and leave your clothes over the curtain to dry."

She tipped her head at me and the smile she gave was more cheerful than I would have been had I been caught in the rain with a dead car and forced to spend the night with a stranger. But she just said, "Go ahead and finish up then. I'll take a shower. Thank you, Sam."

I nodded and ducked back out the door and into the hallway, then made my way downstairs and back to the bookstore, trying hard not to think about the woman in my apartment, who would soon be naked in my shower. And then wearing my clothes. She would use my shampoo; she would smell like me. And my clothes would smell like her.

She was the first woman, aside from my mother and Jeanne, who had set foot in my apartment since I'd moved in. And it wasn't that I didn't want to share the space with anyone—far from it. But after enough bad experiences with women using me to get at my brother, I'd learned to be very protective of my space.

But I liked Ellen. She was open, and friendly, and she seemed to like me. And most importantly, she seemed to have no idea who my brother was.

At the front of the store, I ducked behind the counter and lifted the first of the boxes up onto the desk, then pulled the knife from my pocket and sliced open the packing tape. Time to finally get this over with.

I ripped open the top of the box with perhaps slightly more force than was strictly necessary, and the stack of freshly printed books spilled across the counter. The face on the cover looked up at me, Caroline's face, a reproduction of the painting done in the thick, bold brushstrokes of my brother's signature style. Her bright golden hair was depicted with a thousand different hues of yellows, oranges, and browns, and her eyes were a smudge of blue oil paint in a sea of colors that made up her warm skin. I hadn't seen Caroline's real face in more than a decade, not since college, when she was full of tears and explanations and apologies, and then at a few awkward family events when she'd made an appearance on my brother's arm. And then she fell out of his life as well, replaced by him as easily as she'd replaced me. But I'd seen the painting many times since then, over the years, and while the pain was gone, the jealousy and resentment outgrown and discarded, I still never cared to see it.

The title cut a bold swath across the top of the book: *A Life of Color*—and when I flipped it over, my brother's smiling face, so like my own, looked out at me from the back cover.

Hurrying now, I stacked the books around the register before ripping open the second box and starting to build a display on the nearby table of local authors. I wondered if he would ever come see the display—he'd not been here yet, despite currently living not twenty minutes away, but seeing his own work on display had always held strong appeal for Jeremy.

I forcibly chased this thought away, and thought instead of the woman in my apartment. I'd much rather think of her —much rather *be* upstairs with her, than down here letting old bitter feelings get the best of me.

I felt a sudden rush of gratitude that she'd picked tonight of all nights to show up on my doorstep, and that I'd answered the door at her knock, even though the shop had long since closed for the night. I was glad not to be alone tonight; just to have company, someone new to talk to, was a welcome distraction.

And I liked Ellen. I'd liked her immediately, with her friendly, approachable smile and effortless charm. She seemed the kind of person who was friends with everyone, and took easily to strangers, with a kind of trust and openness that I didn't have.

I'd felt something, too, when she'd taken my hand. She had too, I thought. I'd seen the way she looked at me. I wondered, just for a minute, what it would be like to share more than just my apartment with her tonight. God knew I could use some companionship, and I wondered if she would be open to it. I thought there might be a chance.

I sliced open the last box of books and slid a few into place on a shelf before taking the rest back to the storeroom. Caroline's face stared up at me. Ellen really was just my brother's type—bold, striking features, long, thick hair, a laugh lurking in her eyes. What would my brother do in my place? I didn't even have to stop and think about it. He'd charm his way into her bed. He would paint her likeness, and sell it for more than my bookstore would make in six months. Or maybe he'd write a song about her, or she'd become a character in a book. Jeremy had many talents, after all. But either way, he'd get what he wanted, and so would she, and then she'd be on her way the next morning.

And as much as I liked Ellen, and thought maybe she liked me, and maybe there was or could be something there between us...I would never be like my brother.

CHAPTER 3

ELLEN

*S*am was an enigma. *Intensely* attractive, with that thick dark hair and brooding eyes, that square jaw and full lower lip. He didn't seem to like to speak unless he had something to say—a concept I admit I wasn't entirely familiar with—but there was so much going on behind those eyes, and in that ready smile. He was like a lake, smooth and placid on the surface, but with God-knew-what lurking in the depths.

I snorted to myself at my own foolishness and leaned back into the spray of the shower, rinsing the shampoo out of my hair. I was being an idiot, I knew it, but it was hard not to get carried away when I was standing here, in his shower, surrounded by the scent of his soap and shampoo. The man had a presence, that was for sure, and I could feel it just by existing in his space, solid and tangible all around me.

Ugh. Maybe I'd just been single too long. Hell, I'd only met the guy an hour ago.

I shut the water off and helped myself to one of the fresh towels he'd left for me on the rack. Thick and blue like the ones he'd brought down to the bookstore for me, though I could smell him on this one—laundry soap and the faintest hint of cologne. I dried myself with it then wrapped it around my hair, before retrieving his clothes from where I'd left them on the counter. I debated for half a second whether to put back on the underwear or bra I'd been wearing, but they were both still damp from the rain.

His clothes were enormous on me. I had to roll the sweatpants at both the legs and the waist, and the long-sleeve t-shirt came down nearly to my knees. But the fabric was well worn and soft against my bare skin, and I immediately didn't want to give them back.

Sam was still down in the bookstore, so I took the opportunity to wander through the tiny apartment. The space reminded me of the man—quiet and simple, but warm and solid. It was sparsely furnished, but everything there was sturdy, made of solid wood and thick leather, with soft lighting and warm plaid throws on the sofa. It was homey. I'd never lived in a place like that. Hell, aside from San Diego, I'd never stayed in one place long enough to buy real furniture or decorate. Just one of the byproducts of my nomadic childhood.

I turned when I heard the door open, and then the man himself entered, stopping when he saw me. His eyes were unreadable, but I watched as his gaze moved over me and his mouth opened slightly. I held my breath, but he just closed it again and stepped into the room, closing the door behind him and locking it.

"Did you finish your work down there?" I asked to break the silence.

He just nodded and brushed past me into the kitchen, where he filled the kettle that sat on the counter and switched it on. "Would you like anything to drink? I'm making tea. Or eat?" he added belatedly.

"I'd love some tea, thank you. And thank you for letting me stay with you. I really appreciate it."

He nodded again, and I could almost feel the warmth of his eyes on me.

I lingered in the kitchen doorway, watching as he moved easily around the small room, pulling mugs from the cabinet and teabags from the pantry. We were quiet while we waited for the water to boil, but it was an easy silence, not awkward or uncomfortable, and I was too preoccupied watching the contrast between the delicate patterned mugs and Sam's large capable hands to want to fill the space with chatter.

It wasn't until the tea was poured and steeping and we'd settled on opposite ends of the large living room sofa that I finally broke the silence.

"So, how long have you owned the bookstore?" I asked, tucking my feet underneath me and turning to face him.

"It was a year last month," he answered.

"Did you always want to own a bookstore?"

He paused for a moment, looking thoughtful. "Yeah, I guess so. It wasn't something I really planned on, but I went to school for business, and moved back here after, and when the building came up for sale, it seemed like a logical step."

I leaned toward him, wrapping my fingers around my mug. He didn't seem like the kind of guy who liked to talk about himself, and I found myself feeling unaccountably pleased that he was talking to me.

"Did you grow up around here then?"

He nodded again, his voice low. "Yeah. About twenty minutes away. My parents are still there; grandmother too. And my brother has a house up on the ridge."

I looked at him questioningly and he grimaced. "Fancy part of town."

I hadn't realized this little town was big enough to have a fancy part. I wondered what that would be like, staying in one place your whole life, with the same people and your family just a short drive away. I started to ask, but he changed the subject before I got the chance. "What about you? Are you moving for work?"

I untucked my feet and stretched them out in front of me, and noticed that his eyes followed my movements. "I guess so. I'm a freelance illustrator. Children's books, advertisements, a bit of everything. I can really work anywhere. I had a job in San Diego that kept me there, but I decided to go back to freelancing when I moved to Phoenix."

"So, what's in Ohio, then?"

I took a sip of my tea. "My friend Dana lives there. I've known her since college, and she's going to let me stay with her for a bit while I figure out where I want to go next. Maybe out east? I'm not sure yet."

He raised an eyebrow. "You're not sure yet? Where have you lived so far?"

I gave an involuntary laugh. "What, altogether? Or just since college?" I thought back, ticking each place off on my fingers. "Since college I've lived in Georgia, San Francisco, Texas, a handful of places in Europe, New York, San Diego, and Phoenix. Ohio next, I guess."

His eyes were wide, like I wasn't what he expected and he wasn't quite sure what to make of me. "And how long has it been since college, exactly?"

I counted back. "Um, eight years? Yeah, I think that's right. I didn't graduate though."

He paused, looking at me like I was a puzzle he was trying to piece together. Finally he said, "Where did you grow up then?"

I snorted before I could help myself, and his mouth quirked up on one side. "Add another fifteen or so places to that list. I don't think we stayed anywhere more than a year or two."

"Army family?" he asked, and I shook my head, taking a long drink of my tea. "No, my parents were...'free spirits.'" I made air quotes around the words. "They thought culture and worldly experience was better for a child than a stable location and standard education. I think I spent the majority of my childhood in a van. But, on the plus side, I guess I've been about everywhere and experienced a lot of things I might not have otherwise."

He was silent a long moment, his intense eyes trained on my face, and again I felt that pull between us, the urge to lean into him the way I had when he'd taken my hand in the bookstore growing even stronger. After a moment he took a drink of his tea and asked, "And was it?"

"Was it what?" I asked.

"A better experience."

I opened my mouth to answer, but nothing came out. This was usually the part of the conversation I tried to skip past quickly—how cool that must have been, where all had I been, what had I done? In my few brief stints of being enrolled in a regular public school, which never lasted long, kids had always treated me like a celebrity—so worldly, how lucky! Wish my parents were as cool as yours—and while I didn't particularly like the attention, or the uncomfortable insinuation I should be feeling grateful, and not like I was missing out, still I'd grown used to it. But never before, in all my years of meeting new people and the million questions I'd been asked, had anyone ever thought to ask what *I'd* thought of it, or even if I'd wanted it at all.

"I guess I don't know," I said finally. "I've never had anything to compare it to."

He nodded slowly, still watching me like my face was saying more than my words were, and I shifted under the weight of his gaze.

Finally, he looked away and drained the last of his tea,

sitting the mug on the coffee table. He yawned, stretching his arms up over his head, and his shirt rode up to reveal a sliver of skin above the waistband of his jeans. The skin looked soft and warm, and for a second I wanted nothing more than to reach over and hook my finger over the edge of his pants and see if I was right.

When he lowered his arms and saw me looking, I didn't flush or look away. Sam was gorgeous, all hard edges and solid muscle, and I wasn't ashamed to be caught noticing. I considered for a second, if I made a move, would he go with it? I'd felt the weight of his eyes on me all night, seen the intensity in the way he looked at me. And I supposed I might be reading into it; maybe he looked at everyone that way, but it was a chance I might be willing to take.

Honestly, it would be the perfect situation. One night with a hot guy, much needed, no strings attached. A *really* hot guy, one I was more attracted to than anyone I'd met in a long time. And here I was, by some twist of fate, stuck with him in his apartment. I'd be on my way tomorrow, free and clear with no time for feelings or regrets. Should I seize this opportunity?

Before I had a chance to say anything one way or the other, Sam rose to his feet and grabbed my empty mug from the coffee table, carrying it with his into the kitchen. "I'm going to turn in," he said over his shoulder, and just like that, the moment was lost.

I rose to my feet and followed him, tamping down my disappointment and clicking off the light in the living room as I went. It was probably better this way. I really had only just met the guy. "Guess I should as well. Hopefully I'll be on my way early tomorrow."

He rinsed out the mugs and put them in the sink, then turned off the kitchen light and escorted me down the short hallway to my room. We both paused there in the doorway, the dim light from the hall casting his features into shadow, and my heart sped up at his nearness.

"Is there anything else you need?" he asked, and the low, gravelly sound of his voice rumbled inside me like distant thunder.

You, my mind answered, and I was too afraid to open my mouth in case the word slipped out, so I just stood there, frozen in place. But he didn't turn to leave either, and after a long moment his hand came up, and snagged the edge of the towel I had completely forgotten was still wrapped around my hair. A little tug, and the fabric came loose in his hand, sending my hair falling free around my shoulders. A strand caught on my lip and he reached to gently pull it free, and when his thumb grazed my mouth I reacted without thinking, parting my lips and letting my tongue dart out to taste him. He sucked in a breath and I couldn't see his eyes, shadowed as he was in the darkness.

I don't know who moved first, but his mouth was on mine between one heartbeat and the next, and my arms came up to circle his neck even as his hands came to my waist, fingers splayed wide as he held me. His hands were huge and warm through my shirt—his shirt—and I let out an involuntary moan at the feel of them gripping my waist. When I let one of my hands drift up and tangle into his hair and give a soft tug he pushed me back, pinning me against the wall, his tongue teasing at my lips until they parted, letting him in, and everything was lost in a tempest of sensation and heat.

CHAPTER 4

SAM

I hadn't been able to stop myself. My clothes looked ridiculous but perfect on her, and I needed to see her hair out from under that towel. And then the feel of her tongue had shocked me, slick against my thumb, sending a lance of heat slicing through me, and I'd been lost.

She was perfect in my arms—soft and warm—and the sounds she made drove me wild. She wouldn't have stopped me, I knew it, could feel it in the grip of her fingers in my hair, her other hand fisted in my shirt, and the voice in my mind that cautioned that this was a bad idea was growing less and less insistent. It was only when I felt the smooth glide of her hand on my skin, under my shirt, and realized my own hand was gripping her leg where it wrapped around my waist that I realized how fast things were moving and the voice came roaring back.

This was a bad idea. I didn't do one-night stands, and I *wouldn't* be like my brother. I barely knew Ellen, but I knew enough to know she deserved better.

I broke the kiss and pulled back with a groan, resting my forehead against hers. Her breathing matched my own, and I could feel her heart pounding where her chest was pressed against mine.

"We have to stop," I whispered, tracing her jaw with my fingers to take the sting out of the words.

"We do?" she whispered back, which made me smile. I bent my head and kissed her again, long and sweet, savoring the feel of her soft lips against mine, before pulling back again to look at her. Her face was flushed, and she looked so beautiful.

"We do," I confirmed. I felt like I should apologize, but I wasn't sorry that I'd kissed her. Nothing had ever felt as good as she had in my arms. So instead I stepped back, and just said, "Sleep well." It wasn't enough, and I knew it, but if I stayed a second longer, I would give in. So, I turned away and walked to my room, closing the door firmly behind me.

* * *

That night was a testament to my self-control. I nearly left my room to seek her out a hundred times, but each time I reminded myself that as much as I hated living in my brother's shadow, the last thing I wanted was to embrace his negative traits. Still, every time I closed my eyes, I remembered the way she looked in my clothes, and felt in my arms, and sounded when I kissed her.

I was up with the sun the next morning, and out the door for a run to clear my head in the cool morning breeze before coming back to quickly shower. Ellen wasn't up yet, so I was able to mostly keep myself from thinking about how she'd been the last person in my shower before I hurried downstairs to open the bookstore.

Geoff, one of my three employees, was there when I went down, busy opening up the cafe. The bookstore did all right, situated where it was right on Main Street, but we still made more on coffee and pastries than we did on books. Geoff usually got up around four in the morning to bake, using rented space I paid for in an industrial kitchen before carting his delicacies across town, the smell of warm cinnamon and honey wafting in his wake. On weekends he was sold out by noon. I didn't deserve Geoff; he could do so much better than the corner of a tiny bookshop; maybe even open his own cafe. Fortunately for me, he hadn't realized it yet.

It was cinnamon rolls today, as big around as my hand, and I could smell them the second I walked in the door. He handed me one as I went by on my way to the office, and I slapped him on the back appreciatively, then studiously ignored his sympathetic expression as I walked by a display of my brother's books. We worked well together, Geoff and I —I never told him what to bake and gave him free reign of the cafe, paid him well, and he kept me in customers who sometimes happened to buy books.

It was a Wednesday, and therefore slow, customers coming in fits and starts to buy coffee and cinnamon rolls and peruse the shelves. I kept an eye on the back door as I went about my work, turning the register over to Rachel, my part-time employee, and accepting a donation of used books, always alert to the presence of the woman upstairs in my apartment, wondering when she would come down, and if it would be awkward when she did. Would she be angry with me? Hurt, or offended? Did it matter if she was? She was leaving today, after all.

As luck would have it, Ellen showed up just as my cell phone began to ring. The light of day had done nothing to dim the beauty I'd succumbed to the night before. Her hair, now dry and brushed to a gleaming shine, was a dark auburn color, with hints of red and coppery brown that I hadn't seen while it was wet the night before. She was wearing her own clothes again, rumpled, but dry now, and I forced myself not to be disappointed that she was no longer wearing my t-shirt and sweats. She paused in the doorway, looking around, then her eyes lit with a smile when she found me across the store, causing my stomach to lurch in a not-unpleasant way.

I smiled back, pulling my phone out of my pocket and answering it as she reached my side. "This is Sam."

A second later I handed the phone to her. "It's Tony, about your car. He forgot to get your number last night." I turned back to the books I was unboxing, giving her privacy to talk. The conversation took longer than I expected, and I tried not to listen, but her side of the conversation gave little away.

"Uh-huh."

"Of course."

A laugh. "Well, I have no idea what *that* means."

"No, I can work with that."

"Sure, no problem. Thanks Tony, I really appreciate it."

She ended the call and handed the phone back to me.

"What's the verdict?" I asked.

She grimaced. "I barely know what he was talking about. Something about alternators and spark plugs. It sounds like there are a few different problems, but he seems to think that's reasonable for a seventeen-year-old car."

I raised an eyebrow. "Your car is seventeen years old?"

"*Anyway*," she said with a glower, "he says he can fix it, but he'll have to order some parts, and it might take a few days, maybe even a week or more."

I immediately shut down the feeling of satisfied pleasure I felt at the thought of her staying for a week. "You're welcome to stay with me," I said, but she was already shaking her head.

"No, I can't impose like that. I appreciate it, really, but that one hotel had an opening. I can stay there for a few days."

I protested, but she shut me down again, with a mean-ingful look, and her voice was softer when she said, "No, really. I think...I think it might be better if I didn't stay with you."

I didn't push it. She was probably right. I didn't know if I'd hurt her feelings or not, but I did know that I'd barely made it a couple of hours before throwing myself at her, and it would be much safer with her out of easy reach. As attracted to her as I was, I wasn't looking for a one night stand, and there was no reason to get in over my head with someone who was just passing through town.

"Well, let me know when you're ready, then. I'll take you to pick up your stuff from your car and drive you to the hotel."

She nodded. "I'll just call and make sure that room is still available. And I guess I need to call Dana again, and tell her I won't be there today either."

I headed back to my office to give her space, and she found herself a corner of the cafe and settled in to make her calls.

Geoff caught me on the way back to my office. "She with you?" he asked, cocking his head in Ellen's direction. I'm sure it hadn't escaped his notice that no one ever came through that back door except me.

I shook my head. "She's just passing through. Her car broke down last night and she's staying in town for a bit while Tony fixes it."

He eyed me. "Where'd she stay last night?"

"In my spare room." I glared at him. "Nothing happened." Not exactly true, but unfortunately much truer than I would have liked.

He didn't say anything, just eyed me appraisingly before walking away. But the next time I looked, a cinnamon roll had appeared on Ellen's table next to a steaming cup of coffee. I shot Geoff a look, but he ignored me. I watched as she sent Geoff a dazzling smile, and then took a bite. When her tongue poked out to lick a drop of glaze off the corner of her mouth, I had to look away.

Stop it, Sam. She's not for you.

It wasn't much later before Ellen came to find me in my office, where I was updating inventory on the computer.

I pushed the keyboard away and sat back in my chair. "Any luck?"

"Yep, that room was still available. I booked it for a few nights. The Traveler's Inn."

I nodded. "Give me a second to finish up here and I'll take you over."

She smiled that dazzling smile again, and my heart skipped a beat. "Thank you, Sam. For everything. Oh, and hey, whoever made those cinnamon rolls...never let them go."

* * *

The Traveler's Inn was a little dingy-looking hotel, located right off the interstate on the main road that led into town. The place was noticeably run-down, with chipped paint and torn blinds in some of the windows, but the front desk staff was friendly, and the room seemed clean.

"And it's cheap enough," Ellen said as we started pulling boxes out of the back of my truck. "I didn't exactly budget for a week in a hotel."

I reminded myself that it was much better this way, but the words were out of my mouth before I could stop them. "You're welcome to stay at my place for free," I said, but she only shook her head.

"You've done more than enough for me already. I'd rather not impose." She winked. "Besides, if Geoff keeps making those cinnamon rolls, you'll see me every morning anyway."

I wanted to say that I wanted to see her every morning because that would mean she'd spent the night in my bed, but

I reminded myself again that it had been my decision to stop things last night before they progressed too far. And it was still the right thing to do, I thought. There was no reason to get attached to someone who was just passing through, and I could already tell there was no way I'd be able to avoid getting attached if I slept with her. I liked her too much already.

It hadn't taken long to pick up her belongings from the trunk of her car in Tony's lot; she really did only have a handful of boxes to her name. I couldn't imagine living like that, but she didn't seem to think anything of it.

"I tend to rent furnished apartments," she explained as we carried the boxes up the stairs. "So, I really don't need much. Some clothes, a few mementos. Honestly, most of these boxes are art supplies I couldn't bear to part with. Even though I mostly work digitally these days."

"That's right," I said, holding the door open for her at the top of the stairs. "You're an illustrator, you said. Do you have a job lined up in Ohio then?"

She shook her head. "It's just a stopgap while I figure out where I'm going to go next. I'm working on a couple of small projects right now, but I was hoping to pick up more along the way. I've got a lead on a magazine looking for an illustrator, and there's a children's book publisher I've worked with before who may have some new projects."

She passed ahead of me through the door, hitching the box higher on her hip. We arrived at the room and I watched her for a moment, her long hair cascading down her back as she balanced the box and pulled the room card from her pocket. It took two hands to unlock and open the door, so I shifted my box to one arm and lent her a hand. So close, I could smell her hair—the scent of my shampoo, and under that, the fresh clean scent of her. It probably really was best she was staying in a hotel.

"Have you always wanted to be an illustrator?" I asked as we set the boxes down in the corner and went back to my truck for another load.

She looked thoughtful. "I think so. Drawing has always been a big part of my life. When I was a kid…well, I didn't have a lot of friends, so I used art as a way to escape, and then I really fell in love with it. Plus, I wanted to find something I could do anywhere, so I wouldn't be tied to one place."

"Why didn't you have many friends?" I asked, hoping I wasn't being pushy. I just found I wanted to know everything about her. She seemed like such a happy, upbeat person, but I could swear sometimes I caught a glimpse of something sad behind that wide smile and twinkling eyes.

She shrugged. "I guess that's not exactly true. I had a lot of friends, just not that I was close with. It's hard to get too close to people when you move a lot."

I thought about that. Aside from college, I'd lived my whole life in Fairfield. The idea of having to make all new friends every year or two seemed so foreign.

"Did you like moving that much?" I asked.

"Mostly yes, I think I did. It felt very glamorous, as a kid, and a part of me liked having all these experiences that no one else my age had."

We worked together again to open the door and stacked our boxes on the growing pile in the corner before heading back down for the last few.

"What kind of experiences?"

"Oh, I don't know. I speak a few different languages—French, Spanish, a little bit of Mandarin. I've traveled through every state and every Canadian province, and I think I've been to every National Park. My mom went through a phase where she liked to take weekend classes, like workshops on different subjects? So, when I was a teenager, we tried everything. And I mean everything," she said with a laugh. "Welding, woodworking, yoga, gardening…lots of other stuff. But just in bits and pieces. I think she wanted me to try everything so I had a lot of options."

I was quiet at that, using the excuse of checking the truck to make sure we'd gotten everything and locking it up to cover my reaction. Multi-lingual, world traveler, many hobbies…yes, she was exactly the sort of woman my brother would pursue. The sort of woman who had a taste for adventure, and no use for a small-town bookstore owner who hadn't left the state more than a handful of times and had never traveled outside the country.

I held the door for her as we made our last trip up the stairs and tried not to be affected by her grateful smile. *Don't get attached,* I reminded myself. *A guy like you has nothing to offer a woman like that.*

CHAPTER 5

ELLEN

*I*t had been fun spending the morning with Sam. I'd been worried that things would be weird or strained between us, after he'd turned me down mid-kiss the night before and left me alone in his spare room wondering if I had done something to upset him. I didn't think so—he had seemed as into it as I had, but clearly something had spooked him.

But then this morning things had been as effortless and easy between us as they had yesterday evening. And yet, the sexual tension was still there, coiled tight as a wire, vibrating with energy.

I did my best to ignore it—the intensity of his looks, the way our bodies moved around each other like orbiting planets. And we'd had fun, retrieving my belongings from my poor, broken car. Even though he didn't seem to like to talk much about himself, conversation had been easy, and I'd enjoyed answering his questions and telling him more about myself.

Until now, that was. I was used to people being overly interested in my bizarre childhood experiences. Usually people found my life exciting, and wanted to hear stories, and while I certainly didn't like being fawned over, I did enjoy sharing some of my more bizarre experiences. But Sam had gone quiet, and I couldn't read his expression. Or his mind.

We made our way up the stairs with the last load of boxes and sat them down on the stack in the corner. Slightly out of breath from all the exertion, I collapsed in one of the chairs by the window, and after a second, he took the seat opposite me.

I was just beginning to wonder if I'd mis-stepped again and upset him somehow when he asked, "Do your parents still move around as much as you do?"

I tilted my head to the side, looking out the window as I pondered his question. "Well, yes and no. My dad passed away almost a decade ago, but my mom still travels. Less, though. She's been in South Korea for the past few years, teaching English as a second language, but she actually just moved back to the States about six months ago. She's living in Florida right now, I think."

"You think," he repeated, the barest smile tugging up a corner of his mouth.

I gave him a shrug and a smile. "You never know with her."

He leaned back in his chair and laced his hands behind his head. I tried not to notice the way it made his shirt stretch across his chest.

"So, tell me about one of your crazy childhood adventures," he said. And there it was. One of the standard questions everyone asked me. And yet, from him it was different somehow. His mouth was still quirked in a half-smile, but his eyes were serious, and I got the feeling he wasn't just asking because he wanted to hear a crazy story. There was something more there, something I couldn't identify.

"Well," I said, leaning forward to brace my elbows on my knees as I thought. "There was one time, when I was about nine, that I had a toothache. We were passing through somewhere in Montana, heading east, and my parents stopped and took me to a dentist. I don't know what the dentist did, exactly, but I left with half my face numb. By the time I got feeling back in my face, my tooth hurt even more. We were in South Dakota at that point, so we stopped again at a new dentist, and he went on about how the first dentist had messed it up. So, he did something else to my poor tooth and I guess he messed it up too, because we went to another dentist in Iowa and then another in Illinois. Each one thought the others had screwed up and *they* were going to fix it. I've hated dentists ever since."

Sam looked at me incredulously for a moment before bursting out laughing. "*That's* your crazy childhood adventure story?"

"What?" I said defensively, though I was laughing as well.

"I was expecting something about skydiving in the Andes or taking a train across Canada, and you tell me about your toothache."

I shrugged, but he was still smiling, and his eyes had softened a little. "So," he said, "did the dentist in Illinois get it right? Did your tooth stop hurting?"

"Well, I don't know if he got it right, but I didn't have a tooth after that, so there was nothing left to hurt." I gave him a broad smile and tapped on my fake premolar.

He continued to chuckle, a low gravelly sound that made my insides clench.

"So, tell me about yourself, then," I said, shifting in the hard hotel chair. "You mentioned you had a brother. What does he do?"

And just like that, his whole demeanor changed. His

chuckle stopped and his face closed, like a shutter had dropped behind his eyes, erasing the softness I'd seen there.

"He's an artist. And writer. Sometimes musician."

"Wow, that's a lot."

"You'd probably like him."

I tilted my head. "I'm not sure about that. Anyone with that many talents must have an ego to match."

His face softened a fraction. "Ah, he's not so bad. Besides, it sounds like you've got plenty of talent yourself."

I couldn't stop the laugh that burst out of me at that. "I said I'd tried lots of things. I certainly didn't say I was any good at them."

He smiled at that, and I pushed up to my feet, stretching my arms above my head. I didn't miss the way his eyes followed the movement, and a shiver tingled down my spine. Suddenly I became very aware of the fact that we were alone together in a hotel room, sitting next to a large, very empty, very welcoming bed.

A second later he rose as well and took a step toward the door. His face was slightly flushed, and I wondered if his train of thought had taken the same turn as mine. "I should probably get back to the bookstore," he said, and there was a faint apology in his words.

"Of course," I said. "I've kept you here long enough. Thank you again, so much, for everything you've done."

His eyes were warm again when he nodded. "Anytime." He paused awkwardly for a moment, and I acted without thinking, crossing the few steps and wrapping my arms around him. His came up around me as well. Just a hug, a thank you, between two friends. Safe and warm and comforting, and maybe going on slightly longer than necessary, but the muscles of his back were so hard beneath my hands, and I buried my face in his shoulder and breathed in his scent—and okay, maybe that wasn't *exactly* what friends did when they hugged, but his arms were tight around me and his breath warm on my hair and I couldn't seem to bring myself to let go.

He let go first, and I felt a rush of guilt. Despite our mutual attraction, he had set clear boundaries the night before, and I had just overstepped them. "I'm sorry, Sam, I—"

But I couldn't get the words out before he was kissing me, his mouth hot and firm against mine. I'd been half convinced that last night had been a fluke, that since he'd left when I'd been so turned on, I must have exaggerated the feel of his kiss in my mind. I'd been kissed plenty of times before, and there was no way he could feel as good as I remembered. But I'd been wrong. Nothing had ever felt this good. His stubble scraped against my skin as he deepened the kiss, his hands were in my hair, and my blood was molten metal as it pulsed through my veins, spreading a hot twist of pleasure deep within me.

I kissed him back for all I was worth, and I wondered what was going to happen. Would he stop this again? Would he regret it if he didn't? Would he—

A harsh jangling sound shrilled loud and we jumped apart as if doused with ice water. It took me a second to get my bearings and realize the terrible racket was coming from the phone on the bedside table. I chanced a look at Sam and found he was breathing as hard as I was, and with his hair mussed from my hands and the sleepy, hooded look in his eyes, I barely stopped myself from hurtling back into his arms. But his mouth quirked at me and he nodded his head toward the phone, and reluctantly I crossed to the table and lifted the receiver, silencing the awful ringing.

"Hello?" Good, not too breathless.

"Miss Price? This is Cynthia from the front desk. I just checked you in a few minutes ago?"

"Yes?"

"I'm very sorry to have to tell you this, but we've had a report of bedbugs from someone on your floor, and we've just verified it to be true."

"Aaah!" I leapt back away from the bed, and the phone pulled off the desk and crashed to the floor. Sam looked mildly alarmed. You might think, with my extensive traveling, that I would be used to all manner of creepy-crawlies and would not freak out at the mere thought of bedbugs not a foot away from where I was standing. You would be wrong.

"Miss Price?"

"I'm here!"

"Unfortunately, we're evacuating the floor as a precaution. If you'd like to stay, we're happy to transfer you to a new room on another floor that has been checked and cleared, or if you'd prefer not to stay I can offer you a full refund, with our sincere apologies."

My answer came out as a garbled squeak.

"I'm sorry?"

"Refund!" I cleared my throat. "I'll go with the refund. Thank you for letting me know. I'll be right down."

I hung up the phone and darted across the floor, grabbing Sam's hand along the way and hauling him behind me. "What the—"

I only answered once we were safely in the hallway.

"Bedbugs."

He started to laugh.

CHAPTER 6

SAM

The suggestion to stay at my place came from Ellen this time, and I readily agreed. I had tried to do what was best, I told myself—give her space so she wouldn't feel like she was imposing, and give myself distance from this woman who was so quickly getting under my skin—but if fate had decreed that she would stay with me, who was I to complain? Besides, you couldn't argue with bedbugs.

It was unfortunate that we had to lug all of her belongings back down the stairs and reload my truck, only to haul them all back up the stairs when we reached my apartment, but we laughed as we did so and it ended up being more fun than I'd had in a long time. We didn't talk about the kiss—either kiss—and both of us focused on the task at hand. But I could feel my defenses weakening.

I left her upstairs to unpack and get settled—and, I suspected, shower obsessively after the bedbug run-in—and I went back down to the store, checking in on my employees and making sure everything was running smoothly. She came down a while later and parked herself at the cafe with a laptop. I gave her space, focusing on my work as I left her to hers, but I couldn't help my awareness of her, the comfort of knowing she was there as I moved around the store. In the end I decided to head out early, leaving Rachel, my cashier, in charge of closing the store. My announcement was met with dumbfounded looks and inquiries as to the state of my health, since I had only ever left early once before, and that was when I'd had the flu. But I ignored Rachel's mocking hand on my forehead, and it was all worth it for the look I got when I leaned over the little table in the cafe and said, "Hungry? I thought I might make dinner."

Ellen's answering smile was wide and lovely. "Ooh, and he can cook! Or, well, I guess I don't know that yet. But I'll give you a chance." She closed the lid of her computer and leaned close, lowering her voice conspiratorially. "To be fair, I am pretty hungry; my standards might not be very high."

"Oh, good, then I don't have to try very hard," I joked, and she laughed as she followed me through the store.

Upstairs, she made herself at home in my kitchen, setting out plates and pouring wine as I threw together the one thing I knew I could handle—spaghetti and meatballs. I was no gourmet chef, but after years of living alone, I could hold my own.

Being with her was easy and we worked together well. She chattered amicably as we cooked and didn't seem put off by my quiet nature. In turn, I found her stories charming and her voice soothing. We moved around each other easily; she reached across me to grab the strainer and nudged me aside to reach the knife to chop vegetables for a salad, and it was like we'd been living together for years.

When dinner was ready, we sat together at my tiny dining room table and ate together in comfortable silence.

"This is delicious," she said after a while, and I nodded my thanks, trying not to lean across the table and wipe a speck of sauce from her lip. Finally, we finished, and I sat back, taking a long sip from my wine glass.

"So," she started. "I already know what you're going to say to this, but I'd really like to pay you for letting me stay with you."

"That's not necessary."

"I would be paying to stay at a hotel, and you've gone out of your way already."

"You're not costing me anything," I protested. "The room is just sitting there."

"You cooked for me," she pointed out. "And I took you away from your work today to help me move."

"I won't take your money," I said firmly.

She leaned back in her chair and looked at me shrewdly. "I thought you might say that. So, I was thinking…"

I raised an eyebrow.

"Would you be interested in a trade?"

I took another drink of wine and narrowed my eyes. "What did you have in mind?"

"Well, you have that huge blank brick wall in the store. It's a focal point, this huge empty wall that dominates one whole side of the space. It's the first thing you see when you enter the store, and it's just…empty. Even the second floor balcony doesn't extend that far."

I raised an eyebrow. "Go on."

She eyed me, clearly uncertain as to how I was going to react, but she pushed on regardless. "Well…what would you think about a mural that covers the wall?"

I blinked and leaned back in my chair, trying to picture it. "That's an interesting idea." It *was* an interesting idea. It would be a huge feature that customers would see the second they entered the store, something completely unique. It would also give my mother fits that it had been painted by someone other than my brother. "What did you have in mind?"

"Oh, I...well, I hadn't thought that far yet." She blew out a breath. "I wasn't sure you'd go for it. It would change the whole feel of your store. But if you would really consider it..." She started to look excited. "Well, I'm sure we could come up with something amazing. Plus, then I'd feel like I'd repaid your kindness in letting me stay with you."

I thought it over. It really would be an amazing feature in the store. It would give her something to do while she was stranded here, and another unexpected bonus—she wouldn't be able to leave town until it was complete. I didn't have to think long.

"I'm in."

Her smile lit the room.

"On one condition," I added. "We won't be trading. You have to let me pay you for it."

Her eyebrows furrowed. "No deal. Then I'm just indebted to you again."

I shook my head. "I don't know what the going rate is for a two-story painted mural, but I'm betting it's more than a couple of nights in a seedy hotel."

"Hey, your apartment isn't seedy," she protested. "You don't even have bedbugs!"

I quirked a smile, but held firm. "That's my offer. We can find another way to trade if you want, but if you're painting my store, I'm paying you for it." I held my hand out across the table, and she scowled at me for a moment before reaching across and gripping my hand. "Deal."

"Deal," I repeated. Her hand was soft and small in mine, and I held it just a moment longer than necessary before releasing it.

* * *

The next morning, she jumped in with both feet. Watching her work was actually rather amazing. I eventually just gave her the keys to my truck and told her to get whatever she needed, and she was back a few hours later with all kinds of supplies—gallons of paint, brushes, drop cloths, not to mention scaffolding that she'd procured from God-knew-where. She was quick and efficient, and paint was flying before the afternoon was out.

I hadn't considered what a draw just having her there working on it would be, but the number of customers steadily increased throughout the day until by late afternoon, people were openly standing around watching. We'd spent the evening before perusing her portfolio and deciding on a design, and finally settled on an amalgamation of imagery from famous books, better to fill the space than a single large design. She was working in the bottom corner at the moment, roughing in the shape of Moby Dick arcing out of the ocean in a spray of water as Pequod rode the waves in the background.

I couldn't imagine how much time a project of this size and complexity would take, but the longer it kept her around, the less I was complaining.

Smiling to myself, I stepped around a cluster of people who were obviously only there to watch—well, and to buy coffee and pastries from Geoff while they did, so I wasn't complaining—and made my way back to my office, where I had paperwork awaiting me. I'd no sooner sat in my chair and pulled the keyboard close when my phone rang, vibrating in my pocket. One glance at the display and I wasn't sure I wanted to answer, but I knew if I didn't, she would just call again. And again.

"Hey, Mom."

"Hi, Sammy. How are you? You haven't called in a while."

I'd spoken to her just days before, but it wouldn't be my

mother if she didn't start right in with a guilt trip. I didn't rise to the bait. "I'm fine, Mom. How are you?"

She ignored my question. "I heard you're having someone paint the store."

My mouth dropped open. How could she possibly know that? Ellen had only started that morning. The curse of living in a small town. "Yep. I'm having a mural done on the brick wall, you know, the big one in the back?"

A pause. I gritted my teeth. Wait for it…

"I don't know why you didn't ask Jeremy." There it was. My mother was nothing if not predictable. "He *is* an artist, you know," she added. As if I could forget.

"I think he's probably a little out of my price range, Mom."

She scoffed. "Oh, come now, he's family. He wouldn't have charged you." I bit my lip to keep from laughing out loud at that. "Anyway," she went on, "I just thought it might be nice, you know, having his artwork on your wall. It would really be a family store then. Besides, it would be good publicity, you know."

She was right; it probably would increase sales and exposure to have a huge Jeremy Whitaker mural on the wall of my store. But the store was *mine*. The one thing I'd done all by myself, for myself, and I intended to keep it that way.

"Sorry, Mom. I didn't plan it; I only met her a couple of days ago."

"Who's *her*?" She sounded suspicious. Better shut that down. "The artist." I said. "She came into the store." Technically correct.

My mom sighed. "Well. I hope you've at least put out Jeremy's new book. He's really counting on you for promotion." I nearly laughed at that, too. Jeremy's big-name publisher was more than capable of promoting him without the help of a tiny bookstore in Nowhere, Indiana, even if it was the writer's hometown.

"Yes, Mom. I put the book on display. I've already sold a few."

I could almost see her satisfied nod through the phone.

"Good. Even if you don't share your brother's artistic talents, it's good to see you supporting—"

"Did you need anything else, Mom?"

"Oh, so I can't call just to check in with my son?"

I waited, and finally she sighed.

"In case you forgot, Dylan's birthday is coming up, and we're throwing a party at the house. I hope you can come. It's a week from Saturday."

Dylan. Of my brother's many accomplishments, soon-to-be six-year-old Dylan was the only one I really cared about. It was Dylan who brought my brother back to town after years of gallivanting around the world, determined to raise his son in his hometown. And though his marriage hadn't lasted out the year, Jeremy had stayed—so far—and his amazing kid had stayed as well. Providing my parents with their only grandchild had only served to raise my brother even higher in their eyes, but I couldn't fault them for that one. Dylan was pretty great.

"Of course I'll be there. Just let me know what time."

"It's at four. Bring a picture of the mural. Even if it's not as good as what Jeremy might do, we'd still like to see it." Like it would kill them to drive twenty minutes and come see it themselves. I ignored the barb and said my goodbyes, stepping to the office door as I hung up the phone.

Ellen had finished the rough shape of the whale and had climbed up onto the scaffolding, where she was busy blocking in the sweeping vista of Hogwarts Castle. By the looks of it so far, the mural was going to be almost as beautiful as the woman painting it.

CHAPTER 7

ELLEN

I'd painted a handful of murals before, but never one of this size or scope. I'd been worried that I might have agreed to something over my head, not to mention the added pressure because I really cared about Sam's reaction to it, but in the end I was enjoying myself more than I could have imagined. It was nerve-wracking at first, especially as a few people gathered around to watch— I'd never had an audience watch me work before—but their enthusiasm was palpable, and it just fueled my own excitement.

I hadn't thought he would actually go for the idea. But when he had, I'd been so excited I threw myself into planning, brainstorming book-themed ideas with him, mapping out the layout, making supply lists. We'd both been so tired at the end of it all that we'd fallen into bed—separately— without a repeat of the kiss in the hotel room. Part of me had been disappointed—the attraction I felt to this man was so strong it was like a relentless itch under my skin—but another part of me was slightly relieved. If nothing got started between us, it would be so much easier when I left.

No disappointment, no feelings, no attachment. Besides, I was afraid the time to sleep with Sam just for the enjoyment of it and walk away with no strings attached was rapidly passing. I liked him too much. We would have to keep this professional.

So, I didn't dwell on Sam, and focused instead on the mural.

I lost myself in the work, translating the rough sketch I'd developed the night before into a well-balanced design on a massive scale. Huck and Jim floated on their raft down the Mississippi; Winnie the Pooh danced with Christopher Robin and his friends in the foreground while a forest of *truffula* trees filled the horizon. Alice chased the white rabbit through the tea party; Hamlet clutched Yorick's skull; Dorothy and the Scarecrow skipped down the yellow-brick road; the fiery peak of Mount Doom rose out of the land-scape. I hid Easter eggs throughout, imagining some kind of literary treasure hunt—a scarlet letter "A" carved into a tree, Poe's raven perched on a limb, the tiny figure of Peter Pan flying through the night sky.

I paused only to scarf down some food from the cafe, and gave a distracted nod when Sam told me the store closed in half an hour, and another vague wave of acknowledgement when he told me he was heading upstairs an hour after that.

When I finally surfaced from my creative fog, I had no idea what time it was, and while Sam had left the lights on for me, the sky outside the windows was pitch black. My back popped and groaned as I stretched it out, and I made my way down the scaffolding to the floor, feeling like I was climbing up out of the bottom of a well. It had been a while since I'd been this lost in a project.

Back on solid ground again, I walked clear across to the other side of the store and turned to take in my work. It was disheartening to see just how little I appeared to have accomplished, though I knew I'd gotten much more done than it seemed. It was a huge space, and this was a big project, and though they may not look impressive, the rough shapes and guidelines I'd established today would go a long way toward making the rest of the work go smoothly.

Satisfied, I moved my supplies out of the way as best as I could and shut the lights off, before making my way up to Sam's apartment. I'd half expected him to be asleep when I got there, but instead I heard the shower running in the bathroom. In the kitchen I found that Sam, ever the thoughtful host, had left me a covered plate containing an enormous sandwich and a bowl of still-warm vegetable soup next to a note with my name written on it in a bold scrawl.

I inhaled the sandwich like a starving wolf and was just about to demolish the soup when I heard the tap in the bathroom shut off. A moment later he appeared in the kitchen doorway and I froze, spoon lifted halfway to my mouth.

Any thoughts I'd had about keeping things professional evaporated as if they'd never existed.

Sam fully dressed was a sight to behold. Sam wearing nothing but a towel slung low on his hips, water droplets still clinging to the ends of his hair, muscles gleaming in the light from the hallway...well. That was something else entirely. The soup tipped out of my spoon and ran back into the bowl.

"I thought I heard you come in," he said. I couldn't seem to form the words to respond, and a moment later the corner of his mouth pulled up. A little more. Then the other side, and then the smile gave way to a very poorly suppressed bout of laughter.

Suddenly I realized how I must look. I had tied my hair up hastily at some point and rammed a paintbrush through it to hold it in place out of my way. I couldn't seem to remember if the brush had had paint on it. I was wearing my work clothes, which were more holes than fabric, and were held together largely with dried paint at this point. My t-shirt sported a drawing of a cartoon pencil with the phrase, "2B or not 2B" emblazoned across my chest—fitting, I'd thought, for this project—and both it, and my skin, were spattered with fresh stains in every color of the rainbow. I'd inhaled my sandwich so fast I likely was wearing half of it on my face, and I was still holding up that damn spoon.

I let the spoon clatter down into the bowl. Sam was laughing so hard he was clutching the counter to hold himself upright, so I did the only self-respecting thing I could think of. I balled up my napkin and threw it at him. It bounced harmlessly off his shoulder—that *shoulder*—and without missing a beat, he grabbed it from the floor and threw it back. It hit me in the forehead and when it hit the floor again, it was smeared with green paint. Sam just laughed harder.

So, I looked down, jammed my hand into a blob of scarlet paint on my shirt, crossed the room to him, and ran my hand in one smooth motion down the length of his torso, smearing a thick trail of red down his chest. His skin was hot and still damp from the shower, and the laughter died on his lips.

Our eyes met and held. Scarcely daring to breathe, I took another blob of paint—blue this time—and smeared it slowly across the first, savoring the feel of his skin under my finger-tips. I trailed it down, my hand moving of its own volition, until my fingers hovered just above the edge of his towel. His lips parted on an indrawn breath and my eyes dropped to his mouth, and less than a heartbeat later he had grabbed my shoulders and pulled me to him. Our lips crashed together, and my senses were overwhelmed with the feel of his lips, his tongue sliding against mine, the taste of him, the feel of his shoulders, smooth and damp under my clutching hands.

His hand came up behind me and pulled the paintbrush

from my hair. His fingertips came away green and my hair tumbled around my shoulders and down my back. He buried his fingers in the strands and gave a light tug, pulling my head back so his mouth could move to my jaw, trailing a line of kisses there, and I moaned at the sensation, the sound catching deep in my throat.

He stepped closer, until we were touching all along our fronts, and then without warning he bent and lifted me up, sitting me on the edge of the counter. His hands came to my thighs, and I parted my legs, wrapping them around him and pulling him closer to me. His answering groan lit my body on fire.

When his hands came to the hem of my shirt, dipping underneath so his fingers could trail a line of goosebumps along the skin at my waist, I nearly melted in relief. He wasn't going to stop. Whatever had spooked him that first night wouldn't stand in our way now.

Because I *wanted* this. I didn't want another night lying awake in bed knowing he was just steps away down the hall.

He broke the kiss long enough to pull back and meet my eyes. His were dark and steady, but there was no mistaking the question there.

"Yes," I breathed, and then he tugged my shirt up and over my head, smearing paint across my skin in the process. His mouth was back on mine, hungry and hot, as my bra joined my shirt on the floor, and then his hands slid up my sides to skim over my breasts. My nipples hardened into sensitive peaks against the rough skin of his hands, and he dipped his head, trailing wet kisses down the column of my throat before capturing a nipple in his mouth. When he swirled his tongue around the tip, a bolt of heat rushed straight through me, and I clutched at his back, feeling the hard muscles shift beneath my hands.

I tried not to dig my fingernails into his skin, but I didn't have complete control over my body, and my head tipped back as he switched to the other breast, kissing and sucking until I squirmed against him, shifting, trying to gain friction where I wanted it most.

"*Ellen.*"

His voice was a low growl against my breast, reverberating through me, and I arched forward into him. The movement pulled his towel loose and it fell in a heap to the floor. He pulled back, breathing hard, staring at me with an intensity that made me feel like my skin might catch fire.

I glanced down, and only got the barest glimpse of hard muscle, smooth skin, bold smears of paint all over his arms and torso where he'd been pressed against me, before he hoisted me up into his arms with one smooth motion.

I let out a surprised squeak and wrapped my arms and legs around him tight, and then his mouth was on mine again as he carried me down the short hallway and into his bedroom.

The comforter on his bed was soft, and that was all I had time to notice before his hands were at the waist of my jeans, and then they were sliding down my legs along with my underwear. A moment later the warm weight of him was on top of me, and then inside me, in one, long, slow, delicious movement, and then we were moving together, my hands touching every inch of skin I could reach, tangling in his hair and sliding down his back, paint staining the bedclothes, and when at last the pleasure was too much and I couldn't hold back a second longer, I could feel his dark eyes on me, watching as I let go, and he closed his eyes and followed a second later, my name on his lips.

CHAPTER 8

SAM

I hadn't intended to have sex with her. Not the first time, or the second, when I rolled over in the night, only half-awake and confused at the unfamiliar weight in my bed, only to find soft skin and warm lips curved in a sleepy smile.

The third time, when my alarm went off and I returned from the bathroom to find her in my bed, hair matted and stiff with dried paint, covers pulled up under her chin and eyes wide with what looked suspiciously like panic in the cold light of day—well, that time I meant it. I wasn't even sure my body would cooperate again after what I'd put it through the night before, so I erased the look in her eyes with my mouth between her legs, and the sounds she made suggested it was the right choice. But then she slid down my body—all smooth skin and soft hair—and returned the favor, and my body cooperated just fine after all. And by the time we'd both showered and dressed and made our way downstairs to the shop, there was no trace of panic left in her eyes.

Geoff didn't say a word when we entered the store together, but he narrowed his eyes at me. I ignored him and his raised eyebrow as he brought a chocolate scone into my office and left it on my desk, but when he dropped another scone off with Ellen where she was setting up her paint in the corner, whatever he said to her made her blush so brilliantly I could see it across the store. He shot a smirk at me and didn't seem at all bothered by the glare I sent back.

The day dragged on, and I tried to ignore her, I really did. I tried to get my work done and help my customers and act normal, like there wasn't a magnet on the other side of the store pulling my attention away from my job every five seconds. But it was really hard to pretend when said magnet was perched on a rickety metal platform halfway up the wall, pulling the eyes of not just myself but every single person in the place. Which was a lot of people, come to think of it.

There were easily twice the number of people I usually saw in the store on a weekday afternoon, with more coming and going regularly. Most people were standing around not even pretending to do anything other than watch Ellen work. I wasn't sure if I should be offended or grateful, but I had to admit, sales were up so far that day, so I settled on grateful.

It was around four o'clock in the afternoon, and I was half reorganizing a table full of mystery books and half watching the Cheshire cat's smile take shape in the leaves of a tree when I heard a familiar voice by my side.

"So, that's Fairfield's new artistic protégé, hm? Think she'll replace your brother as the town's creative darling?"

I snorted and turned to look at Jeanne.

"Hardly. I doubt anything could replace Fairfield's one big claim to fame. Besides, she's not staying, just passing through. She's doing the mural to pass the time while she waits for her car to get fixed."

"Not staying, huh?" My ex-sister-in-law tilted her head as she watched Ellen work. "That's too bad. Everyone seems pretty enamored with her."

I glanced back to the scaffolding and realized Jeanne was right. While much of the crowd seemed content just watching Ellen work, I realized I'd seen more and more people coming up to talk with her, asking her questions about herself and her work. In a quiet little town like ours, any hint of excitement or change was pounced upon immediately.

"What about you?"

"Hmm?" I said distractedly.

"Are you enamored with her as well?"

I looked sharply back to Jeanne, then resumed stacking books on the mystery table. "What are you talking about?"

"Just wondering," she said idly. "Only, most people in here are watching her paint, but you seem mostly to be watching her."

I glowered at her and she laughed. "Oh, calm down. Come on, Sam, come have a cup of coffee with me so I can pretend I stopped by to see you instead of spy on your artist."

Giving in, I left the mystery table in disarray and followed her over to the cafe, waiting while she perused the small case with its array of baked goods.

Jeanne's marriage to my brother had only lasted for eleven months—a whirlwind wedding after she found out she was pregnant, then just enough time to realize they actually had nothing in common, before hastily filing for divorce. She was a dentist, and, at first glance, exactly the kind of girl Jeremy usually went for—gorgeous, funny, and sweet. But then it turned out she was also a fair bit smarter than his usual conquests, which meant that she had her own thoughts and opinions, including ones that didn't entirely mesh with his. The marriage ended amicably enough though, and when Jeremy decided he wanted to move back home to raise Dylan in Fairfield, Jeanne agreed without protest.

Despite her questionable taste in men, I had to admit

Jeanne was a wonderful person—sharp, with a quick wit, and a good friend to have. What's more, she was my one ally in the family. Since my mother would never forgive her for her clear mistake in divorcing her flawless son, it was rather refreshing to not be the only one who constantly fell short. Still, I always felt like Jeanne seemed to handle it better than I, not having grown up with it.

Geoff had already left for the day, but my other part-time employee, Marian, was working in the cafe. She slid our drinks across the counter with an amicable, "Hey, boss."

I took the coffees while Jeanne grabbed the plate with her slice of cheesecake, and we settled in at a small table in the corner.

"So, I'm guessing your mom called you about the party? You'll be there, right?" she asked, taking a bite of her cheesecake. I'd never met a dentist who ate as much sugar as Jeanne did.

I nodded. "I'll be there. I wouldn't miss the little guy's big day." I took a sip of the scalding coffee. "Besides, it'll give my mom something to focus on other than my failures."

Jeanne smiled. "Failures like hiring someone other than your brother to paint your wall?"

Jeanne always was one step ahead of me. I shrugged. "She pitched the mural idea and it sounded good. I wasn't thinking about how my mom or my brother would react."

"From your tone, I'm guessing your mom already brought it up."

I rolled my eyes. "Of course she did. Good publicity, support your family, et cetera." I couldn't keep the bite out of my voice.

Jeanne snickered into her coffee then looked appraisingly at where Ellen was mixing paint.

"Well, I like her. Anyone who pisses your mom off by default has my approval."

I narrowed my eyes at her. "Approval for what?"

She blinked guileless eyes at me. "Oh, nothing. Just approval."

"Mm-hmm."

She took another bite of cheesecake and her mouth curved in a devilish grin. "You should bring her to the party next Saturday. That would cause quite a stir."

I stared at her incredulously. "Why on earth would I bring her to Dylan's party? She's just someone I hired to paint my wall while her car gets fixed. It's not like I'm dating her."

Jeanne just looked at me. "Oh, sure, I know. Just a thought."

* * *

It really *wasn't* like I was dating her. We were just two people, working together in the bookstore...checking in with each other...eating lunch together...going upstairs to our apartment to make dinner together...possibly touching each other a little too long, maybe sneaking kisses.

Ellen made good progress on the mural that day, finishing most of the work of blocking in all the major scenes and characters and setting herself up to start detailing the next day. When I told her I was closing the store and heading upstairs for dinner, she started cleaning up her paints and brushes and joined me.

I had no intention of throwing myself at her, but we'd barely made it into the apartment before she grabbed a fistful of my shirt and pulled me to her. One kiss turned into two, then three, and I only just managed to get her out of her clothes before I ended up covered in paint again.

By the time we got around to dinner it was pushing midnight, and we ate naked in my bed, wrapped in sheets and blankets, trading bites and stories and laughter. It took me a while to identify the tight feeling in my chest as happiness.

"So," Ellen said, leaning back on her hands. "Who was the lady sitting with you at the cafe today?" The sheet shifted with her movement and fell, exposing one breast, and her skin glowed golden in the light from my bedside lamp. She saw me staring and smirked, deliberately shifting again so the sheet fell all the way to her waist. I realized I had completely missed her question and tried to drag my eyes back up.

"What's that?"

She smiled. "The blond lady in the cafe. You guys were talking for quite a while. Is she a regular or something?"

I liked the thought that she'd been watching me enough to notice me sitting with Jeanne. "No, that's Jeanne. She's my sister-in-law. Well, ex-sister-in-law. She divorced my brother about five years ago. She came in to invite me to her son's birthday party." I didn't add that Jeanne had also come to check Ellen out.

I looked up at her face. It was open and happy, nothing there beyond curiosity at how I spent my day, but I couldn't resist teasing her. "Why, are you jealous?"

She laughed. "Well, if I was going to be, she'd be a good choice. She's gorgeous."

I nodded. "Yeah, just my brother's type."

"Gorgeous isn't really a type."

"That's true," I conceded with a grin. "His type is actually sweet, but kind of vapid and not too bright. Jeanne may be sweet, but she isn't any of the rest, so I guess that's why they didn't work out."

She tilted her head. "It doesn't sound like you and your brother have much in common."

I felt my mouth pull up on one side. "Thank you."

She laughed again. "Do you get along with him?"

My smile fell and I shrugged. I leaned forward and snagged a lock of her hair, toying with the strands as I thought it through. I didn't generally like talking about my family, but I felt the need to answer her honestly. I let the strands of her hair run through my fingers like water and sat back. "It's complicated, I guess. My brother isn't a bad guy, and we get along well enough. But it's like you said, we don't have much in common, and that's always been to my detriment."

She looked at me closely. "What do you mean?"

"Well, he's very talented. He's an artist, like I told you, and a writer. Dabbles in music, too. To hear my parents tell it, he can also cure the sick and walk on water."

She ignored my sarcasm. "Are you suggesting that you're not talented?"

I shrugged. "I know I can't walk on water."

"Seriously though. You're a really great person. I don't know about your drawing or writing abilities, but I've only known you for a couple of days, and I've already seen enough to know you're amazing."

I quirked a smile at her. "You're sleeping with me. You have to say that."

She attempted to stifle a smile, and opened her mouth to argue again, but I cut her off. "No, I know my brother is not objectively better than me. I guess I've just always been in his shadow, and after a lifetime of being compared to someone and coming up short...it just starts to get old, that's all."

She shifted on the bed, rearranging her legs as she seemed to mull this over. "I've always been an only child. I guess I can't imagine what it would be like to have a sibling in the first place, let alone one that you always got compared to," she said quietly. "But I do know what it's like to be the odd one out. I'm really sorry your own family makes you feel that way."

I gave a half shrug. "I guess I'm used to it."

"Your brother has a son, too, you said?"

"That's right. Dylan. He's turning six on Saturday, so I'll get to spend the day listening to my mom compare her sons. Oh, and hear about how terrible I am for not having my brother paint my wall."

"What?!"

I gave a wry smile. "Yep, sorry. Apparently, you made me betray my brother."

She scowled. "Who is your brother, anyway?"

"Jeremy Whitaker."

I watched her face, which she worked to keep neutral, but her quick indrawn breath gave her away. I felt a twist in my gut. "You've heard of him."

She nodded, almost apologetically. "He's pretty well known. I saw one of his exhibitions when I lived in San Francisco. I didn't realize he'd written a book."

I gave a quiet laugh, and rose from the bed, not bothering to take the sheet with me. In the living room, I retrieved my brother's book and brought it back into the bedroom, handing it to her wordlessly before climbing back beneath the sheets.

She took it and stared at the cover, tracing her fingers over the brush strokes visible in the paint. "Wow," she said softly.

"I know."

"Who is she?"

"What?" I asked, but I knew what she meant.

"The girl in the painting. Who is she?"

"Her name is Caroline. She was my brother's girlfriend." *And mine,* I didn't say.

"Have you read the book? What is it?"

I nodded. "It's a series of short stories. Each chapter starts with a painting, and then has a story based on the theme of the artwork. It's pretty good, actually," I admitted grudgingly.

"Are all the paintings of women?"

"Not all of them."

Ellen traced the image on the cover again. "I guess you were right. 'Gorgeous' might be your brother's type."

I reached out a hand and stroked a finger down the soft skin of her shoulder. "You're more gorgeous than any of them."

Her breath caught and she met my eyes. Hers were fierce with emotion. "And you have just as much value as your brother."

I let my fingers trail over her collarbone and down to cup the soft skin of her breast. Her breathing stuttered and I felt her nipple pebble under my touch. I ran my thumb lightly over the peak, back and forth, and watched as her eyes fluttered closed.

Then they opened again. "Are you sorry you didn't have your brother paint your wall?" she asked quietly.

I moved my hand away from her breast and lifted it to her mouth, running my thumb over her lower lip. "Not a bit," I said, meeting her gaze so she would know I was serious. "I wouldn't trade your mural for anything. Your work is beautiful and unique."

I leaned in and replaced my thumb with my lips.

"And so are you."

CHAPTER 9

ELLEN

*B*y the time the weekend and much of the following week had flown by, I realized that I scarcely recognized my own life. I didn't know when I'd fallen into this routine of domestic bliss, but if I closed my eyes and didn't think too hard, I could almost pretend it was real. Each day that week we woke together, and eventually made our way out of bed and into our clothes and down to the bookstore. Geoff—who was quickly becoming my favorite person—was always there to greet us with something delectable, a kiss on the cheek for me and a smirk for Sam. I worked on the mural while he ran the store, and at the end of the day we went upstairs and made dinner before falling into bed together. Meanwhile, the bed in the guest room stayed pitifully empty.

My panic after that first night, my fear that I had messed up and gotten in over my head, hadn't disappeared, exactly, but I had successfully filed it away under "Things to Deal with Later."

And for the time being, that was working. Days passed, and nothing interrupted our happy routine. Tony called only to say he was still waiting on a part for my car, but he expected everything would be done by Thursday or Friday. Dana called to tell me she was excited to see me, and though I apologized profusely for leaving her hanging, she insisted that I should take all the time I needed, and her house was there when I was ready. I got an email from the children's book publisher I had worked with previously, wanting to hire me on for a series of books by a new author, but the project wouldn't start for a few weeks yet. And so, I put all those little bits of real life aside, and focused instead on the mural and on the wonderful feeling of being with Sam.

He really was wonderful. Beneath the quiet intensity of his exterior was a warm and generous man. He was both thoughtful and sweet, and I knew that while I would be sad to leave, these would be memories to treasure for a lifetime.

When Jeanne came into the store on Tuesday afternoon, just as I was putting the finishing touches on the hazy figure of Dickens' Ghost of Christmas Past, Sam beckoned me down to the cafe to meet her. She shook my hand, heedless of the paint streak I left on her palm and said, "So, you're the artist everyone in town is talking about. Your work is beautiful. You're doing a wonderful job on both the mural and my brother-in-law here."

I liked her immediately. I even forgave her for being a dentist when she admitted that she hated dentists, too. Though considering the amount of chocolate she ate while we sat together, I thought I might be able to guess why.

We talked about art, and the bookstore, and a little bit about my past—she had moved quite a bit in her life and sympathized—and she showed me pictures of her son, Dylan, who was, unsurprisingly, a very handsome kid. And after she left, Sam looked at me across the table in silence for a long moment, before blurting out, "Do you want to come to the birthday party on Saturday?"

I blinked. "What?"

He ducked his head to take a sip of his coffee and I could see his ears were slightly pink under his dark hair. "You don't have to, it was just a thought. Jeanne would love to have you there, too, but I know—"

"Sure."

"—you'd probably—wait, what?"

"Sure, I'd love to go. Your nephew seems like a good kid, and I'm happy to provide another line of defense between you and your mom."

Besides, Saturday was only four days away. My car might be finished by then but the mural likely wouldn't be, and I'd rather spend the day with Sam's family than sit in his apartment alone.

"Oh," he said, looking slightly bewildered, like he wasn't sure if he was more surprised that he'd asked or that I'd said yes. "Well, that's great."

I grinned at him and leaned across the table, pulling the paintbrush I'd been using from my hair and wiping a smear of yellow paint down his cheek. I gave him a wink and rose to head back to work. His grumbling protest followed behind me, but I didn't look back.

* * *

To my surprise, the mural ended up taking less time than I expected. Once I got into the swing of things the detail work progressed quickly, and by Thursday evening it was becoming clear that I would have it finished up the following day. I had mixed emotions. Part of me was sad that it was almost over, which meant as soon as my car was done my time here would be drawing to a close. Another part of me was immensely proud of the work I had done. Rather than decrease as the mural became old news, my audience had grown, and more and more people had started approaching me to ask questions. I heard people start to pick out my hidden Easter eggs, exclaiming over finding small literary references hidden in unlikely places. It was thrilling to hear.

Two other people had shown interest in my work, and one—the elementary school principal—had gone so far as to ask my rates and whether or not I'd be interested in doing a mural for the school. I was sad to tell her I wouldn't be staying in town that long, and hoped she would be able to find another artist to do the work.

My heart was heavy that evening as I packed up my supplies, rinsing out brushes and moving everything out of the way. I had torn down the scaffolding that afternoon and borrowed Sam's truck to return it, since everything that was left could be reached with a small step-ladder. I felt subdued that evening, but I tried to keep my feelings to myself. Sam knew what this was; we'd both known from the beginning. He didn't seem upset, so I wouldn't weigh him down with feelings I'd known better than to develop in the first place.

I was right—the mural was completely done by early evening the following day. It was near closing time and the store was quiet, so I cleaned up the majority of my supplies and stepped back one last time to view it from across the store, the way new customers would see it when they walked in. I was happy with how it had all come together in the end, and thrilled that it hadn't taken as much time as I'd feared when I'd started. Sam was out of the store running errands, but Geoff was still there, and Rachel gave me a thumbs-up from her vantage point by the register.

Geoff provided me with a congratulatory chocolate-filled croissant, and joined me in the cafe while I ate it.

"So, what's the plan now?" he asked bluntly. "You ditching us all and moving on?"

I laughed around a mouthful of chocolate. "I dunno. I'm tempted to stay just for your baking."

His smile turned serious. "You could, you know. Stay, I mean. Fairfield isn't such a bad place to live. Small, sure, and gossipy, but we all like you. And I'm pretty sure Sam likes you, and—"

I cut him off with a hand on his arm. "I appreciate it, Geoff, really I do, but I can't stay. I like Sam too, but it's not like that. I wasn't even supposed to be here this long. My friend in Ohio is expecting me, and I've got to move on."

My heart ached when I said the words, and just for a moment, I considered what it would be like to stay. To let what I had with Sam develop into something more. The idea was both thrilling and terrifying. Then I thought about San Diego, remembering what had happened the one time I'd let myself settle down, and I ruthlessly quashed the feeling. What I had with Sam was special; I couldn't let myself stay and ruin it.

Geoff just looked at me, his expression sad. "Does Sam know?"

"Does Sam know what?" came the deep, gravelly voice I'd become so used to in such a short span of time.

"That's my cue." Geoff stood and ducked away from the table, leaving Sam to take his seat.

He looked across the table at me questioningly.

Oh. Wow. I wasn't prepared to have this conversation now.

"Well, the mural is done, so—"

"What?" He looked up sharply. Then his face split into the most beautiful grin I'd seen, and he grabbed my hand and hauled me up from the table. I didn't even have time to protest before he'd dragged me halfway across the store to where he could take it all in.

I watched as his jaw dropped open, and I laughed. "Don't

look so surprised. You've been watching it the whole time, you idiot."

He just grinned and grabbed me around the waist, pulling me close and dropping a kiss on my lips. "It's better than I ever imagined. Thank you, El."

I felt a blush heat my cheeks. "I made you a list of all the books I included, in case you want to do some kind of treasure hunt, or event at the store. It's in your office."

He kissed me again, quickly, then again more slowly, until a throat cleared behind us and he pulled back with a laugh to see Geoff pulling on his jacket. "I'm heading out. I'll see you two tomorrow?"

His question seemed to be aimed at me, but Sam didn't seem to notice, and I just gave a nod before looking down at my feet. As soon as my car was done, I would have to say goodbye to Geoff too, and the thought made my heart clench a little. I always hated this part.

After Geoff left, Sam turned back to me. "I'm going to close up the store, and then we can head up?"

"I'm going to stay for a minute and clean up the rest of my stuff, and then I'll meet you upstairs."

"Sounds good," he said, then smiled at me again. "We'll celebrate when you come up."

I forced myself to smile back, but when Sam had locked the door and turned off the main lights, after I had cleaned up the rest of my supplies, I found myself sitting on the small stepladder I had borrowed and looking around the store. I was an idiot, I told myself. I should be upstairs with Sam, enjoying his company for as long as I could. But I couldn't shake the feeling of melancholy. I would miss this. Not just Sam, but the store, the familiar smell of books and the joy I'd felt at doing such a large, public art project. I had enjoyed that aspect of it more than I'd expected— working in public, having people stop and watch and talk to me as I worked, instead of sitting alone in front of my computer.

My musings were interrupted by a ringing from my pocket, and I pulled out my cell phone. *Tony.* I answered the call.

"Good news, Miss Price, your car is all fixed up and ready to go. I'm sorry for the delay, but we got the last piece in today and you're good to go."

"Thanks, Tony, that's great. I can come by tomorrow if that works for you?"

"That's perfect. We'll be in all day."

When I hung up the phone, my emotions were a tight ball in my chest. Sadness at the thought of leaving this place, of leaving Sam, mixed with the apprehension I always felt at starting a new chapter, no matter how many times I had done it before. Excitement, too. I hadn't seen Dana in years, and I really was looking forward to getting to spend some time with her.

It was time to go. I knew it, and the sadness I felt at leaving was nothing new. It was always hard to leave people and places I'd come to love—I knew that. But there were always new places, too, I reminded myself. And unless I moved on, I would never get to fall in love with those people and places I hadn't seen yet.

The thought bolstered me a little. Yes. I would stay tomorrow, go to Sam's nephew's party with him, and then say goodbye. By Sunday, I would be back on the road.

Still, the heavy feeling in my gut persisted.

I was still perched on the edge of the ladder, holding the phone in my hand, and I flipped it over. I needed someone to help me make sense of all my conflicting emotions, and before the thought had fully formed, I was dialing her number.

"Sparrow, baby!"

My mom was the *only* person I let use that horrible name. And by "let," I mean she used it no matter how much I protested, so I put up with it.

"Hey, Mom. How are you?"

"I'm wonderful, darling. How are you? *Where* are you?"

I laughed a little. Only my mom and I would start a conversation like that.

"I'm in Indiana. A little town called Fairfield. What about you?"

"Oh, I'm still in Florida, honey, but I'm not staying long. I was thinking I'd drive up the coast. Stop in North Carolina for a while." I could hear the excitement in her voice, could almost feel it, and it helped settle my nerves a bit. It was a rush, always, the thought of setting off into the unknown, not sure where you'd end up or who you'd meet along the way. "What's in Fairfield, honey?"

"Oh, nothing much." The words felt like a lie. "My car broke down on the way through to Ohio—I'm on my way to visit my friend Dana, remember her? From college?—so I stayed for a few days while my car got fixed up."

"Oh, that's nice. Do you have enough money for the hotel? I can send some if you need."

"No, that's okay, Mom. I'm actually staying with a friend here. Sam. He owns a bookstore and lives upstairs, and he's been putting me up while I'm here."

"Was Sam a friend from college too?" Mom sounded confused.

"No, no. I just met him here when my car died."

"You're living with a man you just met?"

I rolled my eyes. "I'm not *living* with him, Mom. He just offered me a place to stay. I've only been here a little over a week."

I could hear her moving around in the background. My mother was perpetually incapable of sitting still. "Sorry, sweetie. I'm just making sure you're being careful. Don't forget what happened in San Diego."

Like I could forget. San Diego had been my longest stop in one place, ever. Three years, long enough to have my own apartment, a stable job, and even a long-term boyfriend. Long enough to get complacent. Long enough for him to get bored and cheat on me, to break my heart and remind me why I didn't stay in one place. I didn't blame him, not really. He must have known all along I wasn't permanent. I was never permanent; everything in my life was temporary.

Just like this.

"I know, Mom. It's fine. It's not like I'm dating Sam. I'm just staying with him until my car is fixed."

"When is that going to be? Honestly, Sparrow, I don't know how that car is still running in the first place."

"Hey, don't you say bad things about my car," I said in mock defense. "She's an old lady; you'll hurt her feelings. Besides, she's already fixed. I'll get her back in the morning."

"So, you're heading out tomorrow then?"

"Probably Sunday," I said, shifting my seat on the ladder. "I'm going with Sam to his nephew's birthday party before I go."

There was silence on the other end of the line, and I knew I'd messed up.

"You're going to his nephew's birthday party," she said finally, speaking slowly. "I thought you said you weren't dating this guy."

"I'm not!" I protested.

"But you're meeting his family?"

"I'm doing him a favor. It's complicated; he doesn't get along with—look, it doesn't matter. I'm leaving on Sunday regardless. And you know I don't do long distance relationships. They never work."

I considered it, with Sam, just for a moment. Could we

make this work long distance? But no. Even if Ohio was close enough to visit, who knew how long I would stay there, or where I would end up next. I couldn't string him along like that.

"I'm sorry, sweetie," my mom said, her voice conciliatory. "I don't mean to nag. I just worry about you, and I don't want to see you get hurt again."

"I know, Mom," I said quietly. She was right though. This was all too much. Too fast. I'd moved into Sam's apartment without a thought, fallen into bed with him even though I knew I'd end up getting hurt.

"Well, look, you have fun at the party," she said. "And call me when you get to Dana's, okay?"

"I will, Mom. I love you."

"I love you too, sweetie. Be careful, okay?"

We hung up, and I sat on the ladder, staring at my phone. She was right. I needed to be more careful. With my life, but especially with my heart.

CHAPTER 10

SAM

*T*he mural was more amazing than I'd imagined. It was the first thing you saw when you walked in the door to the bookstore, and it had already increased sales and traffic before it was even complete. I considered doing some kind of unveiling, maybe a special event or open house the following week. If Ellen was still around, that was. My heart clenched at the thought.

Maybe it was time to tell her how I felt. Surely, she already knew. I was half-convinced she felt the same way. But maybe if I spelled it out for her, I could persuade her to stay. She could be happy with me. Happy in Fairfield. I knew it; I'd seen it.

She was still downstairs in the store, so I set about making a celebratory dinner. I set the tiny dining room table with candles and cloth napkins and turned the lights low, before starting chicken for dinner. I tucked the bag Geoff had given me for dessert—a rainbow array of decadent macarons in a variety of flavors—into the pantry where she wouldn't see them.

We would talk later. I would plead my case and explain how I felt. But for now, I would just have to show her.

* * *

The chicken had come out of the oven and the asparagus and potatoes were just finishing up when I heard the door open. The moment she walked into the room I knew something was wrong. It was in the set of her jaw, the light in her eyes, which were closed off and wary instead of open and full of their usual sparkle.

"What's wrong?" I asked quietly.

She smiled at me, but it was stiff. "Nothing is wrong. Tony called; my car is done. I can pick it up tomorrow morning."

"That's great," I said carefully. "What happens next?"

She shrugged and looked away. "It smells great in here. Can I help with anything?"

My heart sank. "No, it's all done." I gestured to the table. "Have a seat and I'll bring it out."

I waited until we were both served and digging in before I broached the subject again. "Ellen, I was thinking—"

"I'll stay for the party tomorrow and leave on Sunday morning." Her voice was soft, but it cut through me.

I tried to keep my voice steady and my eyes level on her. "You could stay, you know."

Her expression was almost sympathetic when she looked at me. "I can't, Sam. You know that. You knew what this was from the start."

Suddenly the candles and the low lighting seemed awkward and out of place. "I knew what this was, yes. But I think over the course of the last couple of weeks, it's changed, don't you?"

She didn't say anything, so I pushed on, food forgotten on

the plate in front of me. "There's something there between us, you know there is. Why not give it a shot?"

"And what?" she returned, setting down her fork. "Stay here? Live with you? We've known each other for barely any time at all!"

I shrugged. "It's been working so far. But no, you don't have to stay with me. You could get your own place. Fairfield is a good place to live. Or we could even try long distance. I could visit on weekends, and—"

"You know, I tried that once," she interrupted, her tone conversational, as if she was talking about the weather instead of ripping my heart out. "I stayed somewhere. I got my own place. I had a boyfriend."

I waited, even though I knew this wasn't going anywhere good. "And?"

"It didn't work. It never works."

"What happened?"

She looked down at her plate. "He cheated on me. He found someone permanent. So, I left, like I should have done in the first place."

I raised an incredulous eyebrow. "You won't give *me* a chance because your last boyfriend was a jerk?"

She shook her head impatiently. "Sure, he shouldn't have cheated, but can you really blame *him*?"

"What? *Yes.*"

She ignored me. "I would have left at some point. It's what I do. I can't just stay in one place forever."

"You *can't*, or you *won't*? Or maybe he just wasn't worth staying for."

"And you would be?" She gave a choked laugh and I jerked back. "You'd be okay putting up with me, always wondering when I'd get bored and decide to take off?"

I was silent a minute, looking at her, but she refused to meet my eyes. "You know what I think?"

She didn't answer.

"I think it's an excuse. I think your parents did you a disservice, moving you around so much, and now you use it as a crutch. If you move, you never have to get too close to people, let them really get to know you."

She shook her head and glared at me. "I let *you* get close. I let *you* know me. And look how well this worked out."

"I think it's been working out fine. Until now."

"Well, sure! It's all great when it's temporary."

I leaned forward, frustration heating my blood. "See, that's exactly what I mean. If you keep everything at surface level, you don't have to put any real effort into it. Real relationships take work. How many people really know you, El?"

"What do you mean? I have plenty of friends."

"Sure, but how many of them really *know* you, beyond seeing you in passing when you flit through town?"

She didn't answer.

"What were you imagining was going to happen here?" I demanded, sitting back.

She looked at me blankly.

"Are we just never going to speak again? It was a fun time, but that's it? Nice memories?"

She winced. "No...I mean, I figured we'd keep in touch..."

"And that's it," I said flatly. "A phone call every once in a while?"

Her eyes flashed and she glared across the small table at me. "Look. I never led you on. We both knew this was going to be temporary from the start. And this is just who I am. Who I've always been. You can't ask me to change who I am!"

I wrestled my temper under control. "I'm not asking you to change. I'm asking you to consider doing what you *want* to do, and not what you think you're *supposed* to do."

"I *am* doing what I want to do," she snapped. "I'm seeing new places, and meeting new people. You think I don't let people really know me, but look what happens when I do— we end up yelling at each other across the dining room table!"

I threw up my hands. "That's what a real relationship is like! It's not all sunshine and rainbows. Sometimes things are hard and you have to deal with it like an adult instead of running away."

Her eyes flashed. "Well, I didn't ask for a *real* relationship."

I stared at her, paint still staining her fingers, hair mussed and cheeks flushed with anger. My heart twisted painfully in my chest.

"Well, neither did I."

CHAPTER 11

ELLEN

I slept in the guest room that night for the first time since I'd started working on the mural. Well, "slept" was being generous. I paced. I cried. I brooded. But I didn't open the door, no matter how much it hurt, and Sam never came, never knocked, never apologized.

I had done the right thing, I kept reminding myself. Not in fighting with Sam; nothing about that was right. But it just served to prove I was making the right choice. It was time to go. And I hoped Sam could forgive me, and we could be friends someday. But my mom was right—I had gotten in too deep, too fast, and it was no one's fault but my own.

Sleep finally came, but it was fitful in the noticeably empty bed, and I missed Sam, missed the weight of him next to me, the solid pressure of his arm around my waist, the warmth of his breath stirring my hair. The thought that he was only steps away down the hallway didn't help—he could have been miles away for how much I missed him. And when the first rays of sun began poking over the horizon and I awoke, heart aching and body stiff, I knew what I had to do.

There was no sound from Sam's room as I rose and

dressed. It didn't take long to pack my bag, and I carried my boxes from where they'd been stacked in the corner down the stairs, leaving them piled near the door at the bottom. I didn't go out of my way to be stealthy, but I was still relieved when Sam didn't wake. After my last trip I returned to survey the empty apartment. Except it wasn't empty—it was still filled with Sam, his books, his dishes, evidence of a whole life. A life that I'd briefly been a part of, then left with no trace except for the scars on my heart. The apartment looked like I'd never been there at all, and while I'd thought that would make it easier, for some reason it just made me hurt.

This is no one's fault but your own, I reminded myself.

I said a soft goodbye to the apartment, and to Sam, and I left a note for him on the kitchen counter where I knew he'd find it.

Then I went out, locking the door behind me, and left out of the back door that led from the stairwell directly into the alley, bypassing the store in case Geoff was already there.

Tony's auto-repair shop was within walking distance, just down the road, and only the barest chill hung in the late summer air. I parked myself outside the office and sat on the stoop, wrapping my arms around myself and trying not to think.

I didn't have to wait long. Tony was an early riser too, it seemed, and though he paused when he saw me waiting, he didn't mention it.

"Ready to go then?"

I nodded and followed him into the office, and after a brief explanation of what he'd done that I didn't understand and only barely listened to, he traded me my keys for the payment and I was back in the familiar interior of my old red car just minutes later.

I parked in the alley lot next to Sam's truck and quickly

loaded my boxes. I was glad not to have to go through the store, glad I wouldn't have to avoid looking at the mural. I wasn't sure why, but I was convinced it would make me cry. I hoped it would bring Sam good memories, not painful ones. He hadn't had a chance to pay me for my work, but I was glad of that, too. I hadn't wanted to take his money regardless. With the last of my boxes tucked into the trunk, I re-locked the back door and was gone twenty minutes after I'd arrived.

I called Dana on my way out of town, partly to keep my mind from running in circles, but also in the hope that her familiar voice might cheer me up. Remind me why I had been excited about this move in the first place.

It was still early yet, but the sun was up, and I remembered Dana had been a morning person back in college. Banking on the hope that not too much had changed in the intervening years, I dialed her number and held the phone up to my ear.

It seemed to ring forever.

"Good morning, *Sparrow*," came the cranky voice at last. Oops, I must have woken her after all.

"Sorry, Dana," I said meekly. "I was hoping you were still an early riser."

"That was before kids," she informed me with a yawn. "And never on weekends. It's cool though, I need to get up anyway. What's up, El?"

I transferred the phone to my other ear. "I just wanted to let you know I was on my way again. My car is all fixed, and I should be there in a few hours."

"Okay," she said with a laugh, and I caught an edge in her voice. "Should I expect you in about six hours, or two weeks?"

I frowned. "I told you I was sorry. I really am on my way this time."

She sighed. "I know, El. Sorry, I didn't mean to snap at you. I just get a new story every time I talk to you. Whenever you get here is fine, really. It's no problem."

Something twisted in my stomach. I'd always considered my spontaneity a positive trait. It meant that I was flexible and always ready for anything. I'd never really considered that maybe I was just *flaky*.

I put on a smile, hoping it would show through in my voice. "Well, I'm on my way now. Maybe we can grab lunch together? I've had a crazy week; I can tell you all about it." It would be good to get another perspective on it all.

"Can't today." Dana yawned again. "I'll be out all day. But I'll leave the door unlocked for you. Just make yourself at home."

I felt disappointment well up inside me, but reminded myself she hadn't known I was coming today. It wasn't her fault. It was my own. Again.

Oh well, there would be plenty of time to catch up with her later. I'd be there for...well, who knew how long. Long enough to start on my book illustration project, but not so long that I was imposing on her. And then I'd be off again. To somewhere new. Boston, maybe. I'd never been there.

The thought didn't fill me with excitement like I expected. Oh, I definitely wanted to go to Boston. Or Rhode Island, or wherever I ended up. Maine, maybe. I just didn't want to go there alone.

I sighed as I signaled and merged onto the interstate, leaving Fairfield behind. It had taken such a short amount of time to fall for Sam. Why did I have the sinking feeling that it would take much longer to get over him?

CHAPTER 12

SAM

I wasn't surprised to find Ellen gone when I woke up. Disappointed, yes. Heartbroken, yes. But not surprised.

I *was* a little surprised that she had managed to get all of her boxes out of the apartment without waking me, but considering how poorly I'd slept the night before, I imagined it would have taken a lot to wake me once I'd finally fallen unconscious.

Waking in my bed alone felt so foreign, so *wrong*, as did eating breakfast alone hunched over the counter, and it amazed me how she had fit herself so easily into my life so quickly.

I found her note on the counter, and after the sense of gut-wrenching loss I'd felt at finding the guest room cleared out that morning, I couldn't suppress the jolt of hope that shot through me when I saw my name scribbled on the paper in her messy handwriting. I held my breath as I unfolded the paper, not even sure what I was hoping for. "Gone to pick up my car, back soon?" "Maybe we can make this work long distance?" Or maybe, "I've changed my mind and I can't live without you; let me give up all my hopes and dreams and stay with you forever in Nowhere, Indiana?" I snorted humorlessly, opened the paper, and read:

Sam,

I'm sorry I can't stay for the party today. I think it'll be better if I'm not there. Tell Jeanne I said hi and tell Geoff I'm sorry I couldn't stay long enough to say goodbye. And Sam, I'm sorry. Not about the party. But for everything else.

Ellen

I folded the paper again with nerveless fingers and let it fall onto the counter. She was sorry. *For what?* I wondered. For her hurtful words last night? For not even staying long enough to say goodbye? Maybe for breaking my heart?

I guessed I would never know.

I wasn't sure it mattered.

Geoff was there when I came down alone to open the store. He didn't say a word, but two cherry Danishes appeared on my desk half an hour later, along with a steaming mug of coffee. I didn't know if that made me feel better or worse.

The morning lasted forever, the interminable ticking of the clock on my office wall loud in the confined space. I stayed in my office, preferring the solitude there to the people that gathered in the store, eager to exclaim over the finished mural. I tried not to look at it. I loved it, and appreciated all the work she had done, for me and for my store; I just didn't want to see it. Not right now. So instead I hid out in my office, letting Geoff and Rachel and Marian deal with the customers, while I sat in silence, pretending to work, vacillating between sadness and anger. Anger at myself for being right the whole time. I had known a guy like me would never be enough for a woman like her. I was no world traveler, no linguist, no adventurer. I wasn't spontaneous or extroverted. Why had I thought I'd be enough to convince her to stay? No, I had known better from the start, and I'd let myself get hurt anyway.

But I stared at my computer screen and tried not to think about how mad I was that I'd gotten myself into this mess. Or about how empty my apartment would be when I went upstairs, or about how she'd only been gone for a few hours, but I already missed her laugh, and her smile, and her presence so much it hurt.

* * *

The last thing in the world I wanted to do was go to the birthday party. But at the same time, I supposed it would be a reprieve from the mindless staring and churning thoughts that had occupied my day so far. So it was with a mixed sense of relief and foreboding that I left the store that afternoon in the capable hands of my employees—who gave me wary and sympathetic looks, but were wise enough not to say anything —and made the short drive across town to my parents' house.

They lived just outside of the suburbs, in the house I'd grown up in, a kind of modern-style farmhouse on a few acres of land. It hadn't changed much since I'd lived there; the house was still largely a shrine to my brother, with framed prints of his paintings lining the walls interspersed with photos of the four of us together. Functionally, it had changed though, as for a few years now it had been occupied part-time by a rampaging toddler, and thus toys and photographs of Dylan were strewn over most surfaces. My brother and Jeanne had joint custody, and yet my nephew spent most of his daytime hours at my parents' house. Or at least he had until he'd started kindergarten the year before. During summer vacation, though, all bets were off, and my parents' house had turned back into Dylan's personal play space once again. School had just started up again, but their house hadn't yet recovered.

It actually cheered me momentarily, seeing Dylan's toys spread over the floor as I let myself in, and then the monster himself was on me, arms wrapped around my waist in a bear hug.

"Uncle Sam! It's my birthday!"

"I know, buddy," I said, dropping to my knees so I could hug him properly. "Happy birthday!"

"Thanks! There's gonna be cake. And presents, too! I know what some of them are, but not all of them. I don't know what that one is," he said suggestively, eyeing the wrapped package I held.

"And you're not going to until later," I informed him. "You like surprises."

He considered this, his dark hair falling over his eyes. He looked so much like my brother, but he had Jeanne's warm gray eyes. "That's true," he said after a moment. "I do like surprises."

And then he was off, darting into the other room at full speed.

I rose to my feet, still smiling, and left my present—a jigsaw puzzle, one of Dylan's current obsessions—on the table with the other wrapped packages by the entryway. I made my way into the kitchen where everyone was gathered, counting down the last few seconds before my family struck.

They were efficient about it, at least.

"Sammy, you made it. I wasn't sure you'd remember."

"Hi, Mom." I dropped an obligatory kiss on her proffered cheek and took a seat at the kitchen island. I had called during the week to tell her I was bringing Ellen with me, and while she'd had a lot to say about that at the time, she seemed to have forgotten now. Though to be fair, I much preferred it that way. I didn't want to talk about Ellen. Or the mural.

Of course, I couldn't be *that* lucky.

My brother Jeremy wandered into the room and gave me a slap on the back. "Hey man, I heard you got someone else to paint the wall of your store. How dare you?"

He winked and grabbed a sandwich from the tray on the island, then settled into a chair next to me. I knew he was joking—my brother wasn't a bad guy, and I knew he was aware of the way my parents compared the two of us, but I think he found it more amusing than hurtful.

My mother looked up at his comment though. "That's right Sammy, you really didn't consider your brother's feelings." Jeremy choked on his sandwich and coughed. "Is the mural done?" she went on. "You said you'd bring pictures."

"It's done," I said shortly. "And sorry, I forgot." I *had* forgotten, but I probably wouldn't have brought them had I remembered. The mural was a work of art, but I certainly didn't need to hear the inevitable comparison.

"Oh, Sam."

"You can always come to the store and see it," I said mildly.

My mother gave me a martyred look—her specialty—and bent to remove a pan from the oven. "Like I have time to come all the way into town when I'm busy chasing my grandson all over the house. I just wanted to see what you had done. It's good that you're trying to cheer up your store. I've always thought it was awfully—"

My father poked his graying head into the room, effectively cutting her off. "Have you seen my newspaper—oh, hi Sam, didn't hear you come in. Say, have you read Jer's book yet? Real work of art." He didn't stay to wait for a response, just wandered back out in search of the crossword puzzle he had no doubt abandoned.

"That's right," my brother informed me with a grin. "A real work of art."

"Now don't be modest, Jeremy," my mother started. "You know you—"

At that moment a hand reached over my shoulder and a full glass of wine appeared on the counter in front of me. I grabbed it without hesitation and took a long drink, shooting a grateful look to where Jeanne was pulling out the chair on my other side.

"Jeanne!" my mother exclaimed. "This is a child's birthday party."

"I didn't give any wine to Dylan," Jeanne said mildly. "Just thought Sam might like a drink."

"Why would Sam want a drink?" my mom asked suspiciously, but her attention was captured a moment later by Dylan, racing through the kitchen and colliding with her legs.

"So, where's Ellen?" Jeanne asked in a low voice. "Didn't you say she was coming?"

"She couldn't make it. She said to tell you she was sorry, and it was nice to meet you." I worked hard to keep my voice and expression even, but I must not have succeeded, because Jeanne's eyes widened.

She lowered her voice further. "Is everything okay?"

"She left," I said tersely.

"Like…left left?"

"Yes. You knew she was only staying until her car got fixed." I took a long drink of my wine.

"Well, yes. But I mean…I thought that might change."

"Well, it didn't."

Wisely, she let the subject drop, and after a minute I rose from the island and went to help my mom carry dishes into the dining room. I felt Jeanne's eyes on me though, all through dinner, though I successfully avoided sitting next to her.

The evening dragged. We ate dinner—all of Dylan's favorite foods, which made for an interesting spread of macaroni and cheese, tater tots, French fries, and buttered noodles.

Dylan had had another party earlier in the week with his friends, so this one was family only, and with just the six of us—my parents, Jeremy, Jeanne, myself, and Dylan—I had hoped the focus would stay on my nephew. And while he did command much of the attention, there was still plenty of time left over for my parents to question my life choices, for Jeremy to poke fun at me and graciously accept praise from our parents, and for Jeanne to send sympathetic glances my way. By the time we'd finished Dylan's birthday cake and turned to opening presents, I wanted nothing more than to lock myself in my apartment, alone, and never come out. Well, maybe not alone, but that was the only option at present.

I'd been filled in on Jeremy's travel schedule for the year, his book signings, art exhibitions, and future plans, and every word he said just reminded me more of Ellen. They really would have been perfect for each other, I thought bitterly. They had so much in common—the love of travel, of art, and the willingness to jump into something new at the slightest distraction. It was a wonder my brother had stayed married to Jeanne as long as he had.

I glanced her way and found her watching me, and she rose and crossed the room, finding a seat on the sofa by my side as her son ripped open presents across the room.

"You look terrible," she said bluntly.

"Thanks."

"Seriously. You look like someone ran over your dog. I'm surprised no one has noticed."

I raised my eyebrow at her. "I'm not."

"Okay, I'm not either," she conceded with a smile. "Seriously though, tell me what's going on."

I'd only had two glasses of wine, and I wasn't drunk, far from it, but the combination of the loose feeling from the alcohol and the sympathetic ear of someone who actually cared drove me to honesty.

"I can't believe I messed up so bad."

"What do you mean?" she asked.

I sighed and leaned back against the sofa. "I knew what Ellen was like from the beginning. She's adventurous and independent. A world traveler. Spontaneous. I mean, those are all things I love about her, but she was never going to be happy with a guy like me. I just didn't expect to fall for her the way I did."

Jeanne narrowed her eyes at me. "What do you mean, a guy like you?"

I waved my hand vaguely. "You know, someone…I don't know. Boring. Quiet. Whatever the opposite of spontaneous is. Someone who hasn't accomplished anything."

"Oh, you mean like getting the first master's degree in his family? Or buying a building and opening a successful business by age thirty?"

I shook my head. "You're missing the point."

"No, I'm not." She flipped her blond hair over her shoulder and fixed me with a stare. "You're not boring, and there's nothing wrong with being quiet. And you're spontaneous. You invited Ellen to stay with you two seconds after meeting her. That's not only spontaneous, but kind, too. You let her paint the entire back wall of your store with barely any consideration. I think you two have more in common than you think."

I shrugged. Dylan had finished opening his presents and was now elbows deep in a train set. My father was down on the floor, reading the instructions while Dylan spread the pieces out in front of him. My mom had vanished back into the kitchen, and my brother had taken over Dad's crossword puzzle. No one was paying any attention to me and Jeanne.

"She needs to be with someone like Jeremy. Someone on her level." I sighed, draining the last of my wine, and cast a glance over at my brother. "At least that way when one of them moved on to something new and sparkly, no one would get hurt."

Jeanne laughed. "It's true, your brother's attention span was never his strongest attribute."

I glanced over at her. It had been nearly six years, and both she and my brother seemed fine with the roles they had, but still, I could sometimes see the sadness in her eyes. "I'm sorry he hurt you," I said. "I don't think I ever told you that."

"Oh, Sam. I appreciate that. But that's not why Jeremy and I didn't work out."

"No?"

"No. Jeremy and I just weren't right for each other. He would have stayed with me, I think, if I'd pressed it. But we weren't good together. But you and Ellen—you were. I know I only met her once, but you two were good together, you really were."

I looked down into my empty glass. "It didn't matter in the end."

"I'm sorry this happened," Jeanne said quietly. "I really am. But if she left, it was because of her issues, not because of you."

We were quiet for a long moment, until finally I said,

"You know, I never even got her phone number. It never occurred to me, and she left so fast."

Jeanne put an arm around my shoulder. "I know it's cheesy, but it's true. If what you had was real, she'll come back on her own. And if she doesn't...well. I guess you won't be any worse off than you are now, huh?"

CHAPTER 13

ELLEN

*I*nterstates all looked the same. Especially in the Midwest. Just long expanses of flat, endless pavement, cornfields only broken by small, identical towns stretching to the horizon, which never grew any closer. There was nothing new to look at, nothing to grab my attention, nothing to keep me from thinking about Sam. From remembering how he'd looked the first night I saw him, tall and broad-shouldered, emanating an aura of calm competence. I missed his soothing energy. His dark eyes and the intensity of his expression, which made me feel like when I spoke, he was really listening.

For the first hour or two, every time a thought of Sam entered my mind, I pushed it away. I blocked it out, and filled it instead with thoughts of the future, of Dana, of my mom, *anything*. It didn't work. So instead I gave in, and I wallowed. I pictured him in my mind, his dark hair, the slow curl of his mouth when he smiled. I pictured waking up next to him in the morning, his sleepy protests when I tried to get out of bed, his arm around my waist, pulling me closer. His lips on mine. His lips everywhere.

When my phone rang, it startled me so bad I had to stop myself from jerking the steering wheel and running the car off the road. I answered the call without checking who it was.

"Hello?"

"Sparrow, darling!"

"Hey, mom. What's up?"

"I just wanted to check in with you, sweetie. Did you go to the party?"

"No, mom, I didn't. I ended up leaving early." I glanced at the clock in the dashboard. The party would be going on right now. I couldn't be very far from Dana's at this point.

"Oh, did you? Honey, I think that's probably for the best."

"Uh-huh." My voice sounded flat to my own ears.

"Are you in Ohio, then?"

"Yeah. I don't have too far to go, I don't think."

"That's good. Drive safe, sweetie. I'm on the road again, too. North Carolina, did I tell you?"

"Yep, you mentioned it," I said.

"Well, it's lovely. You should come down here some time. Oh! I nearly forgot! You'll need to be free in the last week of August."

"Why's that?" I asked.

"I'm getting married!"

This time, I did jerk the steering wheel. I quickly swerved back into my own lane as a horn sounded behind me.

"What?!"

A semi rushed by as I changed lanes, heading for the upcoming exit ramp. I shouldn't be driving during a conversation like this.

"What the hell do you mean you're getting married? To *who?*"

"To Scott, darling. I'm sure I've told you about him."

"You most certainly have *not.*"

"I could have sworn—oh well, I'm telling you now. He's wonderful," my mother trilled. "We met in Florida, and he's meeting me here in North Carolina. I don't know where we'll be for the wedding, but you have to be my maid-of-honor."

"I—sure, Mom, of course, but who *is* he?" I pulled into a gas station and cut the engine.

"Who, Scott?"

"*Yes*, Scott!"

"Oh, I met him at the grocery store. He's a real sweet-heart. He used to fly commercial jets, but he's retired now, and—"

I tuned her out. I mean, I still listened, and responded appropriately, but my brain had short-circuited midway through. So, I just let her go on for a while, congratulated her, promised I would check in again soon, then ended the call. I felt shell-shocked.

My mom was getting *married*? That wasn't even the real kicker. I mean, of course I wanted my mom to be happy. I was glad she'd found someone, and I was honestly happy for her. But what really hurt was that I hadn't even known she was dating anyone. I wondered how long this had been going on. She hadn't even been in Florida that long. Less than a year, I thought. Maybe six months?

Abruptly, I felt sorry for Scott, whoever he was. My mother meant well, she always did, but she'd never even mentioned him any of the many times I'd spoken to her since she'd been back.

I'd always known my mom was flighty. My dad had been the more level-headed of the pair. But this seemed like too much, even for her. Had she really forgotten to tell me about him? Or had she maybe left him out of our conversations intentionally, knowing this was how I would react?

I dropped my phone into the passenger's seat, wondering

if the marriage would last. At least it sounded like the guy enjoyed travel and could keep up with my mom's whims, but I wondered how *real* it could actually be if I'd never heard of him before now.

What a way to treat a guy, I thought. *I* wouldn't want to be the person dating my mom, so unimportant that I didn't even come up in conversation with her daughter. But it was typical of my mom, selfishly letting the world organize itself around *her*.

My stomach suddenly dropped.

But wasn't that exactly what I'd done to Sam? Kept him at arm's length, treating him as temporary and unimportant? Like he didn't figure into my plans, so his feelings didn't matter?

Tears pricked behind my eyes. And what about my *own* feelings? Didn't they matter either?

Did I really want to end up like my mom? To be fair, she was happy. My mom had always been happy with our life-style—my dad, too. But I couldn't honestly say I'd been *happy* leaving my home every time I got settled, leaving friends I'd just gotten to know. I'd just been *used* to it. Maybe I'd thought the feeling of setting out into something new was happiness, but really, was it just the safety of something familiar?

I closed my eyes and leaned back against the seat. I missed Sam. A lot. More than I'd ever missed anyone I'd left behind before, and it had been less than a day.

Again, I let myself imagine for one brief moment what it would be like if I stayed. Could I really see myself in Fair-field, Indiana, putting down roots? Sam and I would argue, and it would be scary, and would he still like me if he got to know me even better? Would I be able to deal with his parents, who probably wouldn't like me on principle?

I thought the answer to those questions might be yes. And

what was the worst that could happen? I'd give it a try, and maybe it wouldn't work out. And it would hurt, but then I'd move on. Like millions of couples did all the time. Like I'd done before.

Maybe my mom wasn't crazy and flighty, I thought, opening my eyes and staring up at the sky through the windshield. Maybe she was brave. My dad had been gone for years, and he and my mom had been so perfect for each other. She was taking a risk on someone new, but maybe it was worth it, and even if it didn't work out, she was going to marry the guy and give it all she had.

Did I really want to end up like my mom? Yes, maybe I did.

I started the engine and pulled out of the gas station, and when the ramp to the interstate came, I took the second turn, and headed west. The way I'd come. Back to Fairfield, Indiana.

I had messed up, and I prayed I wasn't too late.

* * *

I had just crossed the border between Ohio and Indiana when I realized I had another call to make.

"Hey, El, what's up? You close?"

"Hi Dana. Look, I'm really sorry, but I'm not going to be there today after all. In fact, I'm not really sure what's going on yet."

"Oh? Everything okay?"

"I think so. I hope so. I'm heading back to Indiana. I shouldn't have left yet, and I owe someone an apology. I'll fill you in soon, but I wanted to let you know I wasn't coming."

Dana's laughter was a little resigned. "It's okay, El. I didn't really expect you today anyway."

My voice was quiet. "I'm really sorry Dana. I really do want to see you."

"I know, El. I want to see you too." There was a pause, and I tried to think of what to say, but then she sighed. "Don't worry, I'm not mad, I get it. I know you, El. You'll get here when you get here. Or not. My house is always open to you, now, or next year, or in five more."

"I—" My throat felt tight, and I didn't know what to say. "Okay. Um. Thanks, Dana."

"No worries. Don't forget to call sometime and tell me what's going on in Indiana."

I hung up the phone feeling even worse. Was I really that bad of a friend? She hadn't expected me to show, even though I'd called her with every update, to try not to inconvenience her too much. I swallowed the lump in my throat.

I wasn't spontaneous and adventurous. I was inconsiderate and rude. And selfish.

Sam had been right. Real relationships took work. From both sides. That meant friendships too. And he hadn't been asking me to change, but maybe he should have.

I didn't deserve a friend like Dana, and I hoped I'd be able to make it up to her someday. But for now, I needed to make it up to Sam. I pressed down on the gas pedal, and my little car sped down the interstate.

It started to rain just as it was getting dark. With my windshield wipers smearing the oncoming headlights into blobs of light in my vision, I drove as fast as I safely could, the rain slicking the pavement and slowing the traffic.

With every mile that passed, I became more sure of my decision, more certain that Sam had been right and I had messed up. What a poor way to treat someone, especially someone I cared about as much as I cared about him. I hadn't gone with him to the party even though I'd promised, and I'd known he was going to have a hard time there. I'd said hurtful things to him the night before. I'd left, and hadn't even said goodbye. I really hoped he didn't hate me now. I was doing enough of that myself.

It seemed like an eternity had passed when my headlights lit up the big, green sign. Fairfield, five miles. *Finally.*

I took the exit, relief warring with trepidation in my chest, and made my way down the long, winding road that led into town. When I passed The Traveler's Inn, I couldn't keep the smile off my face. I hoped they'd been able to deal with the bedbugs. So many changes in my life, sparked by something so seemingly insignificant.

It seemed like forever before the distant streetlights of town wavered into view, then finally the rows of storefronts appeared, their familiar awnings stretching cheerfully over the sidewalk. The antique shop, the barbershop, and there, finally—Sam's Books.

The bookstore was closed, as I had anticipated, so I turned the corner and parked in the back alley, where the outside door led directly into the back hallway that led up to Sam's apartment. When I pulled on the handle, I found that door was locked as well, and when I glanced around I realized his truck wasn't parked in the alley lot. Looking up, I saw there were no lights on in his apartment.

He wasn't home.

All of my elation at finally making it back drained out in a rush, leaving only exhaustion and worry behind. What if Sam didn't forgive me? What if he decided I was more trouble than I was worth? I couldn't really blame him. What if I had overinflated his feelings for me, and he hadn't really been that upset to see me go in the first place? I hadn't talked to him since our argument the night before, after all. The what-ifs spiraled in my head, gaining traction in my thoughts.

I forced them down and turned my head up to the rain, letting the cool water wash over my face. The rain had lightened to a gentle mist, and it felt good after the stuffy interior of my car, so I lowered myself down onto the steps, groaning as my stiff joints protested, and leaned my head back against the door.

It was fine. It had to be. I'd come all this way; for Sam I could wait a little longer.

CHAPTER 14

SAM

*S*pending the evening with my family was just as frustrating as I'd expected it to be. But while on any other day I would have found an excuse to leave early, today I was finding even my mother's snide remarks more appealing than the thought of returning home to my empty apartment.

So, I stayed, after the party had officially ended and my brother had gone home. It was Jeanne's turn to keep Dylan, but my parents had asked if he could stay with them for the night, so eventually Jeanne left as well, giving me a hug and ruffling my hair on the way out. My dad retrieved what was left of his crossword puzzle and my mom parked herself in front of the television, in search of a home improvement show, which left me and Dylan to dive into the jigsaw puzzle I'd brought him.

The puzzle had seven hundred pieces and was possibly a bit advanced for him, but the picture on the front depicted a battle scene between a group of dinosaurs and an army of armor-clad Vikings, and honestly, who could pass that up?

He cheerfully ignored my suggestion to look for edge

pieces and instead started hunting for dinosaur faces, and we passed the time in content concentration until my mom announced that it was Dylan's bedtime and I decided I couldn't avoid my apartment any longer.

I hugged my dad and kissed my mom on the cheek and ignored her advice to, "Have your brother come do a book signing at your store, it'll be good for business,"—even though she was probably right—and headed out to my truck.

It had started raining sometime while I'd been at my parents' house, and while it wasn't coming down too hard, the sky was dark, roiling clouds blocking out the moon as I carefully made my way back into town.

The weather matched my mood. I wasn't angry anymore, and after talking with Jeanne, I wasn't feeling sorry for myself any longer, either. I was just sad. Sad because I'd finally found someone who really seemed to get me, who was fun and silly, who was smart and kind and sexy. Someone I had an immediate connection with, and really seemed to feel the same way…but in the end, it hadn't been enough.

I would get over her, I supposed. Though having that mural taking up a whole wall of my store certainly wouldn't help. The problem was, I didn't *want* to get over her.

The rainstorm had picked up slightly during my drive into town, and I pulled carefully into my space in the alley behind the bookstore, readying myself to make a run for the back door.

I almost didn't see her there, sitting on the stoop, illuminated by the single security light shining through the rain. But she shifted when I turned the truck off, rising to her feet on shaky legs, and all thought fled my mind.

She came back.

The rain faded to background noise, and I climbed out of the truck, ignoring the droplets of water quickly soaking into my clothes. I walked toward her on numb feet, my eyes scanning over her and my mind processing every detail.

Her clothes were wet, and while they weren't soaked, I was reminded of the first time I'd seen her, dripping in the doorway to the store. But the wet clothing was the only similarity. This time instead of the ready smile and sparkling eyes, her face looked red, her eyes puffy. I stopped in front of her and she tried to smile at me, but it was tremulous, and I could see the hope and fear on her face clear as day. She didn't say anything, and was clearly terrified of how I was going to react, so I did the only thing I could. I reached out and pulled her into my arms, lowering my head to press my lips against hers before my heart exploded.

Her mouth was soft, and I raised my hands to cup her face, pouring all the emotion of the day into the kiss, all the frustration, and longing, and fear, and sadness, and she wrapped her arms around me tight, and I hoped she'd never let me go.

When I finally pulled back she was crying in earnest, and laughing too, and all she could get out was, "Sam, I'm so sorry," before I reached around her and unlocked the door, clumsily walking her backward into the stairwell before she stood on her tiptoes and dragged my head back down to hers.

I'm not sure how we made it upstairs. Stumbling and staggering up one step at a time, stopping to press her against the wall, sliding my hands beneath her shirt to feel her chilled skin, slipping on the water that puddled beneath us when we stopped, finally picking her up and carrying her up the last few steps and into my apartment.

I swallowed her apologies with my mouth, and she dragged her fingers through my hair, pulling harder when I groaned against her, tracing her jaw with my lips.

Our clothes were hard to get off, clinging damply to our

skin, but we did it together, laughing, between kisses and gasps and groans, and finally I had her skin under my hands. I touched her everywhere I could, warming her with my hands and my body, and she responded just as fervently, running her hands over me like she would never get enough, holding me tight like she would never let go.

We didn't make it past the couch.

* * *

Hours later, we came up for air. We'd moved to the bathroom at some point, where I'd urged her to take a shower to warm up. She dragged me in after her, and we warmed up together before ending up in the bedroom, wrapped in towels.

We sat facing each other on the bed, and I couldn't keep myself from touching her, tracing the shell of her ear with a finger, or tucking a strand of hair over her shoulder, or lacing her fingers through mine. She raised our joined hands to her lips and gently kissed the backs of my fingers.

"You were right, Sam," she finally said, her voice quiet. "It was an excuse. When I get scared or overwhelmed, I run away. I'm not used to...having real relationships. I'm sorry I left the way I did."

I nodded, her words warming me more than the hot water of the shower had.

"I'm sorry too," I said. "I shouldn't have expected to you to just drop everything, all your plans, just to be with me. I said I wasn't asking you to change for me, but I guess I was. And that wasn't fair."

She shook her head and looked down. "I think I could use some change," she said quietly. "Some growing up, maybe. I think I'd like to learn what a real relationship can be like."

I tucked a finger under her chin and tilted her head up to look at me. "I want this to work, El. I want to be with you."

Tears welled in her eyes, but she blinked them back. "I want to be with you too. I want to stay here, in Fairfield, and make it work."

I wanted nothing more. "But I don't want you to change who you are," I said. "You're adventurous, and fun, and independent, and *that's* the woman I fell in love with." Her breath caught, but I pressed on. "I don't want to tie you down and make you feel stuck." I tilted my head and looked at her. "Maybe all you need is a home base."

Her voice was thick but her gaze was steady on mine. "Would you come with me? When I travel? Then we can always come home together."

I tightened my fingers around hers. "You know I will."

She leaned in to kiss me, and I could feel her smile against my lips."Maybe I've been looking at it wrong all along. Maybe my home isn't a place," she murmured against me. "Maybe it's a person."

"Maybe it's you."

FOLLOW YOUR HEART

CHAPTER 1

BRIA

*N*umerous scientific studies have shown that there is no actual link between the full moon and increased hospital admissions. But as anyone who has worked in an emergency department will tell you—that's bullshit. Everything's crazy during a full moon.

Which meant that after a case of kidney stones, a bad dog bite, two cases of the flu, one of strep throat, and an elderly lady with chest pain, coupled with the fact that I'd eaten nothing more than peanut butter crackers since my shift started over ten hours ago, I was understandably tired and grumpy.

It hadn't helped that Dr. Ashvale had been on duty when I'd arrived, and he'd been in rare form too, full of barked orders and scathing comments. At least he was off shift now.

"You're all good to go," I told my chest pain patient, who I had just spend the last ten minutes walking through how to take her medication and what to do if her symptoms persisted, and handed her discharge papers across to where she sat perched on the bed. She gingerly took them, making an obvious effort not to make contact with my tattoo-covered hands, as if the decoration might be catching. I suppressed both an eye roll and a scathing comment, and left her there to head back to the nurses station, where I sank gratefully into a chair. The change in hospital policy to allow visible tattoos was recent, and fortunate, as I wouldn't have been offered the job otherwise, but I had forgotten how close-minded small towns could be.

"Will this day ever end?"

My coworker, Claire, threw herself down next to me and slouched dramatically. "I swear, you'd think it was Friday the thirteenth, and a Monday, and a full moon all rolled into one!"

I snorted. "Friday and Monday at the same time; that'd be something else. Besides," I nudged her shoulder. "You've only been here for two hours."

"Yeah, well, it feels like a million," she said through a yawn. A second later she sat up, squinting at the camera set into the desk which showed a view of the hallway leading from triage. "Uh-oh."

I glanced at the screen and sighed in commiseration. It looked like there was no reprieve to be found just yet. We both watched the hunched figure in the wheelchair, rolling down the hallway with the guidance of Kristen, the charge nurse. I rolled my shoulders and tilted my head to the side, cracking my neck. Only just over an hour to go, I reminded myself.

Claire, who had been leaning over my shoulder just moments before, seemed to have conveniently disappeared by the time Kristen had escorted the hunched figure into a room and came out to assign his care. I schooled my glower into a resigned shrug, accepting her answering apologetic grimace, then squared my shoulders and headed toward the room.

Mr. Templeton was one of the small handful of patients

the nurses tended to refer to as "frequent fliers." I couldn't even count how many times he'd been in to the emergency department already this year, and it was only going to increase as the weather got colder. It was a tricky situation. On one hand, he took staff and resources away from other patients, tying up rooms and often wasting the staff's time. But on the other hand, November in Indiana was no joke when you were homeless. And it would only get colder from here.

"Oh, it's you," he grumbled in his gravelly voice as I pulled back the curtain and entered his room. He looked me over with his trademark sneer, his milky eyes catching on my tattoos. "You know that skin came from God. You insult Him when you deface it."

The effort it took to keep my face pleasant was monumental. Probably deserving of an award. I consulted his chart. "What seems to be the problem today, Mr. Templeton?"

As if I didn't already know.

"My back is killing me. I need something for the pain."

"Well, let me check your vitals and we'll get the doctor in here to see what he can do for you."

Mr. Templeton was in rare form that morning. He cursed at me and called me names as I checked his pulse ("Degenerate! Blue hair is unnatural!"), spit out the thermometer ("Useless untrained idiot wasting my time!"), and knocked the blood pressure cuff out of my hands twice before I was able to wrap it around his scrawny arm and get a reading ("You look like a felon!"). As usual, all his stats were normal, and aside from the nearly overwhelming stench of alcohol wafting from his pores, which was nothing new, he seemed to be in reasonably good condition for a sixty-something-year-old homeless alcoholic.

I closed my ears to his insults and was only shaking a

little by the time I finally made my way out to the nurses station. I leaned over the desk and took a few deep breaths. It's nothing new, I reminded myself. I'd heard it all before, from him and many others.

And it was true. I'd been hearing it for years. Ever since I'd moved back to small town Indiana after years in the city. Even though I'd grown up here—not in Fairfield, but another small Hoosier town not far away, nearly identical in both population size and small-town mindset—it was still a bit of a culture shock moving back again.

My parents had both grown up in big cities—Chicago for my mom, New York for my dad—and moved to Indiana for my father's teaching job when I'd been a toddler. Splitting my time between our home in Indiana and visiting grandparents in the cities, I'd learned quickly that I preferred the anonymity and relative cultural freedom of the metropolitan environment.

The teasing started in middle school. As I grew bigger, my hometown seemed to grow smaller around me, the teasing increasing as the differences between me and the other kids grew, and it wasn't until I left home for college in Chicago that I began to finally find a group of people I fit in with.

That was when I'd gotten my first tattoo. It had been on my eighteenth birthday, a tiny rose picked off the wall and applied to my hip, my terrified hand clutching tight to my laughing roommate as I put on a brave face and tried not to pass out.

I'd laughed when the artist had warned me that tattoos were addictive and people rarely stopped at just one. Not for *me*, I'd told him. One was all I'd ever need.

That had lasted less than two months.

It certainly hadn't helped when my roommate began to date a tattoo artist. And when the tattoos had led into piercings, and then colored hair after that, well, they were all just different forms of self-expression, right? Just new ways for me to feel at home in my skin, something I'd never managed to accomplish before. A collection of beautiful artwork that conveniently covered up my differences.

Besides, it had never seemed like any big deal at the time. I'd never felt out of place in Chicago. When I came home to visit my parents, they'd just roll their eyes and shake their heads and ask what I'd done this time, and I'd enjoy the ease of their non-judgmental company before escaping back to the city.

I certainly hadn't imagined I'd ever end up back in rural Indiana.

Claire appeared next to me at the nurses station, shaking me out of my reverie, and I reminded myself that not everyone here was as judgmental as Mr. Templeton.

She sent me an apologetic glance and squeezed my arm. "Sorry I left you with Mr. Templeton. The last time I had him he puked on me."

I shuddered in sympathy. "Oh, man. Usually he holds his alcohol better than that."

"Yeah. Back pain again?"

I nodded, and forced myself to think charitable thoughts. "I think last night was the first drop below freezing, too. Poor guy's probably cold. I might just let him sleep for a bit after Dr. McClimon checks him out."

"'Poor guy?' Have you heard the way he talks to you?" Claire gave me a look. "Besides, we're not a hotel, you know."

"I know," I sighed. "But we've got the room, at least until the next wave comes in. I'll discharge him when we need the space."

We were a small hospital, with an even smaller emergency department, but by some luck the full moon rush seemed to finally be quieting down. At the moment I had two of my assigned beds empty, and my only patients were Mr.

Templeton and a new guy who had just been brought in from an ambulance and shown into room five. It couldn't hurt to let the man rest for a bit before kicking him back out into the cold. Even mean, judgmental people deserved a break, though sometimes it was easier to tell myself that than others.

I ducked away from Claire's disapproving look and went to check on my new guy. Less than an hour to go now.

"Geoffrey Ashvale? I'm Bria, your nurse—"

I was reading the chart to get an overview of the patient as I pushed past the curtain—bad knife wound on his arm, likely needed stitches—and was therefore unprepared for the panicked gasp of the wild eyed, messy-haired young man perched on the edge of the bed as he cut me off mid-sentence.

"Who's the doctor on duty?"

I eyed him strangely. "It's Dr. McClimon," I answered, checking him over. He wore jeans and a long-sleeved green t-shirt, one sleeve of which was currently soaked through with blood. He was clutching what appeared to be a dish towel tightly around his forearm, and his eyes were wide and slightly manic. I was just beginning to wonder if I'd need to call for a psych consult, when the man let out a long exhale and sagged back against the bed, closing his eyes.

"Okay, thank you," he said in a much calmer voice. "I'm sorry I interrupted you."

I waited a beat. "Is…that okay?"

"Yes, yep, that's fine. Sorry."

What a weirdo. I guess the full moon brought in all types.

He opened his eyes then, and I saw the moment they landed on me. It was hard to miss the slight double take, especially when you were used to it. I waited. What was it going to be? Insults? Condescension?

"You have blue hair."

Ah. Stating the obvious. Well, that was the least offensive option. Aside from just, you know, treating me like a normal person and not saying anything. But that never happened.

I ignored his statement, and instead moved around to his uninjured arm, unwinding the tangled cord of the blood pressure cuff from the wall and wrapping it around the arm with possibly slightly more force than was strictly necessary.

"Sorry, that was rude," he said after a moment, glancing at me.

"Mm," I responded, squeezing the bulb. "Your blood pressure is fine," I informed him, entering the numbers into my notes.

"I like it. It suits you," he said a moment later, still looking at me, and I glanced up in surprise. That was a new one. I eyed him warily. The last thing I needed was a patient hitting on me. But his gaze was apologetic, not flirtatious. He offered me a small smile, and even the slight change in expression seemed to alter the serious set of his face. It was a nice face, the smile infectious.

To keep myself from smiling back, I held out the thermometer. "Here, put this under your tongue." As he obeyed, I couldn't keep myself from taking a closer look. He was tall, fairly slender, but with long, ropy muscles. A body like a runner rather than a weight-lifter, I decided. His messy hair was dark and soft looking, over a face with serious eyes that crinkled when he smiled.

Reign it in, Bria. Hunger and fatigue must be affecting me more than I thought.

The thermometer beeped, and I practically snatched it back.

"You've got a tattoo," he blurted in surprise, and I followed his gaze to where the bold patterns of ink peeked out from under the long-sleeved shirt I wore under my scrubs and ran across the backs of my hands.

"Are you for real?" I demanded, raising an eyebrow.

He closed his eyes and held out his injured arm. "I'm sorry. I'm making an ass out of myself. Just cut my arm off so I can get out here."

When he opened his eyes again and saw the scissors I was holding, he yanked the arm back out of reach. "I wasn't serious!"

I fought to keep my mouth from twitching. Despite his penchant for speaking the obvious and embarrassing himself, I found I liked the guy. He was making my stressful day more entertaining, at any rate.

"I'm going to cut off your sleeve so I can see your wound," I informed him in my most patient voice. "Your shirt is ruined anyway. So, tell me what happened."

He did as I cleaned out his wound. It turned out he worked in a small downtown bookstore and rented space in a commercial kitchen to make pastries for the bookstore's cafe. He'd sliced his arm open in the kitchen and, to his great embarrassment, had passed out when he saw all the blood. The wound wasn't that serious, but he hadn't realized one of the other chefs there had called for an ambulance until one had shown up.

As he spoke, I watched him covertly watch me, his eyes taking in the ink on my hands, as well as the thin veins of filigree I knew were visible above the collar of my shirt.

The words were out before I could bite them back, and I could hear the defensive note in my voice. "They're just tattoos, you know."

Rather than flush, or look away, as I expected, he met my eyes squarely. There was no apology there this time, just a bit of hesitation and a kind of open honesty. For a second, my breath caught as his gaze trapped me in place. "They're beautiful."

Surprised, I cleared my throat and stepped back, feeling

both flustered and annoyed at myself for feeling that way. "The doctor will be in to stitch you up, and then we can get you on your way," I informed him. Then I fled the room before the flush rose in my own cheeks.

The doctor hadn't been in to see Mr. Templeton yet, but I headed down the hall to check on him anyway, in an effort to compose myself before I returned to the nurses station. I was pretty sure a patient had never called my tattoos beautiful before. And they had certainly never looked at me with dark soulful eyes while doing so.

I shook my head to clear away the foolishness as I pulled back Mr. Templeton's curtain, but the man was gone. He must have checked himself out rather than wait for the doctor. The pity I felt for the old guy, back out in the cold, warred inside me with the relief I felt at not having to deal with him again.

Claire was leaning against the nurses station when I returned.

"Were you with Knife Wound Guy? I saw them bring him in. He's cuuuute," she said, drawing out the word and waggling her eyebrows as she nodded down the hall in the direction of my patient.

"He also has no filter," I replied in a grumble, coming around the desk to join her.

"Oh no, one of those." She winced in sympathy. "What did he say?" She affected a low, mocking growl. "'Tattoos are the devil's mark. You shouldn't ruin your skin. That's not very professional.'"

All things I'd been told before, but I shook my head, feeling my cheeks heat slightly. "He said my hair suits me." I fingered my shoulder-length locks, black at the roots before transitioning to a brilliant cobalt blue at the tips. "And he said my tattoos were beautiful." *And he looked at me and I couldn't look away.*

"Ooooh." Claire's eyes grew wide. "That's romantic."

"Awkward," I corrected her, and myself. "It's awkward. And inappropriate."

She winked. "Not when he looks like that it's not."

She had a point. I leaned over the computer, inputting information into his chart, and suddenly his name caught my attention at the top of the screen. I'd seen it on the chart, but it hadn't registered. Suddenly the guy's concern over which doctor was on duty made sense.

"His name's Geoffrey," I informed her, pointing to the incriminating words at the top of the screen. "Geoffrey *Ashvale.*"

Claire glanced over my shoulder to verify. "Oh no, you don't think…"

"Does Dr. Asshole have a son?" I wondered aloud. I pitied any potential relation of the horrible man. He may be an effective ER doctor, but he'd earned the nickname fairly from his staff, who tended to try to avoid interactions with him at all costs. More than one nurse had transferred out of the ER after a handful of shifts with Dr. Ashvale.

"I dunno. But now that you mention it, they do kind of look a little alike." She sighed. "Okay, you were right. More awkward than romantic."

"It would explain the lack of filter though," I pointed out, and she nodded.

"That's for sure. Well, never mind then. That erases the attractive factor, too."

I wasn't sure I agreed with that one, but one thing was true. If Cute Knife Wound guy was Dr. Asshole's son, he was best avoided at all costs.

CHAPTER 2

GEOFF

The morning could hardly get any worse. Some careless knife work and I'd passed out in front of another chef at the commercial kitchen—my squeamishness around blood was *not* something I liked to admit to people— woken up in the back of an ambulance on the way to the last place on earth I wanted to be, and then made an ass out of myself in front of the nurse. With my day off to such a spectacular start, I shouldn't have been surprised to hear the familiar voice echoing down the hospital corridor as I tried to make my escape.

"Geoff?"

I briefly considered what would happen if I ignored him and kept walking, before letting out an aggrieved sigh and turning around. "Hi, dad. I didn't think you were working this morning."

"I'm not, technically. I came back in for some files."

I shouldn't have been surprised; the man practically lived at work. Which usually made it easier to avoid him.

He frowned at me. "What are you doing here?"

I gestured vaguely with my newly-stitched-up arm. "Just cut my arm. Not a big deal."

His frown deepened. I was pretty sure my father never reached his full frowning potential. There was always another level of frown for him to reach. "Let me see."

I pulled my arm back out of reach. "Dr. McClimon already stitched it. It's fine."

"Who was your nurse? Was it properly cleaned?"

I sighed in exasperation. "I think her name started with a B. Blue hair. She cleaned it out. It's *fine.*"

Another level of frown. "Oh. *Bria.*"

I didn't much like the judgmental way he said her name, and I felt an inexplicable urge to defend her, but I quashed the feeling. Arguing with my dad was a good way to lose an hour better spent on something less awful. Like clawing my eyes out. Besides, I never won.

"Look, I have to go," I said, edging away. "I'm late for work."

His only farewell was a tight nod before he turned and headed down the hallway, and I breathed a sigh of relief. As far as encounters with my father went, I'd call that one a success. He hadn't insulted my chosen profession; he hadn't belittled my work at the bookstore; he hadn't told me what a disappointment I was. Of course, he hadn't needed to. It was all there in the set of his jaw and anyway, I'd heard it all a million times before.

Back outside in the cold, I called a cab to take me back to the kitchen, and on the way I tried to block out the judgmental look on my father's face by remembering the nurse instead.

Bria.

She was both gorgeous and intriguing. When she'd come in with my discharge papers I'd noticed another line of ink running beneath the neckline of her shirt and across her shoulder. Fascinating. I wondered where those patterns went. Was all of her skin covered like that?

By the time I made it back to the kitchen and found my phone, which I'd inadvertently left behind in the rush, I had three missed calls and a handful of texts from my boss, Sam. I called him immediately, and he answered on the second ring.

"Hey, man, are you okay?"

"Yeah, I'm sorry. I cut my arm open in the kitchen, and I had to go to the hospital, but I forgot my phone so I couldn't tell you I was going to be late."

"Whoa, what? Slow down. The hospital? Are you okay?" His voice was concerned.

"Yeah, I'm fine. Just a handful of stitches. I'm sorry I didn't let you know earlier. I can be there in twenty minutes, but I won't have anything for the cafe today."

There was a pause, and then an incredulous laugh. "Dude, that's the least of my worries. You don't have to come in. Marian is covering the cafe. Just take the day off. You sure you're okay?"

"I'm fine. I don't need to take the day off. I'll be there soon." I ended the call.

I knew Sam had a point. He probably didn't need me today, and it would likely be smart to go home and rest. But what the hell would I do there? Work was what I *did*. I baked all morning, and then I spent the rest of my time at the bookstore. Technically my shift ended at one in the afternoon, but more days than not I hung around, often 'til close.

I tried to imagine it, having a day off, as I drove across town to Sam's store. If I was stuck in my house all day, honestly, I would just end up baking. I had a new shortbread recipe I wanted to try anyway. But then I wouldn't be able to serve them in the store, because they weren't made in a certified kitchen, and I wouldn't be able to eat them all myself, so they would just go stale and end up in the trash. No, better I should just go to work. Much less wasteful that way.

When I got there, Marian was behind the counter at the cafe and she tried to insist she had it all under control.

"Geoff, you just came from the *hospital.* Look at your arm! You don't need to be here." I tried to glare, but she just laughed. My look must have turned pleading though, because finally she rolled her eyes and took pity on me, sliding out from behind the counter and throwing her dish rag over her shoulder at me as she left.

The display was looking sad with only a smattering of Danishes and the leftover cheesecake from the day before. I made a mental note to make things I could freeze in case this ever happened again, and then I got to work, cleaning out the coffeemaker and wiping down the counters.

It wasn't long at all before Sam came over. He just looked at my arm and sighed. He wouldn't try to send me home. He'd made an effort on the phone, and he knew I would just ignore him if he tried again, but the look on his face made it clear he thought I was an idiot. He was probably right.

"You sure you're okay?"

"Yep, just had to get a few stitches." No need to mention the passing out. I pulled the blender away from the wall to wipe behind it. I was a little anal about cleanliness in the cafe. In the kitchen, too.

"Hey, stop cleaning. Marian's already been through all that. Come sit down for a minute. As long as you're here, I wanted to talk to you about something."

That sounded ominous. Reluctantly, I put down my dishrag and poured two mugs of coffee before joining Sam at one of the little wrought iron tables. My leg bounced under the table with the effort of holding still.

Sam eyed me. "Was your dad at the hospital?"

"Yeah," I said shortly. I didn't need to elaborate. Sam got it

—I wasn't the only one who had trouble living up to parental expectations.

He winced. "Sorry. Look, I've been meaning to talk to you. I'm planning a kind of open house…party…event type thing. To celebrate our first year in business."

I'd been with him since two weeks after he opened. I counted mentally. "You've been open for sixteen months."

He shrugged. "Okay, a year-ish. Anyway, I wanted to do an open house. A big holiday sale, show off the mural, maybe have a raffle, prizes, promote my brother's book. You know."

He shrugged again, and I eyed him. "That sounds…fancy." Sam was a hard worker, there was no doubt about that, but he was also as laid back as they came. Elaborate parties didn't really seem like his style.

"It was Ellen's idea. She's handling the details."

Ahh, that made much more sense. Ellen was Sam's new girlfriend. She'd swept into town only months before, putting her stamp on the bookstore in the form of an enormous floor-to-ceiling mural, before Sam convinced her to stay and put down some roots. Already, it was like she'd been here for years. I liked her immensely. I especially liked what she did for Sam. She was vivacious and outgoing, everything he was not, but they balanced each other perfectly, softening his hard edges and calming her scattered flightiness. She really must be having an effect on him if he was considering an event to promote his brother's book. Sam and his brother didn't have the easiest of relationships. I could sympathize. Though at least they could stand to be in the same room as each other, which was more than I could say for me and my father.

"Okay," I said. "When is this open house?"

"Next weekend, I was thinking. That'll give us enough time to throw up some fliers and put the event online, but not enough time that Ellen can get too carried away."

I laughed and drained my mug of coffee. "Good plan."

"I was thinking Saturday evening. Pretty laid-back, you can dress up if you want, maybe some food, possibly a cash bar. I was hoping you could help out."

I nodded. "Okay, well you know I'm in. I can serve if you need, and run the register if we'll be selling."

Sam raised an eyebrow. "Man, I'm not asking you to run the register."

I furrowed my brow. "Um, okay?"

He rolled his eyes and I shifted uncomfortably, suddenly aware of where this was going. "I want you to *bake*. I want you to cater it."

I was already shaking my head. "Hell, no. We've talked about this. I'm fine making small things for the cafe, but this is *big*. How many people are we even talking about here?"

Sam shrugged. "A few hundred, probably. Over the course of the evening. Maybe more if we're promoting my brother."

"A few *hundred?*"

His brow creased. "I'd pay you for the extra time, of course. I thought you told me once it wasn't hard to scale up."

"It's not that." I shook my head again. "I can make more food easily. It's that...it's..." I had no idea how to explain.

Sam narrowed his eyes at me and leaned forward across the table. "You're good enough, you know. Everyone freaking loves your food."

I looked down at my empty mug on the tabletop. Sam was a great boss, and a great friend, but I hated how easily he could see through me.

"You know we make more from cafe sales than we ever do from books," he went on. "I keep telling you, you could open your own place easily. I don't even know why you work here."

Just the thought of having my own place made my throat

feel tight. Here, baking was just a hobby. Just something I could do to help Sam out, so he didn't have to buy pastries from somewhere else. But my real job was running the cafe. There was no pressure there. Just an easy job I could enjoy while I figured out what I really wanted to do.

Sam was watching me, his eyes intent, and for a second I had the uncomfortable feeling he could read my thoughts.

"Why? Why don't you want to do it?"

"What, open my own bakery?" I asked incredulously.

"No," he said impatiently. "Cater the open house."

I opened my mouth, but nothing came out. Because he was right. I *did* want to. But the idea was terrifying.

"Right." He sounded satisfied. "Look, just think about it. I'll pay you whatever you need." He eyed me. "I don't even have to tell anyone it's you, if you don't want. Your food is amazing, and it'd be a shame, but you can remain anonymous if you want."

I hesitated. It was tempting. Anonymity was appealing, but it was still only half the battle. Selling a handful of Danishes throughout the day to people buying books was one thing. Catering a party of hundreds was something else entirely. If I failed, *I* would still know who was to blame.

Sam waited me out, quiet and patient, until I couldn't take it anymore.

"Okay. I'll do it." My voice sounded a little hoarse to my ears. I knew this wasn't nearly as big a deal as I was making it out to be, but at the same time it felt huge. This opportunity would force me to admit to myself how much baking meant to me, and I wasn't sure I was ready for that.

Especially not today, after the look of scorn on my dad's face as I explained I'd cut my arm. I hadn't said it, but he knew it had happened while baking pastries for Sam's cafe. Possibly the least manly of all possible activities, in his opinion. And that was just my most recent failing in a lifetime of not being the tough, manly son he'd always wanted.

But then I remembered the nurse from the ER. I remembered the way she'd stiffened when I'd called attention to her hair and her tattoos, as if she was used to people's poor reactions.

Abruptly, I was embarrassed. Here was someone who knew what made her happy, and wore it on her skin for all to see, even though she clearly got ridiculed for it. And here I was, afraid to be ridiculed for my passions to the point of not even trying, even with a promise of anonymity. Maybe my dad was right; I *was* weak and pathetic. Just not in the way he thought.

I squared my shoulders and met Sam's eye. "I'll do it," I repeated, my voice clear and firm this time.

An approving smile spread across his face and he leaned across the table to clap me on the back. "Awesome. Make some of those little tiramisu square-thingies, yeah? They're Ellen's favorite."

CHAPTER 3

BRIA

"*R*emind me again why I let you talk me into this?"

I was at Claire's house, watching as she leaned close to the mirror and applied a layer of pale pink lipstick to her pouting mouth.

"Two reasons," she informed me, blotting her lips on a tissue. She met my eyes in the mirror and held up a finger. "First, because you never go anywhere, and you desperately need to get out. What were you going to do tonight, eat Chinese takeout and watch TV?"

"No," I responded archly. I'd been planning to eat Thai takeout and watch a movie. Not that I had any intention of admitting that.

"Second," she said, holding up another finger and giving me a look as if she knew I was full of it, "*Jeremy Whitaker* is going to be there, and I can't meet him alone."

"Who?" I asked blankly.

"Seriously? Jeremy Whitaker. Everyone here knows who he is."

"I'm not from here," I reminded her.

She rolled her eyes. "I don't care how long you've been in Chicago, you grew up what—an hour away? It's no excuse."

"So, who is he?"

She went back to examining her makeup, touching up her eyeliner with a practiced hand. "He's an internationally famous artist. He's well known for painting amazing portraits of women." She slid a look my way. "Usually ones he's sleeping with. Anyway, he just put out a book, and his brother owns the bookstore, so he'll be there doing a signing tonight."

I nodded in amusement. "So, you're going to get your portrait painted and be famous, huh?"

She shrugged and winked at me. "Who knows what might happen?"

I smothered a laugh. She might be right. With her dark blond hair caught up in a twist and her elegant floor-length pale green dress, she looked like a supermodel. If Claire had her sights set on him, the poor artist wouldn't know what hit him.

I met the eyes of my own reflection in the mirror and had to suppress a smile. I couldn't look more different from Claire if I tried. Maybe I hadn't wanted to come tonight, but at least it gave me an excuse to get out of my scrubs and get dressed up, and I had to admit I looked good.

My dress was a gorgeous calf-length swing dress with a subtle black-on-black plaid pattern and a thin belt. Beneath it, just visible below the hem, I was wearing a violently red crinoline that made the dress swish out around me in voluminous folds as I walked, and emphasized my waist. The crinoline matched the bright crimson stain of my lipstick, and my blue hair fell past my chin in a carefully crafted mess of waves. The dress was sleeveless as well, and though I had a black shrug thrown over top to ward off the chill, the tattoos on my chest as well as the ones on my legs were plainly visible.

"Maybe you'll meet someone there tonight, too," she suggested, watching me size myself up in the mirror.

I turned from my reflection. "At a bookstore?"

She shrugged. "Hey, it's a small town. This is a big event for us. I expect half the population will be there."

My heartbeat ratcheted up at the thought. I liked socializing, and I liked meeting new people, but only in small doses. I was an introvert at heart, and was much better with a small group of friends than a big crowd. Unfortunately, I hadn't been living in Fairfield long enough to find a real group of friends, so currently Claire was what I had to work with. I liked her quite a bit, but honestly, we were really only friends by virtue of working together. And so, if she wanted to go to a big party, to a big party we went.

"Ready to go?" she asked. I nodded and we both donned our coats and grabbed our purses. I waited by the door while she locked up. It was freezing cold outside, but thankfully dry, so I didn't have to worry about slipping on ice in my heels and ending up spending the night in my own ER.

I left my car in the lot at Claire's apartment and joined her in her green SUV, where she set the heater to blasting and we made the short drive downtown to the bookstore.

She hadn't been kidding. The store was *packed.* Either this Jeremy guy really was famous, or Claire had been right and there was nothing else to do in a town this size on a Saturday night. Possibly both.

I followed close on Claire's heels as she slipped through the crowd milling outside and into the store. I'd never been to Sam's Books before. I knew of it, one of the old brick storefronts on Fairfield's cute tree-lined Main Street, but my job kept me busy and I hadn't had much time for exploring.

Inside, the store was warm and festive, decorated for the

upcoming holidays with garland and sprigs of pine draped around the displays of books and across the fronts of the registers. I took my coat off, folding it over my arm as I scanned the store. Tables lined the periphery, one set up with what appeared to be a cash bar, another piled high with amazing looking desserts of every variety. Across the back of the store, a two-story brick wall had been painted with an enormous mural, stretching all the way to the ceiling, with bright splashes of paint depicting more literary scenes and characters than I could count. I gaped, and Claire laughed.

"I forgot to tell you about that. They were just finishing it up when I was in here last, a couple of months ago. Pretty cool, huh?"

That was an understatement. "Did the artist guy do it? Jeremy?"

Claire shook her head. "No, it was a woman. I can't remember her name, but I think she's dating the owner."

Man, everyone really did know everything about everybody in a town like this.

There was a cluster of people milling about over in one corner surrounding a display of books I couldn't see, and Claire tilted her head toward the group. "I think he's over there. Come on, let's go look." Not waiting for an answer, she turned and started making her way across the room. I tried to follow, but seconds later she had disappeared, her blond head swallowed by the crowd.

The press of bodies made me feel slightly lightheaded, as if there wasn't quite enough air in the store for all of us, and for a second, I wondered why I had come. I didn't know anyone here except Claire, though I did recognize a couple of patients. The old woman near the dessert table who'd had kidney stones. The young man at the bar with asthma.

"Bria?"

The voice was warm and deep like melted chocolate, and

I turned in surprise, only to come face to face with another patient, none other than Geoff Ashvale, son of the infamous Dr. Asshole, who totally hadn't crossed my mind at all in the time since he'd left the hospital. Certainly not every time I had a run-in with his dad, causing me to wonder at the differences between them. Granted, I'd only spent about fifteen minutes in Geoff's company, but he certainly hadn't *seemed* anything like his father.

Tonight though, my eyes widened at the sight of him. He was wearing a charcoal gray suit over a black shirt. The suit fit him flawlessly, fabric clinging to his broad shoulders and draping over his lean, muscular physique. My eyes followed the shape of him, from his clean-shaven jaw all the way down to his shiny black shoes. It was a big change from the somewhat scruffy man I remembered from the ER, and I felt my insides clench.

Then he cleared his throat and my eyes flew back up to his face. *Busted.* I could feel the flush burning on my cheeks, but his cheeks were red too, so I smirked and decided to own it.

"You look good in a suit," I said with a teasing smile, which startled a laugh out of him.

"If I have my way, this is probably the only time I'll wear a suit this decade." His eyes crinkled, and I couldn't keep myself from smiling back. Upon closer inspection, I realized he wasn't as flawlessly put-together as I'd first thought. His shirt was open at the collar and his hair was a mess, as if he'd been running his hands through it all evening. Somehow it made the effect even better.

His eyes were bright, and a little wide as he tried to subtly take in my appearance.

"You look incredible," he said, and his soft voice sent a surprise wave of goosebumps rising all along my skin. Geoff was nothing like the majority of guys I knew—my friends in the city had all been a little rough around the edges, loud and heavily tattooed and quick with a dirty joke. By contrast, Geoff seemed…soft. Sweet. Utterly foreign.

"Thanks," I managed.

He cleared his throat, and pulled his eyes away from where they'd snagged on my lips. "Here, you can put your coat in the back if you don't want to carry it. Come with me."

Gamely, I followed him to the checkout counter, where he raised a hinged panel and held it open for me. With a quick glance around, I slipped through and he guided me back into an office where a small coat rack was hung with what were clearly employee coats.

"Are you sure we can…" I broke off. "Wait, do you work here? I thought you worked in a kitchen. Isn't that where you cut your arm?" I was confused.

"Both," he said, gesturing at me to hand him my coat. "Kitchen in the morning, then I run the cafe here after that. I'm not working tonight, though."

It was warm with the store filled with people, and I slipped the shrug off my shoulders as well, handing it over with my coat. He took them from me, but made no move to hang them on the rack. When I glanced up, I found his eyes locked on my shoulders, and understanding filled me. Honestly, half the time, I forgot I had any tattoos at all.

He clearly found them fascinating though, and I suppressed a smile, waiting for him to ask me about them. But instead of speaking, he slowly took a step toward me, and tentatively raised a hand. My breath stuttered and ground to a halt, and I held utterly still, afraid to make a move and scare him away.

It had been many years since I'd gotten my first visible tattoo, and in that time, I had come to one big realization. People liked to touch tattoos. My artist had warned me of this, but I'd ignored him as surely as I'd ignored the warning that they were addictive. Of course, he'd been right. I don't know if it was just that people needed proof they were real and wouldn't wipe away, or if they didn't even realize they were doing it. But just like pregnant bellies, if a tattoo was visible, you could be sure someone was going to touch it without warning or permission. I didn't like it, but I'd grown resigned to it.

This was different though. I'd had people grab my arm and pull it close to take a look, or turn my body to see the rest of the design, but Geoff simply reached out a finger, then hesitated, his fingertip a hair's width away from my shoulder, hovering over my skin until I could almost feel the electric current running between us.

I held my breath, nearly shivering with anticipation as I wondered what it was about this serious, hesitant man that made me welcome a touch that I would have scorned from anyone else. But then my mind went blank when finally, *finally*, he began to move his hand, his fingertips moving with glacial speed, tracing the artwork that curved over my shoulder and down my arm without ever actually making contact. The anticipation built inside me, tension rising with every second that passed as I waited for the heat and pressure of his touch, until I felt like I might combust.

The touch never came, and I nearly climbed out of my skin when he lowered his hand and took a deep breath, stepping back out of reach.

What was this guy *doing* to me? I felt like I had just run a marathon.

He glanced slowly up to my face, looking scandalized as he realized what he'd done, and I waited for an awkward apology like the ones he'd delivered at the hospital when he'd made surprised comments about my appearance there.

But to my surprise, none came. Instead he simply held my eyes with his, the same gaze that had held me captive in the

ER, and said in a low voice, "Do they cover your whole body?"

I blinked in surprise, and watched as his cheeks reddened, as if he was as surprised by his own forwardness as I was, but he held his ground and didn't break his gaze.

For a brief second, I imagined letting him figure out the answer to that question himself, and the air left my lungs in a long wheezing trickle, before I pulled myself together. "I still have some blank skin left," I informed him, sounding much calmer than I felt.

He chuckled, a surprisingly sinful sound, and opened his mouth to respond, but I never got to hear what he was about to say. Instead we were interrupted by a big, harried-looking man with dark hair and dark eyes.

"Geoff, you'll have to clear out. There's not enough room for us all to hide out in here, and there's way too many people in my store. Did you know—" He caught sight of me and broke off. "Oh, hey, sorry. Didn't mean to interrupt."

"You didn't," Geoff said, much to my mingled relief and disappointment. "I was just hanging up our coats. You can hide out all you need to." He finally moved to hang my coat on the closest hook, then gestured at me. "Bria, this is Sam. Sam, Bria."

I glanced at the big man with interest. "Sam, as in Sam's Books?"

He nodded. "I'm not sure why I thought a huge party would be a good idea, but thanks for coming."

Geoff grinned at him, the twisting smile that lit his face and softened his serious eyes. It made my heart stutter. "Because you couldn't say no to Ellen. Besides, it *was* a good idea. You've sold a ton of books, and your brother is in his element."

Oh, right, the brother. I wondered if Claire had found him.

"The food is doing quite well, also," Sam said with a significant look at Geoff, then he glanced at me. "You should try it if you haven't yet. Bria, was it?" I nodded. "The pastries are amazing."

Geoff shot his boss a look I couldn't quite interpret, but the bigger man just laughed. "Oh, calm down. You're doing great. Have another glass of wine and you'll make it through the night just fine."

I looked to Geoff in bewilderment, but he just took my elbow and steered me out of the office and back into the crowd. The noise level increased exponentially and I immediately missed the privacy of the office. And the maddening sensation of his skin *notquitebutalmost* touching mine.

"Have you been here before?" he asked as we made our way through clusters of milling people.

I shook my head. "I've only been living here for about eight months. I've been meaning to see more of the town, but I haven't had the chance yet. Tonight seemed like a good opportunity to check out the store." I decided to omit the part where Claire had to practically force me to come.

"What do you think?"

"The mural is incredible. I'll have to come back on a quieter day to check out the books, though."

Geoff laughed. "So, you aren't just here to get a signature from Jeremy Whitaker, huh?"

"I didn't even know who he was before tonight," I confessed. "But my friend Claire is here for that express purpose." Though she was probably after more than a signature.

We came to a stop in front of a display of Jeremy's books. The cover really was striking, a portrait of a beautiful blond woman painted in bold brushstrokes. "Honestly," I lowered my voice confidentially. "I'm more interested in those desserts Sam was talking about."

Geoff's face seemed to get a little red, but it might just have been the heat in the store. He held out an arm though, indicating that I should lead the way toward the food tables lining the back wall. I did, and found myself caught in another cluster of people crowded around the overflowing tables.

The food looked amazing, more befitting the window of a French patisserie than a bookstore in Indiana. I took a small plate off the stack at the end and made my way along the table, piling it high with little carefully crafted delicacies. Geoff followed along behind me, but he didn't say anything or choose anything for himself to eat. I wondered for a moment if he was going to stay with me all evening, and then wondered why the thought not only didn't bother me, but was actually rather appealing.

We found a relatively quiet spot in the corner where two shelves met and we could hear each other over the din, and I selected one of the desserts on my plate, a relatively innocuous looking circular pastry with a kind of puffy top. I took a bite and felt my eyes roll back.

"My god, have you tried these?"

Geoff was still looking slightly flushed, but he nodded.

"I don't know what the hell they are, but they're unbelievable."

"They're Kouign-amann," he told me, his mouth shaping bizarre syllables I'd never heard before.

"I have no idea what you just said, but I could eat fifty of them."

He smiled. "I'm not surprised. They're basically just butter and sugar."

I raised an eyebrow at him. "Well, if everything is like this, I'm going to gain fifty pounds tonight."

"So," he said, changing the subject as I took a bite of a small, square, layered cake that was every bit as good as whatever I'd just eaten. "You said you just moved here a few months ago. Where did you move from?"

"Chicago," I said around a mouthful of pastry. "I grew up in Rushton, just an hour or so north of here, but I went to school in Chicago and I've been there ever since. What about you?"

"Good old Fairfield, born and raised," he said with a sarcastic twist to his tone. "What brought you back?"

"My grandmother got sick, and I moved home to help my parents take care of her. She died a couple of months ago, but…" I shrugged. "I guess I'm staying."

"How come? Did you not like Chicago?"

"Oh, no, I loved it. But…I don't know. I'm close with my parents, and I guess I don't want to leave them again. Especially with them getting older. I would have stayed in Rushton, but I found a job here."

I had demolished the food, and Geoff took the empty plate and set it on a small table nearby. "Must be nice to be close with your parents."

I'd almost managed to forget who his dad was, but at his tone I looked up, remembering. "You don't get along with yours, then?" I couldn't begin to imagine being close to Dr. Asshole, and I wondered what kind of a relationship the two must have. This evening had only reinforced my observation that Geoff seemed nothing like his father. But then again, I only saw the work side of Dr. Ashvale. Maybe he was a different person in his private life.

Geoff gave a stifled sort of laugh at my question. "Not exactly. Do *you* get along with him? You must know who he is."

I felt like he was testing me. "Yes, I know. And no, he's… um. He can be…difficult to work with."

He smirked at that. "I can imagine. He can be difficult to be related to as well."

"What about your mom?"

"Oh, she's in Florida. They're still married, but they don't really get along. She doesn't like the cold, so she spends the winters down south." He shrugged. "Every year she tries to get my dad to go with her, but he won't leave the hospital. She doesn't mind going on her own though. I'm not really sure why they're still married."

I wanted to ask more, but just then I felt a slight gust of air as another figure ducked into our little alcove behind the bookshelves. I turned to find a tall, impeccably-dressed and very handsome man clutching a glass of wine in one hand.

"God, Geoff, I'm freaking exhausted," the stranger said, taking a long swig of wine. "I've known most of these people my whole life, you wouldn't think they'd *all* need signed copies. I think my hand is going numb!" Suddenly his eyes swiveled to me and his eyebrows raised with interest.

"Well, hello there."

CHAPTER 4

GEOFF

I knew Sam's relationship with his brother was strained, but I'd always found Jeremy to be pleasant enough, if a little bit self-important. Right then though, I wouldn't have been upset if a meteor had fallen through the ceiling of the store and wiped him out. Not only did he deserve it for interrupting my conversation with Bria, but at least then I wouldn't have to stand here and watch the way his eyes traveled a slow circuit over her body before landing on her face with undisguised interest.

The way yours did not twenty minutes ago, you mean? my inner voice asked. I told it to shut up.

"Jeremy Whitaker," he said, holding out a hand to her, which she accepted, and he raised it to his mouth, pressing a kiss onto the back of her hand. Good lord, what was this, a Jane Austen novel? But honestly, what a very Jeremy thing to do.

"Bria Kohler," she replied, flushing slightly as he lowered her hand but did not let it go.

"It's wonderful to meet you," he said smoothly, then looked her over. "You have a very distinctive look."

I watched as the wall slammed down behind her eyes, the same way it had when I'd brought it up the first time we'd met. Her answer was every bit as polite yet emotionless as it had been then. "Thank you."

Jeremy was not one to be deterred though. "I don't think I've ever worked with someone with such a unique style before. Have you ever had your portrait painted?"

I waited in agony to hear her response, but before I got a chance, I felt a tap on my shoulder. It was Sam's girlfriend, Ellen, looking flushed and pretty and entirely in her element.

"Sam's looking for you," she told me with a smile. "Apparently you're out of something chocolatey and he wanted to see if you had any more in the back. I think he's hiding out in the office again." Someone tapped her arm on the other side, pulling her away, and I excused myself, grabbing a glass of wine from the bar on my way to the office and covertly slugging half of it back.

Damn Jeremy. I didn't have any right to be mad at him; he was just being Jeremy. And besides, I hadn't even talked to Bria for more than half an hour; it wasn't like I had any claim on her. I should be grateful, I thought, taking a drink of the wine as I wove through the crowd. Between the two of them, I'd barely had any time to freak out over the food.

By the time I reached the office, most of the wine was gone and the careful buzz I'd been maintaining throughout most of the evening was back in full force. Sam took one look at me and laughed.

"Oh man, is it that bad?"

"It's fine," I said shortly. "Ellen said something about chocolate?"

"Yeah, we're out of the chocolate mousse. Is that all there was?"

"Yep, I already put out all I brought. In fact, I don't think there's much of anything left in the back at this point."

Sam leaned back in his office chair, looking pleased. "Well, I think tonight has been a success on all fronts."

I had to agree. It had been nerve-racking as hell, but I didn't seem to have poisoned anyone yet, and all the comments I'd overheard had been good.

"People have been raving about your food all evening," Sam said as if reading my mind. "I told you you could do it." He paused, then lowered his voice. "Look, I love having you here, man. You keep the cafe running and you probably work as many hours as I do, not that I think that's a good thing. But…if you ever decide you want to try something else… something for yourself. Something bigger? You know I'd support you completely."

I felt my throat constrict. Sam was a great boss and probably the closest friend I had, but he wasn't the most emotional guy. I knew he wanted more for me and I knew he believed in me, but it was still a bit of a shock to hear him say it.

I just nodded and looked down. "Thanks. It was just one event, huh? Let's not get ahead of ourselves."

Sam just sighed and changed the subject. "Who was that woman you were in here with earlier? Bria, you said?"

"Yeah. She was my nurse in the ER the other day."

"Oh yeah? She works with your dad?"

"Apparently. Anyway, I didn't know she was coming tonight. I was just letting her hang her coat in here." I glanced toward the coat in question, a dark teal wool coat with carved wooden buttons. Her short black sweater was thrown over top, and just looking at it made me remember her shoulders when she'd taken it off. She had tattoos covering her chest as well—a beautiful geometric piece in the center framed by ornate filigree designs that crawled over her collarbones and up just slightly onto her neck. The filigree had transitioned into floral designs as it ran over her shoulders and down her arms, then back into geometry when it reached her wrists and hands. Aside from her hands and just a bit peeking out of her collar, I hadn't seen any of it in the hospital—it had all been covered by her scrubs, and I'd tried with everything I had not to stare at her chest when she'd removed her sweater this evening.

Sam started chuckling just as Ellen poked her head in the doorway. "You guys can't hide out in here all night, it's—what on earth were you two talking about?" She stepped fully into the room.

Sam smothered his laughter. "Nothing. Geoff was just telling me about his nurse in the ER."

She turned to me. "She must have been something else, judging by the expression on your face."

I tried to carefully erase whatever my face was doing without my permission, but it just made Sam snort again.

"Apparently she's here," he informed her, not helping my cause at all.

"Oh really? I'd like to meet this—oh no. She was the one I pulled you away from just now, wasn't she? The one Jeremy was putting the moves on?"

"It's fine," I told her. "I only just met her. She can talk to whoever she likes." I kept my face carefully blank, and only realized I was failing when Sam and Ellen both looked at me with matching expressions of pity. Damn that wine, it was messing with my face.

"C'mon, man, go ask her out," Sam advised. "You know if Jeremy gets his hooks in her, she's gone forever." His voice was tinged with bitterness and I remembered that he had cause to know. It was his ex-girlfriend's face gracing the cover of Jeremy's best-seller out there.

Ellen disappeared from the office and reappeared only seconds later, another glass of wine in her hand. She pressed it into mine. "Drink this. Then go ask her out. Seriously."

I did as instructed.

* * *

By the time I found her again, with the wine running through my system like a warm river, Bria was standing with another woman by Jeremy's book-signing table. Jeremy had recaptured her hand—or had possibly never let go in the first place—and was talking to her, gesticulating with the other hand and smiling his trademark charming smile. The other woman, a tall, elegant-looking blond, was too busy glaring daggers at Bria to notice my approach.

Bria did, however, and I couldn't quite read the look she gave me. Relief? Annoyance? The wine was clouding my head, but I decided to use it to my advantage. The night had clearly been a success. Sam had sold a bajillion books—not even all of them by Jeremy—Ellen had another mural lined up at the elementary school, and I had to admit, my baking had gone over even better than I'd hoped. Now all I had to do was get this amazing woman away from Sam's brother, and this might just qualify as the greatest night of my life. And if she said no, if she looked at me in horror and told me to get lost, well, at least I'd have until morning before my head cleared and the regret and embarrassment set in. It was win-win.

Waiting for a lull in the conversation, I stepped close, gathered my resolve, and wrapped my hand around Bria's elbow. Her skin felt blazing hot against my palm, and I tried not to lose myself in the sensation. She managed to pull her hand out of Jeremy's grasp, and turned to look at me. I still couldn't read her expression, so I barreled on.

"I'm getting ready to leave," I told her. "And I was wondering if you might like to come." All three pairs of eyes looked at me. *Oh no, that didn't come out right.* "Er, with me," I amended. "Come with me." *Shut up Geoff, that's even worse.* I cleared my throat, and tried again. "Would you like to leave?"

Huh. So the wine wasn't saving me from embarrassment after all.

Bria was clearly trying not to laugh, which I took as a good sign. Her blonde friend was no longer glaring, and Jeremy had actually turned away, and was now busy signing a copy of someone's book.

"I'd love to," she said, and my embarrassment melted into elation. "Claire," she said, turning to her friend. "I don't need a ride; I can find my own way home. Are you good here?"

The blonde—Claire—nodded and gave Bria a kiss on the cheek, and then she turned and we were heading back toward the office. I belatedly realized I was still holding her elbow, and I forced myself to let go, instantly mourning the soft feel of her warm skin.

The office was empty when we got there—thank god—and before I could reach for our coats, she turned to face me.

"Thank you for that," she said. "I wasn't sure you could hear the 'help me!' signal I was broadcasting into the room."

I raised my eyebrows. "I thought Jeremy was every woman's dream man. You passed up a much-sought-after opportunity there," I joked. Well, half-joked.

She laughed. "I think I might have alienated my only friend if I'd said yes to him." My spirits fell for a second, but she continued. "Besides, he's not my type at all. Very charming though; I can see the appeal. But it's not exactly flattering to only be wanted for the way you look."

Oh god, I hope she didn't think that of me. I opened my mouth to clarify, but before I could get a word out, she said, "Thanks again for the rescue though. I think I can duck out now. I'll call a cab to get home."

My heart plummeted into my shiny, uncomfortable shoes. She thought it was a ruse, that I was just helping her escape from Jeremy's advances. Well, there was no way to salvage this now; I would have to let her go.

I stepped back to give her access to the coat rack, but she didn't move, her eyes still on my face.

"What?" she asked.

"*What* what?"

She laughed. "You look like someone just ran over your cat. Did I miss—oh. Oh. You were serious, weren't you?"

Nope, definitely no way to save face now. It seemed all I did around this woman was embarrass myself. I cleared my throat. "Erm, about what?"

She winced, and I mentally scolded myself. *Fucking man up, idiot.*

I took a deep breath. "I...worded it in the worst possible way, and no, you don't have to leave with me, but yes. I was wondering if you wanted to...um. Go out. With me. Some-time." *Not smooth, but better. Serviceable. I might not have to shoot myself when I sober up.*

She was smirking at me, her eyes dancing with suppressed amusement, and I forged ahead, barely pausing for breath. "You said it's not flattering to only be wanted for the way you look, and I hope you don't think that's what *I* want. Er, think. I mean, I like the way you look, don't get me wrong, but it's certainly not—" I stopped when she stepped forward into my space and laid her hand across my mouth.

"Yes," she said, and I was too stunned by the feel of her fingers against my lips to react. "I would love to go out with you. Are you free right now?"

She removed her hand, but she was still so close.

"Really?" I asked. "You want to go—"

I broke off again when her forehead creased, and she leaned closer for just a second, breathing in. Then stepped back. "Are you drunk?"

Oh shit. "I'm not drunk," I said loftily. "I prefer the term, 'soberly impaired.'" Well, I'd known this evening was too good to be true.

But after a second she just held out her hand. "I guess I'd better drive then. Give me your keys."

CHAPTER 5

BRIA

*I*t was late enough that almost everything was already closed, and it seemed presumptuous to invite Geoff back to my apartment, or invite myself over to his, so we ended up walking down Main Street together. It was cold outside, but the moon was bright and beautiful, and my nerves were keeping me warm, at least for the time being.

After a long moment, he reached out and took my hand in his. We were both wearing gloves, but the weight of his fingers interlaced with mine was comforting, even through the fabric.

The noise of the party was long behind us now, and the night had an eerie, silent quality about it.

"So, why are you drunk?" I asked. Maybe too blunt, but I wanted to know. It hadn't seemed like *that* kind of party, and while I had nothing against alcohol in moderation, I had plenty of experience—both at work and back in Chicago—in seeing what too much of it did to people.

He gave a slight chuckle. "I'm not really drunk. Just a little…uninhibited, maybe. But to answer your question, I was very nervous about tonight."

I raised an eyebrow and smirked. "How come? You didn't even know I was coming." His cheeks were ruddy with cold, his hair mussed from the wind, and the effect was surprising in how it affected me.

He laughed outright at that. "Thank god for that. I might not have come at all if I'd known you'd be there."

"What?" I feigned outrage. "I'm not that scary."

"You're a little intimidating," he informed me, a little shyly. You have a very…no-nonsense air about you. Also, you make me act like an idiot, in case you hadn't noticed."

I laughed to myself. "It's my job, I imagine. I have to put up with a lot at work."

"Do people give you a lot of trouble?" he asked, and I suddenly didn't think he was talking about the job itself.

I shrugged. "Sometimes. It's a small town. Some people are more accepting than others. Especially in healthcare. It wasn't long ago at all they wouldn't have hired me, looking like this."

He slanted a glance at me. "It would have been their loss." He swung our arms between us and let the silence stretch for a moment. It hadn't escaped my notice that he hadn't actually answered my question, and I wasn't sure whether or not to push it, but finally he spoke again, his voice quiet in the chill air.

"I was…nervous about the food."

I glanced sideways at him, confused.

"I…I made it. I catered the event."

My eyebrows shot up and I turned to stare at him. "You what?!"

He nodded, looking down at the ground as we walked. "You know I work at the kitchen co-op? Well, I bring in pastries for Sam's cafe each morning. It's not really part of my job exactly, but I like to bake, and try out new recipes and stuff."

I stepped around a fire hydrant without letting go of his hand. My toes were starting to go numb in my shoes, but I didn't want to interrupt our conversation. "The food tonight was *incredible*, Geoff. Surely you know that."

He went on as if he hadn't heard me. "Sam's been after me for a while now to do something bigger. Cater an event, even open my own place. Tonight was my…trial run, let's say." He shrugged, then shot me a crooked smile. "I was pretty nervous. Wine helped."

Ah, that explained the alcohol. I raised an eyebrow. "You realize it was a huge success, right? Everyone I walked past was either talking about Jeremy Whitaker or your food."

He gave a self-deprecating laugh. "Yeah, it went well. But I'm glad it's over and I can get back to normal. I've been stressing about this for days."

"Well, I'm really impressed," I told him. "You could do whatever you want with baking skills like that. You must be really proud. Sam, too. And your family."

He glanced over at me again, and his smile was gone. "Yeah, not so much. You know my dad. I imagine he's as excited about my baking as he is about your tattoos."

* * *

We ended up at a tiny coffee shop at the end of the street, with a "Going out of Business" sign in the window. Fortunately, they hadn't gone out of business just yet, and had late weekend hours, even though the place was largely deserted. I tumbled gratefully through the door and my feet screamed in relief as they began to slowly thaw in the warmth. A fireplace was burning in the corner, sending sparks flickering up the chimney, and after ordering at the counter, we chose a small booth nearby. I slipped my heels off under the table, waiting while Geoff went up to the counter to retrieve our drinks.

I winced as I thought about what he'd said. I knew exactly what Dr. Asshole thought about my tattoos, and my hair as well. He wasn't exactly stingy with his opinions. I didn't know what kind of relationship Geoff had with his dad, but it didn't sound like an easy one. He'd avoided my questions when I'd pressed for more details, so I'd let him change the subject.

With drinks in hand, he slid back into our booth and passed my chai latte across the table. I wrapped my fingers around the mug, letting the warmth seep into my hands as I waited for the foamy drink to cool.

Geoff, however, pushed his own drink out of the way and reached out, looking at me for permission before capturing one of my hands in his. He turned it over so the back was facing up, and examined the intricate patterns there.

"How do you decide?" he asked, tracing his fingers along the lines of ink. It felt like a line of fire followed his touch, and I shivered with the sensation. "I mean, do you have something in mind when you go in to get one? Do they all have meaning to you?"

"Some yes, some no," I said, a fluttery feeling taking up residence low in my stomach. "Some of them have a lot of meaning—they represent people in my life, or events, or places I want to remember. Others...I just like the artwork. Sometimes I just have an idea and I let the artist run with it. A lot of it is just finding an artist you trust."

"Do you have any you regret?"

I thought about it for a minute. "I don't think so. I have ones that I like more than others, but all of them have meaning to me, one way or another."

He looked so fascinated, I had to laugh. "You obviously don't have any, huh?"

He released my hand and glanced down, seemingly embarrassed. "Sorry, I'm full of questions."

I was used to fielding questions about my tattoos, and while Geoff's weren't judgmental at all, I still had to fight the defensiveness that seemed to be ingrained in me. "No, it's okay," I assured him. Usually I didn't like it when people called too much attention to my appearance. It wasn't anything I did for recognition; it was for me, a way to make myself feel comfortable in my skin. But from Geoff, it was different somehow. He made me feel special, rather than weird or different.

"A lot of people have them, you know," I told him. "I see tons in the ER, people you would never imagine have a tattoo."

"I know," he said. "I've just never seen anyone wear them the way you do. Like they're a part of you."

A shiver ran down my spine at his words. Abruptly he looked up and met my gaze, and the intensity in his dark eyes stole my breath.

"I really want to know the answer to the question I asked you earlier," he said, his husky breath nearly a whisper.

"What was that?" My voice came out strangled. I couldn't look away, but if I didn't, I might fall into his eyes and never resurface.

"Do they cover your whole body?"

There was a long pause, and the air between us was charged, alive with crackling electricity.

Finally, I found my voice. "Would you ask me that if you were completely sober?"

His expression didn't change. "Probably not," he admitted. "But that doesn't mean I wouldn't still be wondering."

A rush of warmth spread through me at his words.

He hadn't even touched his drink, and my chai latte was only half gone, but he didn't spare them a glance when I reached out my hand and pulled him to his feet. He wrapped my coat around my shoulders and seconds later we were out the door and back into the cold.

But this time I barely felt it.

* * *

I drove his car to my apartment, second guessing myself the entire way. I wasn't a put-out-on-the-first-date kind of girl. And I definitely wasn't a one-night-stand kind of girl. And yet, it was pretty obvious where this was headed. If I brought Geoff back to my apartment, he was going to end up in my bed; it was inevitable.

But instead of worrying if this was going too fast (it was), or if I would regret it in the morning (I might), or if *he* would regret it in the morning (God, I hoped not), my thoughts were focused elsewhere. Instead, all I could think was, what did the body under that suit really look like? Would I spontaneously combust when he touched me? Good lord, I hadn't even *kissed* him yet. What was I *doing*? Would he—

My train of thought derailed as he put a hand on my knee. I jerked the wheel a bit too hard as I turned into my apartment complex and pulled into my space, turning off the engine with shaking hands. The sudden silence was deafening.

"I had a great time with you this evening," he said. "And you don't have to invite me up." His voice dropped low even as his face flushed slightly. "But I'll be honest—I'd like to kiss you. I'd *really* like to kiss you."

The contrast between his obvious shyness and the bold words made a molten river of lava run through me.

"But," he went on in a quiet voice before I had a chance to respond, "I won't, if you don't want me to. And we certainly don't need to do anything more than that. I'm happy to drop you off and head home, if that's what you want."

"You can't drive; you're drunk," I informed him in a husky voice.

He sat back a little. "The alcohol bothers you, doesn't it," he said, and I mentally cursed how observant he was.

I took a breath. "I used to date a guy with a drinking problem," I said bluntly. "I also see a lot of alcoholics in the ER. It's your life, and your choices to make. But I'm not going down that road again."

He nodded slowly. "I don't drink often," he said, "usually just when I'm stressed. Or around my dad."

I wondered what that meant. With my job, if I drank when I was stressed, I'd be drunk all the time. Besides, if I'd learned anything from my time with Alec, it was that you couldn't trust what people said when they'd been drinking.

I opened my mouth to respond, but the corner of his mouth twisted up in a lopsided smile. "Besides," he said, pinning me again with the intensity of his gaze, "I'm not drunk anymore."

I turned to face him fully, shifting sideways in the driver's seat, and decided to let it go for now. "And you still want to kiss me?"

His eyes darkened as they dropped to my lips. "More than anything."

I leaned in. I couldn't have stopped myself if I'd tried. Our lips paused, almost touching, less than the space of a breath between us.

His hand came up, and just as they had earlier that evening, his fingertips hovered, millimeters from my skin, without touching. They traced the shape of my jaw, the curve of my cheek, and I shivered, waiting expectantly for the warm pressure of his touch that never came. My senses heightened, waiting for the contact, tension and anticipation ratcheting tight within me. His fingers ghosted down the column of my neck, moving around the back and then finally, *finally*, he made contact, cupping the back of my neck before threading his fingers into my hair.

I breathed out a shaky sound of relief.

His mouth was so close to mine I could feel the fan of his breath across my lips as he whispered, "I was right."

Unable to form words, I made an inquisitive sound, and he chuckled against my lips. "Your hair is as soft as it looks."

Then he moved forward a fraction of an inch, and our lips met. It started so slowly; just a leisurely slide of skin, gentle friction, the barest pressure, touch building on touch. The barest sweep of tongue, the nip of teeth on lip, a shudder and a gasp.

It was like this shy, soft, serious man knew exactly how to read me, just how to build anticipation. Just as he had with his ghosting touches, his kisses built the same way, teasing, slow, until I couldn't take it anymore and found myself twisting and writhing in my seat. And then he would ratchet it up a notch, a long slide of his tongue on mine, his fingers tangled in my hair to tilt my head just right.

I'd never been kissed like that before. Any hesitation he'd shown earlier didn't carry over into his kisses, and I felt like my blood had turned to fire, like I might combust at any second.

I'd never known anyone who could read me so perfectly, could control my reactions and keep me wound so tight, and I didn't even realize how much he was being affected as well until he groaned, long and low in his throat, his breath a shuddering gasp as he moved his mouth to my jaw. The power I felt in that moment was exhilarating, but quickly forgotten as I melted into his touch once again.

I don't know how long we sat in the car. It might have been minutes or hours. Long enough for the cold to seep in and turn my fingers and toes to ice, until not even the heat of his kisses could thaw them. While the thought of staying here forever and slowly freezing to death in his embrace had a certain appeal, finally I forced myself to break the kiss and lean my forehead against his. We were both breathing hard, and his face was flushed in the dim illumination of the moonlight.

"As much as I enjoy making out in the car like a couple of teenagers, I don't think frostbite is very sexy," I told him.

He sat back a little, eyes dark on my face as he caught his breath. "Thank you for tonight," he said. "I really—"

"Please," I cut him off. "Come upstairs with me."

He didn't protest, didn't say another word. Just pressed another lingering kiss to my swollen lips and pulled back, climbing out and locking the car. The loss of his touch was jarring, but he was back almost immediately, hands warm on my back even through my coat as he followed me into the building and up the stairs to my second-floor apartment. We were kissing again before we made it to the door.

CHAPTER 6

GEOFF

*N*o one had ever been as sexy as Bria. Her hair was mussed from my hands, her lips red from my mouth, her face flushed, and I barely got her in the door before her coat was puddled on the floor, wicked-looking cherry red heels kicked beside it. She lost three inches of height without them, but she still seemed to fit me perfectly.

Her lips fitted to my throat as she pushed me backward down a short hallway toward what I assumed was her bedroom. Her hands fisted in my suit jacket, pulling it off my shoulders and tossing it carelessly to the floor. We shed clothing as we went, dropping them heedlessly in our wake, until I found myself in her room, the side of the bed pressing into the backs of my legs, wearing only my suit trousers, shirt unbuttoned and hanging on by one sleeve.

I barely remembered the trip down the hall, lost in a hazy fog of tangled limbs and sliding lips, heavy breaths and soft skin.

She still wore her dress, but her sweater had been abandoned along the way, and one of her straps had fallen down over her arm. Her eyes were as bright as stars as she reached behind her for the zipper to the dress.

"Wait," I said hoarsely. "Stop." She froze, fingers still poised behind her.

"Wait," I said again, softer this time, and the corner of my mouth pulled up. "Don't ruin the suspense."

She rolled her eyes. "You and your suspense." But her hands fell away from the zipper.

I watched her for a moment, all flushed skin and parted lips. So beautiful. Then I lunged. I caught her around the waist, and she gasped out a laugh as I tossed her onto the bed, face down. She made to turn over and I climbed up as well, straddling her legs and pinning her down, surprising myself with my own actions. This woman seemed to bring out a side of me I hadn't known was there, but I couldn't seem to help myself. No one had ever turned me on the way she did. Leaning forward, I swept her hair off her neck and bent to press a kiss to her hairline. She went still, spreading her arms out at her sides and waiting to see what I would do.

I did the only thing I could, what was quickly becoming my favorite thing to do. I touched her, just a brush of fingertips at the nape of her neck, where the finial to a sweeping flourish of filigree ended. I felt her shiver against me, and I took it as encouragement, tracing my finger down the line of ink. The design spread out across her shoulder blades, and my fingers did as well, following the patterns etched into her skin.

She arched into my touch, grinding back against me in a way that nearly derailed me entirely, but I persevered, tracing over the lines until they disappeared under her dress. I needed to see more. I needed to see everything.

I grasped the zipper in one hand and began to pull it down, one slow inch at a time, and she whimpered, her hands fisting into the blanket. I watched as the design was revealed. It spanned her entire back, a wash of color, sweeping lines and shapes that formed a scene of such beauty I was astonished at the quality. I'd had no idea tattoos like that were even possible. With a slide of fabric, I pulled the dress off completely, the rustling crinolines as well, and the tiny scrap of lace beneath them, before sitting back to admire the view. The artist had taken care to emphasize her figure, and the design followed her curves, sweeping down the expanse of her back, curving in at her waist before flaring out again at her hips.

I couldn't help myself. I leaned down, replacing my fingers with my mouth, pressing kisses all along the length of her spine, tasting her skin, breathing her in. She squirmed against me, and finally I lightened up the pressure, giving her space to flip over to face me.

"You're so beautiful," I told her, and she reached up for me, snagging what was left of my shirt and pulling me down to kiss her. She hitched a leg up over my hip and I could feel the wet heat of her, pressing exactly where I wanted her.

I wanted to see the rest of her artwork too, because in my brief glimpse I could see she had bold patterns splashed across her torso as well, spanning her waist and down both legs. I wanted to freeze time so I could stop and look, admire and touch and taste every square inch of her, but the friction of her was more than I could handle. My breathless impatience was growing to match hers, and when she reached down between us and fumbled with my pants it was all I could do to help, kicking them off and pulling her close again. Her hand slipped in between us and wrapped around me, a startling jolt of pressure that made my breath catch in my throat, and then our lips were together again as she guided me, sliding me into the slick heat of her body, and the feel of her was overwhelming.

I would have time to look at her later. To touch her

everywhere and ask a million questions, about her ink, her job, her family, her friends, her *life*. Because as we moved together, hands clutching, breath coming fast, bodies slick, all I could think was, *I'll never be able to get enough of her*.

* * *

Sunday was usually my day off from the bookstore, and while any other week that wouldn't stop me from spending my morning working in the kitchen and bringing a tray of freshly-baked something-or-others over to Sam's, for the first time in over a year, on this morning I had other things on my mind.

Other things that took the form of long smooth legs that tangled with my own. Arms that twined around my neck and pulled me close. Soft lips and soft hair and soft skin. Low, dirty laughs and breathless gasps.

When the sun came streaming in through the open blinds and she lay sprawled, still asleep, across the tangled blankets, I finally got a real look at her. I'd never seen anything like her. I'd been right—the ink covered her front as well, an intricate scene that tied into the one on her back, leaving only her nipples bare.

Unable to help myself, I reached out and traced a finger around one nipple, watching it tighten into a peak, before widening my circles to take in the weight of her breast. She shifted in her sleep, then slowly blinked awake, dark lashes revealing sleepy blue eyes.

"Good morning," I said hesitantly. The previous night had been amazing, but this morning I had no idea where we stood. No idea what she would be thinking, or how she would react. Had it been too fast? Undoubtedly. Did I regret it? Not one bit. But that didn't mean she felt the same way.

She stretched languorously in the sheets before sitting up,

but she didn't move to cover herself, which I took to be a good sign. But then she just looked at me for a long moment, blinking owlishly, and my uncertainty returned.

When she did finally speak, her voice was a demanding bark. "Coffee!"

I couldn't help but laugh. Not a morning person then. "Coming right up."

Half an hour later we sat together in bed, partially dressed and drinking coffee, and as she began to wake up, we talked. My fears began to dissipate as she showed no sign of regret or apprehension, and I hung on her every word, eager to know everything I could about her.

I learned that she suffered from vitiligo, a disease that caused her to lose pigment in her skin in blotches, turning her naturally creamy skin to a stark white. It mostly affected her legs, and she'd been teased mercilessly about it as a teenager.

"Is that why you started getting tattoos?" I asked.

She shook her head. "Not at first. My first was here, on my hip." She had commandeered my dress shirt from the night before and was wearing it, partially unbuttoned, leaving me only with my suit pants to put back on. My shirt came down nearly to her knees, and I had to admit, seeing her in it was something I could get used to.

She pulled up the black fabric and indicated a tiny faded red rose near her hipbone that had since been worked into a larger design. "I didn't really think about using tattoos to cover the pigment loss until my artist suggested it. He was dating my roommate in college, and she knew I was pretty insecure about my legs. She must have told him about it because one time when we were together, he mentioned that I could cover the skin with tattoos, and no one would notice the vitiligo."

She pointed to an area of skin on her calf, covered over

with a bright cluster of flowers in an art nouveau-style frame, and while I could see the patches of discolored skin, she was right, I would never have known if she hadn't pointed it out. I told her so and she nodded and smiled.

"I think that was the beginning of the end. I started covering my legs, and I never stopped."

"Is the vitiligo still spreading?" I asked, lightly touching the skin on her leg, tracing the line of pigment loss as it disappeared behind the bold flowers. She shivered but shook her head.

"No, it seemed to stop in my mid-twenties. But I was too far down the tattooing rabbit hole at that point."

I took a drink of my coffee and looked at her with a thoughtful expression. "I would imagine," I said carefully, "that you probably get more attention from the tattoos than you did from the vitiligo."

Her face hardened slightly, but she nodded. "I do. But... it's different. I was just a kid then, and kids are mean."

"Are people not mean about the tattoos?"

"Sure, they are. It might be worse, even, because these are adults, and I think it comes more from prejudice than from ignorance, like it was when I was young. But..." She paused to think, pulling absently at a loose thread on the edge of the blanket. "It's different, you know? These were my choice. I hated the vitiligo; I hated how it made me look different. And I know I still look different, but I love the way I look now. *I'm* happy with myself, and I wasn't before. Does that make sense?"

I nodded. It really did. I could completely understand the desire to make choices for yourself that made you happy, even if they upset other people. I only wished I had the guts to flaunt it openly the way she did.

"I think that's really admirable," I told her. "It takes a lot of courage to do what you want and not care about what other people think." I paused for a second. "What do your parents think?"

"They like them," she told me. "Or, at least, my dad does. I'm not sure my mom cares either way. They're not originally from around here, and they're both pretty open-minded. It helps. A lot, really. I don't know that I would have pushed it so far if I hadn't had their support from the beginning."

I nodded, shifting on the blankets as I thought about her words. I wondered how my own path might have been different if I'd had support in the beginning from the people who mattered.

She seemed to follow my line of thoughts, because after a minute she said softly, "You said yesterday that your dad didn't approve of your baking. Has he always…"

She trailed off, as if she wasn't quite sure how to finish the question. I mentally filled in the options. Been overbearing? Been judgmental? Disapproved of all my choices? It didn't matter. The answer would be the same regardless.

"I was supposed to be a doctor," I told her. She raised an eyebrow. "Maybe a lawyer, or an engineer, those might have been okay too, but doctor was always the first choice."

"His, or yours?"

I shrugged. "Both, I guess. He was always pretty strict growing up, and I've never been much of a rule-breaker, not really. It was always easier to just try to make him happy. I always failed, because I was never the tough, manly kid he wanted, but at least I figured I could give him that. So, I always assumed I'd be a doctor, too. I made it all the way to med school."

Her eyes went wide in surprise. "What happened?"

I looked down at my lap. "I've always been kind of squeamish around blood. Turns out that's not something I could easily get over. I dropped out after one semester."

She winced. "I imagine your dad was upset."

I laughed, but there was no humor in it. "That's one way to put it."

"So, why baking?"

I leaned back on my hands. I wondered if she was as interested in me as I was in her. It was too bad my story wasn't as interesting as hers was.

"My grandma loved to bake," I said. "I was a sensitive kid, and if I got picked on, at school or at home, I'd go to her house. I spent a lot of time with her, and she used to teach me to bake when I was a kid. I guess it's always been a hobby. My undergrad degree is in chemistry, which my dad thought was a good plan for med school, but I got really interested in applying it to baking. It can be pretty scientific, learning how ingredients work together and how they react." I shrugged again. "I needed a job after I dropped out of school, and I ended up finding work in a bakery. I was there for a few years, then Sam opened his store, and…I dunno. It's good to do something I enjoy while I figure out where to go next."

"Where to go next?" She looked at me closely.

"Well, sure. I'm not going to work at the bookstore forever. Someday I'll get a real job. I'm just not sure what it'll be yet. I'll need to save up for another year or two, but I've been thinking about applying to law school."

I felt like I'd stepped into some alternate reality. One where a really amazing guy wanders into my life, asks me out, takes me home and screws me senseless, then—gasp—sticks around, asks me about my life, shows interest in all its mundane details, and wants to see me again. It was like the plot of some cheesy rom com. Well, either that or things were about to go spectacularly wrong—like I'd find out he was secretly married and a father to quintuplets, or he had an obsession with women's shoes, or he was on the run from the mob. Or more likely, I thought with a pang, he had an abusive childhood, or a secret drinking problem.

It had to be something. Things like this just didn't happen to normal people.

But, at least for the time being, it seemed to be happening to me. We spent almost the whole day together on Sunday, in and out of bed, eating takeout on the couch, ignoring the movies we let play in the background. While I had managed to get him to open up at least a little about his family and his job, it was obvious he didn't like to talk about either, and tended to change the subject when they came up. But I learned lots of other useful information about him—like the fact that he didn't care to wear a lot of clothing around his apartment, something I certainly wasn't complaining about. Those shoulders...

I also learned that while he loved to bake, he didn't seem to like to cook, and ate out as much as he ate in. I learned that he had studied abroad in France for a semester in college, and while his French was absolutely terrible, I still couldn't keep my hands off him when he tried to speak it.

That Sunday was one of the best days I'd had in a long, long time. In the evening, forced out of our isolated bubble and back into harsh reality, Geoff drove me to pick up my car from the parking lot outside Claire's building, where I hoped she hadn't noticed it had been sitting since the night before. I left with no small amount of apprehension, worried that the magic of the day would dissipate with any amount of distance. Had I overinflated our connection? Was it just a fun one-time thing and now that it was over would he want to move on? Was I being *that girl* right now, overanalyzing everything?

My apartment felt cold and empty without him there, but with evidence of him everywhere, from the empty takeout containers in the kitchen to the rumpled sheets on the bed that still smelled like him. My apartment had never seemed so foreign.

In the end, I hadn't been home more than half an hour when my cell phone rang. When I saw his picture on the display, I let it ring three more times before I answered so as not to seem too eager, feeling completely idiotic the whole time.

He didn't even say hello.

"I miss you," he informed me. "How can I miss you? It hasn't even been an hour."

I put on my best condescending tone, even as relief swept

through me. "Seriously, Geoff? That sounds pretty needy. I don't think we should see each other again."

An awkward pause followed this, and I worried for a second that he'd taken me seriously and I may have hurt his feelings. Claire sometimes told me my humor was too blunt.

But a second later he replied, "I'll admit I don't know you that well, but I think I'm getting the hang of your sarcastic streak. You'd better be joking or I'm going to need to hang up and go die of shame."

I grinned, and when I spoke, I could hear the smile in my own voice. "I miss you too. Come back. My bed looks so empty without you."

"Don't tempt me. Your bed is much more comfortable than mine anyway."

"All the more reason you should come back," I said. "I'll call in sick tomorrow. I'll call in sick forever and we can just live in sin."

"Until we end up homeless and freeze to death together on the streets."

"At least we'd be together."

He chuckled. "When do you get off work tomorrow?"

"Seven. I'll be useless though; it's a twelve-hour shift."

"Let me bring dinner over and we can be useless together."

"Deal."

There was a long pause.

"This is too fast, isn't it?" I asked.

"Yes," he said. Then, "Do you want to slow down?"

"No."

"Me neither."

"I'll see you tomorrow."

* * *

After that, the days began to run together in a kind of blissful fog. Claire had indeed noticed that my car had never made it home on Saturday night, but I managed to sidetrack her with questions about Jeremy, who, it seemed, had finally suggested he might like to paint her at some point. Unfortunately, she'd lost his attention when his ex-wife had arrived with his six-year-old son in tow, but Claire thought there had definitely been something there between them.

I returned home that night exhausted and filthy and sweaty, as I ended most work days, and fell into Geoff's arms. It took me longer than necessary to shower, despite his assistance—maybe *because* of his assistance—but eventually we found our way onto the couch together. Our bowls were filled to their brims with chili he'd cooked after work—it turned out he *could* cook, just preferred not to—and we swapped stories about our days. He'd even brought me one of the pastries he'd made that morning for Sam's store—something with a totally unpronounceable name that seemed to consist mostly of thin flaky layers of pastry sandwiched with cream. It was indescribably good. He watched me eat with hooded eyes, tensing every time I licked my lips or moaned in delight, until finally he just took the plate away and took me to bed, rubbing the soreness of the day out of my muscles until his touch became too much to take, and I climbed on top of him to demonstrate I wasn't as tired as all that.

Our days fell into a kind of pleasant routine. The weather outside grew colder and work was…well, the challenge that work always was, but at the end of every day somehow I still had Geoff, and I found that nothing else really seemed to matter all that much.

* * *

"Good news, Mrs. Burris, the X-rays show it's just a bad sprain, not a fracture. I'm going to wrap your ankle for now, and you'll need to try to stay off it as much as you can for the next couple of days, but it'll heal up on its own."

Mrs. Burris, a somewhat uptight-looking woman in her mid-sixties who had glared disapprovingly at my tattoos as they wheeled her in, gripped my hand in relief at this news. "Oh, thank you so much dear. I don't have the *time* to deal with a broken ankle."

I smiled and handed her the discharge papers. "Well, all the info you'll need to take care of it is in here. I'll go over it with you, and then you can call your primary physician with any questions and to follow up in a few weeks."

She took the papers and flipped through them as I wound the bandage securely around her ankle.

"Oh, and Mrs. Burris, please try to have a spotter if you're going up on ladders. It really could have been so much worse."

"I will, dear," she said dismissively, patting my hand. Then she looked at me sadly. "Such a pretty girl. Why you would ruin your skin like that, I'll never know."

"You're good to go, Mrs. Burris," I said, working to keep my face pleasant. "Have a nice afternoon."

Back at the nurses station, Claire was holding a flyer, printed on thick, pale yellow paper.

"What's that?"

"Annual fundraiser," she said, handing the paper to me as I came behind the desk. "They're combining it with a holiday party this year though, so maybe it'll be fun."

I snorted at the thought, but took the flyer from her anyway. Claire had already warned me that the fundraiser would be coming up. According to her, they were always dreadfully dry and boring affairs, full of people with too much money and sky-high opinions of themselves, schmoozing with hospital executives who were all far too similar to the donors they were attempting to woo. But apparently, they strongly encouraged whatever staff wasn't working to attend, so it didn't look like we had a choice.

I skimmed the flyer, phrases jumping out at me. "Black tie." "Silent auction, all proceeds to benefit the hospital foundation." "Hors d'oeuvres and light appetizers provided."

And just like that, I had an idea.

* * *

"Absolutely not."

"It's a wonderful idea."

"It's a terrible idea. Baking for the entire hospital foundation and staff and donors...not to mention my *dad?* Nothing about that sounds even remotely like a good idea."

We were lying in bed at Geoff's apartment, one of the few times we'd come to his place instead of mine—it was true, my bed *was* more comfortable than his. I was snuggled in his arms, and he was looking at me like I'd grown a second head.

"Has your dad ever actually eaten anything you've baked?" I asked, pushing up to sit against the headboard.

"No. And it's so much better that way."

"How is it better that way? If he knew how good you were, surely he would understand—"

Geoff cut me off. "Understanding isn't exactly something he excels at."

I glared at him. "You know what I mean. Besides, this has nothing to do with your dad."

"It doesn't?" He raised a cynical eyebrow.

"No," I informed him. "Don't you remember how you felt when Sam's party was a success?"

He hesitated, and I sat up straight, ready to make this argument in earnest. "I've seen the way you look when you bake, Geoff. I see the way you watch people in the cafe when they eat your food, the way you watch *me*. You don't just love baking. You love baking *for other people*."

He looked vaguely uncomfortable. "I—" But he broke off and I didn't let him finish.

"You keep telling me you're thinking about law school, but you *can't*, Geoff. You can't do something you'll hate just because it'll please your dad. Hell, it probably *won't* even please him. He probably wouldn't be satisfied if you were a doctor, the chief of surgery even. You should *do* this, Geoff. You know you can, you proved that at Sam's open house. You should do it for *yourself*."

"This would be way bigger than the open house," he protested weakly. "You can't compare them."

I could see he was starting to waver, and I decided the wisest move was to back off, at least for now.

I leaned in close, brushing my lips over his. "Just think about it, okay? It would be a huge opportunity." I bit lightly on his lower lip, then sucked on it gently. "Just think about it?"

He gave me a look, suggesting that he knew exactly what I was up to, but he let me get away with it anyway. "I'll think about it," he promised, then kissed me back.

CHAPTER 8

GEOFF

*T*hey were all conspiring against me. Bria had been careful not to bring up the fundraiser again since our talk two days before, but when I received a surprise phone call that morning from the hospital Foundation, I knew she'd still been busy, if not direct. And when Sam cornered me at the bookstore that afternoon, it seemed like the whole world was working against me.

"So…I heard something about a catering job you were considering." He was stacking books on an endcap near the cafe, carefully busying himself with his work and not meeting my eyes as he tossed out his comment in the most nonchalant manner.

I snorted out loud. "Very smooth, Sam. So, I'm considering it now, am I?"

He dropped the pretense and looked at me directly. "Are you?"

I paused. I mean, no, obviously I wasn't going to do it. Why would I set myself up for failure? But in the privacy of my own imagination, I had to admit I'd thought about what I might make. The chocolate mousse again, definitely—that had been a big hit. Probably an array of macarons, maybe some eclairs? Would it be too messy to make single serving trifles? I'd already built mental supply lists, tallied costs, thought about things like timing and fridge space.

But those mental exercises, while fun, were unrealistic. I'd done the open house because Sam was a friend, and my boss. It had been a favor, and a success, but it was only a matter of time now before I would need to get serious, and figure out what to do with my life. Bria had been right; I would be a terrible lawyer. But that wasn't the only option. Besides, maybe I'd been too hasty to dismiss med school.

"Geoff?" Sam prodded, and I realized I'd been silent a little too long.

"No," I told him, turning to organize the bags of coffee. "I'm not."

Rather than be put off, Sam came over and laid his hands flat on the counter, leaning toward me. I scowled at him and reached for the cleaning spray. "Why not?" he asked bluntly.

The cafe was deserted, the store quiet. Why were there never any customers around when I needed them?

I sighed. "I did the open house, didn't I? Why do I need to prove myself again?"

Sam frowned. "It's not about proving yourself. No one doubts your abilities. We want you to do it because *you* want to."

I raised an eyebrow. "I do, do I? Is that why I keep saying no?"

He paused, narrowing his eyes at me. "How many people are they expecting at this event?"

"They've sold about two hundred and fifty tickets so far, so with the hospital staff, probably around four, maybe five hundred total. It's a pretty big fundraiser; it brings in people from some of the surrounding towns that don't have their own hospitals."

He leveled his gaze on me. "And how do you know all that?"

I felt the flush creep up from my shirt collar and spread across my face.

"You've talked to them about it," he stated.

"Bria had one of the Foundation members call me," I confirmed, frowning as I wiped down the counters. "When I brought it up, she got defensive, and we haven't talked about it since." Yet another reason not to do the event; I didn't need it adding stress to my relationship as well as to my life.

Sam heaved a sigh, moving his hands out of my way. "Look, man, I'm not trying to trap you or back you into a corner. If you want me to drop it, I will. But tell me honestly, do you really not want to do it?"

I let the dishcloth fall from my fingers and sagged against the counter. It felt like all the breath was draining out of my body. Sam came around to the other side of the counter and leaned next to me. I kept my gaze on the floor so I wouldn't have to look at him.

"Of course I do," I said quietly. "The lady at the Foundation says she needs an answer from me by the weekend. I already know how much it'll cost, and mostly what I'd make. I just…"

"Just what?" he prodded, and I looked up.

"Jesus, Sam. No one goes against my dad's wishes. Ever. Even my mom does what he tells her. I've spent my entire life trying to make him proud of me. How can I flaunt this in his face? It's one thing if I cater your open house, or a wedding, or even if I opened a bakery. But to come to where he works, at their biggest event of the year, and throw my failure in his face? I just…how could I possibly do that to him?"

Sam slouched down to sit on the floor, his back against the counter, and was quiet for a moment. I slid down next to him, waiting for him to speak. "You really think he would see

173

this as you flaunting it in his face? You don't think he'd see how much of a success it was? How the hospital Foundation agreed to work with you at such a huge event even though you're relatively unknown and untested?"

I shook my head, then leaned it back against the counter. "He wouldn't see it that way. He takes my working here as a personal affront. He thinks I'm wasting my life baking and serving coffee."

"Do you see it that way?" He sounded genuinely curious.

I hesitated. "I don't know," I said honestly. "I love what I do, so I don't regret it, but sure, sometimes I think he's right. I should be doing more."

"Don't you think catering the event would qualify as doing more?" he asked.

"Not to him."

"What about to *you*?" Sam's face was serious as he looked at me. "Maybe you should consider that it's not about him. It's your life, and your choice to pursue something you love. And if it's bothering *you* that you're not taking risks and moving up, then maybe this is the opportunity you're looking for. And whether or not your dad will be there, or what he'll think, shouldn't factor into it."

I opened my mouth to respond, but a voice came from the other side of the counter.

"I'm sorry, sir, I don't know why there's no one over here. Geoff must have—oh! There you two are."

Marian's face appeared over the counter, upside-down in my view, next to a confused looking older gentleman.

Sam rose to his feet, then offered me a hand, hauling me up beside him. "Sorry, sir," he said smoothly. "Just having a staff meeting. What can we get you?"

Marian shot us a bemused look. "I've got it. You guys can go talk in the office if you want to. It's probably more comfortable than the floor."

Sam shook his head. "I think I've probably said all I can. But Geoff," he said, pulling me to the side as Marian ducked behind the counter and started taking the man's order. "Don't be too upset with Bria about this. She really cares about you, but I think she's afraid that since you two are so new, you might not listen to her."

I sighed, thinking about how I'd blown her off the same way I'd tried to blow off Sam. How would I have reacted if she'd made the same arguments he had? He was right, I probably wouldn't have listened to her.

"I really like her," I told him.

He clapped a hand on my shoulder and grinned. "She really likes you, too. Now get back to work before I fire you."

* * *

Bria didn't bring it up again, and neither did Sam, but his words kept echoing in my head. My dad's opinions aside, did I feel stuck in my job? Maybe I did.

When Friday finally rolled around and I had looked at the dilemma from every possible angle, argued myself to death, and changed my mind a hundred times, I finally gave up and delivered my problems into the hands of fate. Then I called the Foundation.

CHAPTER 9

BRIA

*G*eoff was manic, and I'd been giving him space. I didn't know what Sam had said to him, but whatever it had been, the magic words had worked, and Geoff had signed a contract with the hospital Foundation. In the intervening weeks he'd been wound more and more tight, and now, with the fundraiser only one day away, he'd been spending so much time at the kitchen co-op I wasn't even sure he was sleeping.

I was elated that he had taken the job, and would be catering his desserts at the fundraiser, but I wouldn't deny a small part of me was looking forward to things going back to normal in a couple of days. That amount of stress couldn't be healthy. Also, while Geoff seemed to want to talk about the job, running through lists and baking desserts for me to taste test, I found myself hesitant to ask questions for fear he would snap at me. Geoff was an easy-going guy by nature, but this had him on-edge, and he didn't seem to have an outlet for the pressure.

These thoughts were turning over in my head as I headed into the hospital to start my shift on Thursday morning. I assumed he would be at the kitchen until all hours of the night and I probably wouldn't even see him until the fundraiser. I missed the easy routine we'd fallen into, meeting in the evenings after work to eat together, share our days and relax.

Fortunately, it was a busy day at work, patient after patient, and it helped to keep my mind busy so I didn't spend my long shift worrying about Geoff. Just another day and it would all be over, and I could have back the gentle, laid-back man I'd been so quickly falling in love with.

I only hoped everything would go smoothly for him over the course of the next day. Unfortunately, in all my worry for Geoff, it didn't occur to me to hope things went smoothly for *me* as well.

Thankfully, disaster waited at least until the very end of my shift to strike. It took the form of a uniformed police officer in his mid-fifties with thick-rimmed glasses and an unreadable expression. I was standing at the nurses station with Claire, who was just coming on shift, and Dr. Asshole had just finished with a patient and was typing on the computer. I wondered idly if he had any idea his son was catering the fundraiser. I wasn't sure how often Geoff even talked to his father; he so carefully tried to avoid talking about the man. Come to think of it, I was pretty sure Dr. Ashvale didn't even know I was dating his son. *I* certainly hadn't brought it up.

The officer approached the desk and looked between the three of us.

"Are any of you familiar with a man by the name of Philip Templeton? Late sixties, in a wheelchair?"

"I think everyone in the ER is familiar with Mr. Templeton," Claire quipped, but the officer didn't crack a smile.

"I need to know when he was last seen here, and I need access to his medical records."

Dr. Ashvale looked up sharply. "What is this about?"

The officer's expression still didn't change. I exchanged an uncomfortable glance with Claire. "Mr. Templeton is dead, and the cause of death is under investigation. I have authorization to review his records."

I sucked in a sharp breath, but Dr. Ashvale just held out a hand and accepted the papers proffered by the officer. He glanced them over, then said, "Come with me. We can talk in my office."

The two men left together, and Claire and I stared at each other in stunned silence.

"Poor Mr. Templeton," I said at last. "What could have happened?"

She just shook her head. "I'm not one to speak ill of the dead, but it'll be much quieter around here with him gone."

I didn't get a chance to respond before she was called away to see to a new patient. I only had half an hour left on my shift, but I still had work to do, and I found it hard to focus. What could have happened to the poor man that involved the police?

In the end, I didn't have to wait long to find out. I was just gathering my coat and purse when Dr. Ashvale came out of his office, heading directly over to the nurses station.

"Bria." His voice was as cold as ice, and I felt a chill run up my spine. "Come with me."

He didn't wait for a response, just turned and headed back into the office. I followed.

When I entered the office, the police officer rose to his feet. He shook hands with Dr. Ashvale, his expression never changing. "Thanks for talking with me, Dr. Ashvale. I'll be in touch with the hospital security department for a copy of those records." He didn't even glance my way as he walked out of the office.

Somehow the departure of the police officer did nothing to calm my nerves.

"Sit down, Bria," Dr. Asshole said. He waited while I gingerly perched on the edge of the seat before getting right to it. "Mr. Templeton died from an overdose. He had lethal amounts of alcohol and morphine in his system when he was found. His death was reported by another homeless man, who reported that apparently Mr. Templeton had been here, in the emergency department, roughly twelve hours before his death, and was turned away and refused treatment."

I stared at the doctor in shock, and he leveled a gimlet eye on me. "His records show you were the last one to see him, on November eighteenth."

"What?!" *That wasn't possible.* It took a moment for the gears in my head to grind to life. Frantically, I cast my mind back to late November. Days in the ER all ran together, hell, most of the days in my *life* ran together, and I couldn't pull a specific date out of my memory.

I tried very hard to keep my voice calm, but still I could hear the tremble in it. "There must be some mistake. It's been weeks since I treated him, but I never would have turned him away, overdosing or not."

"No mistake," Dr. Ashvale said, his voice like steel. "I've heard the way Mr. Templeton is discussed at the nurses station. I realize he is in rather frequently, but there is no excuse for this kind of mistreatment."

I was trembling now, and I sat on my hands to keep them still. There *had* to be some kind of mistake. If only I could remember..."Can you look up who else I treated that day? If I can remember the specific day..."

I trailed off, and Dr. Ashvale turned to the computer, swiftly tapping in a few keystrokes. "Gloria Elridge, presenting with chest pain. David Meyer, the child with flu symptoms." Yes, I remembered both cases, but—

Dr. Ashvale's expression changed to one of scorn. "My *son*, with his *knife wound*."

My breath stopped, and it all came flooding back, every minute of the day I would never forget. Yes, of course. Mr. Templeton had been here at the same time as Geoff. It had been a full moon and we'd had the first snow of the season the night before, and he'd come in complaining of back pain, and—

"No!" I said, leaning forward toward the desk. "I remember that day. Check my notes! He was complaining of back pain and I took all his vitals. He wasn't overdosing; he'd been drinking, but he was *fine*." I kept going, urgently trying to get it all out before he stopped me. "It had just snowed, and we were busy from the full moon, but it had finally slowed down, so I was going to let him rest inside while we had the bed space, but when I went to check on him again, he had already left."

Dr. Ashvale just looked at me, and it took everything I had not to quail under his unyielding stare.

"Clearly you overlooked something. It shows here he wasn't even checked by a doctor before he was discharged."

"I didn't discharge him! He left AMA. You can't think I would—"

But Dr. Ashvale simply sat back in his chair and looked away, his gaze dismissing me in his signature move. "It doesn't matter what I think," he cut me off. "I sent Officer Brady up to security for a copy of the records. I imagine he will want to question you once he has reviewed the files more thoroughly. In the meantime, I am going to recommend to the board your suspension until this matter is settled."

My heart seemed to stutter, stop, then begin a freefall, dropping out of my chest and crashing down through my body. A *suspension?* How was any of this happening?

"You may go," Dr. Ashvale told me. He had turned his attention back to his computer, and clearly had no interest in the fact that my life was being ruined right in front of him.

So, I did the only thing I could. I left.

I ignored Claire calling my name as I hurried across the floor, not even bothering to put on my coat as I left the building. I climbed numbly into my car, and drove home in a fog, hazy thoughts tumbling in my head. Something was missing; some piece of the puzzle. The police were wrong, or the autopsy was wrong, or, or, or Dr. Asshole was setting me up because he's always hated me.

I felt sick.

Could it be true? Had Mr. Templeton really been over-dosing? Could I really have missed it, let my own prejudices get in the way? Could I really be at fault for a man's death?

I narrowly made it home without throwing up.

It took me three tries to get my key into the door with my shaking hands. Once inside, I didn't even bother to turn on the light. I dropped my purse on the floor, crawled into bed, pulled the covers up over my head, and cried myself to sleep.

It took a long, long time.

*O*ne more day. One more freaking day and this would be over, and everything would go back to normal, and I'd be able to breathe again. At this point, I wasn't sure I even cared if it was a success or not, I just wanted it to be over.

And it would be in—I checked my watch, as I had been doing compulsively for hours now—just over ten hours. Seven hours to go before I would need to get everything over to the convention hall and set up. Another hour after that before the fundraiser started. Two hours of what would either be intense panic because it was all out of my hands, or blissful relief because it was all out of my hands. And then it would be over, and I could go home, drag Bria into bed with me, and sleep for a week.

Bria. She'd probably be as glad as I would when this was over. I wondered if she regretted pushing me into it. I hadn't even spoken to her in two days now. She hadn't called me after work last night, nor this morning. I missed her, but I knew she was giving me space to work.

I knew I hadn't been great to her over the past couple of

weeks; I'd been trying hard not to take my stress out on her, but I wasn't sure I'd been successful. But if I could just get through tonight, I could apologize, and things could go back to the way they were. Because they'd been wonderful. *She'd* been wonderful.

I took a long pull from the glass of bourbon I had sitting next to me on the counter, feeling the blaze of heat trailing through me as I swallowed. I'd promised myself I would stick to wine to calm my nerves as I worked, but the wine bottle was empty, and my nerves were still jangling. To be fair, the wine bottle hadn't been full to start with, and I was taking the bourbon slow—this was only my second glass.

The timer on the oven beeped, and I started, the spatula I'd been holding motionless in my other hand falling to the countertop. I mentally chastised myself. *Pull yourself together. Ten hours, then you can daydream.*

I pulled the last tray of custard tarts out of the oven, setting them on the stove top to cool, then got back to my mixing bowl. This was it, the last of it. Everything else was done, filling the fridge and stacked on the counters, waiting to be packed up for transport. I had macarons in five flavors, eclairs, and mille feuilles, and I'd gone ahead with the mini-trifles. I also had the custard tarts, shortbread cookies, and squares of honey-drenched baklava.

The only thing I'd left to the last minute had been the chocolate mousse, which didn't take long to make and always seemed to taste best when fresh.

I already had the chocolate melted together with butter and coffee, cooling on the countertop. The bowl in front of me, sitting over a pot of simmering water, held practically more egg yolks than I could count, and I began to whisk them, adding in water and a generous splash of rum. I'd used up my current bag of sugar in the tarts, so I dug another bag out of the cabinet and poured sugar into the mix, whisking until my eyes began to glaze over.

I took another quick sip of bourbon to keep myself awake —funny that it seemed to be having the opposite effect—and moved the bowl into an ice bath before beating it further. Fortunately, I could make chocolate mousse in my sleep, so I beat in the chocolate mixture, beat the egg whites with some more sugar and a splash of vanilla, then folded it all together in record time. It took longer than I'd hoped to portion it all out into individual servings, but I got it all into the fridge with plenty of time to chill before I had to leave.

There was still more to do—cleaning up and packing everything for transport, but I desperately needed a break. There should still be enough time. Taking my bourbon with me, I sank down to the floor, where I leaned back against the counter and let my head roll back. My breath escaped in a long, low sigh.

A few minutes later I roused myself just enough to set an alarm on my phone, before letting myself drift off again.

Just a few more hours to go.

* * *

When the alarm on my phone went off, I jumped so high I nearly smashed my head on the lip of the counter. My glass of bourbon had fallen out of my hand at some point and was now a sticky puddle spreading across the floor. Thank god I was the only person using the commercial kitchen today. This wasn't exactly a good look.

It was best that I hadn't drank it though, I thought as I mopped up the spill; I needed to be sober enough to get to the convention center.

Shaking the fog of sleep from my head, I staggered to my feet and forced myself back to work. This was it, the home stretch. Packing containers. Loading the van I'd rented. Back and forth between the van and the kitchen a million times.

A quick stop at my apartment to shower and get dressed, and then I was off to the convention center. More trips back and forth from the van, unloading, transferring food to the huge fridges there, setting up displays, sneaking sips of bourbon as I hurried back and forth from the kitchen.

The big ballroom they'd chosen for the fundraiser looked amazing. With the holidays approaching fast, they'd gone all out with the festive decor—twinkling lights, wreaths on the doors and pine boughs on the tables, an enormous, ceiling-high tree in one corner decked out with glittering tinsel and ornaments. Long tables covered with decorative cloths framed the perimeter, one entire wall set up for my delicacies, a drink station in one corner. Another long table for the other caterer who was providing hors d'oeuvres. The tables along the other walls were all set up with displays of local artwork and other donated items for the silent auction. The center of the room was filled with small tables and chairs, suitable for mingling and schmooz-ing. I felt very out of place, and my head was feeling a bit fuzzy. I was glad I would be spending my time primarily in the kitchen.

The doors opened at precisely seven o'clock, admitting a throng of well-dressed hospital patrons into the ballroom. I scanned the crowd for Bria, but her blue hair was nowhere to be seen. She must not have arrived yet. I did see her friend Claire's blonde head though, and caught a glimpse of my father just in time to make a beeline for the kitchen.

At first, I hadn't been sure if I should tell him I would be catering the event, or even if I would be there at all. And while I dithered about it, unable to decide which option would be less painful, the mayhem of preparation had taken over all my attention, until suddenly the fundraiser had started and I still hadn't spoken to him. Well, it was too late now. Maybe I could hide out in the kitchen the whole—

"Geoff?"

Shit.

Apparently, I hadn't been fast enough. I turned, a little too quickly, and the room wavered alarmingly in my vision. I focused on the frowning face of my father and tried to stay calm. I wished Bria were here, holding my hand so I could pull her support into myself by osmosis. I tried to think of what she would tell me. *She'd tell you to calm down. She'd tell you your baking is amazing. She'd tell you that you don't need his approval.* I took a deep breath.

"What are you doing here?" my dad asked, his features set in their requisite frown.

"I, um." I wished I could be anywhere else in the world. The beach in Florida with my mom. The North Pole. Maybe home in bed with the rest of that bottle of bourbon.

"Speak up. Don't stammer."

Suddenly I caught a flash of blue over by the door, and relief swept through me like a wave. Bria had arrived. I heard her voice in my head. *Dammit, stand up for yourself.*

I tried again, and my voice was stronger this time. "I'm the caterer."

"You what?" He looked at me like I was speaking gibberish.

The room was filling up, the noise level rising, and people were beginning to drift toward the dessert table.

"I catered the fundraiser." I tried to match his expression. Like *he* was the idiot here, not me. "The desserts. I made them."

His eyes inched up. "You *cater* now? What happened to the bookstore?"

The word "bookstore" sounded like "trash heap," but I soldiered on, keeping my voice calm. "I still work there, I'm just branching out a bit. The hospital Foundation offered me this opportunity, and I thought it would be good."

"Good? Good for what?"

"Good for the future. I don't want to stay at the bookstore forever."

His lined face relaxed minutely. "Oh, thank god. You've come to your senses."

"Yes," I said, feeling strangely defiant. "I've been thinking about expanding into catering. Possibly opening a bakery at some point."

His face hardened again, and I could see a vein throb in his temple. Why had I thought it would be a good idea to have this conversation here? Oh, right—because he wouldn't kill me in public. Where had Bria gone?

"What are you talking about? You—" He broke off as a colleague waved from across the room, and when he spoke again, his voice wasn't angry, it was dismissive. The knife he had planted in my chest twisted painfully. "Don't be ridiculous," he said. "We'll talk about this later. Right now I have to—"

He broke off again at the sound of a commotion from the far end of the room, a raised voice, then two. We both turned, and I caught sight of Bria, standing only a few paces behind us, also turned toward the commotion. I had only enough time to register that she didn't look like herself—sick, or upset, I couldn't tell, but *something* wasn't right—before the raised voices from across the room suddenly became clear.

An elderly woman in a long, stately red dress had her hand over her mouth and was coughing, her face a shade to match her dress. My dad started across the room, not sparing me a glance, and I followed close on his heels. Only when we got closer did I realize what was happening. Whatever residual effects I'd been feeling from the alcohol evaporated, cold sobriety washing over me like a tidal wave.

The woman in red was holding one of the small glasses of chocolate mousse in her hand, gesturing wildly with the spoon she held clutched in the other one. "What *is* this?" she gasped out between coughs. Another man at the far end of the table began to cough as well, discreetly spitting something back out onto his plate.

"What's *wrong* with it?"

"Oh, that's vile!"

My heart plummeted like a stone.

My father, upon realizing that no medical assistance was needed, turned to look at me, his eyebrow raised in condescending speculation. Without looking away from me he reached out, helping himself to one of the tiny decorative glasses filled with chocolate mousse that I'd spent the afternoon working on, each one topped with a swirl of cream and a mint leaf. He lifted the spoon and took a bite. It seemed to happen in slow motion.

I watched the expression on his face slowly morph into one of disgusted horror, but he made himself swallow before setting the glass carefully back on the table.

I didn't wait for him to speak. I grabbed my own glass, digging out a spoonful and shoving it in my mouth.

Salt.

It was immediately obvious. I'd used salt instead of sugar. I must have opened the wrong bag, and not bothered to check. What a completely ridiculous, novice-level mistake. Something that only would have happened to an idiot who was too busy drinking and panicking and feeling sorry for himself to pay attention to what he was doing.

My father opened his mouth, but I didn't wait to hear what was going to come out. Something I would agree with, no doubt. I set the glass on the table, turned, and fled into the kitchen.

"Geoff!" Bria's voice sounded behind me, but I ignored her as well, mortification burning in my chest.

In the kitchen I grabbed the biggest tray I could find and headed back out into the ballroom. At the dessert table I ignored the stares, the tactful whispers and less tactful comments, and loaded the tray with all the mousse. The damage had clearly already been done, but I said a few reassuring words to the crowd, doing what I could to salvage whatever vestiges of pride I had left, then headed back into the kitchen with the ruined mousse. My father, thankfully, was nowhere to be seen.

The rest of the food was fine; I knew that, I had sampled it all. Like any decent pastry chef would do. I don't know why I hadn't tasted the mousse. Because I was an idiot, obviously. I didn't know if anyone would be brave enough to try the other desserts at this point, but I wasn't going to stand around and watch to find out.

Bria was waiting for me when I finally retreated back into the kitchen with the tray of mousse, which I unceremoniously dumped on the counter.

Her eyes were wide. "Geoff, what *happened?*"

I tried, but I couldn't keep my voice even. It boiled out in an angry whisper. "What happened? I proved my dad right, that's what happened. I messed up, just like I knew I would. I should have stayed in med school."

Her face was twisted in sympathy. "What, you think no one messes up in medicine?"

"You're right," I snapped. "I would have messed that up, too. I shouldn't have done this. I *knew* better, but you and Sam wouldn't let up, would you?" I couldn't stop. I could see her expression hardening into stone, the emotion draining out of her face, and I tried to halt the flow, but it was too late.

189

The embarrassment, the failure, the anger, it was too strong, and it poured out of me along with the words. "You both thought you knew what was best for me, even though I *told* you I didn't want this. I knew this wouldn't end well."

"That's right," she said, color blazing bright in her cheeks. "Something went wrong, so you'd better give up, right? You made a mistake, so your dad must be right about everything." Her hands were fisted on her hips, the air practically crackling with energy around her. "Don't listen to the hundred people telling you your food is great, just listen to the one saying you're worthless. What do *we* know anyway? We're not validating your insecurities, so we must be full of shit, right?"

I rolled my eyes impatiently. "That's not what—"

But she didn't stop. "I guess if you stop baking, you'll be looking for a new job, huh? Maybe we can job hunt together, if I'm not in prison by then!"

She hurled the final words at me and turned to leave, but my hand shot out reflexively, grabbing her by the arm. "What are you talking about?"

She spun back to face me, so fast her arm ripped out of my grasp, and I realized I could see tears in her eyes. She blinked them back, still clearly furious and trying to hold herself together. I suddenly felt like I had lost the thread of this argument. What the hell had I missed?

When she spoke again, she bit out the words in a trembling voice. "One of my patients died and there's a police investigation. I'm under review for inappropriate treatment. They suspended me yesterday pending an investigation. Best-case scenario—I'll lose my license. And I'm not holding my breath for the best-case scenario."

The tears spilled over and she jerked her face away from me, then turned, and fled out the back door.

*G*eoff caught up with me in the parking lot, looking like he'd been hit by a freight train. A small, hidden part of me felt guilty—that probably hadn't been fair of me, to hit him with everything like that, especially when he was still reeling from the failed mousse and the confrontation with his father.

But the larger part of me, the angry, hurt part, felt vindicated. How dare he blame me for this? I hadn't forced him to take the job. Yes, I'd had the Foundation call him, but only to offer him the chance. He'd made the decision by himself. Hell, I hadn't even brought it up again after I'd talked to Sam. Obviously, I'd thought it was the right thing for him to do, but I'd let him come to that conclusion on his own. And if he wanted to find someone to blame for his failure tonight, maybe he should blame the alcohol that was still painfully obvious on his breath.

Dammit. My tears dried up in the heat of my anger, and I swiped a hand across my eyes, probably smearing my makeup. I hadn't even wanted to come tonight. The last thing I wanted to do was put on a dress and spend an evening socializing with the very people who were all no doubt whispering about me behind my back. It had been obvious from the second I'd walked through the door tonight, faces turning in my direction, alternatively speculative and pitying. I never would have come, except I had to support Geoff. I knew what this meant to him, and I had to be there for him. And then he threw it all right back in my face.

I stopped when he caught me by the arm, swinging me around to face him. I looked down, refusing to meet his eyes.

"Bria." His voice was urgent. "Tell me what happened. Tell me everything." His eyes were wide, illuminated by the lights in the parking lot, just beginning to come on in the gathering dusk. He sounded bewildered.

The anger still simmered in me, but it had been two days now, two days of fear and confusion, of second guessing myself, and having no one to talk to, and the story began to spill out in a flat voice.

"...and then I had to go to the police station and give my statement. The board put me on paid leave while the police conduct the investigation, and I don't know what happened, but I saw the medical records. I...I didn't think I did anything wrong, but if what they say is true and he died just after he left, and *I* was the last one to see him, then I must have." My chest was tight now with the effort of keeping my voice from shaking. I knew I shouldn't even be talking about this with him, with anyone, but I couldn't stop. "I must have missed something, must have—"

"No." He gripped me tighter, forcing my chin up to meet his eyes. "If you say you gave him the best treatment you could, then you did. There has to be another explanation, and if there's an investigation, the police will figure it out."

The certainty in his voice should have been reassuring, but I still felt cold inside.

"Tell me what I can do," he said. "How can I help?"

The coldness inside me seemed to solidify. Because there was nothing he could do, no way he could help. I had gotten myself into this mess, and it was out of both our hands now. Just like Geoff had gotten himself into the mess inside, with alcohol and self-doubt, and he had to find his own way out of it. We weren't in this together.

I don't know what expression he read on my face, but he started to shake his head. "No," he said, his voice sounding choked. "What—"

"Geoff," I cut him off, and he closed his mouth with a snap. "You can't help me with this. And I can't help you with...that." I waved my hand vaguely back toward the convention center. "I don't..." I squeezed my eyes shut, and my voice was a strangled whisper. "I can't do this right now."

I didn't know what he could say to make me change my mind, but I expected him to *try*. I expected reassurance, or apologies, or even pleading. I certainly didn't expect to open my eyes a moment later and find myself standing alone in the parking lot.

But maybe I shouldn't have been surprised. Maybe giving up was what he did best.

CHAPTER 12

GEOFF

I knew I'd messed up. I'd messed up on every level. I shouldn't have blamed Bria for my mistakes, shouldn't have taken my anger out on her in the first place. And I *definitely* shouldn't have just left her in the parking lot. But I hadn't known what to do. I'd been so overwhelmed, so frustrated and scared, and, I'll admit, not entirely sober, so I'd fled.

I'd regretted it immediately. But when I'd come back out to the parking lot, she was long gone. I couldn't leave until the end of the fundraiser, so I'd called her instead, apologizing and imploring her to call me back. I hadn't expected that she would, but I'd hoped, as I waited for the stupid event to finally end. I was right; she didn't call. Or answer my texts.

On the plus side, at least one brave soul had decided to try the other desserts I'd baked, and once it was discovered they weren't poisoned, word spread through the crowd. I wasn't forgiven for the chocolate mousse disaster, but at least the days and weeks of preparing hadn't been a waste.

My father left without seeking me out, not that I'd made any effort on my part either, and when the last straggler had finally, *finally* cleared out of the ballroom, I tore down my displays in record time, packing up the leftovers to take to Sam's and hightailing it out of there.

I had every intention of heading straight over to Bria's apartment, but with a little distance from the situation, and a little sobriety, I began to second guess myself. What if she didn't want to see me? What if she needed some time? Hoping I wasn't making yet another colossal mistake, I went home instead. I would wait; give her time to cool off and call her in the morning. I wouldn't barge in on her unless she invited me.

But she didn't invite me over the next day. She didn't answer her phone, either. Or return my calls. Or my texts. The day after that was more of the same, and by Monday morning, when she normally would have had a long shift at the hospital, I was practically beside myself. I finally gave in and stopped by her apartment on my way to work. If only I could talk to her, just for a minute, I could ask how she was doing. I just needed to see if she was okay.

But she didn't answer her door, and when I made my way dejectedly back out to the parking lot, I realized her car wasn't even there. Where could she possibly be? The radio silence was killing me.

It only took about twenty minutes of me moping around at the bookstore before Sam came over and dragged me away from the cafe.

"Marian's got it. Come with me. Look at you. You'll make the customers depressed."

I followed him obediently into the office, where I slumped into a worn leather chair. Sam took the rolling office chair, pushing his computer out of the way and propping his elbows on the desk.

"Okay, let's hear it. What happened?"

"What do you mean? I told you what happened. I served

chocolate-flavored salt to half the hospital staff and got to hear 'I told you so' from my dad." I'd called Sam on Saturday morning with an update and an excuse as to why I wouldn't be in that day. The second time I'd ever called off since I'd been working for him. I'd thought it wouldn't take anything less than a knife wound to keep me from work, but apparently heartbreak and embarrassment would do the trick as well.

He rolled his eyes. "Yes, you told me about that part. But that doesn't explain why you look like..." He waved his hand in a vague circle, encompassing my entire state of being. "...*that.*"

He looked at me expectantly and I gave in. He wasn't going to let up until he was satisfied.

"I haven't talked to Bria since the fundraiser. I told you about our argument."

"Have you called her?"

I glared at him. "Of *course* I've called her. I've left about a million messages. And texts. I even went to her apartment this morning, but she wasn't there. I don't know what to do. She won't even give me a chance to apologize."

Sam shrugged. "Maybe an apology isn't what she wants."

"Well then what *does* she want?" My voice came out in an exasperated growl. "I can't read her mind. I know I messed up, but I don't know how to fix it! Besides, she's dealing with all this shit from work right now, and she's cut me out. I can't comfort her, I can't support her, I don't even know what's going *on.*"

Sam blew out a breath and leaned back in his chair, looking thoughtful. "I don't know, man...Bria doesn't seem like a mind-games kind of girl. If she's avoiding you, there's got to be a reason for it. What did she say to you before you left on Friday?"

The words echoed in my mind as clearly as if she had just

spoken them. "She said…she couldn't do this right now. She said I couldn't help her, and she couldn't help me."

Sam's eyebrows drew together, and there was a long pause. Finally, he said, "Well, that sounds pretty clear to me."

"Enlighten me." I couldn't keep the frustration out of my voice.

"Look, man. She's right. There's nothing you can do to help her through this investigation. She has to get that straightened out on her own, and the outcome is out of your hands."

"Yeah, but—"

"And *she* can't help you figure out your shit either. She especially can't help if you don't listen to her, or if you blame her for your mistakes." My mouth, which had immediately opened in defense, snapped shut. "*You* have to do that," he went on, "and maybe what she needs isn't an apology. Maybe what she needs is for you to fix your shit."

"How do I do that?" I said in exasperation. "I thought you guys wanted me to try catering, and I did. But that's not going to work out. Maybe you're all right, and maybe my food tastes okay when I don't fuck it up, but I can't do it again. It's too much stress." I hadn't even realized I'd made that decision until I spoke the words aloud, but it was true. I didn't like who I became when I was stressed like that. I didn't like how I'd treated Bria, or how I'd turned to alcohol to cope with the anxiety. I'd told Bria that I only drank when I was stressed, or dealing with my dad, and I'd told myself at the time that since I didn't drink otherwise, I didn't have a problem. But maybe that was the definition of a problem.

Sam just stared at me like I'd lost my mind. "Geoff, it's not about what *we* want you to do. Who the hell cares what we want? What do *you* want? All that *we* want is for you to do what makes *you* happy."

I just blinked.

"Baking makes me happy," I said slowly.

Sam looked at me with exasperated annoyance, though I could see the corner of his mouth twitch up. "Things are always so black and white with you. You're either in med school, or you're a disgrace. You either have to kill yourself baking for huge events, or you can't bake at all."

I looked down at the floor. He wasn't wrong.

"Look, I know you like running the cafe," he went on, "but you're obviously not completely happy here. You want more, but catering doesn't have to be the only option. Why don't you stop worrying about what your dad wants, or what I want, or what Bria wants, and figure out what *you* want."

What I wanted was Bria. But I understood his point. I spent so much time being afraid of letting everyone else down, and all I was doing was letting myself down in the process.

I thought back over all the time I'd spent throughout my childhood trying so hard to be the person my dad wanted me to be—strong, successful, accomplished. I thought about how I'd always been teased for being who I was—soft, compassionate, emotional. And I wondered for the first time if those things were mutually exclusive.

I rose to my feet, thanking Sam and heading back out to the cafe, to the one place in my life that I felt like I knew what I was doing. His words echoed in my head as I walked. *What do* you *want?*

If I was honest with myself, I knew what I wanted, what I'd always wanted. What I didn't know was how to convince myself that my dreams were worth following.

CHAPTER 13

BRIA

I was lost in a tangle of emotions. Between the situation at work, the meeting with the police investigator, and the argument with Geoff, I was still reeling. Everything had happened so fast, I hadn't gotten a chance to process any of it. And so instead of figuring out how to deal with any of it, I just shut down.

I locked myself in my apartment, turned on the TV in hopes that the sound would drown out my racing thoughts, and then proceeded to ignore the phone when it rang. And rang. And rang some more. It wasn't all Geoff. I didn't answer Claire's calls either, or my parents. But it was mostly Geoff.

At first, I didn't answer because I was mad. Then I didn't answer because I was overwhelmed and confused. But eventually, the main emotion keeping me away was a conflicting combination of guilt and hurt. Part of me was starting to regret the way I had reacted, and the things I'd said. While I knew he was in the wrong, he had tried to apologize. And what's more, I *knew* he hadn't meant the things he'd said. But that still didn't make his words any less hurtful.

And at the same time, it was obvious I'd been wrong. I'd told him there was nothing he could do to help me through the mess with my job. But in reality, I desperately missed his support, his comfort, his sympathetic ear. Effectively having cut myself off from my friends at the hospital, I had no one else I could turn to. And really, aside from his blind spot where his own job was concerned, Geoff really was a generally rational and level-headed guy. He was exactly the sort of person I needed to help me through this.

So why couldn't I just answer the phone?

The weekend seemed to stretch into eternity, and Sunday was even worse. I slept fitfully, tossing and turning and losing track of the time. I ran every second of my interaction with Mr. Templeton over and over in my head. I replayed my fight with Geoff in vivid detail. I drove myself crazy.

It was in the dark, moonless hours late on Sunday night when I decided I couldn't take it any longer. I'd call him in the morning. Or better yet, I'd go see him at work. I'd apologize; I'd accept his apology, and we would get through this mess the way we both needed to—together.

I felt the barest relief at a decision made, but it still took me forever to fall asleep. When the harsh ringing of the phone jerked me awake, it could have been hours later or mere minutes, and I nearly fell out of bed as my heart leaped into my throat.

"Geoff?" I said aloud, my throat scratchy as I lunged for the phone.

It was the hospital.

I barely had time to process that it wasn't him before I'd answered the call, phone clutched tight in my sweating hand.

"Miss Kohler? It's Amanda, from Human Resources. Would you be able to come into the hospital this morning?"

Amanda was the same person who had delivered the news that I'd been suspended. Oh god, was this it? Was I about to be arrested? But no, then it would be the police calling, not the hospital, right? And they'd probably show up at my door, not call first. Was I just getting officially fired, then?

"Miss Kohler?"

I realized I'd been silent too long. "I'm here. Yes, I can be there in about half an hour." My voice shook no matter how hard I tried to control it.

"That'll work just fine. We'll see you soon."

I ended the call, replaying every word in my mind. Should I have asked what it was about? Who was "we?"

One glance in the mirror convinced me that I couldn't leave the house in this condition. I hadn't showered or slept well in days, and it showed. Fortunately, it only took about fifteen minutes to get to work, so I stripped down and showered in record time, brushing my teeth with one hand while attempting to tie up my wet hair with the other. Should I wear scrubs? *No, idiot, you're not going to work. You're going to find out you'll never work again.*

I pulled on clean jeans and a nice top—what *does* one wear to get fired?—grabbed my coat and was out the door seconds later.

I barely registered any of the drive there, I was so preoccupied with the instant replay of the phone call running over and over in my mind, and I didn't realize I was in the wrong place until I had walked into the ER and was halfway to the nurses station.

Idiot, I chastised myself again, ignoring the pang that twisted my heart in my chest. I really was going to miss this place.

By the time I'd made it across to the other side of the building where HR was housed with the other administrative offices, I was late, and I could hear voices coming from inside the small meeting room the receptionist directed me to.

When I opened the door, I barely had time to take in the scene inside before silence fell and three pairs of eyes swiveled to look my way.

Only one of the seats at the table in the center of the room was occupied—by a tense-looking Amanda, a pretty woman in her mid-fifties with graying hair. Standing behind one of the empty chairs was Officer Brady, the police officer who had taken my statement, the same one who had come into the ER on Thursday and ruined my life. Across the table by the far wall was Dr. Ashvale, wearing his scrubs and lab coat, his face pinched in an expression of supreme annoyance.

What was going on?

"Ah, Bria, come take a seat." Amanda half rose, gesturing to one of the empty chairs around the table. I obeyed, clutching my purse tight to my chest. I was so confused. What was—

"We all know why we're here," she started, and my brow furrowed. Had I missed something? But a second later she turned to look at me and continued. "After reviewing the statements and the additional evidence, we have been authorized to lift your suspension, Bria. You can return to work on your regular shift on Wednesday."

"*What?!*" My voice came out in a hoarse squeak.

Officer Brady took over, coming around the table so I could see his face. It was still expressionless—I wondered if the man was even capable of forming expressions—but I was much more interested in his words than his face.

"We've been through the medical records, and it seems there was a mistake." He consulted the file of papers he held in one hand. "Mr. Templeton came into the emergency department on November eighteenth, at 8:17am, complaining of back pain, and was treated by you, correct?"

I nodded numbly, heart pounding.

"He was found and reported to the police early in the morning on November nineteenth. The autopsy showed that he had died from an overdose of alcohol and morphine, and put his time of death at roughly 9:30pm on the evening of the eighteenth."

My brow furrowed. We'd already been over all this. What was going on?

"Apparently that was not Mr. Templeton's only visit to the ER that day."

I looked up, startled.

"It seems he returned to the hospital roughly six hours later, and was seen by Miss Harper."

Claire? Six hours later…I would have been off my shift by then.

"But…but you had his medical records," I said, looking around the room. "Why…"

"Apparently that second visit was misdated," the officer informed me. "It was entered into your computer system as occurring on October eighteenth, instead of November."

My jaw dropped open.

"But when the timeline is fixed, everything makes sense," Officer Brady went on. "Mr. Templeton checked into the ER again at 2:45pm on the afternoon of November eighteenth, and was released without medical treatment. He died approximately seven hours later."

I sat, stunned, waiting for my brain to process all this new information. Finally, I glanced toward the police officer. "How did you figure it out? The dates, I mean."

Apparently, the man could form expressions after all, because I saw the faintest flush of what looked like embarrassment cross his features. "We didn't. Miss Harper called this morning and brought the matter to our attention."

"It's been *four days*," I whispered, half to myself. Suddenly

I felt cold. What would have happened if Claire had never come forward?

There was a long silence, and then Amanda cleared her throat. "Okay, well, Officer Brady, I'll need you in my office. Bria, if there are no other questions, we'll expect you back at work on Wednesday, okay? I'll have paperwork for you then as well."

I nodded dumbly, and the two of them left the room, leaving me alone with Dr. Ashvale.

I expected him to leave as well, but instead he pushed off the wall and turned to face me. "Miss Kohler. I apologize for reporting you to the hospital board and recommending your suspension. I am glad you will be staying. You're a good nurse."

I blinked. Then blinked again, looking into his scowling face with disbelief. I didn't mean to respond, but the words were past my lips before I could pull them back. "I thought you hated me."

Dr. Ashvale snorted, his expression full of that familiar disdain. "Miss Kohler, I don't *hate* you. I do not particularly approve of your...choices." His gaze pointedly took in my hair and tattoos. "I find it unprofessional. I fought the board when they relaxed the rules on body modifications, but I lost. However, it does not appear to affect your abilities, and you are good at your job. It would have been a shame to lose you."

I opened my mouth again, but nothing came out.

I expected him to leave, but a moment later, Dr. Ashvale's frown deepened, and he opened his mouth, then closed it again. I realized suddenly that he had more to say, and I had a sinking suspicion I might know what it was. I waited him out, my mind still reeling from the events of the last half hour, and finally he spoke.

"I understand you've been dating my son."

I winced, and wondered how he'd found out. "Yes, well. I was. I'm not currently sure if I am or not."

Dr. Ashvale raised an eyebrow over his frown, but I elected not to clarify.

"Well, after that embarrassing fiasco at the fundraiser, maybe he'll stop—"

I didn't know how he was going to finish that sentence, and I didn't want to find out. My anger welled up, and I cut him off before I realized I was going to speak. "You know," I said loudly, "the only person at that fundraiser who's opinion he cared about was yours."

Dr. Ashvale scoffed. "Geoff doesn't care about my opinion. He never has."

I looked at him in amazement, my mouth open. "Look, this is none of my business. I don't even know if I'm dating your son or not. But that doesn't make any of this less true: Geoff cares about your opinion more than anything. He works so hard to be what he thinks you want, and never feels like he's good enough."

Dr. Ashvale opened his mouth, but I didn't give him a chance to speak. "Your son is a wonderful person. He's the kindest, most caring, supportive individual I've ever met, and any faults he has are *directly* a result of him trying to make himself into a different person so he can gain *your* approval."

Dr. Ashvale's mouth snapped shut, and I suddenly regretted my outburst. My emotions were too close to the surface, and I was being inappropriate. This really wasn't my place.

I waited for whatever blistering retort the doctor had for me, but to my surprise, he didn't say anything at all. For just a second I thought I caught something more than disapproval in the depths of his frown, but before I could identify it, he gave me a brief nod. "I'll see you on Wednesday." Then without another glance, he turned and left the room.

The door swung shut behind him on silent hinges, but I didn't move. I sat there for a long time, staring unseeing at the wall, letting the events of the past half hour replay in my mind. It felt like a dream, all of it—a four-day-long nightmare that was suddenly, unexpectedly over.

And in the void of all the stress and anger and anxiety, I missed Geoff. I realized my hastily spoken words to Dr. Ashvale had all been true. Geoff *was* the kindest, most caring and supportive person I'd ever met. And I hated that we'd each let our own insecurities and problems come between us. Problems that could have been better fixed together.

I needed to see him.

What seemed like an eternity later I rose to my feet, wiping my damp palms on my jeans, and pulled my coat on. I glanced at my watch. Geoff should be at work right now; I could head straight there. I hurried out into the hallway, where voices from Amanda's adjacent office stopped me in my tracks.

"I didn't *mean* to." The voice was muffled by the heavy door and thick with tears, but I still immediately recognized it as Claire. "He had *just* been in, and it was cold outside; I thought he was just looking for somewhere to stay! We were busy by then; I didn't have an extra bed or the time to waste on him."

Paused outside the door, I cringed at her words, but then another voice answered. It was Dr. Ashvale—he must have gone to Amanda's office after he'd left the conference room. His voice was icy. "If he was overdosing, he must have had symptoms."

Claire's voice came louder through the door. "He was drowsy and uncoordinated, but it didn't seem out of the ordinary. He was always drunk! How was I supposed to know there was more going on?"

I could almost imagine Dr. Ashvale's glare. "By doing

your job! If you'd done any kind of real assessment you would have seen. Just because the man was homeless, and an addict, doesn't make him any less deserving of our care than any other patient."

I blinked. What a human sentiment from Dr. Asshole.

Claire just cried harder though. "I'm *sorry*."

I heard footsteps moving through the room and then another voice broke in. When I recognized it as Officer Brady, I straightened. This, too, was none of my business. There was nothing I could do about it now, Claire had gotten herself into this mess all by herself. Besides, I had a different mess I needed to deal with.

As I made my way down the hallway, my steps picked up, until I was running out the doors and across the parking lot to my car, wrenching open the door and jamming my key in the ignition.

I needed to find Geoff.

* * *

"What do you mean he doesn't work here anymore?!"

I was pretty sure my voice was reaching a register only dogs could hear, but Sam only smiled at me, his dark eyes crinkling in the corners.

"Well, I mean, technically he does, but only for another month or two. He put in his notice. Finally."

My mouth opened and closed like a fish.

It had been four days since my meeting at the hospital, and I *still* hadn't been able to talk to Geoff. When I'd raced over after talking with HR, he hadn't been at work, and Sam had been out running errands. I'd called, but it had gone to voicemail, and despite the message I'd left, he hadn't called me back all that day or the next. On Wednesday I'd gone back to work, and the bookstore had been closed by the time my shift was over. It was now Friday, my first chance to come try to talk to Geoff again in person, and he *still* wasn't here.

"I gave him the day off though," Sam went on, either not realizing or not caring that he was giving me a stroke. "He had some things to take care of."

"Sam," I growled, enunciating my words carefully. "Please. Tell me. Where he is."

Sam relented, his teasing expression softening. "You know Fairfield Roast? The coffee shop down at the end of the street, on the corner?"

I nodded impatiently. Of course I did, that was where Geoff and I had gone on our first "date."

"He's probably still there," Sam told me.

I was practically out the door when I heard his voice call after me, "Good luck, Bria!"

I waved back over my shoulder, then flew down the street.

CHAPTER 14

GEOFF

*I*n the cold light of day, the place was a little more worn than it had looked the last time I'd been in here. Besides, that time, I'd been preoccupied with Bria, sitting in front of me with her killer black dress and red shoes. My heart clenched at the memory.

I still hadn't returned her call from earlier that week. After she'd avoided me all weekend, I hadn't thought I would end up being the one avoiding her. But Sam's words had made me think. He was right. I couldn't blame Bria, or my father, for my own mistakes. And I needed to fix my own shit before I could move forward.

But now here I was, taking the first steps toward doing just that. Maybe it was time to return her call.

I put the thought aside for now and turned my attention back to the coffee shop. Well, ex-coffee shop. Today I could see that the paint was peeling off the walls, some of the light fixtures were broken, and the booths were a little shabby and worn.

No matter. That was all fixable. All that really mattered

was that the place had a huge kitchen, a workable layout, and a great location.

I went behind the counter again, and was kneeling on the floor to assess the state of the cabinets back there when I heard a knock on the front door. The place was closed and locked, lights off, clearly out of business even without the giant "For Sale" sign in the window, so I only spared the door a dismissive glance, before my brain registered the figure peering tentatively through the glass.

Bria.

I sprang to my feet so fast I nearly tripped and flew to the door, my eyes scanning her through the glass, taking in her wide eyes and anxious expression. Her blue hair was messy, strands escaping out of a loose ponytail, there were dark shadows under her eyes, and she pulled at the hem of her coat, fidgeting as she waited for me to let her in. She looked beautiful.

It took more than one try to disengage the locks, my fingers fumbling clumsily with the latches until finally they gave way and I wrenched the door open.

We both spoke over each other, frantic to get the words out.

"I'm sorry."

"I'm sorry."

"I didn't mean to—"

"I shouldn't have—"

"The investigation is over; I still have my job."

"I wanted to—*What?*"

She started to laugh, the sound a soothing balm to my ears, and I gripped her upper arms in both hands, reveling in the feel of her, the solid warmth of her, and pulled her into the store. Her laughter turned slightly hysterical.

"It's wonderful, but it's also terrible, and I needed to tell you—and Sam said you quit your job?! Why would you—"

Rather than answer, I pulled her against me, wrapping my arms around her and squeezing tight. I ducked my head and buried my face in the warmth of her hair, breathing in the clean floral scent of her, and when her arms came up around me as well, my chest eased in a feeling of palpable relief.

Finally, I forced myself to release her, helping her out of her coat and leading her over to the worn booth by the cold, silent fireplace that we'd sat in together what seemed like forever ago.

"Geoff," she started, "what's going *on?* Sam said—"

I reached across the table and covered her hand with my own. "Wait. Tell me what happened first. Tell me about your job."

She flipped her hand over so her palm was against mine and laced our fingers together. Her skin was soft and warm, and I instantly felt more calm than I had in days.

"It's a hell of a story," she warned me, and then the whole tale came out. Tears sparkled in her eyes, and I could feel her pain as she told me about Mr. Templeton, and what had really happened, about Claire's mistakes, confounded by more mistakes, and I could tell that despite Claire's role in everything, Bria was still deeply saddened by the loss of her friend. She told me what my father had said to her, not to mention what she'd said to *him*, and I blinked in surprise, but let her finish uninterrupted.

When she trailed off, I just sat there, trying to take it all in, before leaning forward and brushing away the lone tear that had escaped her lashes. "I'm sorry I wasn't there for you last weekend," I said. "Or this week. You must have been so upset. I know there isn't anything I could have done to change it, but—"

"It was my own fault," she said, cutting me off. "I shouldn't have said that, anyway. You would have been a huge help." Her voice dropped to a whisper. "I missed you."

"I missed you too," I told her, then looked down at the table. "And I'm sorry I didn't call you back. I...realized I needed to work on myself before I would be able to work on us."

"Is there still an 'us' to work on?" she asked, and I looked back up, meeting her eyes.

"There is," I said firmly, then again, my voice soft. "There is. I'm so glad you came to find me."

She looked up, and then glanced around, as if reminded of where we were. "Now, will you please tell me what's going on? I've had enough surprises this week."

I chuckled softly, squeezing her hand in mine and tracing my thumb lightly over the lines of ink on the back of her hand.

"Well, I've always thought 'Sam's Books' was a pretty uninspired name for a store. So, I don't think 'Geoff's Bakery' is the way to go, but maybe you can help me come up with a good name."

Her uncomprehending stare morphed slowly into a look of astonishment, her eyebrows shooting up as she looked around again, taking in the empty store with new eyes.

Her voice was hesitant. "You...you're going to..."

I grinned at her. "I thought it was time to 'get my shit together' as Sam so lovingly put it. He knows the lady who owns this building, and she let me in to look around. I've got some money saved—you know, for law school," I winked. "—and I was thinking I might put in an offer."

Bria just stared at me.

"Catering..." I started, my grin fading. "I don't think it's for me." Bria opened her mouth, but I pressed on. "It's not just the mistake with the chocolate mousse, and it wasn't just serving my dad. I...I didn't like how it made me feel—the stress, drinking, snapping at you. That's not who I want to be."

I looked at her seriously. "I met with a therapist on Tuesday. We talked about my drinking, about my relationship with my dad…well, we talked about a lot of stuff. At the end, she mentioned that she would like to do a few sessions with both me and my dad. It took me most of yesterday to work up the courage to call him…but I did."

Bria sucked in a quick, indrawn breath.

"And he agreed. We're going together next week."

Her mouth parted in surprise, and I knew how she felt. I'd felt the same shock when he'd agreed to come to therapy with me. It was the last thing I could have predicted. I pushed on, eager to get everything out. "I wanted to thank you. I don't know what you said to him, and I think it'll take a lot of work to repair the damage between us, if that's even possible at all…but without you, I don't think he would have been willing to try. And I know *I* wouldn't have been."

Her eyes were wide in wonder.

"And this…" I turned to look around the shabby coffee shop, waving my arms vaguely to take it all in. "Well, this is practically what I do anyway. I'll just be able to bake in my own kitchen instead of a rented space, and I won't have to drive everything across town every morning. And I promised Sam I would still bring him pastries to sell, so…"

I trailed off. I was babbling, and she was still staring, and I felt a sudden twinge of uncertainty. Was it too late? Had I already ruined things between us?

"You, uh, you can feel free to say something any time now."

There was a long pause. Her expression turned serious, and I felt my nerves grow. Finally, she met my eyes and looked at me intently.

"You could call it, 'The Rolling Scones.'"

My jaw dropped open, and her serious expression wavered just a little.

"'Stop and Smell the Flour?'" she suggested, her eyes sparkling.

I started to laugh, relief rushing through me.

"'United Cakes of America?'"

"Oh my god," I gasped. "You named Sam's bookstore, didn't you? Those are terrible."

"Hey!" she said in mock offense. "Ooh, ooh, I've got it." She raised her arms in the air like she was framing a painting. "'The Bun Also Rises.'"

I grabbed one of her arms and yanked, pulling her up out of her seat and across the tabletop, where she fell, squirming with laughter, into my lap. I pinned her there with one arm, tickling her mercilessly with the other until she squealed, gasping for breath.

Then I kissed her.

She responded immediately, her soft lips moving against my own, and happiness expanded inside me like a balloon.

"Geoff, I'm so proud of you," she murmured, pulling back a little to look at me, and I felt my heart swell in my chest, a rush of emotion building inside me, growing and growing until I couldn't contain it. I knew we would need to talk more later, to make things right between us and figure out how to move forward together, but that could wait. For now, I leaned into her again, and poured out all my emotion into a searing kiss and she clung to me, matching my fervor with her own, leaving us both breathless.

"You can't name the bakery," I told her between kisses, and she smiled against my lips, sliding her hands over my shoulders and up my neck into my hair. I pulled her more tightly against me, all of her soft curves fitting perfectly as if they were made for me.

She pulled back slightly, gazing at me with dark, sparkling eyes. "Can I at least help to christen it?"

I groaned and pulled her mouth back to mine. "You should probably let me buy it first."

CHANGE MY MIND

CHAPTER 1

MARIAN

I have an addiction to crafts. No, seriously. Some people have hobbies; I have a problem. I was currently adding to that problem by way of a shopping cart piled high with yarn and needles. How had I made it this long without trying knitting?

True to form, I went all-in. I had straight needles in all sizes, circular needles, double pointed needles. I had row counters and stitch markers and swatch rulers. Point protectors and cable holders. And don't even get me started on the *yarn.* I had worsted wools and lace weight silks in every color of the rainbow. Variegated fingerling—I didn't even know what that meant, but it sounded vaguely dirty—and the softest baby alpaca. Super bulky blends with metallic threads woven into the fibers. I was *set.* All I needed to do was learn how to knit.

"Knitting this time, is it?" Sherry, manning the register at Fairfield Hobby and Craft, pushed an unruly lock of gray hair out of her eyes and peered into my cart with disbelief. "Have you really never tried knitting before?"

"I know," I said with a wide smile. Nothing—*nothing*—

made me happy the way buying craft supplies did. "I can't believe I've waited until now. Just making up for lost time."

"Well, pile it all up here," she told me, pushing her scanner out of the way to make room for my haul. "Let's get you checked out."

"How have you been?" I asked as I stacked yarn on the counter, bracing it with my hip so the skeins wouldn't fall off. "Have they scheduled your surgery yet?" I could see the slight tightening of her eyes as she shifted her weight, bending down to grab a stack of bags from under the counter. Sherry was in her early seventies, and had been working at FHC for as long as I'd been coming here—which was a long time. I knew she could have retired by now, but she insisted the discount she got on craft supplies was too good to give up. I didn't doubt it. The thought of taking up a second part-time job here had crossed my mind more than once.

"Oh, Marian, that's sweet of you to ask. Yes, it's going to be the end of May."

"Less than a month!" I exclaimed. "Oh, that's wonderful. You'll be able to move so much better with a new hip."

She nodded, starting to scan my towering mountain of knitting supplies and stuff them into bags. "I'm looking forward to being able to walk my dog again. She's going pretty stir crazy being cooped up. So am I, come to think of it," she added with a wistful smile. Then her eyes narrowed, and she looked me over. "What about you, honey? How are you doing? I won't see you while I'm out for recovery."

"Oh, I'm fine," I said. "I'm actually going up to full-time at the bookstore. Geoff left to open his own bakery, so I'm taking over his shift."

I looked studiously down into my cart, pulling out the last of the yarn, so I missed her narrowed eyes and searching look, but, regardless, I knew they were there. Sherry knew me too well.

"And how do you feel about that?"

I shrugged and laughed a little. "It'll be good, I think. Get me out of the house more." God knew I could use that. The craft store and work were pretty much the only two places I went. "Besides, I like my job."

I looked up at her, and her wrinkled face softened. "I know you do, honey. You'll have less time to learn how to knit, though," she teased, and I laughed.

"That's okay," I assured her. "I've got all the time in the world."

The store was largely empty this early on a Monday morning, so Sherry hobbled around the counter as I loaded my bags and gave me a hug. "Come see me before my surgery," she told me. "You don't have to buy anything, just come say hi." I laughed—we both knew I couldn't set foot in the store and leave empty handed—and returned her hug, promising I would stop by soon.

Then I loaded the bags onto my arms and made my way out into the bright spring sunlight.

My apartment was only a fifteen-minute walk from the craft store. That was good because I didn't own a car, but it also meant that I was forced to limit myself to buying only what I could carry. I was pushing it today, with bag handles wrapped up both forearms, but at least the bulk of it was yarn, which was pretty light. Rain or snow—probably even tornadoes—couldn't keep me away from the craft store, but today it was bright and sunny, the warmth of spring finally breaking through the chill Indiana air. I swung the bags on my arms as I walked, the sunshine bolstering my already good mood.

I'd made this trek a million times, but it was a little different each time, and I made finding the tiniest changes into a sort of game. The grass on the edge of the sidewalk was starting to turn green again after all the recent rain, and the bright yellow daffodils were pushing up around the sign in front of the Chinese restaurant. The gas station on the corner had changed their sign, and the motel next door was in the process of washing the winter grime off their windows.

Beyond that was the strip mall, and flowers were blooming there too, tulips in front of the nail salon and —oh no.

Next to the nail salon, the door to the martial arts gym was swinging open, disgorging a loud group of sweaty men in matching uniforms out into the parking lot. They called to each other, slapping backs and waving, and I deliberately slowed my steps, waiting to see if—yes, there he was.

My eye fixed on the man in the back, and my heart jumped into my throat. He wasn't tall, not compared to some of the other men spilling out of the doorway, though still taller than my diminutive five-foot-three-inch frame. But even without the height, his build was thick and muscular in a way that made everything about him seem menacing—big hands, broad shoulders, and a faint scar that traced over one cheek and down the side of his jaw.

Frantically, unreasonably, I looked for a place to hide. Not easy to do when I was right out on the sidewalk and loaded down by a pile of squeaky shopping bags. He hadn't noticed me yet, so I did the best I could, lunging for the thick trunk of a towering oak tree growing up through the sidewalk, its roots dislodging the heavy cement blocks and forcing them apart at the seams. I pulled the bags in around me as tight as I could and hugged myself close to the trunk, mentally becoming one with the shadows. Then I peeked around the trunk as far as I dared, and watched the group of men—and three women, I now noticed—begin to disperse.

Most of them made their way to cars in the small parking lot, donning sunglasses and throwing duffel bags in trunks. But the man in question—Levi—just nodded farewell to his friends and strolled out toward the sidewalk. He passed not ten feet from my hiding place, and I held my breath the whole time, but he didn't glance my way. I let my breath out in a thin trickle of air, not daring to make a sound, and watched his broad back move away from me down the sidewalk.

Though I knew the men practiced in bare feet, he had donned a pair of tennis shoes, and I could hear his footsteps on the pavement. Just as I'd noticed the tiny changes of spring on my walk home, I couldn't help but pick out the little changes in him.

His hair was messy, sweaty from practice and a little longer than the last time I'd seen him. I noted the way it curled around his ears. The uniform they practiced in was made of heavy canvas, and his was a faded blue, folded over itself in the front and held in place with a long brown belt that wrapped twice around his waist. Faded strips of cloth made stripes on the ends of the belt where it hung down in front, and a new stripe had appeared since I'd last seen him in the uniform, but I had no idea what it meant beyond marking his level.

I waited behind the tree, feeling foolish, until he was far enough ahead of me not to notice when I stepped back onto the sidewalk, continuing at a sedate pace so as not to catch up. It was not the first time I'd passed in front of his gym just as class was letting out, but it was the first time I'd hidden behind a tree to avoid detection. Because I sure as hell wouldn't make the mistake of talking to him again.

I'd done that just once, the day he'd moved in next door to me nearly two years ago. I'd first caught sight of him as he'd been lugging furniture across the parking lot, sandy hair falling in his eyes, sweat soaking through his t-shirt. I'd immediately been struck by the sheer power of a man who could move a loveseat across a parking lot on his own seemingly without effort. It had been impressive to watch. And the hard angle of his stubbled jaw and ropes of corded muscle in his forearms hadn't hurt either.

That evening I'd brought him a small potted geranium, planted in a little ceramic hedgehog I'd found at the grocery store, introduced myself, given him a friendly smile, tried to be neighborly. And he hadn't said a word, just took the plant, stared through me with those icy blue eyes the color of a frozen lake, then shut the door in my face. He hadn't even smiled.

I gave him a wide berth after that, and he was nothing if not consistent. He still never spoke to me, just looked at me with those cold eyes when we passed in the hall. Sometimes he nodded politely, but never a word or a smile.

For a long time, I still smiled at him; I could be friendly even if he couldn't. Even if those muscles were equal parts intimidating and attractive. Even if he was as scary as he was easy to look at. Then one day I passed him on the way to work, and discovered he was a police officer. That should have made me feel safer; at least he was using all those muscles for good. But I could only take so many icy blue stares and monosyllabic grunts before my own efforts to be friendly began to wane. Eventually I began to avoid him entirely.

I'd been so lost in my thoughts that I didn't realize I'd reached my apartment until I arrived at the front door, only to find the very man who had been occupying my thoughts holding the door for me.

Shit! I thought I'd given him plenty of space; I swear I'd started at least a full block behind him. But there he was, door braced open with a big hand as he gave me room to step through.

Oh well, too late now. I hoisted the bags higher on my arm and scuttled around him, keeping my eyes on the floor so I wouldn't have to see the unnerving, cold expression I was sure would be on his face.

And yet I couldn't bring myself to be rude. "Thank you," I squeaked as I passed, making a beeline for my apartment, keys already in hand.

I had no expectation of a reply, so when it came, I froze, my hand motionless on the key thrust into the lock.

"You're welcome," he said, and his voice, which I'd never actually heard before, was deep and smooth and would have made my spine tingle if it hadn't come from someone who unnerved me so completely.

He didn't speak again, didn't even glance my way, just crossed to his own apartment, unlocked his door, entered, and shut it smoothly behind him, leaving me gawking in the hallway.

CHAPTER 2

LEVI

I was pretty sure my strange neighbor was still standing motionless outside her door as mine clicked shut behind me. I headed straight for the bathroom, stripping off my gi, and I flipped on the shower and ducked under the spray before it had fully warmed. The cold water was a shock against my overheated skin, but my awareness of the icy spray was muted as my mind replayed the scene in the entryway just now.

From the look on her face and the way she'd hugged the wall as she'd moved through the door, keeping as much space between us as possible, you'd have thought I had some kind of highly contagious disease.

It had been two years now, and I still couldn't figure out what the hell was wrong with that woman.

To be fair, we hadn't exactly gotten off on the right foot. The day I moved in had already been a shitty one, spent hauling furniture all by myself after my brother had failed to show up to help, and I hadn't known whether to be more angry at him for standing me up or worried when he didn't answer the phone. By the time the rented moving truck was finally empty I'd been sore, exhausted, and somewhere between grouchy and murderous, and when my fifth call to my brother had gone to voicemail, I'd finally given in and called my mom.

My mother was a wonderful person, caring and sweet, but also high strung and anxious, and the last thing I wanted to do was worry her. But instead of concerning her over the disappearance of my normally hyper-responsible brother, I'd instead gotten the full story of exactly why he hadn't shown up to help me move. It was only seconds after I'd hung up from *that* conversation that there'd been a knock on my door, and I'd swung it open in a daze only to reveal a short, smiling redhead with eyes too big for her face, holding a plant stuck into some kind of ceramic rodent. I don't know what exactly happened. I don't know what she said, or what *I* said, if anything, but a minute later I was back in my new apartment, surrounded by boxes and mind still reeling from my phone call with my mother, holding this bushy plant in its weird ceramic pot, and the next time I saw the redhead she would barely meet my eyes.

The water had warmed by now, and I sighed as my stiff muscles, sore from the past hour of punishing exercise, finally began to relax.

It was true enough that I'd been the rude one that first night, and it had been no fault of hers that she'd picked such a bad time to introduce herself to a neighbor. But it hadn't taken too long for me to see that I'd likely dodged a bullet. Because the girl was *strange.* Honestly, what kind of a person hid behind a tree, shopping bags crinkling and plainly visible to anyone with eyes. Had she really thought I wouldn't see her there? And even if I had, what the hell did she think I was going to do?

I shook my head, flinging water droplets around the tiny cubicle, and made quick work of rinsing the soap off my body before shutting off the spray and stepping out of the shower.

Whatever.

I toweled off quickly and made my way into my bedroom, carefully ignoring the overgrown geranium on my windowsill—the only plant in my apartment—as I pulled on my uniform. I didn't need to waste more time on some crazy person's motivation. I needed to get to work.

* * *

"Oh, good, you're here."

I'd barely made it halfway through the door before the chief pulled me into his office.

"There's been another robbery, at Royal's Dry Cleaners," my boss informed me, glancing up over the top of his computer monitor with only half his attention. His bushy grey eyebrows were pulled down over deep-set hazel eyes, and with his thick greying beard, he looked like nothing more than a harried, overworked Santa Claus. "We just got the call. I know you just walked in, but Murphy's doing a presentation down at the middle school and Brady and Jansen are out on another call. Can you take it?"

"Of course, sir," I said, shrugging my arm back into the coat I'd just started taking off. One of the downsides of working in a department this small—it was either dead quiet, or we didn't have enough people. There was never any middle ground.

He filled me in on the little he knew, but I was halfway back to my car before I realized where I was headed. Royal's Dry Cleaners was three doors down from my jiu-jitsu gym, where I'd been not an hour earlier, and only a few blocks from my apartment. Had I been at the gym when the robbery was taking place?

I broke into a jog, ducking into my car and backing out of the parking lot. This was the second robbery in as many weeks. The first place that was hit had been the bank on the corner, just a few blocks away from where I was headed now. I hadn't been the one who responded to the alarm, but I remembered what I'd read in the file—the crime had occurred in the early morning just after the bank had opened, when only the bank manager and one teller had been there. The perpetrator had been wearing grey sweats and a mask, and despite two eye-witness accounts and a bunch of surveillance footage, we hadn't even been able to determine if the robber had been a man or a woman. I wondered idly if the same person was at fault for this new break-in as well.

The door to the dry cleaners flew open before I'd even crossed the sidewalk and I was ushered inside by a frantic looking older woman of indeterminate Eastern European heritage with a long white braid framing a lined face. She closed and locked the door behind me and led me around the counter to a small office where a girl in her late teens was huddled in a plastic chair, wiping tears from her face.

"Sit," the woman ordered me, then followed up her command with a hand on my shoulder, pushing me down into the second matching plastic chair. I managed not to raise an eyebrow and let her push me down, then retrieved the small notepad I kept in my pocket and flipped it open.

"Okay, I'm Officer Mathes, and I—"

"Ana, tell him what happened," the older woman cut me off, turning her stern expression on the young woman across from me, then barreled on before the girl had a chance to open her mouth.

"Lots of people drop off clothes around noon, when they are on their lunch break, but it was only about ten-thirty, and we had no customers. Andras—that's my son, the girl's uncle—had told me there was a delivery coming today, and I…"

I listened to the increasingly convoluted story, taking notes and trying to sort out names and details, and it was probably more than five minutes into the old woman's rant before I realized—

"Ma'am, were you *here* when the robbery took place?"

She paused mid-sentence and stared at me in confusion. "No, I—"

"Was…" I consulted my notepad, "Andras here?"

She glared. "No, but—"

I reigned in my irritation at the flustered and increasingly belligerent woman. "Who *was* here at ten-thirty this morning when the robbery took place?"

"Well…if you—"

Finally, the young woman across from me spoke up, her voice soft and scratchy. "I was."

I shot the older woman my best quelling look and turned my attention to the girl. "Ana, right? Why don't you tell me what happened?"

Once Ana got her turn to speak, the story came out quickly and with an unfortunate lack of detail. She'd been alone in the store when one person had come in, wearing dark clothes and a face mask that covered his—her?—face. No, the person hadn't spoken, just handed a note across the counter, which had instructed her to hand over any cash she had in the register, and threatened that the robber would use a gun if she didn't comply. No, she couldn't provide the note, as the criminal had snatched it back after she read it. No, she hadn't actually seen a weapon. Yes, she had handed over the money from the register, which had amounted to two-hundred and forty-seven dollars.

I couldn't get anything else useful out of either of them, despite the old woman's attempt to chime in with everything from the history of the store to the family's genealogy to whether rain was expected that afternoon and how that might affect me should I need to chase down any potential criminals on foot. I left the pair with a case number and a promise to follow up as soon as I knew anything.

The rest of the day was spent running in circles without more than a minute to sit and catch my breath. I responded to a fender bender out in front of the high school and dealt with a child custody dispute, followed up on a complaint from a lady whose neighbor's dog kept digging under her fence, and then ended my day with a noise complaint from the neighbors of a family whose teenaged son had started a band in his garage. In such a small department as ours, everyone specialized in everything, and calls generally got assigned to whomever was free. And while I always preferred busy days to those spent sitting around with nothing to do— I'd never dealt well with being idle—by the time I arrived home that evening I was tired and hungry and more than ready to be away from other people, especially after a day when it seemed like all anyone was capable of was yelling at each other.

When I stepped through the front door of my apartment building and heard voices, my first reaction was to cringe. The last thing I needed was more people on the way to the solitude I desperately wanted. My apartment was down at the end of the hallway, with the strange plant woman Marian next door. On her other side was a young couple, and directly across the hall from me was an elderly lady who didn't seem to be home very often. A vacant apartment next to her rounded out our floor.

The elderly lady—Mrs. Linsey, I believed—was home now though, her door propped open, and Marian leaned against the frame, the two of them laughing together. A glance their way revealed the woman had a hand pressed against her mouth, and Marian was practically doubled over, tears streaming down her face.

A wave of vague irritation passed through me at the sight, and the knowledge that the noise of their laughter would be clearly audible through my door, cutting into my much-desired silence. Hopefully they wouldn't be long; one of the things I appreciated most about this building was how it was relatively peaceful for an apartment complex—no children, no loud pets.

As I drew closer to the pair, the sound of Marian's laughter filled my ears. Her laugh was low and husky, as if it came from deep inside her and bubbled up uncontrollably. It was an infectious sound, the sort that made you want to smile along, and seemed out of place coming from such a slight figure. The form of my irritation abruptly changed shape.

I couldn't help but notice how friendly she was with the neighbors. I often found her leaving small gifts—homemade cookies, small crafts, who knew what else—for the young couple down the hall, and checking in on Mrs. Linsey when she was home. And not just the neighbors—everyone. I'd see her in the grocery store chatting up the cashiers, or stopping people walking by on the sidewalk to exclaim over their pets. A smile and a friendly word for everyone she passed.

Everyone, that was, except me.

As I passed the women their laughter faded, and they both straightened.

"Evening, officer," said Mrs. Linsey, casting a friendly smile my way, but my eyes were on Marian. There was no smile there, no greeting, just wide eyes watching me out of a face flushed with recent laughter but turned suddenly serious.

I grunted in response and gave a short nod, then let

myself into my apartment and firmly shut the door behind me.

The laughter didn't resume; only silence followed me through the door. And yet it wasn't relief that I felt. My longing for solitude had seemingly evaporated, leaving behind only irritation and resentment, maybe something a little like envy, and perhaps some other feelings I didn't care to identify.

CHAPTER 3

MARIAN

$\mathcal{I}$ waited until Mrs. Linsey's door was firmly closed before I let myself back into my own apartment. The action wasn't even intentional, just an ingrained habit after years of keeping my space completely private. Even the landlord had never set foot in my apartment since I'd moved in. I did all my own repairs and he knew and respected that my space was off-limits. I assume he chalked it up to one of my quirks. God knew I had enough of them.

This wasn't exactly a quirk, though, I thought to myself as I picked my way across the living room floor. The path was narrow, piles of junk towering high on both sides, hiding the furniture that lurked somewhere beneath the clutter. It was a mess of shopping bags, cardboard boxes, plastic containers and tote bags, loose supplies, papers and…anything. *Everything.* I wasn't even sure what all was lost in there anymore. Bags full of stained glass supplies, I knew, from a shopping trip two years ago, hidden dangerously somewhere under the window I thought. The remains of craft projects both large and small, half-finished and barely started and never out of their bags. Unopened junk mail and magazines. Books and fabric.

It had started out so small, so manageable—a row of plastic totes next to the couch and a tall cabinet in the corner, bought to contain the collection of scrapbooking supplies I'd bought when I'd finally escaped my aunt's house and moved into my own place for the first time. Had that really only been five years ago? It seemed a lifetime.

My mother had been big into scrapbooking, with a row of albums on the shelf documenting my childhood and teenage years. I still had those books, lined up in the back of my closet, well away from the mess of my living room, but untouched going on nine years now. Mom had made all her own greeting cards too—beautiful, colorful things with buttons and ribbons attached, that she sent out for every birthday, anniversary, or pretty much any other life event of anyone she'd ever known.

We hadn't had a lot of money growing up—my clothes had all come from thrift stores and our apartment had always been tiny and cramped, though clean. Birthdays and vacations had never been extravagant, and bills were always paid, if sometimes after a couple of threatening reminders, but one thing my mother never skimped on was scrapbooking supplies. She'd had a tall cabinet in the corner of the dining room, and I remembered standing in front of the open doors as a child, marveling over the beautiful array of colored cardstock and patterned papers, the multitude of carefully organized stamps and scissors and pens and markers.

So when I'd turned eighteen and my aunt had informed me—to my utter shock—that my mother, who, contrary to anything I'd ever known growing up, had actually left me a sizable sum of money, the first thing I did was move into my own place, and the second was to buy Fairfield Hobby and Craft out of most of their scrapbooking supplies.

Two days later, I'd remembered the time my mom had tried to teach me origami. I'd been probably no more than six or seven, and driven to tears when I couldn't fold the lines as cleanly as she could, and my paper elephant came out looking like it had been trampled. The next morning, I went out and stocked up on origami supplies—whisper-thin paper in colorful patterns, and delicate folding tools made out of bone and bamboo.

Calligraphy had come next, then weaving, then beading, and by that point I was running out of space, so I piled it all on the couch, determined to find a way to organize it all later. Later had never come.

It had taken about a year for the disaster to spread into my dining room. Then it consumed my spare bedroom, and then spilled down the hall, everything stacked precariously to one side so I could still navigate the narrow space.

My kitchen was still decently presentable though, and down at the end of the hall, a person in my bedroom or bathroom might never know the state of the rest of my apartment. In my bedroom, I could almost pretend I was a normal person. Not that anyone had ever been in there besides me.

Navigating the mess, I made my way into the bedroom and stripped out of my clothes, throwing them into the hamper before pulling on a tank top. I was tired, and it didn't take long to brush my teeth, flip off the lights, and slide under the covers. But when I closed my eyes, a frowning face with messy sandy hair filled my vision.

Levi.

I blinked my eyes open, but in the darkness of the room, the memory didn't fade. Why did he hate me so much? What had I ever done to him?

The memory sneered at me, grunted in the barest

acknowledgment, just as the man in the hallway had done, not just now, but every time I'd crossed his path in the past two years. But above the frown, and beneath the creased brow, his eyes glittered with an expression I couldn't quite interpret, and when I finally fell asleep, those glittering eyes followed me into my dreams.

* * *

Regardless of the mess that was my personal life, working at Sam's Books was a dream job. It was part-time, which gave me plenty of time to myself every day, though that was about to change. I didn't need the money, so it didn't matter that the pay was low. And the people there were wonderful.

Sam, the owner, was a big teddy bear of a man, easygoing and a great boss. His girlfriend, Ellen, was sweet and friendly, and despite having her own apartment nearby, seemed to spend more time than not at Sam's place right above the store. Rachel, the other part-time cashier, was a college student with sparkling eyes and a wicked sense of humor, and we got along well. And Geoff, who manned the cafe, was a culinary wizard. He was in the process of opening his own bakery just down the road, and while I was sure I would still see plenty of him—not to mention the fact that he would still be supplying pastries for our cafe—I was sad to see him go. Sam had offered me the chance to go up to full-time, rather than just hiring a new replacement for Geoff, and I had tentatively agreed. The change made me nervous though. It wasn't that I had anything better to do with my time, and I did love the job, but...it would be different. All change made me nervous.

I was still part-time through the end of the week though, so when I showed up for my shift, it was shortly after noon and the store was quiet. Just regulars at this time of day, and I smiled as I hung up my jacket in Sam's office and went out to shelve a cart full of new inventory.

"Hi Marian!" The greeting came from Mrs. Semmler, a pretty woman in her mid-thirties with her two young girls. They came in at least once a week, and were currently looking at chapter books in the children's section. I smiled warmly before bending down.

"And how are you two today?" I greeted the girls, then paused and dug through the box of books I was currently shelving. It took a minute, but I found what I was looking for and handed the book over. The older girl's face lit at the bright red cover.

"Book four. It just came in. I haven't even put them out on the shelf yet." It was the latest in a series of children's fantasy stories I knew the girl had been waiting for, and she hugged it to her chest before turning to show the book to her mother.

After a few more pleasantries I left them there, moving across with my cart to the mysteries section, where two men were browsing the shelves. One was a man I didn't know, and I gave him a warm smile and instructed him to let me know if he needed any help. He nodded and I moved around him, filling the shelves and straightening the spines until I reached the other man, who was balancing four books precariously in one hand as he attempted to flip through the pages of a fifth with the other.

"Need some help, Gary?" I asked with a smile. Gary was another regular, in his mid-fifties at a guess, with thinning hair and a somewhat hooked nose over a slight frame. He looked up in surprise at my voice, as if he hadn't noticed I was there, but when he saw me, his eyes creased and he waved the book he was thumbing through in consternation.

"Well now, Marian, I can't remember if I've read this one before or not."

I laughed. "I don't think there are many in this section that you *haven't* read. But if you want to come over to the computer, I can at least see if you've bought it before."

He gave me a sheepish look and followed me up to the computer at the register. A few keystrokes later, and I had to laugh.

"Not only did you buy that same book about three months ago, but you already have two of those as well," I said, gesturing toward the stack he held in his other hand.

He looked in surprise down at his books, then gave a rueful chuckle and handed the stack over. "I guess I'll take the other two then. What would I do without you, Marian?"

I smiled and rolled my eyes, then scanned his books and sent him on his way. Gary would be back in a couple of days. I wasn't sure if he worked, or was married, or anything else about the man, but he would be in here buying mysteries twice a week like clockwork.

I passed the cafe on my way back to my abandoned cart, where Geoff was stocking the pastry display. He gave me a friendly wave, and since he had no customers, I wandered over.

"How's the bakery coming?" I asked, leaning against the counter. He gave me a pointed frown and reached for his dish towel. I suppressed a smirk and moved out of his way as he cleaned the fingerprints from the spot where I'd leaned. Geoff was a bit of a neat freak, especially where his food was concerned.

"It's ninety-percent done, I think," he told me. "I'm waiting on the new dishwasher to get installed later this week, and then I'm out of here."

"Are you excited?" I asked, even though the answer was plain.

"Excited, yes. Also terrified," he confirmed with a grimace. "It'll be fine though, I know. I just can't believe it's actually happening." He looked at me and his eyes narrowed. "What about you? Are you ready to take over the cafe?"

I'd been helping in the cafe since I started working for Sam, so my actual duties would barely change. But I knew what he meant. Was I ready for the change to my daily routine, the added pressure? It was ridiculous, honestly, that I was worried about it at all.

But Geoff had known me for a long time, and he correctly interpreted my hesitation. "It'll be fine, you know. You already know what to do. Hell, you pretty much know everything about everyone who walks in the door."

I smiled at him, but it felt a bit forced. "You're right, but it's not that. I know it's stupid, it's just…"

His face softened. His shrewd eyes saw more than I wanted. "*I'll* be fine," he told me gently. "The bakery will be a success. And if it's not, I'll just come back and knock you back down to part-time, right?"

I huffed out a laugh. Part of me was embarrassed that he could so easily see my fears, see how much I worried about the people around me, and how much I feared things I couldn't control, but the greater part of me was grateful for his reassurance.

"I know. It'll all be fine. I'll just miss you." I tried to say it lightly, but Geoff could always see more than I wanted to give away. He leaned across the counter and gave me a quick, tight hug, and it worked. I went back to my work feeling a little bit calmer and more optimistic.

His bakery would be a success, and he would be happy there. Sam would do just fine, even down an employee. And I wouldn't have to worry about either of them.

* * *

My good mood lasted through the rest of my shift, and when I left to make the twenty-minute walk home, the sun was still bright over the horizon. The spring air was warm and thick, the ground only barely damp from recent rain, and I hummed to myself as I noted the little changes around me as I made my way toward home. Bright tufts of green grass poking up through the cracks in the sidewalk. The sounds of songbirds chirping in the trees. A cluster of Canada geese staking claim to the small pond behind the strip mall.

Reluctant to leave the balmy spring evening behind, I opened the windows in my apartment as I made dinner, and enjoyed the gentle breeze as I ate at the kitchen table. I cleaned up immediately afterward, washing my dishes and putting them away before stepping over the pile that threatened to spill through the doorway into the kitchen. See, I'm not disgusting, I told myself. I can't be a hoarder if I wash my dishes.

I debated what to do with my evening. It had been a few days since I'd checked in on Donna and Jake, my neighbors down the hall, but I remembered they were on vacation for the week. Instead, I dug through the bags clustered in the hallway until I found my haul from the craft store the previous day, and took the bags into my bedroom, where I spread the contents out on my bed, booted up my laptop, and lost myself in knitting tutorials and tangles of yarn and the feeling of closeness to my mother that only came from learning new crafts.

Only when it was full dark, and I couldn't suppress my yawns any longer, did I shove everything back into the bag before changing and falling into bed.

I fell asleep with a cool breeze on my skin and a smile on my lips.

* * *

I wasn't sure what awoke me, a sound or a feeling or a glimpse of shifting movement, but I came awake hard and fast. It was pitch black inside my bedroom and I had no idea what time it was, and only through the faintest hint of moonlight shining through the window did I see the outline of the figure that stood at the foot of my bed.

My heart slammed into my throat. Silhouetted in the dark, I didn't realize he was facing away until he turned at my sharp intake of breath, then like a creature from a nightmare, reached an arm out toward me.

The lungful of air I'd drawn in exploded out of me in a scream, and the figure lunged.

CHAPTER 4

LEVI

I wasn't a deep sleeper. It was probably a relic from my childhood, deeply ingrained and hard to break, from years and years of keeping an ear open for my father sneaking in late at night, trying not to wake the rest of us. The later it was, the more money he'd likely lost, and the harder my mother would cry in the morning. He'd been gone since I was a teenager, leaving his messes behind for the rest of us to clean up, but it still took only the slightest sound to pull me from sleep.

So, when a piercing shriek split the night, I was on my feet before my brain had even fully registered the sound.

Mom?

My dad hadn't by nature been a violent man, but if it was late enough and he was drunk enough—and the more money he lost, the more he drank—well, let's just say it wasn't the first time I'd been awoken by a scream.

But no—I wasn't at home in my tiny bedroom, crouching by the door to protect my brother. I wasn't a kid. Had I imagined the sound? Maybe leftover from a nightmare that had dissipated upon waking?

Then the scream came again, followed by a crash so loud it rattled the wall of my apartment, and I realized where it had come from.

Marian.

I sprinted for the door.

Once I'd flung open the door to my apartment and barreled into the hallway, I pulled up short. The door to Marian's apartment was locked—of course it was. I spent a handful of seconds pounding on the door and calling her name before I heard another crash from inside, then turned my attention to the lock. If she had the deadbolt set and I tried to kick it down, I would probably just end up hurting myself, and besides, my feet were bare. Did I have a crowbar? Unlikely. But maybe I could find something I could use to pry the lock off.

I dashed back into my own apartment, just as another scream split the air. *Damn it.* I was a police officer, and if there was one thing I could do, it was keep a level head under pressure, but I also knew time was of the essence. What the hell was happening in there?

I cast my gaze around the entryway of my apartment, and my eyes fell on the screwdriver I'd been using days earlier to change a broken electrical faceplate. Worth a try. I grabbed it, sprinted back down the hall, then wedged the tip of the flat screwdriver into the door jamb and slammed my fist down on it. The lock buckled under the pressure, and I immediately saw the deadbolt hadn't been set after all.

Damn it, Marian.

Another crash sounded from inside, and I lifted my foot and aimed a kick at the door by the lock. It only took two kicks to break through—what the hell kind of shitty materials was this place made of?

I shoved through the splintered door, the light from the hallway spilling in to faintly illuminate my way, aimed for the hallway that had to lead to her bedroom—and promptly tripped over an enormous pile of...something...and went sprawling.

What the hell is all this crap?

Pushing myself back up, I dodged around a staggering pile of junk and navigated the narrow hallway to the bedroom, where I paused in the doorway. It took barely a second for my brain to process the scene in front of me.

A figure in dark clothes stood by the edge of the bed, leaning forward in a menacing posture, though one hand was clamped tight over the other arm as if protecting an injury. Broken glass littered the floor in the corner where a lamp had clearly been knocked off the nightstand, and the drywall was cracked where a body seemed to have been thrown against it. Marian? Or the intruder? I fought down a growl, deep in my throat.

The window was open, curtains fluttering in the soft breeze—well, that explained how the intruder got in—and as my eyes completed their scan of the room they landed on Marian, who was up on her knees on the bed, arms raised defensively. In one hand she clutched—were those *knitting needles?*

In the second I'd spared to take in the scene with one well-trained glance, the intruder turned, sensing my presence in the doorway, and leapt at me. *Good. Away from her.*

I didn't have my uniform—hell, I barely had on any *clothes* —but that also meant I didn't have my gun, or my handcuffs. I hadn't seen any weapons in the hands of the intruder either though, so instead I settled my weight evenly on my bare feet, let the man approach, watched as he raised his arms to shove me back, then at the last second turned, my hands coming up lightning quick between his. I grasped one of his arms with both of mine, pulling him close while I twisted my body, using his own momentum to swing him over and drive him to the floor.

He went down with an "Oof," and I could smell the alcohol on his breath. Ah, well, that was familiar enough. When he landed on his back, I followed him down, pushing in close before he had time to react, driving my knee into his belly. When his arms lifted again to fend me off, I grabbed the one closest to me and quickly snaked my other arm around his neck, grabbing his wrist and pulling his arm tight across the front of his own throat, rolling him to his side as I did.

The intruder strained, bucking—this wasn't a choke hold and he'd stay conscious—but I leaned my weight into his shoulder and the discomfort made him grunt and fall still. I turned my attention to the woman on the bed, my eyes scanning her in a rush, checking for injuries. I didn't see any blood or bruising in the dim light, but what I did see was a thin tank top, the shape of her nipples clearly visible through the flimsy fabric. Beyond that she wore only underwear, skimpy white cotton, and her legs were long expanses of creamy skin that practically glowed in the moonlight. My pulse leaped.

Damn it, Levi, focus.

I forced my attention back up to her face, where her eyes were wide, pupils dilated and breath coming fast, but her gaze where it fell on the man I held pinned to the floor was clear, not panicked. Good.

"Marian, listen to me." I waited until her eyes lifted to meet mine. "First, I need you to call the police. Tell them what happened, tell them Officer Mathes is on the scene and has it under control, but they need to send backup." She nodded wordlessly. "Next, I need you to go into my apartment and bring my handcuffs. They're with my uniform, in the bedroom closet. Can you do that?"

Her eyes were like two moons, eclipsing her face, but she nodded, then wordlessly rose and left the room.

When she was gone, I turned my attention to the man pinned beneath me. It was still dark in the room; I'd have to tell Marian to turn on the lights when she returned, but I could see he had a slim frame and dark, short-cropped hair. He was no teenage delinquent, but he still seemed young—mid-twenties, maybe? He was lying still now, not struggling against me, and with the smell of alcohol practically seeping from his pores I wondered if he was even still conscious. Part of me wished he would struggle, give me an excuse to pull his arm tighter, maybe punch him in his exposed face. A greater part of me was glad he didn't—as much as I *hated* the kind of scum that took advantage of helpless people, I wouldn't let him force me to do anything I'd regret.

Marian must have had trouble finding my handcuffs, because she returned only shortly before the police did, handing the cuffs to me before wordlessly climbing up to sit perched on her bed, squashed into the corner as far as she could get from me and the—I was pretty sure now—unconscious intruder. I didn't have a chance to say anything to her again before the police arrived.

It was Officer Jansen, his eyebrows climbing nearly into his hairline as he took in the scene with me wearing nothing but pajama pants pinning a body to the floor.

"I live next door," I explained tersely.

Jansen flipped on the lightswitch in the bedroom but nothing happened, and I glanced toward the broken lamp on the floor. He backtracked and turned on the hallway light instead, as I gave him a brief synopsis of the night's events. Or what I knew of them, at least. Marian could fill in the gaps in the morning.

Things progressed quickly from there—he asked a few questions, heaving up the unconscious and now faintly-snoring intruder, who appeared to be bleeding, though not badly, from a wound in his arm. Jansen confiscated Marian's knitting needles as evidence, and I assured him she would be fine, and I'd bring her to the station in the morning to file a report.

Throughout this exchange, Marian remained huddled in the corner of her bed, back pressed firmly to the wall, sheet pulled up in front of her body, eyes vacant. I wondered darkly what had happened in the minutes before I'd arrived. She nodded when Jansen asked if she was okay, shook her head when he asked if she was hurt, and he shrugged when I shot him an *"I'll take care of it"* look. Then he hauled off the intruder, who had awoken but looked bleary and confused and went along in a willing stupor. In the light, he looked even younger than I'd guessed. Maybe late teens after all, I thought.

I shot him a death glare, an *"I'll deal with you later"* glare, but my ire was wasted on his retreating back as Jansen shoved the kid ahead of him through the splintered remains of the front door, his voice filtering back down the hallway as he informed the kid of his rights.

Which left me alone with Marian. I took in her tiny form, huddled in the corner, unseeing eyes trained on the floor, and a pang shot through me. I crossed the room and carefully eased down on the side of the bed. I kept my voice soft, trying not to startle her.

"Marian."

At the sound of my voice, her head shot up, eyes focusing on my face before shooting away. I watched as her eyes darted around the room, taking in my shirtless form, the broken glass that littered the floor, the overturned bag by the bathroom, yarn spilling out, and finally the towering mess in the hallway, bags and boxes and junk piled so high it barely left a path wide enough for a person to pass through. Her eyes grew wider and wider as they made the circuit, her breathing speeding and growing ragged, and I began to grow alarmed.

"Marian, you need to—" Her eyes darted back to land on my face, and she erupted in a shriek so loud I barely stopped myself from raising my hands to cover my ears.

"Get out!"

"What?"

"*Out!*"

I stared at her in consternation. "Your door is broken, and there's glass everywhere. You need to—"

"Out! Outoutout *get out!*" She scrambled back away from me, even though there was nowhere for her to go, kicking the bedclothes away in her frantic scramble. "Get out!"

I did the only thing I could. I rose, stepping back out of her space. "I'll be back in the morning. Come get me if you need me," I said quietly. Then I left.

CHAPTER 5

MARIAN

*T*he first thing I did once I'd calmed down was shut the windows and lock them. Which I knew was silly, since the intruder was now in police custody, but I only needed to learn that lesson once. Then I crawled back into bed, pulled the covers up over my head, and replayed the last hour, over and over in my mind.

I relived waking up in the darkness to a shadowy figure standing over my bed. I'd screamed, and he'd jumped, maybe almost as surprised to see me as I was to see him, but then he'd lunged for me and locked his hand around my arm. I'd flailed against his grip, knocking over the lamp, and tumbled us both into the wall. Somehow, I'd wrenched my arm away, stumbling across the floor to where I'd left my knitting and grabbing the bag. There'd been a scuffle then—I could barely remember—and he'd grabbed my leg, knocking me down, and I'd turned, frantically lashing out.

I would never forget the sensation of that knitting needle driving into his arm.

I shuddered helplessly as the vision played out. He'd drawn back with a choked sound and clapped a hand over his wounded arm, and I'd launched myself back up onto my bed, cowering back, screaming again—and then there'd been an awful thump and the sound of splintering wood, and the next thing I'd known Levi was there in the doorway, hair sleep-mussed and shirtless, eyes wild but laser-focused. And then he'd just...dealt with it. Brought the intruder to the floor and pinned him there with the efficiency of a man demonstrating a training move to a class, no wasted movements, barely any effort at all.

Then he'd calmly, rationally told me what to do next, and I hadn't had the wherewithal to do anything more than follow his instructions and wait while the police came and took the intruder away.

But then he'd had to go and ruin everything by coming close, sitting on my bed and speaking to me in that soft, gentle voice like one might use on a wounded animal, breaking me out of my trance, and it had all suddenly hit me like a punch to the face.

He was *here*, inside my apartment. He'd seen it all—my shame, the secret I'd kept for nearly five years, my disgusting apartment—as clear as a flashing neon sign—*"This girl is bat-shit crazy. Look at how she lives. She's clearly mentally unstable."* He'd seen it all. Not to mention me in my *underwear*. The shame and humiliation had crested like a wave, joining with the feelings of fear and violation brought on by the break-in, forming into a toxic mix of panic, and I hadn't been able to do anything but shriek at him to leave.

Smooth, Marian, that'll convince him you're not crazy.

I pulled the covers tighter over my head, trying to block it all out, but the blankets did nothing to stop the images that replayed on the backs of my closed eyelids.

Suddenly I remembered the words Levi had said as I chased him out of my apartment. The door. He'd broken down my door. Which meant I was just as vulnerable now as

I had been with my window open, maybe more. I shouldn't have forced him to leave. But I couldn't go after him now; he was probably back in his apartment, sound asleep.

So, I cowered tighter into a ball, pulling the blanket taut around me in a futile effort to stop my trembling, and let the images cycle through my head until the harsh light of dawn began to filter through my cocoon.

* * *

I wasn't actually sure if I'd fallen back to sleep in the intervening hours or just lay huddled in my blankets, but I rose with the dawn and stumbled into the shower, where I set the water near to scalding and let it wash the feel of remembered fingerprints on my skin down the drain, along with the shame of the police—Levi—*anyone*—seeing the state of my apartment.

Dried and dressed and feeling marginally more human, I went to assess the damage to my front door. It was extensive. A screwdriver lay forgotten on the floor, where it had been discarded after being obviously wedged into the frame by the lock. Splintered wood surrounded the broken lock where I guessed Levi had kicked the door open. There was no salvaging it. The picture it made was almost more terrifying if you didn't consider it had been broken down by Levi rather than the intruder. I shuddered at the thought.

But when I stepped around the wreckage into the hallway to see the damage from the outside, my breath caught in my throat.

A man sat propped against the wall just to the left of the door, his tousled head propped on his knees which were pulled up against his chest. He wore no shirt or shoes, just a pair of navy-blue sweatpants, and the bare skin of his shoulder glowed golden in the early morning light.

Levi hadn't left. He'd stayed, as close as I'd allowed, guarding my broken door. Embarrassment pulsed through me, and not, this time, for the state of my apartment, but instead for the way I'd treated him.

This man had potentially saved my life, and I'd thanked him by screeching at him and throwing him out, and *still* he'd stayed. Maybe he didn't hate me after all. Of course, he *was* a police officer; he might just think it's his job to protect me regardless of whether or not he hates me.

Well. Either way, I owed him.

A soft snore came from the hunched figure, and the corner of my mouth twisted up softly. I ducked silently back through the door into my apartment and went to the kitchen, setting the coffee pot on to boil. I didn't know how he took his coffee, so I brewed it strong and poured it into a huge mug. I made up a tray with a small ceramic pitcher of milk and a bowl of sugar. I added a spoon and then, feeling a little silly, added a couple of Geoff's jam-filled shortbread cookies I'd filched from the bookstore a couple of days before. Then I tiptoed back out through my broken door and left the tray—the peace offering, I hoped—next to the still-sleeping figure propped against the wall. His sandy hair glinted in the early morning light filtering in through the windows at either end of the hallway, and a couple of red strands were visible against the shades of light brown. It looked soft, and I ducked back through the door before I let myself touch it.

Then, with nothing else to do and the need for some sense of normalcy rising within me, I grabbed my purse and set off for the craft store.

* * *

Sherry was there at the register, and while I stopped to say hi and give her a quick hug, I couldn't bring myself to tell her about the events of the night before. Instead, I wandered the aisles of the store, looking for something I could make for Levi as a thank-you-for-rescuing-me-slash-sorry-for-freaking-out gift. I could just make him a card, I thought. God knew I had enough card-making supplies at home, and they might be some of the only supplies I could actually locate, but I hadn't opened that cabinet since I'd bought it, and I couldn't bring myself to go there just yet. Besides, this called for something more than a card.

The idea hit me in the paper aisle. I knew I already had origami paper at home too, but that was buried somewhere in the living room, so I chose a variety of bright, colorful pages in different sizes. Two aisles over I found thin lengths of cloth-wrapped floral wire. I was on my way across the store to look for a vase when I saw a familiar face.

"Gary!"

He looked up in surprise, and his lined face crinkled into a smile. "Well, Marian, good morning!"

I smiled back. "You know they don't sell mystery novels here, right?"

He chuckled, holding up a small package of silver buttons. "That's true, but I lost a button off my jacket, and I don't think they sell those at the bookstore."

We exchanged a few more pleasantries, then I bid him farewell. After a little more searching, I found a copper vase with stamped geometric accents around the base and rim that seemed at least a *little* manly, and I headed back out into the May sunshine, swinging the bags on my arms as I went.

CHAPTER 6

LEVI

*W*hen I awoke, stiff and sore and with an awful crick in my neck, there was a tray sitting next to me on the floor of the hallway. The coffee was still hot, and I gulped it down gratefully. I didn't add any milk from the—was that a ceramic *chicken?* I rolled my eyes—just let the bitter caffeine do its job. I scarfed down the cookies as well— they were great—then knocked on the wall by the broken door. When there was no answer, I peered in, but Marian was clearly out. I wondered if she had gone to work, and how she was doing. I hoped she wasn't too shaken up after the events of the previous night.

I would have to find her later and get her statement, but for now I had things I needed to do. I set the tray just inside the door to her apartment, then headed down the hall to my own place to shower and get dressed. I called the landlord to report the incident, and assured him that I'd take care of the door since I had caused the damage. Then I made some more calls, and finally found a place that was able to come immediately to replace the broken door. Two hours later I was on my way to the station.

The door I'd replaced her flimsy one with might have been overkill, I thought to myself in retrospect. I'd ended up with thick 18-gauge steel over a hollow core of thermal bio-foam to reduce the weight. It even included rows of engineered wood at the top and bottom that the installer assured me made it kick-proof. I added a heavy-duty deadbolt and a chain link, and with a little extra persuasion and lots of confused looks, I was able to get the door painted an ugly, dirty beige color to fit seamlessly with the shoddily constructed doors in the rest of the building so the landlord couldn't complain.

I tried not to think too hard about why I'd gone so far overboard. It wasn't for any specific sense of responsibility. I was a police officer; it was my job to protect *everyone.* Hell, I'd have done the same thing for my mom if someone had broken into her place. *But that's your mom. You wouldn't have done that for just anyone,* my subconscious pointed out.

"Sure I would have," I informed it. Out loud, to make it true. It certainly wasn't because I had any kind of interest in the crazy woman next door. Because honestly, she *was* crazy. I'd seen her apartment. If nothing else, she had severe issues to work through, and those weren't anything I needed to be part of.

Although, she *had* freaked out and kicked me out of her apartment pretty quickly, clearly embarrassed that I'd seen the state of her place. Suggesting that at least she *knew* she had problems, which was more than could be said for a lot of people. But I'd grown up with a father who struggled with addiction, and the last thing I needed was to deal with anyone else's addiction problems. Because hoarding was just as much an addiction for Marian as gambling had ever been for my father.

No. I didn't need to help her with her problems. I only needed to keep her safe. And I'd done that, so all I needed to do now was get her statement and have her file a report, and my job was done.

* * *

When I arrived at the station, I found that the intruder had already been released. Jansen had already ended his shift and headed home, but I found the chief in his office and got caught up with what I'd missed since the night before.

"He sobered up and made bail, so we cut him loose," the chief said, forestalling the angry rant I had ready. "Jansen ran his info—name's Danny Thieman, and his record was clean. No reason to hold him."

"Did he say what he was after?" I demanded. "Was it just a robbery? Was he after the girl?"

The chief actually had the gall to chuckle. "No, we got the story out of him when he sobered up. Get this. He thought it was *his* apartment."

"What?" I sank down into one of the chairs by the desk. Why did I have the feeling this was going to take a while?

"Yeah. Kid went out drinking with his buddies. Stumbled home in the middle of the night. Apparently, he lives over on the other side of your apartment complex, the side that faces West Street? Jansen checked it out on his way home; it looks identical to your side. Anyway, kid gets to what he thinks is his apartment, but the door is locked. Goes outside, finds the window open, lets himself in. Then imagine his surprise when there's someone sleeping in his bed!" The chief threw his head back and laughed, his eyes crinkling under bushy eyebrows.

"I fail to see the humor," I muttered. Which wasn't exactly true, it would have been amusing under different circumstances. But the chief sobered regardless.

"Sorry, Mathes, of course," the chief said. "That woman

was lucky you were next door. Jansen said you had him neatly pinned when he showed up. No one got hurt?"

I shook my head, my anger draining away into tiredness. "No, I don't think so. I haven't seen Marian again since last night, but I'll check in with her when I get home, make sure she's okay and see if she wants to press charges. We can go from there."

The chief nodded.

"Was the kid okay?" I belatedly thought to ask. "He was bleeding when Jansen hauled him out."

"Oh, yeah," the chief chuckled again. "Just a hole in his arm. We got him bandaged up. Nothing too serious, but I'll bet it hurt. Stabbed him with a knitting needle, huh? Haven't seen that one before."

I suppressed a smile. Marian had some fire in her, at least I'd give her that.

"So, you believe his story?" I asked.

The chief nodded, looking thoughtful. "Yeah, I think so. Kid was pretty young—only twenty-one. Once he came around, I think he was pretty horrified at what he'd done."

I scowled. It was no excuse. Marian could have gotten really hurt from that idiot's dumb mistake, and I hoped he wouldn't get off too easy. But I let it go for now.

I thanked the chief and left his office to head to my own desk, where I typed up my report of the night before. I had other paperwork to deal with too, but I must have looked as tired as I felt, because after a couple of hours, he sent me home. I nodded my gratitude and left in a hurry.

Not because I wanted to check on Marian. Not because I needed to be sure she was okay, and certainly not because I was worried that her traumatic experience might negatively affect the cheery friendliness she displayed with everyone she seemed to meet—well, other than me. But because I really did need to get some sleep. A handful of hours propped against a wall in a hallway wasn't really cutting it.

But I would check up on her first, sure. Because it was my job.

* * *

There was something strange sitting outside my door. It caught my attention the second I stepped into the hallway, and I slowed my step suspiciously, glancing around. But the hallway was empty, and when I arrived in front of my door, I found a bizarre flower arrangement awaiting me. Marian's new door was firmly shut, so I hefted the strange gift and made my way inside.

I deposited the arrangement on the dining room table and peered at it. The flowers were all made out of colored paper, folded into intricate patterns. No two of the flowers were alike, and each was attached to a stem of green wire, set into a patterned copper vase.

The gift clearly took some skill—I wasn't even sure how someone could make paper look like that—and a chunk of time as well, and I rolled my eyes in a mixture of exasperation and grudging appreciation. She didn't have to do anything so crazy. She could have just said thank you, or left a card—or better yet—done nothing at all, because I'd just been doing my job. I would have responded to any scream in the night exactly the same way.

And yet, from what I'd seen, this was typical Marian. I'd seen her leave gifts outside of Donna and Jake's apartment down the hall as well, and I knew she brought cookies over to Mrs. Linsey when she was home. I'd just never been the target of her over-the-top focus and appreciation, and I wasn't sure how I felt about that. Flattered? Uncomfortable?

I should just throw the flowers away. I didn't need them,

they didn't go with anything in my apartment, and it seemed excessive. But I couldn't let that much hard work go to waste. I sighed, lifting the vase, and I carried it into my bedroom, sitting it on the windowsill next to the ridiculous hedgehog planter I'd received from the same ridiculous person. I'd figure out what to do with it later.

For now, I needed to check on her, but when I went down the hall and knocked on her door, there was no answer. I waited, knocking again, but she wasn't home. I sighed and left. I would try to catch her in the morning.

* * *

It took me forever to fall asleep. Every time I started to drift off, I would jerk awake, my body tensed as if I'd heard a noise and was ready to leap out of bed. I tossed and turned in irritation, rolling to face the window, trying to find a more comfortable position. The moonlight shone in through the open blinds, casting a long shadow from the paper flowers across the wall, and I grunted, rolling to the other side, twisting the sheets as I went.

What the hell was wrong with me? She was *fine* and I needed sleep. Nothing was coming through that door.

I forced myself to close my eyes and relax, emptying my mind and trying to think of nothing rather than listening for sounds of attack that weren't going to come.

It almost worked, and when the sounds actually did come, I almost missed them. They weren't sounds of attack though, no screams or breaking glass like the night before, only the quiet sounds of crying. I opened my eyes, not even completely sure at first what I was hearing. But as I mentally mapped out the apartment next door, I realized that our bedrooms shared a wall, and by the time the sniffle and low sob came again, I was on my feet once more, moving toward the hallway.

I wasn't sure she'd answer the door. It was nearly one in the morning, and I felt like an idiot, standing on her doorstep in my night pants and bare feet once again—at least this time I'd had the foresight to grab a t-shirt. She didn't answer my first knock, and for a second, I wondered if I'd imagined the crying, if my mind was playing tricks on me and she was just sleeping inside. Maybe knocking on her door in the middle of the night was just going to wake her and scare her all over again.

But just as I turned to go, mentally berating myself for being so foolish, I heard the faint sound of the latch—not the deadbolt, goddamnit—and the door swung open.

She opened it only enough to slide through, then pulled it shut again behind her, preventing me from seeing into the apartment. Even though we both knew I'd seen everything last night.

She stood in front of me, wearing a pale yellow tank top and pants patterned with tiny cacti, and one glance at her face showed me I'd been right. Her dark eyes were red-rimmed, though she'd scrubbed any trace of tears from her cheeks, and suddenly I was glad I'd come over after all.

"Did you need something?" she said.

"What?" I responded automatically, only belatedly realizing I'd been staring and looking away. "I heard you," I hastened to explain. "Crying. Through the wall."

Her face flushed scarlet. "I'm sorry, I didn't mean to wake you."

"What? No." What the hell was wrong with me? "I just wanted to make sure you were okay. You went through some traumatic stuff, and I...well, I wanted to see if you needed someone to talk to."

Her expression softened. "That's...that's really nice of you."

I scowled. "You don't have to sound so surprised."

The edges of her mouth pulled up, just a little. "Sorry. I don't want to keep you up though. You probably have to work early, and I'll be alright."

The hallway was dim, a window at the far end and a lone yellow bulb casting faint illumination down the shadowed length, and I took in her swollen eyes and tousled hair. She'd piled it loosely on top of her head, but strands were escaping down around her face, as if she'd been tossing and turning as much as I had been.

I sighed and put my back against the wall, sliding down until I was sitting on the carpeted floor, the same posture I'd spent the previous night in. I looked up at her and patted the floor next to me. "I'm already up," I told her.

She just looked at me for a long moment, and I almost thought she was going to leave me there and go back inside, but then finally she turned and slid down to sit next to me.

CHAPTER 7

MARIAN

We sat in silence for a moment, the hard surface of the wall cold against my back, and I wondered what we were doing, sitting in the hallway at one in the morning.

Levi just stared at the floor, seemingly unsure of what to say, so I spoke first, my voice soft in the still air. "Thanks for fixing my door."

He glanced sideways at me, his eyebrows pulling together. "I heard you open it just now; you didn't have the locks set. You have a deadbolt now *and* a chain. You should use them."

Aside from the previous night, it was more words than he'd ever spoken to me. "You realize the intruder came in through my window, not the door," I pointed out, raising my eyebrows. "*You're* the one that broke down my door."

His voice was gruff. "Yeah, and if I could, someone else could. Lock your door. And it goes without saying that you shouldn't leave your window open in a first-floor apartment."

I eyed him. "I guess it doesn't go without saying."

He gave a faint huff of amusement. "I guess not. I can

replace the lock on your window, too."

"You don't need to. The lock works fine when I use it."

We lapsed into silence for another short stretch, and I couldn't help but sneak a glance over at him. He was wearing a thin gray t-shirt, and it pulled tight across his biceps where he had them propped over his knees. His hair was sleep-tousled, and I was reminded again of my first view of him, moving in two years ago, and how attractive I'd found him. It was really too bad his personality didn't match his looks. I wondered again why he was here, sitting with me in the dim hallway. Had he really just heard me crying and wanted to make sure I was okay? It seemed so out of character based on the way he'd treated me for years now.

As if he could read my thoughts, he finally spoke up again. "Are you okay? I can recommend a therapist, or—"

"No, no." I tilted my head back to lean against the wall, my hands twisting together in my lap. "I'll be okay. I just…" I squeezed my eyes shut. "I can't stop thinking about what would have happened if you hadn't been there." I heard my voice catch and struggled to keep it smooth. "What…what he was after. What he might have done." I'd been fine all day, crafting and work a welcome distraction from any negative thoughts or worries. But alone in my bed, the darkness pressing in all around and every sound magnified to my over-sensitive ears…well, it had been harder to keep myself together.

Levi glanced up at my words, his eyes focusing on me like he'd just remembered something.

"He wasn't after you," he told me quickly. "I haven't had a chance to tell you. And it wasn't a robbery." My head came up off the wall and I looked over at him. Of course, he'd been in to work while I'd been out today, he would surely know more about what happened.

"Is he…is he still locked up?" I asked.

He hesitated for a split second before shaking his head, and I felt myself tense up. "No, he was released on bail. But the guy wasn't trying to hurt you, at least not intentionally. He thought it was his apartment."

Levi explained what the chief had told him, and what Officer Jansen had found out after the intruder had sobered up. My mouth dropped open as I listened.

"He...thought it was *his* apartment?" I repeated in disbelief. I blew out a breath. "How dumb do you have to be..."

"I think it's more how drunk do you have to be," he said with the barest hint of a smile, more of a smile than I'd ever seen on his face before, and I felt the corners of my own mouth pulling up in response, the tense lines of my face beginning to relax.

His ice blue eyes were intense on mine, that same intensity he seemed to carry with him always, the gruff seriousness he wore around himself like a cloak, and I suddenly felt self-conscious. Why was he being nice to me? He didn't like me, he'd made that clear enough in the past, and if he was just doing his job, he would have waited until I came to the station to file a report. He wouldn't have replaced my door with whatever ridiculous steel contraption was on there now. He wouldn't have knocked on the door in the middle of the night just because he heard me crying. He wouldn't be sitting here with me in the hallway, so close I could feel his warmth all along my side, asking if I was okay. Especially after he'd been in my apartment last night, and seen...well, seen what a mess I really was.

I stiffened again, the embarrassment returning, and lifted my arms to wrap them around my torso. I felt more than saw him stiffen next to me as well, and I glanced over, but his gaze was fixed on my arm rather than on my face.

"What's that?"

His voice came out in a growl, and I looked down in

surprise. "What? Oh...that." I lifted my other hand to wrap around my arm and cover the marks, but his hand was already there, gently lifting my arm so he could see more clearly.

The rough, warm feeling of the pads of his fingers on my skin was a jarring contrast to the murderous look on his face.

"I thought you said he didn't hurt you."

I cleared my throat. "They're only bruises." Five of them, dark purple against my fair skin, where the intruder's fingers had grasped me in a vise-like grip. I gently freed my arm. "It's not like I need a hospital for some bruises. I'm fine."

"Yes, but—"

"Besides, I think I got him better than he got me," I said with a sideways glance, and like I'd hoped, he relented, his murderous expression lightening as he suppressed a snort.

"That you did. Knitting needles, seriously?"

After another pause, he added, "Thanks for the...flowers. Or whatever they were. You didn't need to do that."

"Oh," I said in faint surprise. "You're welcome. Thank you for saving my life. Hardly seems like a fair trade."

He just grunted, a more familiar response, but I chose to interpret it as a 'you're welcome' as well. "Just doing my j—"

"They were origami." I cut him off, suddenly desperate that he not finish his sentence, that he not say he was just doing his job. It was likely true, he would have reacted the same to any screaming neighbor in the middle of the night, but I didn't want him to put words to it, to erase whatever progress we'd made here, in turning him from my scary, grumpy neighbor who hated me into a maybe-almost-sort-of friend.

"What?" He looked confused.

"The flowers. They were origami. Folded paper. I used to make them with my mom." I was so shocked that the words had come out of my mouth I didn't even know how to react, and I stuttered to a stop. I never mentioned my mom. And I certainly never talked about her hobbies or us crafting together. But Levi didn't seem to notice the mini-breakdown happening next to him.

"Oh yeah?" he said. "My mom used to be into crafts as well."

I went still. "Used to?" I asked, keeping my voice neutral, though it took some effort. Did we have something in common after all? God, I hoped not. Not that, anyway.

"Yeah." He tipped his head back against the wall and looked up at the ceiling, seemingly unaware of my held breath. "She used to make these mosaic coasters and picture frames, stuff like that. She quit when my dad left and she needed the money for me and my brother. I got a job as soon as I was old enough, so things weren't so tight, but she never got back into it."

I let my held breath flow out in a trickle of relief. So, his mom was okay. His statement just made me more curious though. Why had his dad left? He had a brother? What was his family like? I bit my tongue though, keeping the questions inside, and we lapsed into silence again. It wasn't uncomfortable or strained though, and slowly, in his company, my stress began to ease.

I rested my head back against the wall again, and tipped it to the side so I could see the window at the far end of the hallway. Outside the window the branches of a tree swayed in a gentle breeze, its leaves sending dappled shadows across the floor. I stared, mesmerized, my eyes tracing the moving shadows as I relaxed into the feeling of Levi's solid warmth only inches away from my side. His solid weight was more reassuring than I would have guessed, like some immovable object standing between me and the rest of the world, protecting me, even if it was only because he was paid to do so.

"Marian?" His voice was low, and I hadn't even realized my heavy eyes had started to drift shut. I slowly rolled my head in his direction.

"I'm awake."

He chuckled softly, but still didn't break a smile. I wondered vaguely if he *ever* smiled. I'd always assumed he just never smiled at *me*, but now I wondered if he was even capable of the expression.

"No, you're not. Come on, let's get you back to bed. I think you can sleep now." His warm hand came under my elbow, helping me rise to my feet, and when I'd regained my balance I didn't pull away, letting him steer me drowsily toward my door. But it was only when he opened the door and made to step inside that I realized he intended to walk me in, and I came fully awake in an instant.

"No! I mean, um, thank you." I pulled my elbow out of his grip and pushed ahead of him, sliding through the narrow opening, leaving no room for him to follow. I quickly turned back, feeling slightly panicky. His face was expressionless as I forced a smile. "Thank you," I said again. "I'll see you in the… well…I'll see you."

I ducked back and swiftly pulled the door shut, my heart pounding. Logically, I knew he'd been inside before, but still…I just couldn't. Remembering his words, I set the deadbolt, then paused, unlocked it again, and cracked the door open. He still stood there in the hallway, staring at the door I'd slammed in his face.

"I, uh, I set the deadbolt," I informed him.

His mouth twisted into an expression I couldn't quite identify. Pity? Disgust? It seemed I'd undone any progress we'd made. But all he said was, "Set the chain, too."

I closed the door again, and did as he instructed.

* * *

To my intense relief, I didn't have any trouble falling asleep after that, and though I was still a little short on sleep, I awoke the next morning feeling cautiously optimistic. I really wanted to be able to put the break-in behind me and move on. It had only lasted mere minutes, I hadn't been hurt, and it didn't seem fair that something so short and quickly resolved should have a lasting effect on my mental well-being. Though I knew from firsthand experience that it only takes a second for something to utterly disrupt your life for years to come.

But I didn't dwell on that this morning, focusing instead on the bright sunshine outside the window and the good mood I'd unexpectedly found myself in. One step at a time.

I knew I still needed to file a police report, so I did that first.

On any other day I would have avoided the police station like the plague, terrified I might run into Levi and be subjected to one of his frowning glares. But today I found myself more nervous than afraid, both hoping I might run into him and that I wouldn't. If I did, would he frown and grunt a monosyllabic greeting, or even worse, ignore me altogether? Or was there a chance he might look at me now like I was something more than a bug he'd accidentally squashed underfoot and had to scrape off his good shoes? A human, perhaps? Maybe almost a friend? Someone worth speaking to in words, possibly complete sentences?

I didn't get a chance to find out, because to both my relief and disappointment, he wasn't there. Officer Jansen was though, and he took my statement and helped me file a report. Reliving the experience wasn't enjoyable, but at least he made it as quick and painless as possible.

After my visit to the police station I had to work, one of my last few half-day shifts, and so it was the following morning before I got a chance to go to the craft store.

The sky was dark when I awoke, after a somewhat more fitful night of rest than the one before—with no midnight-hallway conversation to ease me into sleep—and a steady drizzle was falling when I made my way outside. Not the best day to be walking back and forth from the craft store with bags on my arm, but I couldn't help it. I'd been thinking about what Levi had said about his mom, and her mosaic coasters and picture frames. I'd never tried mosaics before, but a quick online search and some time spent watching tutorial videos convinced me it couldn't be that hard.

I was sure I'd get an earful from Sherry coming back so soon after my last visit—usually I tried not to go more than once or twice in a week, and it had only been two days—but when I ducked under the awning in front of the store, shaking my umbrella as I pulled on the handle, the door wouldn't budge. Surprised, I looked up, and the yellow sign on the door immediately caught my eye.

Closed.

What? It was—I checked my phone—just after nine-thirty in the morning. They should have been open for about half an hour now. And the lights were on. What was going on?

I hunched and peered through the glass, and caught sight of Sherry, her back to me as she spoke with another employee who was gesticulating with her hands as she talked. I stood up straight, thinking I should just leave and come back later, maybe the next day, when Sherry turned and caught sight of me through the window.

Gesturing to the other employee, she came and unlocked the front door, stepping out to join me under the awning.

"Hey, honey, I'm sorry, I can't let you in right now," she said, her lined face apologetic.

"Sherry, what's going on? Is everything okay?"

She glanced back toward the store, then lowered her voice. "We were robbed."

CHAPTER 8

LEVI

I was halfway to the station when I got diverted. Another break-in, and once again, only blocks away from where I lived. It wasn't the most comforting feeling. I swung the car around in the opposite direction though, and put on my lights, if not the sirens.

Only minutes later I pulled up in front of Fairfield Hobby and Craft. It took me longer than it should have to recognize the small figure with auburn hair who was standing outside, her arm wrapped around a slightly stooped older woman with short, curly gray hair. They were huddled together under the awning, and I ducked under as well, shaking the rain off my shoulders.

"Marian?"

She spun at my voice, and I looked between the two women. Marian clutched a brightly-colored umbrella in her free hand, but her hair was still slightly damp, water droplets glinting on the strands as she turned. Her eyes were wide, and she seemed surprised to see me as well. The older lady cleared her throat, and I swung my attention to her. She wore an employee nametag pinned to a blue vest, so I addressed my question to her.

"Everything okay here? I got a call about a break-in."

The older woman nodded. "I'm Sherry," she introduced herself. "It must have happened overnight. There's an alarm system, but it looks like it wasn't set, because the back door was open when I got here."

"Alright. Let's go in and you can show me." I glanced back to Marian, who shifted her weight before turning back to Sherry and reaching up to give the older woman a quick hug.

"You take care, okay?" she said. "I'll come visit you in the hospital."

Sherry squeezed her back before opening the door and ushering me through. I caught a quick flash of color as Marian opened her umbrella before scampering off into the rain. I wondered briefly about the relationship between the two women. Were they relatives? Or just friends? It seemed a bit of an odd friendship—Marian had to be decades younger than the craft store employee. But then again, Marian seemed to be friends with absolutely everyone. Except me, that was. I thought back to our strange night in the hallway, and wondered if that was changing. Likely not. She'd been just as eager to keep me out of her apartment that night as the one before. And for an understandable reason, I reminded myself.

I turned my attention to Sherry again as she led me through the store.

"Hospital?" I inquired politely. "Is everything alright? Were you here when it happened?"

She shook her head and flashed me a smile. "Just surgery. I get a new hip next week. This one's about done putting up with me."

"Ah." Now that she'd called attention to it, I noticed she

walked with a limp, favoring her left side. "Best of luck with that."

"Thank you. This is Jenny," she said, as another woman appeared by the door at the back of the store marked "Employees Only." The new woman looked to be in her mid-forties, and was tall with dark hair and thick glasses.

"Officer Mathes," I introduced myself, and the women nodded in greeting.

"We both start our shifts at nine when the store opens," Sherry explained, leading us through the storeroom, "but I arrived first and found this door open." We'd arrived at the back entryway, where a heavy metal door led out to an alley.

"Is this where you came in?" I asked, checking the door. The lock was intact, with no marks or scrapes around the latch.

"No, I came in the front," Sherry said.

"No one ever comes in the back," Jenny put in. "I don't think anyone ever uses this door."

"How did you know it was open, then? You said the alarm didn't go off?"

Sherry nodded. "I'll show you." She turned and started limping back toward the front of the store. I followed, with Jenny bringing up the rear, and Sherry explained on the way. "Someone had clearly been in the store, and gotten into the register. And since the front door was still locked, I checked the back, and found it open."

"Does the door not shut on its own?" I asked.

"No, you have to pull it shut. That's one of the reasons we never use it," Jenny said. "If the door doesn't shut, the alarm won't activate. It might have been open all night for all we know."

That seemed like negligence more than foul play to me. I wondered who was going to get in trouble for not checking the back door before they left.

Sherry showed me the register—an older model—that had clearly been forcibly opened. According to Jenny, who it seemed had been the last one in the night before, only four hundred dollars had been inside, and after a walk-through of the store, we determined that nothing else had been stolen.

I sat down with the two women and got as much additional info as I could—which wasn't much. Apparently, the store was owned by a widower named John McNeill who owned three other similar craft stores around Indiana. Jenny, who had called the police, had called him as well, but he was currently visiting family in Colorado and would not return until late the following week. She had apparently also notified the manager, a woman named Carla, who was on her way in. I decided to wait and talk to her as well, just in case she had any other useful information for me.

Eventually, Jenny left us to reopen the store, and I was left alone with Sherry in the small break room. She had answered all the questions I could think of and I was just finishing up my notes when she turned a nonchalant eye on me and said, "So, how do you know Marian?"

I glanced up in surprise at the abrupt change of subject. "She's my neighbor."

"Ahh, I wondered if that might be the case. Your first name must be Levi, then, Officer Mathes." Her mouth quirked slightly, as if she was suppressing a smile.

I raised an eyebrow, unsure how to respond. Marian had mentioned *me* to this woman? Marian, who was friends with everyone in the world, *except* me, had mentioned me to her friend? I cringed, wondering what horrible things she would have said when describing me.

But before I could think of what to say in response, Sherry rose from the table and headed toward the door. "Carla should be here by now; I'll send her back to talk to you, shall I?"

* * *

Back at the station, I typed up my notes, sifting through the information in my head.

It was similar to the two previous break-ins, I thought, insofar as only cash was taken, and not a lot of it at that. No real property damage—minus the register—and nothing else missing. It seemed like a whole lot of risk for not a lot of reward.

The robberies at the bank and the dry cleaners had both taken place during the day, with employees present, albeit only one each time, and despite this I still didn't even know the gender of the perpetrator. But the craft store break-in had taken place at night. Did that mean it was a different criminal? Or maybe just the same person getting more savvy? I had a hunch it was the latter. All three stores were within walking distance, only blocks away from each other. And besides, Fairfield wasn't big enough for multiple crime sprees to be going on at the same time, and this hadn't been widely publicized enough yet for a copy-cat.

I leaned back in my chair, balancing on the back legs. What about Marian's break-in though? Was that related, or a one-off? I know the chief and Jansen had the story from the kid that he had been drunk and thought it was his own apartment, and while I knew the drunk part was true enough, I wondered about the other. I hadn't gotten a chance to talk to the kid, after all. Even if his story was true, it didn't preclude him breaking into other places.

I sighed, letting my chair fall forward to the ground. I knew it likely wasn't related—the two situations were too different—but I resolved to look into it further anyway, just in case. By the time I shut down my computer and headed home, my mind was still churning with questions.

I went to bed early that night, determined to make up the

sleep that I'd been missing over the past few days. But when an hour had passed and I was still lying there, eyes wide open as I glared at the ceiling, I knew I wasn't going to be catching up on sleep tonight.

I watched the clock on my bedside table click over to eleven. I wondered if Marian was asleep on the other side of the wall. I wondered what she'd been doing at the craft store. Shopping? Visiting her friend? I wondered how she was doing after finding out the store had been robbed, and how she was recovering from her own scare.

Then I berated myself for wondering. I pulled my pillow over my head, which successfully blocked out the light, but unfortunately didn't do anything to stop my thoughts.

Why was I so aware of her? Why did I notice stupid things like the patterning on her umbrella, or the water droplets in her hair? I resented the fact that I was aware of her at all. I'd spent the majority of my childhood and most of my adult life dealing with other people's problems, cleaning up after their messes. The last thing I needed was another broken person in my life.

Every time I visited my mother, she asked me if there was a girl in my life, and every time I brushed her off like it was the last thing on my mind. My job was too demanding. I was too busy. But in reality, this town was just too small. I already knew everyone worth knowing, and as a police officer, I already knew way more than I needed to about most of them. How could I find a "nice girl," as my mom put it, if everyone in town was such a mess?

Not that I didn't have my own share of issues—I certainly wasn't blind to my own faults. But I didn't know where my mother thought I was going to find this "nice girl" who didn't have a drinking problem, or three kids from different guys, or an arrest record, or a history of flings with married men. That perfect woman didn't exist. Not in Fairfield, anyway.

And to make things worse—when I closed my eyes and tried to picture this impossible woman, all I could see was dark red hair and oversized brown eyes.

Damn it.

The clock ticked over to midnight and I threw off the sheets and sat up, grabbing a t-shirt and pulling it on over my head. This was ridiculous. I wasn't getting any sleep anyway, I might as well just get up and be useful.

Useful, it seemed, took the form of cleaning my already clean apartment. It ticked all the boxes, I figured. It was boring as hell, and physically demanding, so it would wear me out. And keep my mind occupied, hopefully.

I tried to be quiet, remembering how sound carried through the walls, and had just stepped down off the ladder after changing the burnt out lightbulb in the kitchen when I heard the slightest shuffling sound outside in the hallway. I froze in the act of folding the small ladder and listened hard. Was there someone out there?

It was a long moment before the sound came again, muffled through the door, and I leaned the ladder against the wall and moved to peer through the peephole in my front door.

My vision filled with a distorted fish-eye view of Marian, standing just outside the door. Her hand was raised and poised to knock, but she didn't move, just stood there frozen like a statue as indecision flashed across her face.

I sighed, realizing I was losing this battle. Even if I worked hard to block her from my thoughts, she just showed up in person. And yet I couldn't explain the warm feeling in my chest at the sight of her, and the tightening somewhere deep inside as I took in her sleep-rumpled form and messy hair.

Taking a deep breath, I stepped back and pulled the door open.

CHAPTER 9

MARIAN

I wasn't sure how long I'd been standing in the hallway, waffling between whether to knock or go back to bed, when the door swung open.

Levi's broad form filled the space, and he looked huge and menacing with the light spilling out from the room behind him, illuminating his silhouette and casting his face in shadow. And yet the relief I felt at his presence alarmed me more than his intimidating shape.

"I hope I didn't wake you up," he said. "I was trying to be quiet."

"What?" I wrinkled my brow in confusion. "I didn't actually knock, did I? I don't think I did."

He huffed out what could have been a laugh. "No, you didn't. I was up anyway, and I heard you outside the door."

"Oh." I chewed on my lower lip. "You were already up?"

"Yeah. I was cleaning." He gestured me back a step and I moved out of the doorway, giving him space to join me in the hallway. He didn't invite me in, and I didn't ask him to, but he pulled the door shut behind him and leaned against the wall next to me.

"Couldn't sleep?" I asked, eyeing him sideways.

He sighed. "Nope. What about you?"

He turned to face me fully, and his narrowed eyes took me in from the top of my messy head to the bottoms of my bare feet, leaving behind a warm tingling awareness everywhere his gaze touched. "You look like you've been asleep."

Flustered by the intensity of his eyes, I leaned against the wall and slid down to sit, pulling my legs in tight, and he joined me on the floor, each of us taking up a position that seemed almost familiar.

"I was for a little while," I admitted. "Had a bad dream and couldn't get back to sleep after that."

Neither of us commented on the fact that my first reaction was to seek him out.

When he spoke again, his voice was low. "You wanna tell me about it? Your bad dream?"

I didn't, not really, so I hesitated, shaking my head, then did the next best thing, giving quiet voice to my fears.

"I don't usually watch the news," I began haltingly, "or keep up on local events, but Sam had the news on in his office at the bookstore this afternoon. I saw...I saw there had been a break-in a few days ago too, at the dry cleaners. The one next to your gym?"

There was a pause, then Levi slid a glance my way. "There was one before that too, actually. About three days earlier."

"Where?" I gasped. The lady on the news hadn't mentioned that. Or at least, not while I'd been standing there. I hadn't lingered long.

"Fairfield Financial." He watched my face as he said it, as if gauging my reaction.

I tried to control my shudder, but wasn't sure I was entirely successful. Someone had robbed the *bank*? "Did anyone get hurt? Do they think it was the same person? At both places? And the craft store too?"

He shook his head. "No, no one got hurt. Though the first two didn't happen at night. But it's likely it was all the same person. We don't know a lot yet. It's still being investigated."

I let my voice drop low, almost afraid to speak my thoughts aloud, lest they become real. "Do you...do you think it could be related to my break-in?"

He paused, just a hair too long, and I ducked my head, burying it in my hands. He'd said that guy was out on bail, just out there somewhere. And not just *somewhere*, I realized —he lived on the other side of our apartment complex. What if he was behind the store robberies as well? What if he started hurting people? What if he *came back*?

I felt the warm circle of Levi's fingers around my wrist, and let him pull my hands away from my face. His face was close to mine, his eyes serious, and when he responded it was as if he could hear my thoughts.

"We don't know anything for sure, but it's really unlikely that it was the same person. There's no reason to think that guy's story wasn't true." He pulled my arm down between us but, after a moment of hesitation, didn't let go of my hand, instead threading his fingers through my own. My shock at his action pulsed through me, his hand warm and calloused on mine as he continued. "And regardless, he's not coming back here. Not with that new unbreakable door. Not with *me* here."

The last words twisted his face almost into a snarl, and I thought about the difference just a few days could make. I'd seen that snarl before, more than once, and it had always scared me. The intensity of his expressions, his thick, muscular form, the silvery scar on his jaw—he'd never been anything to me but intimidating. But knowing that ferocity was focused on my behalf, rather than *at* me...it changed everything.

It made me wonder if I'd always misread him. Had he

really always hated me, as I'd assumed? Or was he this serious and surly with everyone? And had he always been that way, or had something happened to make him like this? Because as we sat together in the hallway, his hand strong and reassuring on mine, I realized I'd *still* never seen the man smile.

* * *

Levi was the first to fall asleep in the hallway this time, his breaths evening out into a slow, heavy rhythm as his head lolled back against the wall. I watched as the frown lines between his brows relaxed, the creases smoothing away, and I realized I'd never seen him look peaceful before. I didn't even notice how much tension he carried with him until it was gone, and I suddenly felt loathe to wake him up and steal away the ease he never seemed to find while awake. My hand was starting to go numb though, trapped under the unconscious weight of his, and I couldn't just leave him in the hallway overnight again.

Besides, I needed to get back to bed. Tomorrow would be my first full-time shift at the bookstore, and while the stress of that had likely contributed to my bad dream, I didn't want to oversleep and show up late on my first full day, either.

Carefully, I detangled my fingers from his and slid my hand out of his grasp. The glide of his warm dry skin on mine was more romantic contact than I'd had in years, and the thought made my throat feel tight. Not that I thought whatever was going on between us was romantic. For all I knew he was still just comforting a scared neighbor. I had no idea what was happening between us, at least on his end. I had a vague suspicion I knew what was happening on *my* end, but I wasn't sure I wanted to examine it too closely, lest it slip through my fingers.

Leaning over, I shook his shoulder, and watched as his eyes came open, the furrow between his brows creasing back into its familiar position. His face was only inches from mine, and from up close I could see that his serious blue eyes had dark flecks in them.

"Time to go in, I guess," I said softly, and he nodded but didn't move, his eyes shifting between mine.

His hair was mussed, his eyes cloudy with sleep, and my gaze dropped, tracing over his features to his mouth. His lips were parted slightly, and they looked soft and full, and suddenly I was gripped with an overwhelming desire to lean forward and bridge the gap between us.

Did I dare? Could I—

"Marian," he said, and though his voice was low and soft and filled with gravel, it jerked me back to awareness. What was I *doing?* Blood suffused my features as I hastily moved back and levered myself to my feet. There was nothing I wanted less than to hear the rest of that sentence.

"Marian, what are you doing?"

"Marian, don't take this the wrong way, but..."

I didn't meet his eyes as I offered him a stilted good-night, and fled back into the safety of my apartment.

With the door safely closed between us, I leaned back against the wall and took a deep breath.

It had taken me years to settle my life into the safe, boring routine that it was, and suddenly everything was changing, flying out of my control. An intruder in my apartment. Robberies in stores all up and down my block. Sherry, dealing with a break-in at work on top of an impending surgery. Sam, losing an employee and having to rely on me to pick up the slack. Geoff, taking a huge step into the unknown. And Levi, going out of his way to take care of his crazy neighbor.

It bothered me to think that one of the things that was

changing the fastest—my relationship with Levi—was also the one that was offering me the most comfort, and to think I'd almost just ruined it.

Between my tangled mess of nerves, worry, and anticipation, there was no sleep to be had after that. I spent an hour tangled in yarn as I continued on my journey to learn how to knit, then spent another hour after that sifting unsuccessfully through the mess in my spare bedroom looking for a bag full of needlepoint supplies I remembered buying at one point before my poor over-stimulated brain finally calmed down. It wasn't yet dawn, thank god, so I set every alarm I had as a precaution and finally fell into bed and into a deep, blissfully dream-free sleep.

* * *

When I woke, rather than feeling exhausted from my missed hours of sleep, or nervous about the impending day, I felt surprisingly refreshed, as if my body had rallied all of its resources. I was determined to do my best today, to show Sam he wasn't making a mistake in letting me take over Geoff's shift and all the extra duties.

As I rushed through my shower, I kept reminding myself that I'd been working at the bookstore for quite a while now, and this wasn't anything new, but in the back of my mind I knew the extra responsibility was real, and I resolved not to let Sam down. I'd be in charge of opening the store, of taking the morning deliveries as they came in, of running the cafe through the morning rush. And while Sam was always right upstairs if I needed him, I promised myself I wouldn't go up to his apartment unless it was an emergency. I wouldn't be a burden.

I took the time to dry my hair and put on one of the forest green Sam's Books employee t-shirts over a pair of dark jeans. We weren't required to wear the shirts—as long as we had our name tags on, Sam didn't really care what we wore—but it seemed like good luck for my first day. Then I fixed myself a sandwich to eat for lunch, tucked it into my purse, and headed out into the bright early morning light. It was a full hour before my shift started, but I had nothing else at home to kill time, and I just wanted to get the day moving as soon as possible.

To keep my nerves from jangling, I looked for the little changes on the way in. I noticed that the grass along the edge of Pike Street had been freshly mowed. I saw that Jerry's Carwash was offering a spring sale. I watched as a landscaping company spread a fresh layer of mulch around the garden display outside Moody's Supermarket.

Another block, a left turn, and I was on Main Street, the brightly colored awnings of the shops swinging into view. Antiques on Main, not yet open for the day. The stoplight where Sam's girlfriend, Ellen's car had died, leading to their first chance meeting.

I reached into my purse for my keys, fishing them out as I crossed the street and—

Oh my god.

Halfway across the street I broke into a run, dashing forward then screeching to a halt in front of the bookstore. Glass littered the sidewalk where the big front window had been smashed in. The lights were still off inside the store, not a soul to be seen inside or out, but shards of glass winked up at me from the interior as well.

Sam didn't have an alarm system. Damn it, how was this happening? There was no *crime* in Fairfield!

My breath came fast and shallow. When had this happened? Could the person still be here?

My racing thoughts slowed just enough to spur me into action. I stepped back away from the door, mindful of the broken glass as I rushed around the side of the building. My phone was in my hand, numb fingers calling the police even as I did the one thing I'd promised myself I wouldn't need to do on my first day—and rushed up the back stairs to pound on the door to Sam's apartment.

CHAPTER 10

LEVI

*M*y eyes sought her out the second I stepped through the door. Jansen had responded to the call as well, and he went to work collecting evidence—dusting the registers for fingerprints, checking the ragged edge of the busted window for traces of blood or clothing—while I made a beeline for the two figures huddled in the office.

A large, dark-haired man had Marian tucked under his arm and was talking to her in a low voice, and I had to keep my spine from stiffening as I saw them together.

"Levi," she gasped as she saw me, wriggling free and gesturing. "This is Sam. My boss. Sam, this is L—Officer Mathes." I shook Sam's hand as my eyes raked Marian from head to toe, but I didn't see any signs of harm.

"Tell me what happened."

To my great aggravation, the story took no longer to tell than it had at any of the three previous stores. The window was busted when Marian arrived—my gut twisted at the thought that the perpetrator might still have been in the store—she called us and rushed up to find Sam, who apparently lived upstairs, but hadn't heard anything. No, there was no alarm system. No, nothing appeared to be missing other than money, no damages beyond the shattered window and the registers at both the front and the cafe. All told he lost just shy of six hundred dollars across three registers.

I sighed when the questions ran down, scrubbing my hand through my hair. I was glad no one had been here when the crime had happened, but that meant yet again that no one had *seen* anything. And with no alarm system, Sam sure as hell didn't have cameras either.

I bit back an angry comment about the oversight, but the damage had already been done, and I had a feeling after today it wasn't a mistake he would make twice.

After making sure everything was under control, I reluctantly left Marian to help Sam clean up the broken glass and headed back to the station. Jansen met me there and after a gesture from the chief we piled into his office to fill him in.

"That makes what—four now?" he asked, his thick eyebrows pulled together over a frown. "And we still have practically nothing to go on?"

I could feel my own dark expression mirroring the chief's face. "Well, we have video footage from the bank, both inside and out, but it's not good enough to even tell gender, much less identity. We're running prints from each location, but nothing useful there yet. The first two break-ins were during the day and the second two at night, but it's almost certainly the same perpetrator—minimal damage each time, only thing taken was whatever money was in the registers."

"Which is always practically nothing," Jansen put in. "A few hundred. Seems like a lot of trouble to go to for practically no reward." That had been my thought as well, but I also knew from experience that some people were willing to risk a lot more for a lot less. It all depended on the circumstances.

"Could be money for drugs," the chief offered, mirroring my own thoughts. "Or debt. Who knows what kind of trouble they're in."

We all fell silent for a minute, then the chief sat forward and pounded his fist on his desk. "Come on, there has to be more. What are we missing? What else do these places have in common?"

"All walking distance from each other. Within a radius of a few blocks." I put in.

"Right, so maybe the perp doesn't have a car. Maybe homeless? What else?"

I sat back, feeling helpless and frustrated. I'd been over and over this in my head, and was getting nowhere.

"What is it?"

I glanced up in confusion, but the chief was looking at Jansen instead of me. I followed his gaze and saw Jansen was looking thoughtful.

"Well, what about that girl?"

"What girl?" the chief demanded, but I felt my stomach clench.

"Well, you remember that girl whose apartment was broken into earlier this week? The one who lives by Levi?"

Had that really only been earlier this week?

The chief nodded, and Jansen went on. "Well, she works at the bookstore. And didn't you say she was there when you responded to the call at the craft store too?" He looked to me and I gave a tight nod.

"What, you think her break-in was tied to these?" the chief asked.

"Well, no..." Jansen said slowly, "I don't think that was the same guy, but doesn't it seem like she's involved in all this?"

"What, you think she's being targeted?" I asked, working to keep my voice even.

"No...I was actually wondering if she was...*involved*." He emphasized the word.

My chest was growing tight. "Involved. Like, she's the perp?"

Jansen shrugged and looked to the chief. "Maybe, right? We know she lives within walking distance to all those places, and she works at the bookstore. Hell, she was the first person on the scene. Who knows if her testimony is truthful? And she was at the craft store right after that break-in, too. It's just a lot of coincidence, is all I'm saying."

"By that logic, the perp could be me," I put in angrily. "I live there too, and I can walk to all those places."

Jansen shot me an odd look. "Oo-kay. I'm just saying, it's an angle we should consider."

The chief opened his mouth to respond, but I barreled over him. "Besides, she doesn't have any ties to the bank, or the dry cleaner."

"Well, we don't know that, do we?" the chief asked, looking between us. "Has anyone checked to see if she's a customer at either place?"

Jansen shook his head. "No, I only just thought of all this."

"This is ridiculous," I muttered under my breath. I knew I was overreacting, but I couldn't seem to stop myself. I wasn't even sure why I was so outraged—their points made sense, and it was a reasonable line of thought, it was just so *wrong*. They didn't *know* her. Marian was as harmless as a freaking kitten. She was already struggling enough to deal with all of this, the last thing she needed was to think she might be a suspect.

"Besides," Jansen went on, "the woman's clearly got problems. You should have seen her apartment," he told the chief. "She's a hoarder or some shit; she's got trash piled to the ceiling. Maybe she needs money to buy more shit."

Blood pulsed in my veins, turning my vision red, and I

opened my mouth without any regard for what was going to come out. But before I had a chance to do more than draw breath, the chief cut in, turning to face me.

"You live next door, right?" He waited until I wrestled myself under control and nodded tightly. "Talk to her. It's one of the only leads we have. Find out what you can."

I choked down the responses that rose in my throat like bile. It wouldn't help. Instead I rose and gave a curt nod, then left the office, ignoring Jansen's questioning glance and hero-ically managing not to punch him in the face as I went.

The anger roiled in me, hot and metallic, and I wasn't even sure who or what was the real source of my anger. I was mad that these break-ins kept happening, more and more damage to innocent people's property and livelihoods, and I was no closer to the answer now than I had been at the beginning. I was mad that Jansen was pointing the finger at Marian, who was just another victim in this list of crimes. I was mad at myself, for reacting the way I was in the first place. Why did I care so much? I told myself I just wanted to solve the case, just have this all over with. And while I honestly believed that Marian wasn't involved, why had I acted that way in front of the chief? Why was I turning into an idiot where she was involved?

Because Jansen was right. She *was* a hoarder, and an addict, and clearly had problems. And I shouldn't care about her beyond the care I felt for any member of the public I was protecting.

And yet I was forced to admit the truth that was becoming more and more apparent with every passing moment. Regardless of whether or not I wanted to—I *did* care.

* * *

That night I didn't make any pretense of going to bed. I hadn't seen her since the break-in at the bookstore that morning, and I wasn't going to lie there and pretend I didn't care if she was alright. I crossed the hallway and pounded on her door, and the swiftness in which she answered it showed me she couldn't have been doing anything but waiting for me.

When she came out into the hallway, pulling the door shut behind her, I let my eyes drink her in. She looked tired, her eyes drawn, worried creases framing her mouth. But the warm brown of her eyes immediately put me at ease, tension releasing that I didn't even realize I was carrying.

The lone light bulb at the end of the hallway had gone out, leaving only a dim light filtering in from the stairwell at one end of the corridor and through the window at the other. The shadows played across her face as I moved to make room for her, both of us collapsing against the wall into our familiar poses.

She was wearing pajamas—a tank top and thin pants covered in cartoon cupcakes—I suppressed a smile *and* an eye roll—and had her hair piled on her head, but she'd clearly not yet been to bed. Soft tendrils of hair fell from the elastic to frame her face and catch on her lip, and I folded my hands in my lap to keep from reaching over and freeing the strands.

"Are you okay?" I asked, watching her face for any shifting flashes of emotion, but if anything, her expression relaxed as her lips curved into a sad smile.

"I'm okay. We got all the glass cleaned up and Sam had someone in to replace the window. He's going to keep the store closed tomorrow and reopen on Monday."

"That's great," I said, "but what about *you?* Are *you* okay?"

CHAPTER 11

MARIAN

I'd known what he meant, but I didn't want to admit to how much the whole situation was bothering me. I couldn't stop replaying the horrified look on Sam's face when he'd vaulted past me down the stairs to see the damage to his store. I knew it wasn't my fault. I knew it was a complete coincidence that it had happened on my first day opening the store. But none of that eased the pain I felt when I saw his stricken face as he took in the broken glass.

Levi leaned close and nudged his shoulder against mine, the warm pressure bringing me back to the present. "Talk to me," he said.

"I...I'm worried. About Sam. And Sherry." My voice dropped. "And you."

He looked at me strangely. "Me? Why are you worried about me?"

I shrugged, looking down to keep from meeting his gaze. "Well, it's your case, right? Four unsolved break-ins now? I imagine that's pretty stressful."

He just looked at me, and I could feel the intensity of his eyes boring into my head until I finally looked up at him.

"Don't worry about me," he told me. "For one thing, stress is part of my job, and I've had way worse. For another thing, I'm *going* to solve this. It's just a matter of time."

The conviction in his voice was reassuring, and I gave a faint nod.

"You don't think…" I trailed off, and he prompted me with another little nudge.

"What?"

"You don't think this…has anything to do with me, do you?"

He looked at me closely. "What do you mean?"

I shrugged, feeling a little foolish. "I don't know. Just… well. I mean, today it was the place that I work. Yesterday it was the craft store I go to all the time. Before that was the bank I use. And the dry cleaners is practically next door to the craft store. It's almost like someone is targeting me."

He was quiet for a moment, then said, "Do you use Royal's Dry Cleaners?"

I shook my head. "No, I've never been there. But I pass it all the time. I know it probably has nothing to do with me, it's just…I don't know. Scary."

"*Could* it be someone targeting you? Do you know anyone —relatives, friends, acquaintances—who might have a motive?"

I thought for a moment, looking down at my lap, then shook my head. "I don't really have any relatives. Just an aunt, but she lives over in Glassbury. As for friends or acquaintances…" I shook my head again. "It doesn't really make sense, I guess. If someone *was* targeting me, why would they rob all these random places I shop at?"

"Exactly."

I glanced over, and caught the slight curve of his lips and sympathetic glint in his eye.

"It doesn't make sense." He repeated my words. "I know

it's scary, but I really think it's just a coincidence." He paused, watching me, and I saw his face soften. He lifted a hand to my face, pulling a strand of hair free from my cheek and tucking it back over my ear, before lowering his hand back to his lap. My breath caught at his touch.

"I'm sorry you're scared," he said softly. "But it won't last forever. We'll catch him. I promise."

I eyed him, still feeling the brush of his fingers against my cheek.

"You're really nothing like I thought you were." The words were out of my mouth before I could stop them.

He raised an eyebrow. "What did you think I was like?"

I shrugged, looking away, before letting the truth out in a mumble. "Scary. Intimidating." I snuck a peak over at him. "Mean."

He grunted noncommittally, and I couldn't read his expression.

I felt my cheeks flush. "I'm sorry. I didn't mean…"

He shook his head, and while his face was still expressionless, I thought I could detect a tightness in his voice that sounded a little like hurt. "No, it's fine. *I'm* sorry. I never meant to be…mean. Or scary. It wasn't personal."

I peeked at him out of the corner of my eye, looking at the way the faint light from the far end of the hall illuminated his profile, casting his face in sharp angles and making the scar on his jaw stand out in silvery relief. He *looked* scary. Solid muscles, big hands, deep set eyes, scruff on his jaw. And what I knew about him didn't lessen his intimidation. He'd chased people down, arrested them, shot people, been shot *at*. Hell, he threw people around as a *hobby*, practicing at that martial arts gym. There was nothing about him that wasn't scary.

Except that wasn't true, was it? He wasn't scary when he sat with me in the hallway, giving up sleep so I could feel safe. He wasn't scary when he'd hooked his fingers through mine and listened to me talk about my fears. He wasn't scary when he brushed my hair off my cheek and leaned so close I could see the flecks of color in his eyes.

Or maybe he was a whole different kind of scary then.

"What?" he asked in a low voice, and I realized I'd been staring at him.

I blinked, but didn't look away. "What happened?" I asked hesitantly. "That first night when we met, when I came over to introduce myself." He just looked at me, and I went on. "Because you *are* scary, and intimidating. But I was wrong. You're not mean. So, what happened?"

He looked away, and silence fell between us. I'd just decided he wasn't going to answer, and I should let it drop when he spoke again, his voice a near whisper in the darkness.

"I grew up here in town," he said. "Out past Cherry Park, me, my younger brother Mason, my mom, and my dad."

I knew where he meant. It was a poor part of town, small houses packed tightly together on tiny plots, cars in driveways propped on cinder blocks and broken chain-link fences.

"My dad...he was an addict. Gambling, primarily, which led to alcohol. I didn't realize anything was wrong for the longest time. When I was a kid he would just stay out late at night, and when he came home, sometimes he and my mom would argue. I shared a room with my brother, and while he always seemed to be able to sleep through anything, sometimes the shouting would wake me up. I thought it was normal. Families argue, right?"

I kept quiet, afraid if I said anything, he would stop. He leaned his head back against the wall.

"I think the day I realized it wasn't normal was the day I woke up for school and saw my mom had a bruise on her jaw. They'd been arguing the night before, and it didn't take a lot of guesswork to figure out where it had come from."

I drew in a breath, and he tilted a glance my way. "It didn't happen a lot. He wasn't inherently violent. Well, not back then, anyway. He got worse the more he drank, and the more he lost at gambling the more he drank, so…it was just a kind of slow escalation, over time. At first, he just went out after holidays, or tax season, or whenever he had some extra cash to throw away. Then he started going out more after his paychecks came in. And then it was all the time. He got into debt, so he'd go more, and then he'd drink more, and get further into debt, and drink more, and hit my mom."

He trailed off, staring out across the hallway, but his eyes were unfocused, and my heart hurt at whatever he saw there in the past. I slid my hand over to where his lay on the carpet between us, and linked my fingers through his. His hand was big and warm, and his fingers tightened convulsively on mine, pulling his attention back to the present, but he didn't let go, just shook his head and looked down, his forehead creased.

"It doesn't matter. He left when I was in high school. Just went out to the casino one night and never came back. Well, actually, he did come back once during my senior year, begging my mom for money, but he didn't stay. He was drunk then, didn't even care that we'd thought he was dead for the past three years."

He shifted, pulling his hands into his lap, my hand following along as he didn't relinquish his grip. Of necessity, I scooted a bit closer and angled my body to face him, watching the play of expressions across his face as he continued.

"After he left, things were better, but they were also worse. He left us saddled with some pretty heavy debt that my mom didn't even know about. She was already working full-time as an administrative assistant, and things were tight even before. It was hard. I got a job as soon as I could, and I worked full-time all through high school. I barely graduated, then joined the police academy the second I got out. Every penny for years went toward my dad's debts, but we made it through. It was close, but we even kept the house."

I blinked down at my lap, unable to process the emotions his story churned up inside me. I'd always considered my life to be pretty hard—I knew there was a lot of grief and hurt inside that I'd never managed to process—but listening to Levi made me realize how easy I had it. Despite what I'd been through I'd never had to worry about money, or paying off debts, or where my food was coming from. I'd never had to care for another person, or worry about someone else's wellbeing. I felt suddenly very spoiled, and ashamed. I'd never really had to work hard a day in my life, and here he was, working since high school and never looking back.

"What about your brother?" I asked. "Did he have to get a job in high school too?"

For the first time since he'd started speaking, the crease in his brow vanished as his expression softened. "No, I wouldn't let him. My brother…he's a good kid." He glanced at me and his mouth twisted in the ghost of a smile. "So smart, so focused. Always straight As. He was young during the worst of it, and I don't think he always knew what was really going on at home. He was only in sixth grade when my dad took off. I didn't want him to end up like…well, like me."

He frowned and the crease in his brow returned. I longed to reach up and smooth it away with my finger.

"I wanted him to have choices, opportunities. Have fun. Enjoy his life. Not to work himself to death and worry all the time."

"So, what happened? Where is he now?" I asked quietly.

"He and my mom still live over in that shitty little house

past Cherry Park. But he's in college now. Studying engineering. He lives at home to save on room and board, and I still send money each month for tuition." His mouth quirked, and I could see the pride reflected in his shadowed eyes. "He's going places. Following his dreams."

"What about you?" I asked. He glanced over and his brow furrowed in confusion. "What about *your* dreams?" I clarified. "Do you have any?"

He didn't answer for a long moment, just looked at me with that intense expression I'd come to realize wasn't meant to be scary or intimidating; it just meant that he was focused, that you actually had his whole attention.

I held my breath, but he didn't answer. He just squeezed my hand tight where it lay against his leg, and after a moment said, "You asked what happened on the night that I moved in. Why I was…mean to you."

I opened my mouth to stop him. To say it didn't matter, that I already knew he wasn't the person I'd thought he was, but he kept going.

"My brother was supposed to come help me move that day. He's very responsible, Mason is, so when he didn't show, I started to worry about him."

My stomach dropped, but I didn't interrupt.

"He didn't answer his phone all day," he went on. "I hadn't wanted to call my mom to ask where he was, because I didn't want to worry her, but when I was done moving and still hadn't heard from my brother, I gave in and called her."

He blew out a breath even as I held mine, not sure I wanted to hear where this story was going.

Levi looked over, catching my eye, and his voice was low and gruff. "My dad had showed up that morning."

My jaw dropped slightly.

"After being gone for *years*, he showed up out of nowhere. Drunk again, *of course*, broke, asking for money. He got rough with my mom, and my brother stepped in, tried to break it up. My dad took off, but the neighbors had called the police, and when they showed up, the story got confused, the neighbors were there, everyone was yelling, and the police thought my brother had hit my mom, and they arrested him.

"*What?*"

Levi turned to face me, and I saw the closest thing I'd ever seen to a smile flash across his face. "Yeah. And right after I hung up from *that* phone call, there was a knock on my door, and I opened it to see this crazy girl brandishing a freaking hedgehog with plants sprouting out of its back at me."

I choked on a laugh.

"I don't even know what you said to me that day," he told me, "and I certainly don't know what I said to you. Hell, I probably slammed the door in your face."

That wasn't far from the truth.

He released my hand and turned, lifting both of his to frame my face, and I froze, my breath caught in my throat, my blood pulsing beneath his fingertips.

His face was so close, his eyes serious and his voice soft. "But I'm sorry for whatever I did or said, that made you feel afraid of me for two years. Because if you'd caught me on any other day, or if I'd had any sense at all, I wouldn't have run you off. I would have done this."

And he lowered his head to mine, his fingers against my jaw a rough counterpoint to the softness of his lips as he pressed them firmly against mine.

CHAPTER 12

LEVI

I hadn't even realized how much I'd wanted her until I felt her mouth against mine. She was soft and warm and her brief sound of surprise transformed almost instantly into a breathy sigh.

Her hands came to my shoulders, gripping tight as I slipped one hand around from her jaw to the back of her neck, holding her to me, my fingers twining in the soft hair at the nape of her neck.

I'd meant for it to be a short kiss, something sweet and gentle to gauge her interest, to make sure I wasn't overstepping. Any second now, I'd let her go.

But her small hands fisted in my t-shirt and pulled me tight to her, and at the feel of her warmth pressed against my chest I couldn't resist.

With a groan I pulled, lifting her into my lap, and the kiss turned sloppy, breathless, all sliding lips and tongues and hot breath, and I didn't remember kisses ever feeling like this before. Her legs settled on either side of my lap and I could feel the tension in them, muscles taut with strain as her hands moved down my chest, leaving a trail of fire in their wake. I desperately wanted to feel them on my skin.

I didn't know where to focus my attention, caught between the heat of her hands on my chest and the pull of her lips, catching mine in soft, sliding kisses, or the feel of her hair tangling under my hands. I lost myself in the swirl of sensation, the heat and softness of her small body, until with a gasp she jerked against me, a small, involuntary thrust of her hips against mine that sent a wave of lust coursing through me, and with a monumental effort, I forced myself to pull back, breaking the kiss.

Her eyes were glazed, and I leaned my forehead against hers, letting both of us catch our breath, even though that was the opposite of what I wanted. I wanted to rip off the clothing that separated us, pull her mouth back to mine and swallow the sweet sounds she made until she was gasping my name. I wanted to feel the softness of her skin sliding against mine. I wanted...I *wanted*.

I was a heartbeat away from pulling her back in when she sighed, lifting her forehead away from mine and sliding off my lap. I immediately felt cold and empty, though she took my hand with her as she went, tangling our fingers together again as she settled back against the wall at my side. The only indication that anything had happened at all was the lack of space she left between us—the feel of her shoulder against my arm, her thigh pressed against the length of mine and our linked hands a reassuring indication that maybe I hadn't gone too far after all and scared her even more.

I didn't know what to say, didn't know *how* to say any of the thoughts that swirled in my head, but if there was one thing we'd gotten good at over the past few days, it was comfortable silences, spaces that didn't need to be filled, and we settled into one now.

I glanced over at her, and she had her eyes closed, her face soft and peaceful. I tipped my head back, letting it rest against the wall behind me and let out a breath, and a few minutes later she spoke.

"I wish you *had* done that when we'd first met."

I gave a startled laugh. "You don't think that might have been scarier than me slamming the door in your face?"

She smiled, opening her eyes. "Maybe. But we've wasted a lot of time hating each other, I think."

I turned to look at her, lifting my free hand and letting a finger trace down her jaw. "I never hated you."

She met my eyes. "Me either," she admitted. "Misunderstanding each other, then."

I nodded. That was the truth, I thought. At least for me. I'd never taken the time to try to see past my own prejudices. I'd classified her as crazy and weak, strange right off the bat, and never bothered to see past that to who she really was. Someone who cared so much for everyone around her. A great listener. Someone sweet and strange and giving and completely unique. She wasn't like anyone I'd ever met.

I wondered what her story was. I'd given her mine, fought past the embarrassment and shame to tell her the truth of why I was the way I was. And she'd accepted it—accepted *me* —listening to my words without judgement. Surely, I could offer her the same. If she'd talk to me.

"What about you?" I asked, sliding a glance her way.

"What about me?"

"What's your story? Family? Siblings?"

She didn't move, didn't let go of my hand, and nothing changed in her expression, but I could still feel her pull away. Her answer was slow in coming.

"No. No siblings. No family. Well," she amended softly, "I have an aunt, a few towns over. But we don't really talk."

It was a delicate subject, I could tell that much even if I

didn't know why. I kept my voice easy and light. "Is that where you grew up?"

She shook her head, looking down at her lap. "No, I grew up here in Fairfield. I only moved to Glassbury when I was fifteen."

She trailed off, not volunteering any more information, and I didn't know what to ask. I wanted to know more about her—*anything* about her. But I didn't want to force it if she didn't want to talk to me. Her fingers convulsed slightly in mine, and I reached over and tilted her chin up so I could see her face. Her eyes were damp and shining, though she was clearly working hard to keep the tears from falling, and I felt slightly taken aback. I'd barely asked her anything at all.

"I'm sorry," I told her. "You don't have to tell me—"

"No," she said quickly, rubbing a hand impatiently over her eyes. "Don't be sorry. I want to—I'm not…" She bit her lip and my eyes fell to her mouth, watching her teeth work at the tender flesh.

"Look," she said finally, her voice breathy, and I dragged my eyes back up to hers. "Can you just kiss me again?"

That I could do.

* * *

I'm not sure either of us got any sleep at all that night, but it didn't stop us from meeting in the hallway the following night as well, and the night after that. I wasn't making any progress on the case—though there hadn't been any new break-ins, thank god—and she wasn't volunteering any additional info about her life, but none of it seemed to matter when I had her in my arms, squirming and panting, her soft sounds driving me insane as I ran my lips over every inch of skin I could reach.

It occurred to me in a vague haze that I should just invite

her into my apartment. It would certainly be more comfortable and private than the hard, carpeted floor of the hallway, but part of me knew she'd say no. This stretch of dingy hall, for whatever reason, had become our safe space, and neither of us wanted to upset the balance. So we made out in the hallway like idiot teenagers afraid to wake our parents, and I thought longingly of my big empty bed and instead contented myself with running my hands up the soft skin of her sides, feeling the swell of her breasts beneath the flimsy fabric.

We talked too. She told me about her friends and coworkers—Sherry at the craft store, Sam and Geoff and Rachel at the bookstore. She was full of funny stories, and it amazed me how much she noticed about everyone around her. The regulars at the bookstore—Gary who came in twice a week to buy mysteries he'd already read, Mrs. Semmler and her two daughters who fought over books. Our neighbors Donna and Jake, who were trying to have a baby, Mrs. Linsey across the hall who would probably be moving out soon to go live with her daughter in Missouri. She knew everything about everyone.

I didn't have nearly the stories that she did, but I told her about my mom and my brother, and the guys at the station and some of my friends at jiu jitsu. She seemed fascinated by everything, drilling me for information about everything from what it had been like training to be a police officer to how the belt leveling system worked in jiu jitsu. Her curiosity was insatiable, and the more I got to know her, the more I let her in, the more I wanted *her* to let *me* in. I wanted to ask her about the family she didn't talk about, about the apartment she wouldn't let me inside, about the bags I knew were piled up inside, about her fear of change.

But I didn't push it. Even though I wanted to.

On the plus side, Sam had gotten the windows replaced at

the bookstore, as well as installed a high-end security system, so I no longer needed to worry about her at work. She had been settling well into her new full-time position there, as everyone other than her had known she would.

I decided, as I lay awake in bed late on Wednesday night after leaving her, my hands tucked under my head and my senses still reeling from the sensation of her soft lips and smooth skin, that I would surprise her the following morning. She'd told me that she'd started stopping by Geoff's bakery in the mornings on the way in to work, picking up pastries he had ready for her to sell at the bookstore cafe. I could meet her there, under the guise of picking up donuts for the station, and if nothing else, I could meet one of her friends. She spoke a lot about Geoff, and I knew she worried about him, just starting out with a new business. If I could kill two birds with one stone—meet her friend and support a new business, maybe it would bring her one step closer to letting me in. Besides, it would give me an excuse to see her again before the following night.

I'd meant to rise early and walk with her, but the sleepless nights must have been catching up with me because I overslept my alarm. When I did finally wake, I rose and dressed in a hurry. I knew she liked to stay a while and chat with Geoff before the bookstore opened, so there was a chance I could still catch her there.

The morning was bright but chilly, and I could feel an unfamiliar lightness in my chest as I drove the few blocks to the bakery. Spring had arrived in full, it seemed, the chill air of the morning giving way to a mild breeze, and the air was thick with the smell of mulch and newly blooming flowers.

I'd never been inside the store when it had been a coffee shop, but Marian's friend had done a good job with the place. It was small, but warm, with dark wood floors and local artwork on the walls, and the smell of coffee permeated the air and made my mouth water.

A bell over the door announced my entrance, and a tall man behind the counter—Geoff, presumably—glanced my way with a welcoming nod. He was serving another customer, but to my relief, Marian was still there as well, deep in conversation with another man standing by the display case.

She looked up at my entrance as well, and the surprised smile she gave lit her face and caused something tight to ease within my chest. I could feel my own face relaxing in response, and I started to move into the room, but at that moment the man she'd been speaking to turned to glance my way, and I froze.

It may have been close to a decade since I'd last seen Gary, but I recognized him in an instant. The same scrawny build. The same hooked nose. His face lit up too, not so much with simple recognition as with horror, and I watched as the panic-driven thoughts played across his face. His eyes darted around, and I saw him arrive at a decision in the split second before he moved.

"Wait—"

But it was too late. He bolted, faster than I'd expected, across the room and out the door before I could react.

"Hey—"

"Levi, what—"

Fuck no, he wasn't getting away.

I ignored the confused babble of voices from behind me as I turned to give chase, barreling out the door and back into the bright sunshine. I pushed myself as hard as I could, my shoes pounding on the cement sidewalk as I chased after the slight figure of the fleeing man—damn it, I wasn't in uniform. I didn't have my gun—even as my mind worked to put together the pieces.

The last time I'd seen Gary, he'd been where he always was, with my dad, coming out of a casino, face slack and eyes bright with alcohol and God-knew what else. While my dad had always brought his money troubles home to his family, Gary and Jack, my dad's closest friends, had brought them elsewhere, turning to dealing drugs and petty theft to stay afloat. The last I knew, Jack had been arrested and shipped off to prison—where I assumed he still was—and Gary had fled town. It had only been another month or two before my father had disappeared as well.

I couldn't imagine what had made him return, but from the looks of his sallow skin and prematurely aged face, there was no doubt Gary was still in the same trouble he'd always been in. And from the shock on his face when he'd recognized me in the second before he'd fled, there was also no doubt who was behind Fairfield's string of recent robberies.

And he'd been talking to *Marian.* I felt the rage inside me burn hotter. I remembered her lighthearted stories from the night before of her friends and acquaintances. Gary from the bookstore. It was no stretch now to figure out why the man couldn't remember what books he already owned. I was surprised he had enough brain cells left to read at all.

I snarled, pushing myself faster to close the space between us. I could see the slight limp in his step and hear the ragged draw of his breath; he would be no challenge to catch.

But I needn't have bothered. Not even three blocks from the bakery he abruptly pulled up short, spun to face me, and fired off two rounds from the gun he held close to his side.

I heard a scream from behind me as I fell.

CHAPTER 13

MARIAN

*T*he first thing I heard when I opened the door was the beeping sound of a heart monitor, and for a moment I was terrified of what I was going to find. What if he looked nothing like the man I'd come to know? What if he was small and fragile in the hospital bed, tubes and wires sticking out of him, a shadow of the man that just last night had pulled me across his lap and dragged his mouth across mine in a way that made me feel special and cherished and *desired?*

"Calm down," Geoff told me, squeezing the arm he had slung around my shoulders. "Stop freaking out. I can hear you overthinking from here."

I took a deep breath.

"I already told you, it was a clean shot, he did fine in surgery, and he's going to be okay," Bria, Geoff's girlfriend, informed me. "He's awake now."

"Just go in and talk to him," Geoff said. He removed his arm from my shoulder, gave me a nudge forward, then stepped back and let Bria lead him down the hallway. I forced another breath through my tight throat, then stepped cautiously all the way into the room.

I needn't have worried. Levi may have been lying in a hospital bed, and he might have tubes leading from the back of his hand up to a bag suspended above the bed, but frail was not a word I would use to describe him. He looked too big for the room, shifting with restless energy and seemingly barely hampered by—or even aware of—the thick wrapping of gauze that wound around his left shoulder. He looked tired and his eyes were glassy, and the scowl that creased his brow was so familiar I nearly laughed with relief.

He turned to face me as he became aware of my presence, and his scowl seemed to soften, but only marginally. He glanced me over, head to foot as if checking to be sure *I* had come to no harm, but then his scowl hardened again, and he looked away from me toward the far wall.

"Levi," I breathed, approaching the bed. I twisted my hands together in front of me, unsure what to do with them. I wanted to reach for him. I wanted to check his wounds and be sure he was really okay, brush his hair off his forehead, climb into his lap and make new memories to erase the sound of gunfire and the sight of him crumpling to the pavement. Erase the feel of my pounding heartbeat and the scream I couldn't suppress. Erase the sight of Gary—*Gary?*—tearing down the sidewalk out of sight, even as blood pooled under Levi's motionless body.

But instead I stood there, feeling awkward and out of place as he glared sightlessly at the far wall and refused to meet my eyes. It was as if all the progress we'd made over the past weeks had been erased. As if I was still afraid of him and he still communicated in monosyllabic grunts and he'd never held my hand or clutched my face and kissed me as if he were drowning.

"Gary's in custody," Levi finally said, wrenching his gaze off the wall with an effort to meet my eyes. His were dull and glassy, unfocused, and I wondered just how many painkillers were in his system right now. The surgery on his shoulder had taken hours, and I'd felt small and uncomfortable in the waiting room, like I had no right to be there as strangers came and went. Other police officers in uniform, talking quietly with the doctors, then a tall lady with wide, tear-filled eyes and an even taller man whose appearance indicated he couldn't be anyone other than Levi's brother. The pair of them sat together on the opposite side of the room, and I'd watched them with fascination, feeling torn between the idea that I should go introduce myself, and the thought of how ridiculous and inappropriate it would be if I did.

Bria came to check on me and bring me coffee, and I asked myself a hundred times why I was there at all, until finally, *finally*, the doctor came out and I listened as he told Levi's mother that he was out of surgery, everything had been successful, and she would be able to come see him as soon as he woke up and got settled in his own room.

Half an hour later, a nurse called them back and Levi's mother and brother disappeared through the doors, and still I sat, unsure if I should leave or stay or attempt to sink through the floor. Why was I even *there?*

I watched as the two uniformed officers from earlier returned and disappeared down the hall, then another one I hadn't seen yet, then finally a couple of guys in plain clothes I thought I recognized from Levi's jiu jitsu class. And when they'd all left, still I sat, wallowing in embarrassment and indecision until Geoff had shown up and grabbed my hand, manually hoisting me out of my chair and propelling me down the hallway to Levi's room. Where I now stood, still not sure I should be here at all.

"Officer Jansen found him a couple of hours ago at his apartment," Levi went on, pulling me back to the present.

"He hadn't tried to flee or anything," he scoffed, then muttered as if to himself, "I *told* you he wouldn't have any brain cells left."

I looked at him in confusion. "How did you know? Who he was, I mean."

"Gary Hensley." He spit out the name as if it were rotten. "He used to be a friend of my dad's. Gambling. Alcohol. Drugs." His eyes lost focus again. "I don't know why he came back. Must've been in debt again. God, I'm tired."

He let his head fall back against the pillow, but his eyes didn't close, just swiveled to look at me under heavy lids. "You're safe now," he mumbled. "We're all safe."

I shifted my weight. I wasn't sure how to reconcile my image of Gary, the sweet man in the bookstore who was clearly short a few marbles but seemed harmless enough, with the man who had run from the scene with a gun, the drug dealing criminal who had been terrorizing our town for weeks now.

And I wasn't sure what to do now. Should I stay and try to talk to Levi? Should I go and let him sleep? I was terrified that if I left, now that this was over, that would be it between us as well. What if he really had just been trying to protect me, and we'd just gotten carried away? We'd have no reason to sit in the hallway together now, no reason to see each other at all.

I couldn't let that happen.

I pushed down the doubt, trying to gather my confidence.

"Levi," I started, then trailed off. His eyes had closed, and his hand had relaxed where it lay on the blanket, slipping to hang off the edge of the bed. I moved forward and picked up his hand, letting myself feel the solid warm weight of it in mine for a moment as I slid it back onto the bed at his side. He jerked slightly and his eyes opened into narrow, unfocused slits.

"Marian? You can go away now." His voice was slurred, heavy with sleep. "The case is over; you don't need me anymore."

"What? That's not true, I—"

His eyes opened all the way and looked directly at me, the blue cold as ice. "Don't you *see?*"

He growled and struggled to sit up, hissing as he wrenched his shoulder. I dropped his hand and stepped back, alarmed. "Stop, you'll pull your—"

"You know you're an addict, too," he said, effectively cutting me off. "Just like my dad, and Gary."

I froze in place.

"I've been in your apartment, remember? Maybe it's not gambling, or drugs—hell, I don't know, maybe it *is*—but it's there, in bags piled to your ceiling."

I was too shocked to react, and he pulled his eyes away and looked up at the ceiling, slouching back down onto the bed. "I can't do this with you. You won't let me *in.*"

I realized he wasn't talking about my apartment. Tears burned the backs of my eyes, but I couldn't move. It was like my feet were encased in ice.

His eyes drifted closed again. "You see how that turns out, right?" he said, his voice thick with the sleep he was failing to fight. "It'll swallow you alive. You'll end up just like them."

The ice around my feet shattered and solidified around my heart instead, and as his breathing evened out, I turned and quietly left the room.

* * *

With Levi's words playing ceaselessly in my mind—*you know you're an addict too...you'll end up just like them*—my apartment was the last place I wanted to go.

I felt numb inside—hurt, confused, offended. How could

he think I was a drug addict? I wasn't anything like his father. Or Gary.

But how could he know that? You've told him nothing about yourself.

I found myself strangely hesitant to leave the hospital, feeling like if I left, it'd all become real. Whatever short-lived happiness I'd found would be over. But if I stayed...*somehow* I could fix this. He'd just been through surgery, anyway. He'd been *shot.* He was on serious painkillers and who knew if he'd even remember what he'd said. Maybe he didn't mean it.

Except that he's right.

I shoved down the tiny voice inside me and tried not to think. Not to *feel.* Just let myself wander the halls, directionless.

I wondered how Geoff was, after the excitement this morning. I wondered about Levi's mother and brother, how scared they must have felt when they'd heard what happened. I thought about Sam, down an employee after I'd called off to spend the day sitting pointlessly in the hospital. I thought about Sherry—

Sherry!

Her surgery was—I wracked my brain, trying to straighten out the days that had all been running together. Two days ago. She might still be here.

It didn't take long to find her. She was in a small but brightly lit room on the fourth floor, with windows lining one wall. A large vase overflowing with flowers sat on one of the windowsills, and a couple of cards surrounded it. I felt bad that I hadn't thought to send her anything yesterday, and tears pricked my eyes, my emotions running close to the surface.

I blinked them back and turned to take in my friend. She was sitting up in the hospital bed, and while she looked tired, her eyes were bright, and her lined face split into a wide smile at the sight of me.

"Marian! It's so lovely to see you, darling."

I opened my mouth to respond...and burst into tears.

"My goodness, I don't look that bad, do I? I know hospital gowns aren't the most flattering, but—"

I snorted through my tears, and she took pity on me.

"Good lord, girl, come here." She guided me around the bed to her right side and pulled me into a tight hug. I wrapped my arms around her, mindful of her stitches, and relaxed into her embrace. A minute later, I got myself under control and she released me. I retrieved a chair from the corner and pulled it up close to her bedside, sinking down into it.

"Now tell me," she instructed, "what's got you all worked up?"

"I'm here to see you, not burden you with my silly problems," I protested. "How are you?"

"Yes, yes," she said with a dismissive wave of her hand. "The surgery went well, I've got a brand-new bionic hip—I'm practically half-robot now, you know—they've got me up walking around the hallways every few hours, and I can go home tomorrow. Now tell me what's happened."

I hesitated. I really didn't want to burden her with my issues. "Well, they caught the man that robbed the craft store," I told her after a moment, realizing that news wouldn't be out just yet. "And the bank and all those other places."

Her gaze sharpened. "Oh, did they now? Well that's good. Though I'm thinking that's not what has you worked up."

"Levi chased the guy down. And got shot," I mumbled. She didn't say anything, but a silver eyebrow climbed up toward her unruly gray hair. My voice dropped to a whisper and I looked down at the floor. "And he thinks I'm more trouble than I'm worth. He said…" My voice caught and I trailed off.

"Ah, now we're getting to it." Her lined face softened. "Come on, I'm stuck in here for another day. You might as well tell me everything."

Haltingly, painfully, I did.

Sherry didn't interrupt, just sat patiently as I told her about the break-in to my own apartment a couple of weeks back, Levi's heroic response and my own reaction to scream and kick him out. About our meetings in the hallway. About what really happened two years ago when we'd first met, and how I'd come to see who he really was, a far cry from who I'd thought he was, and how much I'd grown to like that person. And I told her about the events of the morning, and ended with his harsh words from just now in the hospital.

"And the problem is," I ended, my voice scratchy, "he's right, I know I'm a mess, and if I was anyone else and I saw my apartment, I'd run screaming, too." My voice broke again, and I struggled to hold back a fresh wave of tears. "I have so many problems, Sherry, I'm—" I choked on the words, but forced them out anyway—"a *hoarder*. And he's right, it's an addiction. And I don't let people in. And I worry all the time. And I'm afraid of change. And—"

"Alright. That's enough." Sherry's voice was sharp, but her eyes were kind. "That's enough beating yourself up. You don't have a million problems, Marian, you just have one."

"I know I'm a hoarder, I just—"

"That's not it," she informed me.

I blinked, looking out the window to avoid her eyes. "It's worse than you think," I said quietly. "I haven't let anyone into my apartment in five years, not even maintenance."

"I know, honey," Sherry said gently, pulling my gaze back to hers. "I've known you for years, Marian. I know how often you come into the store, and I know what you buy. Unless you have a side business marking up craft supplies and reselling them on eBay, I can imagine what your apartment looks like."

My lip pulled up in the ghost of a smile.

"But that's not it," she went on, her voice firm. "Everything you listed is just a symptom. The real problem is that you need to learn how to be a little kinder to yourself. You spend all your time and energy worrying about everyone's happiness…except your own."

She reached across and caught my hand, squeezing it gently, her skin dry and papery thin against mine. She didn't let go as she spoke again, her voice soft.

"I know you buy crafts because it makes you feel closer to your mom. I know you lost her young, and I'm so sorry you had to go through that. But you know this won't bring her back. It's not doing anything but hurting you more."

I could barely swallow around the lump in my throat. I could feel her eyes on me, but I stared down at the floor, unable to meet them. Sherry was one of the only people I'd ever even mentioned my mom to, and even she didn't know the whole story.

"Marian," she said gently. "It wasn't your fault."

"You don't understand," I choked out, feeling like a dam was breaking inside me. I yanked my hand out of her grasp, bringing it up to cover my face. "She killed herself, and I didn't even know anything was *wrong*."

I hunched forward, the tears falling freely now, and buried my face in both hands, choking on the bitter taste of the words I'd never spoken aloud. "I found her after school, lying on her bed. She'd overdosed on sleeping pills. I thought it was an accident until I found her note. I remember seeing her lying there, looking like she was sleeping, and I thought, shouldn't I be thinking how peaceful she looks now? Like if life was so terrible and she was so tormented, she should look peaceful and relaxed now that it's all over. But she looked the same as she always did! She always smiled and laughed. How did I not know something was wrong? How could she keep that from me?"

I felt the soft pressure of Sherry's hand on my head, but I couldn't hold back the wracking sobs. "And then she left me all that money, and my whole childhood, I'd thought we were poor. It's like I didn't even know her at all! Like everything I'd ever known was a lie."

I trailed off, and just let it pour out, wrapping my arms tight around myself. Sherry's hand was gentle on my hair, stroking and soothing, and eventually my sobs turned into sniffles, then finally ceased. A few long minutes later, I raised my head.

Tear tracks were drying on Sherry's cheeks as well, and I felt suddenly embarrassed. This was years ago, nearly a decade, and I'd had plenty of time to come to terms with my mother's death. I hadn't meant to let those feelings bubble up and spill all over Sherry.

"I'm sorry," I said quietly. "I didn't mean to unload all of that on you. I know it wasn't my fault, I really do. It wasn't about me at all."

"Oh honey, don't apologize. I'm so sorry. But you see now, don't you?" She reached across and took my hand again, holding it tightly. "It's so true, what I said before. You worry so much about other people. You worry about your friend Geoff at his new bakery. You worry about your boss and how he'll deal with losing an employee. You worry about me, and about your neighbors, and even about strangers in the street."

She paused for a breath, looking at me sadly. "But honey, it's not your job to keep everyone happy all the time. You put everyone before yourself because you're afraid they might struggle, and you might miss it. You're so hard on yourself."

She pulled me forward, until our foreheads were nearly touching, and put her warm hands on both of my cheeks.

"You say you know it's not your fault. But until you act like it, until you really forgive yourself and stop trying to fill the hole inside you with craft supplies and other people's happiness, you'll never be happy yourself."

She pressed a kiss to my forehead as another tear trickled unbidden out of the corner of my eye, then released me. "You're a wonderful girl, Marian. Let yourself be happy."

* * *

It was dark by the time I left the hospital. I'd stayed with Sherry for hours, and we'd foregone the hospital food to order pizza, which we ate together while watching home improvement shows on the tiny television set high in the wall opposite the bed. We made fun of home buyers together and she introduced me to her daughter and granddaughter when they stopped by to check on her.

And by the time I gave her another hug and a whispered thank you and finally departed, the moon was a sliver rising in the sky and the sound of frogs from the woods behind the hospital was an echoing chorus in the night.

I felt calm—or calmer, anyway. Even though nothing had really changed, just the act of actually confiding in someone for the first time had been a release I hadn't known I'd needed, and Sherry's words echoed in my head in time with the bright sound of the frogs.

Stop trying to fill the hole inside you with craft supplies and other people's happiness. Let yourself be happy.

Was Sherry overly intuitive, or was it just that obvious? It didn't matter, I supposed.

I thought about Levi on the walk home from the hospital. Was he awake now, or sleeping? Would he remember the things he said to me? If so, would he regret them? I supposed that didn't matter either. I wanted to be with him. I wanted a chance at a real relationship, not one built on fear and misunderstandings. And the only way that would happen is if I gave it a chance. If I let him in.

Let yourself be happy.

I opened the door to the apartment building, then used my keys to unlock the deadbolts on the heavy new door Levi had installed. He wouldn't have done that if he hadn't cared about me. He wouldn't have gone out of his way to check on me, and sit with me in the hallway. I cared about him, and obviously he cared about me as well. Now it was time to try caring about myself for a change.

I moved through the apartment, flipping on all the lights. Then I went to the kitchen and pulled out the roll of trash bags I kept under the sink. I moved to the living room, sitting cross-legged on the floor in the middle of the thin path that was the only space clear of clutter.

I took a deep breath, and then I started opening bags I hadn't touched in years.

CHAPTER 14

LEVI

he doctors told me I was lucky. The bullet had completely missed my subclavian artery, and the surgical repair of my shoulder had gone well. I was still in for a few months of physical therapy to hopefully regain my full range of motion, but I was released from the hospital two days later with nothing more than a small cluster of stitches to show for my trouble.

But I didn't feel lucky. It was true, I'd had a steady stream of visitors—from my mom and brother, to Jansen and the chief, who kept me up to date on Gary's arrest and the aftermath of the situation—including an impressive array of evidence collected from his apartment—as well as a couple of buddies from jiu jitsu who bemoaned the fact that I wouldn't be practicing with them any time soon. But one person had been conspicuously absent.

I hadn't seen Marian again after that first day when I'd said such horrible things to her. Sure, I'd been doped up on painkillers and fresh out of surgery. And the things I'd said had all had at least a hint of truth to them. But that gave me no cause to be cruel. And I *had* been cruel, there was no doubt about that.

I'd been exactly the person she'd feared I was when we first met. The person I'd been trying for the past few weeks to show her wasn't the real me at all.

That was the only thing I could think about on the way home from the hospital—I owed her an apology.

"So, there was a girl sitting across the room from us when you were in surgery."

My mom had volunteered to pick me up from the hospital and drive me the few blocks home. Despite the fact that the distance was easily walkable, I hadn't had the heart to refuse her.

"At first I assumed she was there for someone else," she went on, either not noticing or deliberately ignoring my lack of response. "But every time your doctor came out, she perked up and leaned forward like she was trying to hear what he said to us."

I blinked. Marian had been waiting there all *day*?

My mother gave me a sidelong glance. "I was just wondering if it was anyone I should know about?"

I just grunted in answer, but she refused to give up.

"She was still there when Mason and I went back. Did she ever go back to see you?"

Yes. And I'd insulted her and made her cry. I called her an addict. I told her she'd end up like my dad. I told her I didn't want to see her. Good lord, I'd be lucky if she was even willing to look at me after all that.

We pulled up in front of my apartment and my mom thankfully let the subject drop. She helped me inside and got me situated, heading back out with a kiss on the cheek and a promise to check on me later.

It had only been a few days, but it felt like so much longer. Like so much had happened since the morning I'd gone to surprise Marian at the bakery. My apartment felt cold and sterile for some reason, and I felt aimless as I wandered through it.

When I drifted into my bedroom though, the first thing I saw was shattered pottery. The geranium in my windowsill had grown too top-heavy and had fallen off the sill sometime while I'd been gone. Clumps of dirt and broken remains of the hedgehog pot littered the carpet, and a tight feeling rose in my chest. The loss of that ridiculous hedgehog struck me harder than I would have expected, and I wondered when the moment had been that I'd started finding her eccentricities endearing rather than weird or annoying.

I bent, picking up a broken shard of pottery and carefully fingering the sharp edge. I wouldn't let this be an omen. My relationship with Marian had barely even gotten started, but I wouldn't let it end so easily, shattered from the same neglect I'd shown this plant. I let the piece fall back to the floor, and without pausing to deal with the mess, I crossed the room and left my apartment, heading down the hall with purposeful strides.

I held my breath and rapped my knuckles sharply against her door.

What was I doing? She'd never let me in. Besides, it was the middle of the day; she was likely at work, and even if not, the familiar space against the wall between our doors was an entirely different landscape in the bright light of day.

To my surprise, her clear voice rang out through the door before I had the chance to turn and leave.

"Come in!"

Come in? Really?

Swallowing down my shock, and the pulse of hope that went with it, I grasped the handle and pushed, then shook my head ruefully—would she never lock the damn door?— and cautiously let myself into the apartment.

Just inside the entryway I froze, and I nearly left again to check and be sure I was in the right place. True, I had only been inside the apartment once before, but it was not the kind of thing you forgot, and this—*this* was nothing like what I remembered.

I looked around in amazement.

A huge swath of space was clear, right down to the carpet. Gone were the bags, the boxes, the loose papers, the *junk.* In the clear half of the room, a misshapen couch was now visible beneath the dusty window as well as some plastic totes and a tall cabinet against the side wall. Trash bags were piled high in the far corner.

I turned, looking toward the hallway, where I could still see a spill of bags cluttering the opening.

"Marian?"

She appeared, stumbling through the mess and kicking things out of her way, a trash bag gripped in one hand, the other raised to push her hair out of her eyes.

"Levi." Her voice was hesitant. "I'd hoped it was you."

I didn't waste a second. I crossed the room, stopping myself just short of touching her. "I'm sorry. I'm so sorry, Marian. I had no right to say those things to you, and—"

"Stop, it's okay." She tilted her head. "Well, it's not okay, but thank you."

She reached out a hand toward me and I grabbed it, the feel of her fingers in mine calming the dread and regret I'd been carrying around for days.

"I'm sorry I didn't come see you again," she went on. "But I had some stuff I needed to start taking care of." She gestured around with a rueful smile.

"Don't apologize," I said insistently. "It's my fault. I had no right to say what I did, and I…" I looked around again, taking in the stark changes since I'd last been here. "I hope you aren't doing this for me. I mean, I'm glad you…but don't…"

"No, it's not because of you. And yes, it is." She smiled, the expression softening the serious look on her face, and my heart unclenched a little further. "Look, come sit. I have some things I want to tell you. Things I should have told you before."

She tugged my hand lightly, leading me toward the kitchen. I went willingly, but my chest still felt tight. I *wanted* her to tell me everything. I wanted her to let me in and to find out who she was. But I didn't want her to think she owed me just because I'd acted like an ass.

"Marian, you don't have to tell me any—"

"I said I *want* to." She took a deep breath, and led me to a seat at the kitchen table. I didn't let go of her hand as she slid in across from me. "They say things get easier with practice," she said under her breath as she folded her legs beneath her. "Let's see if that's true."

And then she told me about her mom. She looked down at the table as she spoke in a quiet voice, and I let her words wash over me.

She'd never known her dad, gone when she was a baby, and it had always been just the two of them. She told me about her childhood growing up, happy on all accounts. About her mom's love of scrapbooking and card making and crafts, and everything they did together. She told me about the day she'd come home from school as a high school freshman, and found her mom dead in her bedroom, a note for her left on the nightstand. My breath caught in my throat as I listened to her describe her complete confusion and numbness, her new life living with her aunt in Glassbury, about an hour's drive away, the surprise of an inheritance when she turned eighteen.

She told me about moving back to Fairfield and into her own place, and the first time she ever went to the craft store, determined to buy some scrapbooking supplies to remind her of her mom. And how everything had spiraled out of control from there.

To my amazement, her eyes remained dry through her story, her voice level, if soft and unsteady here and there. About halfway through I couldn't control myself, and I carefully pulled her around the table and into my lap, where I wrapped my good arm around her silently as I let her speak.

She told me about going to see Sherry in the hospital after she left my room, and the conversation they'd had.

Only at the end did her eyes turn bright with tears. "It was time, you know? Sherry was right. I have to learn how to let go, and be kinder to myself. I…"

She twisted in my lap, turning her face to mine, and I lifted my hand, wiping away a tear that had escaped. "I really like you," she whispered. "And I *want* to let you in."

I barely knew what to say. I'd misjudged her so badly, right from the start, thinking she was weak and silly. But in reality, she was so strong, able to survive such horrible circumstances and still find it within herself to give so much of herself to others. She cared so much about other people, and I couldn't wait to see what she was like when she cared about herself just as much.

I cupped her face in my hands, my thumbs brushing away the remaining tears, and leaned in close, brushing my lips lightly against hers.

"I really like you, too," I told her, and she laughed. "And I think you're strong and amazing and wonderful." I tried to say more, but she cut me off with her lips, soft and pliant against mine, and I couldn't remember what I'd been about to say anyway.

It seemed forever before we came up for air, and she slid off my lap and pulled me up to my feet as well.

"Do you…" I nodded my head toward the hallway. "Do you want my help with that? The cleaning, I mean."

She gave another musical laugh. "You know, at first I thought it was really something I needed to do on my own. Purge everything by myself, and deal with the emotions."

I nodded.

"But I've been at it for two days now, and honestly? I would love the help."

CHAPTER 15

MARIAN

*A*ll told, it took nearly a month. And it was a hard month, too, filled with more tears than I could count—tears of sadness and loss as I found things I hadn't even known I had, things my mom would have loved. Tears of embarrassment as I found things I didn't even remember buying, crumpled and broken under the weight of five years' worth of *stuff*. There were even tears of laughter, as Levi found my old sewing machine in a box with a bunch of half-finished projects and donned a frilly, cherry-printed apron I'd made as he cooked dinner for us in the kitchen.

But by the end of the month, my apartment and I mirrored each other. Both of us were empty, swept clean of five years of accumulated junk, both real and emotional, and only slightly worse for wear. My poor apartment desperately needed new carpet, a fresh coat of paint, and some new furniture to fill the space that had previously been filled with clutter. The spare bedroom was still filled with a selection of bags I was struggling to part with, but as Levi kept reminding me, this was a process, and healing took time. Personally, my body was ready for some new emotions to fill the space that had been cleared of guilt, regret, and self-loathing.

And as unfamiliar as emotions such as love and happiness and optimism might be, I was finding them not at all hard to get used to.

"You're going to keep the knitting?" Levi called from the bedroom. He'd been of limited physical help, due to the restrictions of his still-healing shoulder, but the emotional support he'd provided had been invaluable.

"Absolutely," I called back. "I might need to stab someone with those needles."

"Got a taste for violence, did you?"

He appeared in the doorway, a grin stretched wide across his face, and I tried hard not to melt. The effects of that smile never seemed to lessen.

"What?" he asked as I continued to stare.

"Oh, nothing," I said. "I just was sure for so long that you didn't even know *how* to smile."

He narrowed his eyes and stalked across the room to me, his grin turning into a smirk. "It's not that hard to make me smile," he informed me in a low voice.

"Oh, I know," I told him. "All I have to do is kiss you *here...*" I slid my nose across the underside of his jaw, breathing him in, then pressed my lips to the side of his neck. "Or touch you *here...*" I slipped my hands under the hem of his t-shirt and ran my fingertips up the hard plane of his chest.

"But I'm not smiling now," he said, his voice a low growl that sent heat coiling through me.

"No, I suppose not," I sighed, tilting my face up to meet his. His fingers slipped under the hems of my clothing, one hand questing upward, one downward. His lips met mine in a searing kiss.

"But I think I like this better."

* * *

MEMORY OF LOVE

CHAPTER 1

JEANNE

*T*he last thing I needed to see at the end of a long day was my ex-husband's face grinning smarmily out from a dual-page spread in the newspaper. I knew that look—dark hair flopping over his forehead, dimple in his cheek, twinkle in his eye as if he knew a secret he was dying to share—it was intimate and seductive, as if he was staring directly out of the paper at me. *Hey beautiful. Come talk to me. Come home with me. Let me paint your portrait.*

Oh, no you don't. That'd worked on me once, and on countless other women since then, I was sure.

I scanned the article. *Fairfield's own local celebrity, Jeremy Whitaker...book tour for his recent release,* A Life of Color...*a captivating array of paintings, poetry, and short stories...*

Ugh.

I flipped the paper closed, folded it once, and deposited it neatly in the recycling bin.

"I don't need you to leave the paper for me anymore," I called down the hall to Tris, my front-desk manager. Her laughter floated through the open door to my office, and I rummaged through my purse, needing something to erase the sour taste from my mouth. I found a peppermint candy and unwrapped it, popping it into my mouth and savoring the sweet flavor on my tongue.

I've always gotten a lot of flak from my friends and family for my addiction to sweets. I was the kid that could put away my entire collection of Halloween candy in about an hour if no one stopped me. When I was a teenager, my mother would sigh whenever she caught me liberally sprinkling spoonfuls of sugar over my already sweet Lucky Charms, saying she hoped I'd become a dentist someday…before I lost all my teeth.

So, I guess you could say I chose my profession to spite my mom. Pretty mature, right? Honestly, though, I *love* being a dentist.

I love how something as simple as a teeth cleaning can make my patients feel better. I love the independence and flexibility of my job. I love seeing how a non-judgemental, sugar-addicted dentist helps people feel safe.

And while I definitely learned the importance of good oral hygiene as I got older, still I never lost my sweet tooth, much to my mother's dismay.

It certainly didn't help that my friend Geoff recently opened a bakery that—while not *precisely* on the route between home and work—wasn't exactly out of the way, either. In fact, I'd been thinking about stopping there on my way home to see what he was serving up. E'clairs, I hoped. Or maybe chocolate fudge cake—that was my *favorite*.

"Jeanne, I know that glazed expression. You're thinking about cake again, aren't you?"

Carly, one of my hygienists, as well as one of my closest friends, poked her head around the corner and raised an eyebrow at me.

"I am not," I said with as much dignity as I could muster. "I was thinking about Mr. Riley's root canal tomorrow."

To her credit, she didn't laugh at me outright, though she did roll her eyes. "Sure you were. Well, tell Geoff I said hi. I just finished up with the last patient, so I'm heading out."

I smiled at her. "Have a good night."

"You, too. You have any plans?"

My smile widened. "I sure do. Dylan's at his grandparents' for the next three nights until Jeremy comes home, and I plan to eat as much ice cream as I can handle and fall asleep in the tub. It's going to be amazing."

Carly laughed as she slung her purse over her shoulder. "That *does* sound amazing. He's been gone for, what? Two months now?"

I nodded. "Nearly."

With Jeremy traveling for his book tour, I'd had sole custody of our son, Dylan. And while Dylan was a pretty good kid, all things considered, single-parenting a rambunctious six-year-old over summer break was not for the faint of heart. Jeremy's parents watched him during the days when I had to work, but I hated to ask them to keep him overnight, too. Not only did it seem like an imposition, but Jeremy's mom wasn't the easiest person to get along with. But they'd volunteered to give me a break over the last few days before Jeremy returned, and I certainly wasn't going to say no to the offer of some much-needed alone time.

"Too bad he has to come back at all, huh?" Carly said.

I laughed and tucked my blond hair behind my ear. "Well, if it wasn't for Dylan, I'm sure he'd be on the first plane out of Fairfield, but he's managed to stick around so far."

For all of Jeremy's many—*many*—faults, I had to give him that. He tried to be a good dad.

"Well, you have a good night to yourself. I'll see you tomorrow?"

I nodded. "See you tomorrow."

A minute later I stood and gathered my belongings, shutting down my computer before heading for the door. I called a goodbye to Tris on my way out, then got in my car and headed home, deciding at the last minute to forego the bakery in favor of the ice cream I already knew was filling my freezer. Besides, if I stopped at Geoff's, I'd feel obligated to stop at the bookstore too, right down the block and owned by Jeremy's brother, Sam. And although he was the only member of the family I could tolerate for more than a few minutes at a time, at that moment I preferred the easy company of the ice cream and my bathtub.

I sighed with pleasure as I let myself into the quiet house. Legos and racing cars and puzzle pieces cluttered the floor, and I nudged them aside as I made my way through the foyer and up the stairs. I changed out of my work clothes into a pair of yoga pants and a tank top before heading to the kitchen, where I spent a grand total of thirty seconds perusing the healthy offerings of my fridge before deciding I didn't have anyone to set a good example for that night, and went straight for the ice cream.

Mint chocolate chip. The best.

I curled up on the couch under a throw and worked my way through half a pint while watching crime show reruns. I was getting drowsy and beginning to contemplate that bath when my phone rang.

"Hello?"

"Jeanne?" The voice through the phone was rich and warm, and I couldn't stop the smile from spreading across my face.

"Mark. Hey." I snuggled deeper into the couch and tipped my head to rest against the cushions. "What are you up to?"

"Just missing you," he answered, and I could hear the smile in his voice. "Moving is terrible. Remind me why I'm doing this again?"

"To be near me, of course," I responded.

I'd met Mark Strykowski nearly six months earlier, at a dental convention in Columbus, Ohio. I'd been taking a continuing education course on the human gut microbiome and its influence on oral inflammation, and while the subject matter had been less-than-fascinating, the handsome man I'd been seated next to had been enough to hold my wandering attention. It's possible I wasn't entirely subtle as I snuck glances at him throughout the lecture, because at the end he'd invited me out for dinner.

As coincidence would have it, he was from Indiana as well, where he worked at a large dental practice in Indianapolis. The practice had recently changed owners though, and while Mark had been given the option to stay on, he had instead decided to relocate closer to his aging parents, who lived in Glassbury, only an hour away from Fairfield, and open his own small practice there.

We'd hit it off right away, exchanging stories of small-town Indiana over dinner, dental anecdotes over dessert, and a few flirtatious insinuations over drinks. We'd met up the following night as well, and when after two nights he'd made no move to invite me back to his hotel room, I'd observed with relief how different this all was from the first time I'd met my ex-husband, and thought maybe there could be something here worth following up on.

His soft chuckle brought me back to the present. "Oh, right, how could I forget? But if I'm moving to be near you, then why am I stuck here in Glassbury while you're all the way over there in Fairfield?"

I smiled. "Well, I'd invite you over, but I have the place to myself for the first time in months, and I'm not giving this up."

"All alone, huh? All the more reason you should invite me over," he teased.

I laughed, knowing he was joking and would respect my

boundaries. It was strange—I hadn't seriously dated anyone since my divorce had been finalized nearly six years earlier—between relocating to Indiana, raising a child, and opening my own dental practice, dating had been pretty low on my list of priorities—and I couldn't help but compare him to Jeremy. Jeremy, who certainly would *not* have respected my wishes to have some time to myself, and likely would have shown up uninvited with a bottle of wine half an hour later and had me naked against the wall ten minutes after that.

No, Mark was everything Jeremy wasn't—respectful, courteous, responsible, *grown-up*. If I'd known men like him existed, maybe I would have started dating again earlier.

"I've got plans tomorrow," he went on, "but can I take you out on Friday?"

His voice was a low rumble that made me heat inside, but I sighed regretfully. "I can't Friday; I've got plans with Carly. What about Saturday? I'm free all day."

"Saturday sounds perfect. I'll call you on Friday to set it up." He paused, and his voice dropped even lower. "I miss you, babe."

His words were a simple statement, not a wheedle for an invitation, but despite that fact—or perhaps *because* of it—the warmth inside me began to swirl lower. Maybe I should invite him over after all. We hadn't seen each other at all that week. But no…it was late, and I had to work in the morning. And besides, I really did want that bath, more than I wanted to get laid.

"I miss you too," I said, and we exchanged goodnights and hung up.

I went all out on the bath—candles, bubbles, scented soap, soft music and a glass of wine—and then nearly fell asleep before I had a chance to enjoy it. I laughed to myself as I let the water drain out—clearly, I was too out of practice to even properly enjoy an evening to myself. But the heavenly comfort of my bed was enough to make me not care, and I barely had time to set my alarm before I was out cold.

* * *

I awoke with my heart hammering in my throat and dread coursing through my whole body. What was happening? I didn't know if it was the ear-splitting shriek of the fire alarm that woke me first, or the rasping cough I barely recognized as coming from my burning throat.

Dylan!

It took my addled brain a long moment to remember that he was safe at his grandparents' house. I, however, was *not* safe. My lungs seized against the thick, choking air.

Get out.

I rolled out of bed and crouched low, grabbing my cell phone from the nightstand and yanking the charging cable out of the wall as I hurried to the door. My mind was a confused tumble of thoughts and remembered advice—stop, drop, and roll—*Thank you, elementary school, but I'm not on fire...yet*—smoke rises, so stay low to the ground—have a family meeting place—*Thank God Dylan's not here.*

The doorknob wasn't hot, but the air was thicker in the hallway, and my head felt like a balloon about to lift from my shoulders as I crawled toward the stairs, coughing so hard I thought I might disgorge a lung. I just had to make it down the stairs.

Hold it together.

And across the living room.

Keep moving.

It was hotter down there, smokier, and I pulled my shirt up to cover my nose and mouth. Suppressed coughs fought their way up my throat, leaving me gasping for breath as I stumbled across the floor. The door to the kitchen was a wall of fire, tongues of flame licking up the wall and across the ceiling, and I shied away, keeping low and pressing close to the far wall as I pulled myself toward the front door. Just a little farther…and a little more…and then I lunged forward, wrenching on the doorknob with all my might.

It didn't budge. I yanked at the door, tears of panic and confusion burning my eyes before I realized the locks were set.

I threw the deadbolt and flung the heavy door open wide, practically falling down the front steps into the yard. The air was cool and blessedly fresh, but I was coughing so hard I couldn't even pull the clean air I needed into my lungs.

I scrambled as far from the house as I could, falling to my knees in the yard.

Call for help.

I reached down, struggling to wrestle my phone from my pocket, but the shrill sound of sirens already filled the air. I turned, glancing back one last time to see flames engulfing the roof of the house I'd spent the majority of my adult life in. The house where I'd raised my son. My home.

What the hell am I going to do now?

The phone dropped from my trembling fingers as I collapsed onto my back in the damp grass. The star-studded sky swung drunkenly above me for a moment before my eyes drifted shut.

CHAPTER 2

JEREMY

*T*he seatbelt sign finally went dark when the plane came to a stop at the terminal, and I blew out a sigh. Atlanta was one of my least favorite airports, but it was my final layover before Indianapolis. I couldn't wait to be home.

Don't get me wrong—I've always loved to travel. Loved seeing new places and meeting new people. Having a job that regularly sent me around the globe for gallery shows and book signings was pretty much the most awesome thing in the world. But a small part of me, a part I would never admit to another living soul, always feels a wave of relief when I board the plane to come home. Back to Fairfield, Indiana, to my house, and my bed, and my kid.

It'd been a lot easier when I was young and single, and all I'd cared about was the next exotic location and the next beautiful woman I could paint there. And maybe do more than paint.

Of course, early thirties was still young, and I was still decidedly single, but a lot has changed since Dylan showed up. At this point, any time at all away from the kid was hard enough, let alone two months with only video calls that were limited by his non-existent attention span. The book tour had been a success, taking me to all the major cities up and down both coasts, but I was ready to be home. Besides, I would owe Jeanne big time for two months of single parenting.

Actually, I wasn't even due back for two more days. But one of the signings had been rescheduled, freeing me up early, and my personal assistant had managed to find a last-minute flight home.

I fished my phone out of my pocket as I waited for the flight attendant to let us disembark, and flipped it out of airplane mode. The screen lit up with a flurry of notifications. Speak of the devil...

The messages were all from Olivia, my PA, her tone increasingly urgent as I scrolled through.

1:32pm: *Hey, when was the last time you were on social media?*

2:17pm: *I know you're still on the plane, but give me a call when you land.*

2:19pm: *Everything's fine, by the way, don't freak out.*

2:45pm: *Call me BEFORE you check anything.*

2:50pm: *Have you landed yet?*

Of course, the first thing I did was check social media. I tapped my finger over the tiny icon and my recent posts filled the screen—photos from the convention centers, my own smiling face posing for signatures with happy fans, a stack of my books displayed on a bookstore endcap, the view from the airline window as I'd flown over the mountains from one location to another.

I tapped on the most recent image, posted only that morning—a teaser photo of a new painting, with a suggestion in the caption that even though the book tour was over, new work would be coming soon. Comments stretched out below the photo, and as I read the first one, my thumb froze over the screen.

Don't support this pervert!

Wait, what?

The comment below was no better.

There are plenty of other artists that don't molest their subjects. Buy art from them instead!

What the hell—?

The next comment was even less enlightening, but more troubling. Just, *PEDOPHILE.*

I clicked back and scrolled down to the next photo, an image of myself next to a smiling girl who was holding up a copy of the book I'd just signed for her.

The first comment took my breath away.

Hope he doesn't rape her!

I closed the app then shut off my phone, shoving it in my pocket and grabbing my bag before joining the line in the aisle waiting to disembark. My fingers itched with the need to call Olivia, but this seemed like a conversation better saved for a more private location.

My layover was a long one, so rather than hurry to the other concourse, I sought out a quiet corner of an empty gate and dropped into one of the chairs there. My phone was in my hand before my bag hit the floor, a call to Olivia ringing in my ear.

No answer. Seriously, all those messages and now she couldn't answer her damn phone? Rather than put my phone away and wait for her call like I knew I should, I opened a different app. Notifications filled the screen. Unable to stop myself, I scrolled through them. My name had been tagged in hundreds of different posts, and I thumbed down the list.

#JeremyWhitaker I thought you were better than that.

I always thought there was something off about you. Now I know what it is. #JeremyWhitaker

Stop violence against women! #JeremyWhitaker

On and on it went, and my palms grew sweaty as I scrolled. What the hell was I supposed to have *done*?

Midway down the page, another post caught my eye.

Speak out against abusers! Justice for Emilia Martinez! #JeremyWhitaker

Emilia Martinez? The name was only vaguely familiar, and it took me a minute to place it. Was she—?

Shutting off my phone again, I dropped it on the seat next to me and reached down to drag my carry-on bag closer. I unzipped the side pocket, pulled out a copy of my book, and flipped it open. After two months on tour, I'd spent so much time staring at the cover I was sick to death of the image my publishers had chosen to plaster over the front—a close-up of a painting I'd done of one of my old girlfriends, Caroline. But I hadn't actually looked through the interior in months.

I ran my finger down the table of contents, searching for…there it was. Emilia. Page seventy-six. I flipped through.

While I'd always been an artist, and had dabbled here and there with writing, this book had been my first foray into combining my talents. It consisted of high-res, glossy images of many of my favorite paintings—mostly women, but not all —accompanied by short stories and poems inspired by the artwork.

I turned to page seventy-six, though I already knew what was there. The painting of Emilia stretched the full width and height of the page. It was a good one, not as refined as my current work, but I'd been proud of it.

Emilia had been posing for the painting, but there was no way the viewer would know she wasn't asleep. Stretched out on her stomach, the vivid red of the sheet sliced across her body, covering her from her waist to midway down her thighs. One arm raised above her head, the other tucked in close to her chest, and her face visible only in profile, dark lashes cutting across one high cheekbone, lips painted as bright a red as the sheet. Her hair was a tangled mass of rich brown curls spread over her head like a halo, and the multi-colored brushstrokes of my signature style gave the whole thing a soft, diffuse quality, as if the scene were being viewed through a pane of textured glass.

Every detail, every brushstroke—from the slight smiling curve of her lips to the dip in the fabric of the sheet across her waist—spoke of a woman who had finally fallen asleep after a long and satisfying night in her lover's arms. And while that may be true of any number of the other women in this book, it hadn't been for this one. This painting had been carefully posed and then painted from a photograph. Hell, I hadn't even done more than shake her hand.

I stared at the image and the accompanying poem, waiting as if the painting could explain to me what was going on, when my phone rang loudly from the seat next to me. My heart gave a startled thump in my chest and I slammed shut the book in my lap, jerking the phone up to my ear.

"Liv?"

"Jeremy," came my assistant's breathless voice. "Sorry I missed you; I stepped out for literally one minute."

"What the hell is going on?" I barked into the phone.

"Shit, you went online, didn't you? I *told* you to wait until we talked."

"Well, you didn't answer when I called," I accused, ignoring the fact that I'd checked before I'd even tried to call her. "Anyway, seriously, what the *hell* is going on?"

It was a good thing I was at a deserted gate, because I was having a hard time keeping my voice down.

There was the sound of a door closing in the background, and then Olivia's voice returned louder than before. "Okay, from what I can gather, it all started with Emilia Martinez—the sleeping girl painting from your book."

I growled in acknowledgment and she hurried on. "Anyway, she recently celebrated her birthday and posted a bunch of pictures from the party. It seems someone did the math and pointed out that she would have been underage when you did that painting a few years ago. It blew up from there."

"That's not possible," I said. "You know I always have the models sign release forms. Her age will be on there."

"I know." Olivia sighed. "But it's an older one, and I'm having trouble tracking it down."

"What do you mean? Scott has them all on file." I was admittedly not the best with paperwork, but between my PA and my lawyer, I didn't *need* to be.

"I *know*," she responded testily. "I've already called Scott and left a message. As soon as he gets back to me, I'll get it all straightened out and it'll go away. That's why I wanted to talk to you first, so you wouldn't freak out."

"I'm not freaking out," I grumbled, a bit louder than necessary.

"Obviously," she said. "Anyway, one last thing. I don't want you to do anything before I get hold of Scott, okay? Don't post anything online, don't answer anyone, until I get this straightened out."

"What?" My voice bordered on a shout. "I didn't do anything wrong. And you're saying I can't even defend myself?"

"Look, just let me talk to your lawyer first, okay? I'm sure he'll return my call today. Let me get some proof before you go posting all over the internet. Alright?"

I didn't answer.

"*Alright?*" she said again.

I could see her point, even though I didn't like it. Without that release form, it was my word against hers. "Fine," I ground out. "But make it fast."

"I'm on it," she said.

I sighed. "Thanks, Liv. Sorry to yell at you; you know you're the best, right?"

She laughed. "Just keep calm, okay? I'll take care of it."

I hung up the phone, then immediately dialed Scott's number, growling when it went to voicemail as expected. I didn't bother leaving a message; if Olivia said she was on it, then she was. I shoved the phone into my pocket and the book back into my bag, zipping it with a little more force than was strictly necessary.

With any luck this would all blow over before anyone important got wind of it.

CHAPTER 3

JEANNE

The next time I awoke, it was to the unfamiliar sound of beeping machines, sterile white walls, and a thankfully familiar face bending over me.

"Bria?" My voice was so rough and raw I barely recognized it as my own.

A grin stretched across the face of the blue-haired nurse and she straightened. "About time you woke up. Your brother's been driving me crazy."

I winced, shifting in the bed. "Sam's been here?" I didn't actually have a brother, but my ex-brother-in-law was the closest thing I'd ever had to a sibling, and we'd remained close despite the divorce.

Bria nodded, fiddling with the IV that I only then noticed was hooked up to my left arm. "Sam, and Geoff, and Ellen stopped by, too."

"Good lord, how long have I been out?" I asked.

She laughed. "Not long at all. Word travels fast around here. How are you feeling?" she asked, coming around the side of the bed to peer into my eyes.

I did a quick assessment.

"Well, my throat doesn't feel great," I said, swallowing experimentally and wincing. "And I'm tired, and my head hurts. But otherwise…" I shrugged. "I feel okay."

Bria nodded. "Your throat hurts from the smoke, but luckily we didn't have to intubate you. It looks like you got out before there was any real damage, and you're going to be fine. We'll let these fluids move through," she nodded to the IV, "and then we'll take you down to get some X-rays, but if everything looks good, the doc probably won't keep you here long."

"Thank God," I sighed, then glanced at her. "No offense. Not that I don't enjoy your company, Bria. Just maybe under…other circumstances."

She snorted. "None taken. I'm just glad you're okay. I sure didn't like seeing you coming in on the stretcher."

I shuddered, and Bria's brow creased. "Do you have somewhere to stay? Anyone you want to call?"

That's right. I'd practically forgotten what had brought me here in the first place. "My house…" I murmured.

Technically, it hadn't been my house, just a rental. But I'd moved in after the divorce six years ago, intending for it to be temporary, and had somehow never gotten around to moving out. The place had been conveniently close to work, and had been a good fit for Dylan and me.

Bria looked at me sympathetically. "They got the fire put out after the paramedics came, but I guess it wasn't salvageable. I'm so sorry."

Not salvageable. My God—six years of my life, wiped away just like that. All my clothes, Dylan's clothes, his toys, my furniture—

"Hey, none of that," Bria scolded gently. "I can hear your silent freak-out from here. Take it easy, and deal with it all one step at a time, okay?"

I nodded, trying to take her advice and calm myself down

with a few deep breaths. I gave up when I realized it hurt like a bitch.

"What time is it, anyway?" I asked.

"Six-twenty," she replied. "In the morning. And your phone is here on the table; the paramedics found it in the grass." She nudged it within reach. "I'm going to let you rest for now. You can hit the button if you need anything, alright?"

I nodded again and she backed out with another quick reassuring smile. Groaning, I let my head fall back against the pillow. Who to call first? Not my in-laws, not yet. They would all still be sleeping, and I didn't want to worry Dylan at that point. I also needed to call into the office to let Tris know I wouldn't be in and ask her to reschedule my appointments, but she wouldn't be there for another forty minutes yet.

The phone began to buzz on the table next to me, the vibrations shaking it toward the edge, and I picked it up before it could fall to the floor. I checked the display and felt my heart warm a little. Well, at least that would keep me from having to figure out who to call first.

"Hey, babe," I answered in my hoarse, grinding voice.

"Jesus, Jeanne, are you okay?" Mark's worry was clear through the line.

"I'm fine," I reassured him. "It sounds worse than it is. How did you know I was here?"

"Sam called me. Are you sure you're okay? Can I come down there?"

"No, no," I interjected. "I'm fine, I promise. Don't cancel your plans. The nurse said they won't keep me here long anyway, and I've got to find somewhere to stay."

Just then there was a quiet knock on the door, and Sam poked his head around the frame. He stepped through, relief clear on his face as he saw I was awake, and I held up the phone, gesturing at him to give me a second. He nodded and took a seat in the corner.

"You can stay with me," Mark was saying. "I've got plenty of room, and I can come get you and help you get settled in. Anything you need."

His offer was tempting—between him moving and our crazy schedules I hadn't had many chances to see him recently, and his new rental apartment was spacious, but...

"No, Mark, thank you, that's really sweet of you, but I can't. It's too far from work and Dylan's school, and I need to take care of everything here with the house. I can't move all the way out to Glassbury."

"Are you sure? It'd be expensive to stay at a hotel, and I—"

My thoughts tumbled over themselves as Mark made his case. He was right; I did need to find somewhere to stay. I definitely couldn't move out to Glassbury with him, but Sam's place wasn't big enough for me, especially since his girlfriend Ellen had all but moved in, and I certainly didn't want to stay with my ex-in-laws. I could barely tolerate them for the length of a dinner, let alone live in their house. I supposed I could stay with Carly, but honestly, what I really wanted was a little time to myself to process everything that had happened. Hmm...

An idea occurred to me. It wasn't ideal, not by a long shot, but it might still be my best option.

"It's okay, Mark," I cut him off gently. "I've already got it figured out. I'm going to stay at Jeremy's house."

There was a moment of silence.

"Your ex-husband?"

"Yes."

"Well, I can't say I'm thrilled about that idea."

"You don't have anything to worry about," I assured him. "He's not even there right now, and the place is big enough that I wouldn't even need to see him if he were. Besides, I don't have to stay long." I could stay just for a day or two, I thought, warming up to the idea. I could clear my head and get my feet under me, then leave to go stay with Carly before he even got back.

His disappointed sigh sounded loud over the line, but I hoped he was just worried about me, and not genuinely upset. I knew he trusted me and what I thought was best, and it was so refreshing being with an actual adult I felt like I wanted to crawl through the line and give him a hug.

"Are you sure he won't mind?" Mark asked.

"I'm sure. He already said it was fine." Well, that was a lie, but Jeremy *would* say it was fine, and there was no need for Mark to worry.

"Okay. Well, if you need *anything* you call me, alright?"

"I will, I promise."

I ended the call and looked up to see Sam's raised eyebrows. I'd almost forgotten he was there.

He didn't even wait for me to speak. "You're gonna stay with *Jeremy*?" His voice was thick with incredulity. "In what parallel universe do you think that's a good idea?"

"It *is* a good idea," I said, pushing myself further up in the bed. "It's close to work, close to your parents, and it'll just be for a few days. He's not even *there*."

"Uh-huh. You also told Mark Jeremy said it was fine, which I'm guessing is not exactly accurate."

"Well, I'm sure he *will* say that when I ask him," I said. "The house is just sitting there empty, and I'll leave before he gets back."

"Where will you go then?" Sam asked.

I yawned, my eyelids beginning to grow heavy. "I'll go stay with Carly or something. I'll figure it out."

He crossed the room, then leaned over the bed to wrap me in a bear hug. "You know my place is always open to you, too. And hey, don't you *ever* fucking scare me like that again."

I smiled and returned the hug.

* * *

I'd only been to Jeremy's house a handful of times to pick up or drop off Dylan, and each time I'd managed to forget how completely ridiculous the place was. I mean, even the word mansion wasn't an adequate description—it was practically an estate. Okay, that might be an exaggeration, but regardless, it was a completely unrealistic and over-the-top house for a single guy and his shared-custody child.

But Jeremy was nothing if not impulsive, and it showed in every detail of the place—from the full five-car garage (and who needed five cars in a town you could drive across in twenty minutes?), to the restaurant-quality kitchen (for a guy who didn't cook), to the enormous jacuzzi bathtub in the lavish master bathroom (okay, I wasn't complaining about that one).

Jeremy had given me a spare key for emergencies, but it, like everything else I owned, had been lost in the fire, so Sam had given me a ride over and let me in with his. He offered to stay and help me get settled, but I promised him I would be fine. They'd kept me in the hospital for most of the day, and in all honesty, I was starting to feel a little overwhelmed. Each new minute that passed brought with it a thought of something else I needed to take care of.

I no longer had a driver's license, or a stitch of clothing beyond the smoke-infused pajamas I wore. My car had been in the garage, and had been destroyed as well. I no longer had keys, or a computer. No furniture, no dishes, no books. Everything I owned, lost in the space of a few hours. It was completely overwhelming.

All I had was my phone, and thanks to Sam and a trip by the bank on the way over, I had a debit card again. I also had a promise from Ellen that she would be available all the following day for clothes shopping and any other errands I might need her for. It was reassuring, but after hours at the hospital, many of which were spent on the phone with work and insurance companies and my ex-in-laws—or dealing with a helpful but overenthusiastic social worker—at that moment what I really needed was some time alone to finish freaking out.

Fortunately, Jeremy wouldn't be back for two more days, which gave me plenty of time to figure out what the hell to do.

I still needed to let him know I was here, but I decided I would call him in the morning. I was peopled out for the time being, and anyway, what he didn't know wouldn't hurt him.

With the house sitting empty for the last two months, I wasn't surprised to find the fridge was a barren wasteland. Although I was guessing things hadn't changed that much since we'd been married, so it was likely this was its normal state. Either way, I was glad to find the number of a pizza place that delivered tucked under a magnet on the side of the fridge, and I ordered way more pizza than I could possibly consume and stress ate my way through the majority of it.

Feeling marginally better with a full stomach, I decided the next item on the docket was to get out of those smoky clothes and take a bath. Carting a tall glass of wine I'd stolen from an unopened bottle in the wine cooler along with me, I scoped out the guest bathroom adjacent to the room I'd claimed for myself, and decided that there was absolutely no way I could let the enormous jacuzzi tub in the master bath go to waste. Besides, there was no one here to care.

Honestly, I thought as I dragged myself down the plush carpeted hall towards the master, *this place is just too big*. I couldn't imagine how Jeremy didn't feel lonely living here by himself. Though to be fair, his dating life was probably much more active than mine had been over the past few years, and who knows how much time he *actually* spent 'alone.'

The tub in the master bath certainly wasn't meant for one —and I shuddered to think who else had been in here—but the thought didn't dissuade me from setting the taps to scalding and adding in a liberal amount of scented bubbles.

Besides, the man I'd married had been a slob, and judging by the pristine state of this bathroom—perfectly folded fluffy white towels, scented candles on the double vanity, even the light fixtures polished to a high gleam—he clearly had a housekeeper overseeing the place, which definitely helped reduce the ick factor.

I took full advantage, lighting the candles and helping myself to the scented soaps and lotions in the basket on the vanity, before piling my blond hair on top of my head and sinking neck deep into the bubbles with a blissful sigh.

A huge picture window stretched out to the side of the tub, and I gazed out over the woods behind the house, where the sun was setting and casting rays of red and orange and purple across the cloudless sky. It looked like a painting, and while I certainly didn't think the beauty of the moment was worth the loss of my house and property, well…it was still gorgeous.

Lifting my wine glass from the marble ledge that surrounded the tub, I took a long drink, then settled deeper into the bubbles, closed my eyes, and let the hot water begin to work its magic on my sore muscles. Tomorrow I had endless tasks and worries to crowd my mind, but for that night, I would just sink into the water and enjoy one of the few perks of having such an impulsive, pretentious, and overly extravagant ex-husband.

CHAPTER 4

JEREMY

*G*od, I thought the second flight would never end. I tried not to look at my phone—knowing I couldn't respond to defend myself made scrolling through the slanderous comments and watching more appear in real time as I clicked through my various accounts absolute torture—but I couldn't seem to stop myself. Finally, the flight attendant reminded me with a pointed glare that all phones should be in airplane mode, and I forced myself to turn the damn thing off and tuck it away.

Instead, I spent the entire flight staring out the window, trying not to think about what was happening online. With any luck, Olivia would get hold of Scott while I was in the air. Then the two of them would get the whole thing under control, and it would be over by morning.

God, I hoped so. Building a good reputation in the art world was hard work, and I really didn't want it all ruined over a stupid misunderstanding.

Despite the drama that was ruining the tail end of what had actually been a very successful book tour, I couldn't wait to get home. The last I'd spoken to Jeanne, she'd told me

Dylan would be at my parents' house when I got home. I hadn't bothered to let anyone know I'd be returning early, but regardless, it would be nice to be able to pick him up from my parents' and avoid the inevitable confrontation with Jeanne.

Not that we had anything to actually argue about. We barely spoke as it was. But somehow, we always managed to find something. It seemed like the most innocuous comment from me could set her off, and she seemed to have a talent at getting under my skin as well. No, avoiding her was always the easier route.

To my relief, thinking about Dylan and being home managed to distract me from worries about my reputation, and when the plane taxied into the gate and the seatbelt sign finally blinked off, I didn't even jump for my phone first thing. All I wanted was to get home, take a shower, and relax.

Hmm. I wouldn't even mind some company while I relaxed.

I supposed I could call Susan. She was a substitute teacher at Fairfield Middle School, and she was always game to come over and hang out. But then again, I'd seen her shortly before I'd left on the tour, and I didn't want to give her the wrong impression. Better to keep things strictly casual.

My other local option was Karina, who worked at the antique store downtown, but she was out of town caring for a sick relative.

I rolled my eyes. I was a grown man; I could manage a night alone. Especially after two months on the road, and considering everything that was happening online, my heart wasn't really in it.

Besides, what I really wanted, even more than companionship, was that shower.

My legs were stiff as I wheeled my carry-on down the aisle and made my way through the crowded terminal down to baggage claim, where I had to wait another small eternity for my bag to arrive. I checked my phone for missed calls or texts while I waited—none—but managed to keep myself from logging into any apps.

Eventually my bag showed up, and then finally I was on my way home. I switched the radio on in my car, turning the volume up and letting the thumping bass drown out the noise in my head for the hour-and-a-half drive to Fairfield.

By the time I pulled off the highway and wound through town to the quiet neighborhood where my house perched on a ridge of land overlooking the forest, I was travel-weary and more than ready to be home. When I rounded the bend in the road and my house finally came into view, it was a sight for sore eyes.

To be fair, I didn't exactly *need* a three-story house with a fully finished basement and media room, or an expansive in-ground pool and tennis court. But I hadn't bought the house for the size, and contrary to popular belief, I hadn't bought it to show off how much money I had, either.

Nope—I'd bought it for the view.

Because the back wall of the house faced southwest, over the ridge toward the state park, and every single one of the huge windows along that side of the house gave the most spectacular view of the forest. Especially at that moment, with the sun setting over the treetops and painting the sky in swaths of cotton candy pinks and bright, fiery oranges and reds, broken only by the jagged edges of clouds. That view was one of the few things that made living in such a tiny town bearable. You simply didn't get views like this in the cities, and the paintings I'd done of the view out the bedroom window were some of the best I'd ever done. Not that I showed those ones to anyone though—landscapes were much harder to sell than the portraits I was known for.

Tearing my gaze away from the amazing sunset, I left

the car in the drive and hauled my bags out of the trunk, lugging them up the path and through the front door, where I left them in a pile in the front hallway. I'd deal with them later; at that moment, all I wanted was that shower and maybe a cold beer and a mindless action movie.

I stretched my arms up over my head as I climbed the stairs, working out the kinks in my back, then pulled my shirt off and tossed it in the hamper before making a beeline for the bathroom.

I'd pulled the door halfway open before it really registered that it was closed in the first place. *Was that...perfume?* I only had a split second to register the lit candles and the discarded clothing in the corner before my gaze zeroed in on the naked woman in my bathtub.

What the f— "Jeanne?!"

Her ear-splitting shriek sent me stumbling back, and when my foot met with a puddle of water on the floor my legs skidded out from under me and I went down hard, bashing the back of my head on the side of the vanity.

Spots danced in my vision, and I blinked hard, working to keep myself from passing out.

I stayed there for a long moment, waiting for the dizziness to abate and willing my head not to split open from the pain in my skull. In the background, I was only vaguely aware of the sound of sloshing water as the intruder climbed out of the tub and wrapped one of my towels around herself.

Good, she was coming over to help me up, and probably to apologize for trying to kill me. But when her upside-down face loomed over me, for some reason her expression didn't seem overly apologetic.

"What the hell are you doing here?" she yelled, and I winced as the shrill sound pierced my head.

"Me?" I retorted, staring at her like she was crazy. Which

she obviously was. "This is *my* house. What the hell are *you* doing here?"

"You weren't supposed to be home for *days*," she said, ignoring my completely reasonable question. "Why didn't you call me if you knew you were coming back early?"

"Well, I didn't exactly know you'd be camping out in my house now, did I?" I eyed her from the floor. "Is this what you do when I'm out of town? Crash at my house and use my tub? I know this place is fancy, but that's pretty creepy, Jeanne."

She rolled her eyes. "Oh my God, get over yourself. I don't care about your dumb 'fancy' house. And I don't crash here when you're gone."

Of course, I knew she didn't, but it was so hard not to try to get a rise out of her. Especially when she was standing there, pale hair wet and grey eyes flashing, bubbles still sticking to her damp skin, and with her towel wrapped in a way that I could almost see—

Whoa, hold up there, dude. That ship has sailed.

I forced my eyes back up to her face.

"Well, if you don't want to tell me what you're doing in my house, you could at least help me off the floor and say you're sorry for almost giving me a concussion," I said.

She scoffed. "Please. *You* nearly gave *me* a heart attack. And you're not even hurt; you're just playing it up." But she knelt down anyway, and wedged her free hand that wasn't holding up the towel around my elbow to help pull me up to sit.

My head swam again as I leaned against the vanity. When I felt her hand stiffen under my elbow, I glanced questioningly at her, then followed her gaze down to the smear of blood I'd left on the floor. Gingerly I reached up to feel at the back of my head, and winced when my fingers came away bloody.

"Oh, shit," she whispered. "I'm sorry, Jer. Let me take a look."

I almost smiled at the sound of the nickname on her lips —no one else but Jeanne had ever called me that, and I hadn't heard it in six years—but then her hands were on my head, pulling me away from the vanity so she could take a look, and I winced again as her fingers prodded at the wound in my scalp.

"Ow," I exclaimed, pulling away from her.

"Hold still," she scolded. "I can't see."

"You don't have to pull my hair to see," I complained. "Use your eyes. Ow."

"Oh hush, you big baby. Seriously."

"Did you come over to injure me and insult me, or was there another reason you decided to bless me with your presence this evening?"

She huffed. "It's not bad," she said, ignoring my question. "Just a little cut. It's already stopped bleeding. Let me clean it up and you won't even need a bandage."

"It's fine," I said through gritted teeth as she continued to prod at the back of my head. "I was going to take a shower, anyway; I'll wash it out in there."

"You sure you won't pass out?" she asked, eyeing me skeptically. "It would be just like you to fall in the shower and bash your head a second time."

I glared at her. "How would that be 'just like me?'"

She rolled her eyes. "It'd be just like you to not admit you weren't feeling well enough, then pass out and inconvenience everyone around you by making them take you to the hospital."

I spluttered in indignation. "Look, I don't even know what you're doing here. What the hell do you—" I broke off when I saw the sparkle in her eyes and realized belatedly that she was goading me, the same way I had been to her.

She snorted. "Sorry, you make it too easy."

I heaved an exasperated sigh, pushing off the vanity to stand. My head still ached a little, but I wasn't dizzy any longer. "Just get out of here so I can shower, and then you can tell me what the hell is going on."

She smirked, but did as I asked, reaching over to let the water drain out of the tub. I did *not* notice the way her towel rode up when she bent over, exposing a swath of creamy skin on the back of her thighs.

She grabbed a wineglass I hadn't noticed from the lip of the tub and made her way out of the room, closing the door firmly behind her.

And I got into my much-needed shower, washed the grime of travel from my skin, and tried very hard not to think about how affected I was by the sight of my ex-wife in a towel.

* * *

When I resurfaced again a short while later, feeling marginally more human, my curiosity was at an all-time high. Jeanne and I didn't get along on the best of days, and we hadn't spent any serious time together in years, outside of family events. I couldn't begin to imagine what she was doing here. I knew it didn't have anything to do with Dylan —she would have led with that immediately—but when I tried to think of other options, I drew a blank.

I dried off quickly and wrapped the towel around my waist, then stepped out of the steam-filled bathroom into the bedroom, and stopped dead.

I knew she wouldn't have left completely without letting me know, but I definitely hadn't expected to find her sitting cross-legged in the center of my bed, still wearing nothing but my damned towel.

The sun had set, and the only light in the room came from the small lamp on the bedside table, which cast its subtle glow over her flushed skin. I took in the warm tint of her skin, a tendril of golden hair curling damply against one cheek, the swell of her breast just visible over the top of the towel, the deep bruised-purple shadow of her body cast long over my bedspread, and felt an overwhelming desire to paint her.

But then I remembered exactly who I was dealing with, and mercilessly squashed the feeling. Instead, I exclaimed, "What the hell, Jeanne, are you trying to seduce me or something? Because I thought we'd already decided nothing good came of that."

She jerked her head up to face me. "Holy shit, Jeremy, are you delusional? Of course I'm not trying to seduce you!"

I shrugged and raised an eyebrow. "I'm just saying... you're sitting here, on my bed, in a towel. What's a guy supposed to think?"

Her eyes narrowed. "I'm sitting here in a towel because I don't have any clothes. I didn't want to borrow some of yours without asking."

My brow creased in confusion. "You don't have any clothes? What did you do, show up naked?"

"No, you idiot, I just—" She broke off, and I watched as the anger drained out of her, replaced by an emotion I couldn't quite identify. Sadness?

I sighed and gentled my voice. "Come on, Jeanne, spit it out. What's going on?"

"My house burned down."

"Your—*what?*"

"My house burned down," she repeated.

I crossed to the bed and sat on the edge, frantically checking her over. "What the—holy *fuck*, are you okay?"

"I'm fine, I'm fine," she said, waving away my concern.

"They treated me at the hospital for smoke inhalation, but everything's okay, they let me go. But…" she shrugged, not meeting my eyes. "I lost everything, and I didn't know where to go."

"Why the hell didn't you tell me that in the first place?" I exploded. "Smoke inhalation? My God, why didn't you call me? What can I do? What do you need?"

"Calm down, Jeremy, seriously, I'm fine. I didn't call you because one—you weren't here, and two—it's not your job anymore. We're not married. Or dating." She gave me a look. "Or anything."

Her words gave me pause, as I remembered—"Hey, that's right. Aren't you dating someone? That dentist guy—what was his name? Marvin?"

"Mark," she said with a withering look, and I hid my grin, because of course I knew his name was Mark.

"Seriously though, why didn't you go to his place?"

"Because he lives over in Glassbury, and he's renting a place right now while he sets up his practice and gets settled," she said. "Besides, this place is closer to work, and I was only going to stay here for a day or two to get my feet under me."

"Hmm, that's a lot of reasons not to stay with the guy. Not having trouble in paradise already, are you?" I blinked wide eyes at her, and she glared at me.

"No, everything is fine. It just made more sense to stay here."

"Doesn't he care that you're staying with your ex-husband? Sounds awfully trusting, if you ask me. Maybe too trusting. How does he know I won't take advantage of you? I mean, your first night here, and already here you are on my bed. In a towel." I waggled my eyebrows, and she clenched her jaw.

"Careful, Jeanne," I said with a smile. "I thought dentists knew better than to grind their teeth."

"Oh my *God*," she exploded. "How the hell did I ever put up with you? How does *anyone* put up with you? Seriously, I wouldn't have come here at all if I'd known—"

"Uh, Jeanne," I tried to interrupt.

"—known you were going to be a *dick*, but that's all—"

"*Jeanne*," I cleared my throat and looked at her meaningfully.

"WHAT?" Her glare could have frozen lava. "Am I grinding my teeth again?" she asked, sarcasm dripping from her tone.

I cleared my throat again. "Nope. Just thought you might want to fix your towel. Not that I'm complaining about the view, but seeing as how you have a *boyfriend* and all, I thought—"

Her growl cut me off, her face flushing scarlet as she glanced down and then abruptly jerked her towel back up to cover the curve of her exposed breast.

"You are *such* a dick," she repeated.

"How am I a dick?" I asked innocently. "I was just trying to preserve your modesty. You should be thanking me."

As much fun as it was to rile her up, I was afraid I was about to see steam leaking from her ears, so I pushed off the bed and crossed to the giant walk-in closet to get dressed.

"Seriously though, of course you should have come here," I told her.

"No, I'm sorry to impose," she said. "I was going to call you in the morning to let you know, and I'd planned to leave before you got back. I can go stay with Carly."

I paused and turned toward her again. "You should stay here. The house is more than big enough for both of us. You can stay as long as you want, and I'll help with anything you need while you get everything sorted out." I paused, watching the play of light on her features, then said softly,

"I'm sorry you had to go through that. It must've been really scary. I'm glad you're okay."

She opened her mouth, but shut it again without responding, so I turned back toward the closet. I shut the door as I pulled on some boxers and a pair of sweat pants, then re-emerged holding a clean t-shirt. "You can stay in any of the guest rooms, and help yourself to one of the cars," I said, pulling the shirt over my head. "Is there anything you need for tonight?"

She looked at me with an exasperated sigh, but I didn't miss the hint of a smile that ghosted over her face.

"How about some clothes?"

CHAPTER 5

JEANNE

*J*eremy hadn't changed a bit. He'd always had the ability to make me crazy in a way no one else ever managed. He had a talent for saying exactly the right thing to get under my skin, but then in the next breath he'd turn around and say something sweet and caring, and I'd never known whether to rip his head off or kiss him.

Kissing him was off the table though, so at least I knew where I stood.

Fortunately, after providing me with a pair of sweats and a t-shirt that came down past my thighs, as well as an unopened toothbrush, he left me alone and I was able to flee to the safety of one of the spare bedrooms before I actually did rip his head off. I didn't know why I let him get to me— half of what he said was obviously intended to get a rise out of me, and yet I kept giving him the satisfaction of riling me up.

Fortunately, I'd been right though, and the house really was big enough that I barely even had to see him if I didn't want to. As long as I kept myself from noticing how my borrowed clothes smelled like him—and how familiar that smell was, all cedar and coffee with the undertone of linseed oil—I could pretend I was here alone, just as I'd intended to be.

* * *

Other than when Dylan had been an infant and had kept us awake at all hours, I wasn't sure I'd ever seen Jeremy awake before noon. And sure enough, that also didn't seem to have changed in the intervening years.

There wasn't a peep from his end of the hallway as I got myself up and, well, not dressed, but ready to go at least. Ellen met me at the door at eight o'clock sharp, her dark auburn hair pulled back in a ponytail, and her low whistle when I let her in echoed around the massive foyer.

"This place is ridiculous," she said. "I never believed Sam when he described it."

"It's fitting," I told her, "because Jeremy is ridiculous too."

She grinned and held out a duffle bag. "I brought you a change of clothes. Not that you don't look great in sweats, but I thought maybe you might not want to wear your ex's pajamas out in public."

I had to stop myself from throwing my arms around her. "Holy shit, El, you are *amazing.*"

Twenty minutes later, dressed much more comfortably in a pair of Ellen's jeans and a loose top, I grabbed my cell phone and debit card—the only two things I owned—and we made our way out to the car.

"No lingering effects from the fire?" she asked as we drove into town. "You feeling okay?"

"Yeah, I'm fine today. My throat isn't sore anymore, and the headache cleared up."

"That's good. And Jeremy's not giving you too much trouble?"

I laughed. "Well, yeah, of course he's giving me trouble, but no, he said I could stay as long as I want. My car was in the garage at the house, so it's a total loss, and he's even going to let me use one of his cars until I can get mine replaced. Not that I'm going to stay a second longer than necessary, though. I've already called about my renter's insurance and about the car."

"So, what's the plan for today then?" she asked.

"Well, I've got to go to the BMV to replace my driver's license, and I need to stop by work to make sure everything is covered there." I ticked the list off on my fingers. "I also need to get the fire report from the fire department, and get that to the insurance company, and then get permission to go back to the house and see if anything is salvageable. I need to get my mail forwarded, and look into replacing my passport and Dylan's birth certificate."

Ellen's green eyes were round. "Jeez, Jeanne, I'm so sorry. What a mess. Are you...how are you holding up?"

"I'm f—"

"I know you're fine," she cut in, her voice stern, but gentle, "but how are you, *really?* I mean, you seem to be holding it together remarkably well considering what happened."

I let my breath trickle out slowly. "I...I don't know, I guess. I'm trying to just keep going, you know? Not think too hard about it all. It's...a lot."

Her gaze was sympathetic. "I wish I could do more to help," she said.

"You're helping plenty," I told her. "Seriously, you don't even know how much I appreciate you."

She reached across the console and gave my shoulder a quick squeeze, and I shot her a grateful glance.

"Where are we headed first, then?" she asked.

"I think we should consider the order of importance." I pretended to mull it over. "So, first stop—clothes shopping."

Her face melted into a grin. "Good plan. Just say where."

* * *

Shopping with Ellen was almost enough to make me forget the stress I was under. She was like the sister I'd never had, and we'd clicked immediately when she'd showed up in town nearly a year earlier. I couldn't have asked for a better...ex-sister-in-law? No, that wasn't right because she and Sam weren't married. Yet. Well, whatever else she might be, she was a great friend. Light-hearted and carefree, sweet and loyal, and best of all, at least for today's outing, the artistic eye she had for everything else also translated to clothes.

Replacing an entire wardrobe in one shot was a bit too daunting, so we only hit a couple of stores and got me enough necessities to get through a week or two. After a quick stop for lunch and a not-so-quick stop at Geoff's bakery to load up on sugar, we swung by the BMV and the fire department before ending up at my office.

Tris, my receptionist, had already taken care of rescheduling all my appointments for the day, but there was always more to get done, and I craved the normalcy of being at work, where I could pretend that my life hadn't been suddenly turned upside-down.

"I'll be back in an hour to pick you up, okay?" Ellen said as she dropped me off, and I blew her a kiss through the window as she drove off.

"Oh my God, Jeanne, what are you doing here?" Tris exclaimed when I walked in. "Never mind; I should have known. You're probably the only person in the world who comes to work the day after her house burns down. Are you alright? We really do have everything under control, you know."

I laughed. "I know, I know. You guys could run the whole place without me. I just wanted to stop by. I needed something a little normal, you know?"

"Is that Dr. Halpern?" A voice sounded from the hallway, then Grace, one of my three hygienists, poked her head through the doorway to the reception area. Carly was hot on her heels, and raised her eyebrows when she saw me. "Seriously, Jeanne?"

I raised my hands, laughing. "If I'd known I was so unwelcome in my own practice, I wouldn't have come in."

Grace came around the counter and gave me a hug. "Are you okay? Tris told us everything."

I returned her hug, nodding as she released me. "I'm fine, I promise. Only a little shaken up." Maybe a lot shaken up, but I was trying hard not to let it affect me.

"And Dylan's alright? He was at Jeremy's parents, right?" Carly put in.

"Yes, he wasn't there. Jeremy's picking him up today."

"Where are you staying?" asked Tris. "Can we help you with anything?"

"No, I think I've got everything covered," I assured them. "I'm staying at Jeremy's for now."

You could have heard a pin drop in the silence that followed that statement, and I immediately regretted telling them. Grace was newer, but Carly and Tris had been with me since I'd opened the practice, and consequently, since the divorce.

Carly stepped close, and began examining my clothes.

"What are you doing?" I exclaimed, backing away from her.

"Just checking for bloodstains," she said. "If you're standing here, he must be dead. Otherwise, we'd be checking his yard for *your* body. But there's no way you both made it through a night under the same roof."

I laughed. "C'mon, you're overreacting. We're not *that* bad."

The looks the three of them exchanged implied that we were indeed that bad, but I ignored them. "Seriously, we can manage for a little while. Besides, Dylan will be there, so we'll have to behave. And his house is huge; I can completely avoid him if I want to."

Tris eyed me skeptically from where she leaned on the countertop. "So, you're telling me you spent last night at his house and there was no drama?"

"Well, I mean, maybe not *no* drama," I admitted, shifting my weight. "I *might* have been in his bathtub when he got home, and he *might* have fallen and cracked his head open on the vanity, and there *might* have been some yelling, but we both survived."

"You were in his *bathtub?*" Carly squeaked, eyebrows shooting up under her dark bangs.

"Hey, in my defense, he wasn't even supposed to be home last night. *I* thought he was still in California or Oregon or somewhere."

Tris snorted and glanced at the other two. "Who wants to place bets on how long it takes before they kill each other?"

"Two weeks," Grace offered.

"Ha. Two *days,*" Carly put in with a smirk.

"Hey," I interjected, but our conversation was cut short when the bell over the door chimed, announcing the arrival of a patient.

"Hi, Mrs. Winters," I greeted the older lady, sending a covert glare to the other three, before fleeing to the relative safety of my office.

I spent the next half hour dealing with the paperwork and bills spread out over my messy desk, then catching up on a few journal articles I'd been meaning to read. When the sound of the door chiming again filtered down the hallway I looked up in surprise. Had it really been an hour already?

But when I heard someone in the lobby laughing with Tris, the deep male voice definitely didn't belong to Ellen. I rose from my desk chair and headed out into the hallway.

"Mark!"

A warm smile creased his handsome face, his blue eyes crinkling under close-cropped blond hair. "Jeanne, I had a feeling I'd find you here. You're as much of a workaholic as I am," he teased, and Tris made a face at us both.

"C'mon back." I waited until he'd followed me into my office and the door was firmly shut behind us before letting him pull me into a warm hug. I wrapped my arms around his torso and breathed in the crisp, laundry-fresh smell of his shirt.

"What brings you all the way into Fairfield?" I asked once he'd released me and we'd both settled into chairs by the desk.

"I was worried about you," he said. "I didn't hear from you after you left the hospital, and I wanted to make sure you were really okay."

"Aw, that's sweet. You didn't have to come all this way though," I chastised, though I really was happy to see him. "You could've called."

"I know, but I wanted to see you."

"Well, I'm fine, I promise," I assured him, but he had turned in his chair and was glancing around the office.

"Plus, I've never seen your practice," he said. "Give me a tour?"

"Oh," I said, a little surprised. "Sure, I'll show you around. There's not much to see; it's a pretty standard dental office."

I led him out into the hallway. "Reception, you've seen, and you've met Tris at the desk. Over here are the three exam rooms, and the hygienists are Carly, Grace, and Marisol." I led him down the hallway. "You've seen my office, and here's the bathroom, supply room, sterilization room, lab, and there's a small staff break room at the back." I gestured down toward the end of the hall.

"It's a good-sized place," he observed, poking his head in the supply closet. "Bigger than I expected for just you. You've got room for more hygienists, too. Have you ever thought about expanding? Adding another dentist?"

I laughed and nudged him in the ribs. "Why, you want to come work here?"

He smiled at me. "Maybe. Why not?"

I opened my mouth, then closed it again. Why not? I'd never actually considered that.

He reached up, tucking a loose piece of hair behind my ear. "Just an idea. Something to think about. Anyway, the place looks great." He turned, leading the way back to my office, and I followed, mulling his words over in my head.

"Do you have time for dinner? We could go out?" he offered, but I shook my head.

"I'm sorry; I wish I could. But Ellen will be back to pick me up any minute now, and I want to be home when Jeremy picks up Dylan. I've talked to him about the fire, but I need to explain to him what it all means. I don't think he realizes half of his stuff is gone." I grimaced.

"Oh, I wanted to talk to you about that," Mark said, looking at me with concern. "Are you sure it's such a good idea for you to be staying with a guy like that?"

My brow furrowed in confusion. "A guy like what? Jeremy? He's a flighty artist, sure, but he can be responsible when he needs to be."

"Well, I just mean…are you sure it's safe? For you, or your son?"

As much as Jeremy drove me crazy, I still felt my spine

stiffen at Mark's words. "What are you talking about? Of course I'm *safe*. And Dylan—"

"You haven't been reading the news, then." Mark's mouth turned down in a worried frown.

"No, why?" I felt a rock start to form in the pit of my stomach.

"Your ex is involved in a bit of a scandal," he said. "It's all over social media."

"Well, that's hardly 'the news,' is it?" I grumbled, but I pulled out my phone anyway. I opened up one of the apps I hardly ever used and typed in Jeremy's name. "I don't know that I'd trust—oh my God."

It was a picture of one of Jeremy's self-portraits—the one that graced the dust jacket of his book, in fact—but the word "RAPIST" had been added in violent red right across his forehead. The painted letters dripped down his forehead in a way that uncomfortably resembled blood.

"What the hell *is* this?" I muttered, scrolling through the feed, but it was all accusations with no explanation.

My question hadn't been aimed at Mark directly, but he answered anyway. "It seems he's been accused of sleeping with a minor. And painting and publishing her likeness."

"Well, that's ridiculous," I snorted, glancing up at him. "Jeremy is a complete idiot, but he would never do that."

Mark shrugged, and the expression on his face seemed a little too close to pity for my liking. "It seems there's some pretty good evidence. But either way, I'm not sure I'm comfortable with you staying there."

I barely heard his words though, as I went to grab my brand new purse from the desk. "Look, I've got to go get all this sorted out."

I was halfway out of the office when I felt his hand on my arm. When I glanced at his face, I found his eyebrows pulled together.

"Jeanne, I'm sorry. I hope I didn't upset you. I just care about you, that's all."

I sighed. "I know, it's okay. It's not your fault. I'll get it straightened out."

"Are we still on for tomorrow night?" he asked.

"Absolutely," I said, pushing up on my toes to give him a kiss. "I'll see you then."

"Sounds good," he answered, and with another quick kiss I headed out of the office right as Ellen pulled up to the curb.

CHAPTER 6

JEREMY

$\mathcal{I}$n all the chaos of finding Jeanne in my bathtub and hitting my head, I'd been able to distract myself from the scandal. It wasn't until I received a completely non-informative text from Olivia shortly after ten o'clock the next morning—way too early, if you asked me —that the whole thing came crashing back.

> Olivia: *Sorry I didn't get back to you yesterday. I still haven't heard from Scott. Will keep you posted.*

And then less than a minute later—

> Olivia: *Oh, and stay off the internet!!!*

I snorted. I hardly thought that required *three* exclamation points, especially since I'd already told her I wouldn't post anything. I logged in though. Just to keep informed.

The self-portrait I'd used for my bio in the book was the first thing to fill my screen, and it took my breath away. *Holy shit,* rapist? *Really? That escalated quickly.* I switched back over to the texting app.

> Jeremy: *Have you seen the portrait? Surely that's illegal, right? Slander or defamation or something?*

> Olivia: *I'm working on it.*

I wondered what exactly 'working on it' meant, but another text came through before I could ask.

> Olivia: *It looks like Emilia Martinez is playing it up. I'm trying to get more info while I wait for Scott to get hold of me. Just keep your head down, and I'll be in touch.*

Playing *what* up? There was nothing to play up. I could feel my blood pressure rise as I switched back over to the social media app. I'd been so concerned with what everyone else was saying about me, it hadn't occurred to me to search Emilia's name.

A couple of keystrokes took me right to her page. I skimmed through the most recent posts, and began to feel sick to my stomach.

Thanks everyone for the support. It helps me to feel less violated.

I never want to be a victim again.

I want all women out there to know they should never be pressured into doing something they don't want to do.

I was practically seeing red. If I recalled correctly, Emilia was the one who had approached *me.* At a gallery opening, I believed. I hadn't even asked to paint her; I'd only taken her up on her offer. And then, after she'd signed the same release form all my models signed, all I'd done was take photos of her to use as a reference. I took a deep breath, forcibly relaxing my jaw before I ground my teeth to dust. But I couldn't stop myself from scrolling down.

As if her posts weren't bad enough, the comments were a whole different ballgame. As I'd feared, they were a toxic cesspool of angry rants, calls for me to "rot in prison where I'd get what's coming to me," and demands that all my income should go to Emilia for "emotional damages."

By the time I closed the app, my fingers were clamped around my phone so tight I was afraid the screen would crack.

I forced myself to relax my grip, then called Scott. I left two voice messages, then called a third time for good measure. What was the point of having a lawyer if he didn't answer the phone when you needed him?

I sent him an email, just in case something was wrong with his phone, then dragged myself out of bed, put on my swim trunks, and went downstairs to go burn off some of my irate energy in the pool.

* * *

"Hey buddy, did you miss me?"

I laughed as Dylan flung himself into my arms.

Five minutes later, he was still talking.

"…and Gramma let me put in all the edge pieces, but I let her do the rest, because the middle pieces are *boring*, and Grandpa is teaching me to ride a bike, but he says he hasn't been on one in forever, so I don't know if he's gonna be a very good teacher, and did Mommy tell you about the fire? And I know when you left I didn't like carrots, but I do now, you just hafta make them the right way—Gramma can show you how…"

I grinned as I let him tow me through my parents' house, showing me everything he'd been up to while I'd been gone.

What seemed like a million laps in the pool had taken the edge off my anger and anxiety, but nothing calmed me down or cheered me up like Dylan. Especially after two months without the kid—I hoped I wouldn't have to do that again any time soon.

I waited patiently until he wound down long enough to pause for air, then cut in quickly before he could start all over again.

"You wanna go to the zoo, buddy?"

I was prepared for the ear-splitting shriek of excitement, so I didn't go entirely deaf, and I had to stifle a grin as my mom clapped her hands over her ears.

"You're going to drive all the way to Indy?" she asked a second later, her eyebrows raised.

I shrugged. "It's early enough. And we've got nothing else to do today."

I knew I would probably regret suggesting the zoo after the fourth trip past the penguins—Dylan's current favorite animal—but at least it was guaranteed to get us out of my parents' house faster. I wanted to be gone before my mom started in on criticizing Jeanne. Or Sam. Or whatever her issue of the day was going to be. She never complained about me, at least there was that, but it didn't make her tirades any easier to bear.

"Give Gramma and Grandpa a hug while I put your stuff in the car and we'll get going, okay?"

I watched fondly as he scampered off, feeling the tension in my muscles start to relax for the first time since I'd gotten home.

* * *

Minus the pall of the situation with Emilia hanging over my head, it was as close to a perfect day as I'd had in a long time.

I'd been wrong—the penguins had required *five* trips to visit —but it was bright and sunny outside, the perfect July day. The zoo wasn't crowded, and we'd gotten ice cream and sat watching the sloths as Dylan filled me in on everything I'd missed over the past two months.

I knew Jeanne wanted to talk to him that night about the fire, so I was doing my best to bring him home in the best possible mood to hopefully make the conversation easier.

When we finally left the zoo he was all smiles though, and even managed to fall asleep on the hour-long drive back to Fairfield.

When I pulled into the driveway, he was rubbing his eyes, stretched out in his seat.

"What're we gonna eat for dinner?"

I laughed. "You're hungry again already? We ate like an hour ago."

"That was just ice cream," he corrected me. "It doesn't count."

I couldn't argue with that logic. "Well, let's go see what we've got while we wait for Mommy to get home." The second the words were out of my mouth I froze. *Shit.* Did he know Jeanne was staying here? I wasn't sure what he'd been told at this point. But when I glanced in the rearview mirror, he didn't seem fazed. He yawned, stretching his arms overhead before reaching down to unbuckle his seatbelt.

"If Mommy's staying here, you'll need to buy more desserts," he told me. "At least ice cream. She always has a lot more in the freezer than you do."

I couldn't stop the smile that stretched my face. He wasn't wrong there.

"What do you think, buddy," I asked, opening the car door and helping him out. "Spaghetti?"

The house was quiet as we let ourselves in. Jeanne was clearly still out with Ellen, but I got started on dinner anyway, and had just started dishing the pasta onto plates when I heard the door open.

"Perfect timing," I called, watching Dylan bounce up from where he'd been sitting at the kitchen table, amusing himself with a pile of Legos he'd seemingly conjured from thin air.

He ran out to greet her, and when he reappeared I glanced toward the front hall expectantly. "Dinner's about—" My words faltered when Jeanne appeared in the doorway and I saw her expression. Her brows were pulled together, eyes dark and angry, shoulders tight by her ears as if she were bracing for a fight.

I had just enough time to think *oh boy, here we go*, before she opened her mouth and…stopped. The expression on her face melted into something quizzical.

"Are you…cooking?" she asked.

I eyed her cautiously, but she seemed to have forgotten whatever she'd been riled up about a moment before. Maybe she'd been arguing with Ellen in the car or something. Surely, I couldn't be the only person she yelled at.

I nodded. "Spaghetti. You hungry? I made plenty." I grabbed another plate from the cabinet as she stared at me.

"You made…are those *green beans?*"

I glanced at her in confusion. "Dylan, you still like green beans, right?"

He nodded and I shot another questioning glance her way.

"Sorry." She cleared her throat and finally moved to drop her purse in the corner. "I just…didn't realize you cooked."

Ahhh. That's what all this was about. I smirked at her. "What, you thought when Dylan was over here we subsisted on air and sunlight?"

She glared as she took a seat at the table. "*No,* I…" She shrugged, looking slightly embarrassed. "I guess I assumed you ordered in all the time."

I gave her a wide grin, basking in her obvious discomfort as I slid a plate in front of her, piled high with noodles and meat sauce and seasoned beans. It wasn't gourmet, but I wasn't completely hopeless.

"Sorry to disappoint," I said, blinking wide eyes at her, and she glared at me as I winked, then turned to serve Dylan.

"Legos off the table, honey," she told him, and I braced myself for a complaint, but instead he turned to her with an excited smile.

"We saw *penguins* today, Mommy. And the lady at the zoo said there were *seventeen* different kinds of penguins. But we only saw three—and puffins too, which aren't really penguins even though they look like it. Did you know that? And—"

"Don't forget to eat, buddy," I told him, and he took a dutiful bite before going on to tell Jeanne all about our day.

I sat back and listened as he spoke, eating quietly and watching his expression as he animatedly described everything from the color of the giraffes' tongues to the flavors of the ice cream we'd eaten. It felt so good to have him here again, with his ceaseless chatter and rambunctious energy filling the space. The house always seemed so much bigger and emptier when he was gone.

And Jeanne's laughter when he described the animals, her rapid-fire questions that showed how much she truly cared about whatever he had to say...well. I wouldn't pretend it wasn't nice to have another person around the house as well.

She shot me an appraising glance as she ate her food and miraculously didn't find herself poisoned from my efforts. And when we were all finished eating and I pulled a strawberry cheesecake out of the fridge for dessert, her mouth nearly fell open.

"Where did *that* come from?" she asked.

"I went grocery shopping this morning before I went to

my parents' house," I told her. "I figured with three of us here, I might need more than the stale box of cereal in the pantry." I paused when she continued to gape at me. "What?"

"*You* went grocery shopping?"

I eyed her. "Well, I used to wait for food to magically appear, but then we started to starve, so I figured I should probably just go buy some."

She rolled her eyes, but didn't deign to answer. Instead, she turned to Dylan and her expression grew serious. I straightened, guessing at what was coming.

"Listen, honey, we need to talk about the fire."

I didn't miss the fact that she waited until his mouth was full of cheesecake so he couldn't do anything but listen.

"Like I told you earlier, you and I are both going to be staying here for a little while until we find a new place to live."

Dylan swallowed his bite and cocked his head at her. "Why can't we just stay here? Why do we hafta find a new place?"

Jeanne grimaced and we exchanged a quick glance.

"Because, buddy, your mom wants her own place, for just the two of you, like you had before," I explained.

"But there's enough space for us all here," he protested, screwing up his brows in the same way Jeanne did when she was confused. "Wouldn't it be easier? Then I wouldn't hafta go back and forth."

I opened my mouth, then closed it again. I hadn't expected the kid to try to be *logical*.

Jeanne cut in. "Honey, your dad and I aren't married anymore. We don't *want* to live together. Besides, it'll be fun. We'll get to look for a new house, you and me."

I expected him to argue some more, push the point, but instead he shrugged and took another big bite of cheesecake, then spoke through his stuffed cheeks. "I guess. When will we go get all my stuff from the old house?"

Ah, there it was. Jeanne's wince matched my own.

"Honey, that's what I needed to tell you," she said gently. "It was a big fire, and everything is gone. The house...and everything that was in it."

I braced myself, but Dylan's brow furrowed further. "No, I know," he said. "But my stuff..."

"It's gone, buddy," I said, my voice soft. "Everything is gone. We'll have to get you new stuff, to go with your new house."

"That's right," Jeanne said, shooting me a grateful glance, and for a quick second, I felt a strange sense of deja vu. We'd had this before, fleeting moments in our past, in the midst of our tumultuous relationship, where we'd both been on the same page, on the same side, and things had been easy between us. I'd almost forgotten it could be like that.

"We'll go shopping together," she went on, "and get you new things. You won't even know—"

But then Dylan's huge gray eyes, the same warm, clear shade as Jeanne's, grew impossibly wide and filled with tears, and I knew our luck had run out.

"But what about *Finley?*" he cried out, and I silently cursed. He'd had that damned stuffed shark since he was a year old. It was one of his favorite toys; why hadn't he had it with him at his grandparents' house?

All the color drained from Jeanne's face; clearly she hadn't known either. "Finley was at the house?" she asked, but it was too late.

"And my blanket with the cars on it? The really soft one? And the red toothbrush Grammy got me—my Legos? The puzzles—I hadn't even finished the one with the spaceships —and...and..."

He was full on sobbing at that point, hiccuping and gasping, the tears coming faster with each new realization of what he'd lost. Jeanne scooted her chair back and came around the table to wrap her arms around him, pressing him tight to her chest. Her eyes were damp as well, pained as they met mine, and I hesitated only briefly before joining them, wrapping my arms around them both. I tried not to think about the way the pair of them felt in my arms.

My heart hurt, not only for Dylan, but for Jeanne as well, who had lost just as much as Dylan, if not much more. A whole life to rebuild.

We stayed that way for a long moment until Dylan's hiccuping sobs quieted and he pulled back enough to turn his teary face to peer up at us.

"I want more cheesecake," he sniffled, and though I knew Jeanne was much more careful with his sugar intake than she was with her own, neither of us hesitated before hurrying to grab him another slice.

He was quiet through the rest of the evening, clearly worn out both physically and emotionally, and we convinced him to go to bed early. Jeanne read him a story and I wrapped him up in his second-favorite blanket with a promise that things would look better in the morning.

Even though it was still early, I half expected Jeanne would disappear off to her room for the night, but instead she trailed along behind me as I headed to the kitchen. I sorely needed a drink. If I'd been on my own, I might have gone for a glass of scotch, but instead I retrieved a bottle of wine, turning to hold it up toward Jeanne.

"Do you want a..."

I trailed off. Her expression had reverted to the one she'd worn when she'd walked in the door earlier, all tight and angry and tense. My guard, which had been relaxing throughout the evening, shot back into place.

"What?"

"How could you not tell me?" she demanded, anger simmering behind her words.

She didn't elaborate and I sighed, turning away and digging through a drawer for a bottle opener. Looked like I really was going to need that glass of wine. "Tell you what?"

She rounded the counter to stand facing me. "About this thing on social media. Have you *seen* what they're saying about you?"

Fuck. The bottle opener slipped from my fingers, clattering on the counter. The scandal hadn't slipped my mind, but I certainly hadn't thought to bring it up with Jeanne. I opened my mouth to respond, but she was on a roll.

"They're calling you all kinds of horrible things—rapist, pedophile. And I had to find out from *Mark*, no less. How awkward was *that*, when I didn't even know what he was talking about, and then he starts questioning if it's safe for me to be here, and I—"

"What?" My eyebrows shot up, my incredulity morphing into anger. "What the hell do you mean if it's *safe* for you to be here, of *course*—"

"I *know*, I know," she cut me off. "That's what I told him, but—"

"How *dare* he question that? It's not any of his fucking business what—"

"Jesus, why are *you* getting all upset here? *I'm* the one who's mad," she said, and her statement was so ridiculously illogical I almost laughed. "Anyway, that's not the point. I don't care what Mark thinks of you, or of me staying here. But what the hell is going on? He said you've been accused of sleeping with a minor."

My voice dropped low. "I did *not* sleep with a minor." I bit out each word harshly. How could she even think—

"God, I know that." She rolled her eyes, and I blinked.

"You do?"

It was her turn to look incredulous. "Of course. That's what I told Mark. You're an idiot, but you'd never do anything like that."

"Thanks for the vote of confidence," I huffed, going back to opening the wine bottle. I put my frustration into the task and the cork gave way with a satisfying *pop.*

"Seriously though, Jer, what is going *on?"*

I sighed. "I'm not entirely sure. It seems that one of the women I painted years ago lied about her age. She was probably underage when I did the painting and now she's playing it off like I knew and took advantage of her."

"But...why?"

I stared at her in exasperation. "I have no idea. Maybe she's embarrassed? Maybe she's after something? Or maybe she's just a horrible person."

"Shit," she breathed. "What are you going to do?"

I poured out the wine and handed her a glass before taking a deep pull on my own. "Well, I mean, I *didn't* sleep with her. Hell, the painting wasn't even done live. She signed release forms, so I should be able to prove that she lied about her age if my useless lawyer will ever freaking return my calls." I took another long drink. "But until then, Olivia says I have to stay offline. I can't post anything, I can't even *defend* myself until the lawyer says it's okay."

Jeanne stared at me for a beat. "So...you have to sit there and do nothing while people say horrible things about you?" Her eyebrow raised a fraction, and I caught the barest hint of a gleam in her eye.

"Yeah, pretty much." I dragged a hand through my hair.

She gave a slight cough, then raised her glass to her lips to cover...was that a *smile?* I narrowed my eyes at her, but she looked down, refusing to meet my gaze.

"That's...um, that's..." The smile widened, and she started to laugh.

I stared at her, unsure if I should be offended or amused. "What the hell is so funny?" I demanded, but she just laughed harder. I took the wineglass from her hand before she could spill it everywhere.

"I'm sorry," she gasped out. "It's not funny, it really isn't. But...your poor ego. I can't imagine how hard it must be—" She broke off with a snort, then dissolved further into giggles.

"Yeah, yeah," I said, rolling my eyes. "Hilarious." I set the wineglass down on the counter a little harder than necessary.

"Aw, don't be mad, Jer," she said, trying with what appeared to be a valiant effort to stifle her laughter. "This is just so...*you.*"

"What's that supposed to mean?"

"It's exactly the sort of thing that happens to you," she pointed out with a smile, lifting her glass again. "*Normal* people don't lie about their age just to have someone paint their portrait. But *Jeremy Whitaker, ooh, he's so dreamy.*" Her voice lifted to a falsetto and I had to fight to keep the smile off my face. She was ridiculous, and even standing there laughing at me and insulting me to my face she looked beautiful, her cheeks flushed red with wine and laughter.

"I swear," she went on, "just mention your name and people start to lose their damn minds. Honestly, I don't know why I'm surprised about any of this."

"Uh-huh," I said drily. "I was going to offer you another glass of wine, but from the looks of it, one was more than—"

I broke off when the doorbell rang. I glanced at Jeanne in confusion, but it was clear from her face that she wasn't expecting anyone either.

Crossing quickly to the door, I glanced through the tall glass side panels, then pulled it open.

The man on the step was tall and well dressed, in a dark suit with a neatly-trimmed beard.

"Jeremy Whitaker?" he asked in a deep voice. Behind me I heard Jeanne stifle another snort, but I had a sinking suspicion the next words out of this man's mouth were not going to be *ooh, he's so dreamy.*

I was right. At my nod he extended his hand, holding out a thick packet of papers for me to take.

"You've been served with a lawsuit."

CHAPTER 7

JEANNE

*I*t had been a strange day. Jeremy had been quiet and subdued for most of it, ever since the legal papers had been delivered the night before. It wasn't a side of him I'd ever really seen, and I wasn't sure if the right move was to give him space to process everything on his own, or to keep him distracted, even if it was just through our usual bickering.

In the end I made myself scarce, playing with Dylan as Jeremy swam laps, back and forth in the pool until I imagined he must be exhausted. It was strange being there, in a huge house that wasn't mine, with barely anything of my own, and nothing much to pass the time until I could return to work on Monday.

It was therefore with a great sense of relief that I answered the doorbell at half past five and saw Mark standing there. I was ready for a bit of normalcy.

"Hey, babe," I greeted him, stepping aside to let him in as I finished securing my earring. "Watch out, honey," I cautioned Dylan, who had raced into the foyer at the sound of the door and crashed into my calves, nearly knocking me off balance.

Mark stepped further into the foyer and gave a low whistle as he glanced around. "This is something else," he told me, raising an eyebrow as he took in the ornate crystal chandelier and sweeping staircase with its gleaming wood finials.

"Mm-hmm," I said noncommittally, trying to covertly block him from coming any further into the room in the hopes we could escape before Jeremy appeared. I snatched my purse from the table against one wall and nodded toward the door, but he didn't take the hint, moving instead to face Dylan, who had returned his attention to the toy cars he was careening across the marble floor.

"Dylan," he said, holding out a hand. "How are you this evening?"

I stifled a laugh. Mark hadn't spent much time around kids, but he really was going to have to learn how to interact with them a little better. Dylan, true to form, completely ignored Mark's outstretched hand, his attention entirely focused on the two cars he was racing.

I cringed when Mark tried again. "What have you been up to today?"

When Dylan still didn't answer, I dragged him off the floor and in for a hug. With a little prompting I did manage to get a quick "Hi," out of him before releasing him back to his cars.

"Be good," I told him with a kiss and a last darting glance toward the living room where the patio doors led out to the pool. Still no sign of Jeremy, thank God. "Daddy's by the pool and I'll be back by bedtime, okay?" I grabbed hold of Mark's hand and began towing him toward the front door. "Let's—"

"You two leaving already?"

Shit.

Either Jeremy was some kind of ninja, or he'd deliberately

waited until he knew I thought I was free. For a second I considered simply ignoring him and hustling Mark out the door, but my boyfriend was already moving, pulling his hand out of mine, and I let out a resigned sigh as I turned again to face the room.

My sigh morphed into a groan, even as my face flushed scarlet.

Jeremy wore a familiar wide smile—the one that lit his whole face with mischief—and practically nothing else. His swim trunks were still wet, clinging to muscular thighs, and the towel around his broad shoulders did nothing to hide the smooth expanse of tanned skin across his chest. Droplets of water still glistened on his arms and his hair was—*Fuck, Jeanne, stop ogling him.*

"Did you forget how to put on clothes?" I asked, hoping the sarcastic tone of my voice would offset my still-burning cheeks.

"Sorry," he said in a tone that implied he was anything but, then cast a quick wink in my direction. "I just didn't want to miss the chance to meet your gentleman caller. Mark, right?" He held out a hand. "Jeremy Whitaker. Jeanne's told me so much about you."

Liar. I'd told him practically nothing about Mark. But at least he'd gotten his name right.

"Mark Strykowski," Mark said with a nod, then hesitated slightly, as if shaking my ex's hand was the last thing he wanted to do. Politeness won out though, and they clasped hands briefly before Mark pulled back, trying to surreptitiously wipe the pool water from his now-damp hand onto his slacks. A quick glance at Jeremy told me the wet handshake was no accident, yet he managed not to keel over and die from the force of my glare.

"Strykowski, huh? Polish?"

I winced, knowing Mark was extremely proud of his Polish heritage and would talk for an hour about his ancestry given half a chance, but he surprised me by barely pausing to give Jeremy a curt nod before ushering me to the door.

"Oh, I guess we're going, then. Bye Jer, bye Dylan."

And then we were outside, Mark hustling me down the drive toward his car.

"Bye Jer?" he asked with a frown when I was settled in the passenger's seat and he'd slid behind the steering wheel and started the car.

"Um…should I not have said goodbye to him?" I asked, tilting my head, but Mark didn't appear to be listening.

"And does he usually walk around like that? It's not very…decent."

I snorted. "No one ever accused Jeremy of being decent. But it is his house. And to be fair, he was in the pool, not just hanging around like that."

He grumbled, pulling the car out onto the road and heading toward town. I eyed him for a second, then gave him a smirk. "You're not jealous, are you?"

He turned his head, fixing me with a dark look before returning his attention to the road. "I'm not jealous. I just don't trust the guy."

His usually close-cropped hair was starting to grow out, and a dark blond lock had fallen over his forehead. I leaned across the console to brush it back. "But you trust *me*, don't you?" I asked.

He glanced at me again, then gave a sigh, and his bad mood seemed to deflate. "Of course I do," he said, catching up my fingers and pressing a kiss to the tips before releasing them. "So, where do you want to go tonight?"

With that, the tension in the car eased and I leaned back in my seat. This was what I wanted. Something normal and easy, to help me forget the craziness of the past few days, an evening to simply relax and have a good time.

We ended up at a tiny Italian place on Main Street, only a few blocks from Sam's bookstore. The place was nothing to look at, narrow and cramped with peeling paint, but the food was second to none, and the family who ran it made a point to stop by and chat with every guest.

We had just wrapped up an animated discussion of tooth extraction techniques and I was digging into my eggplant parmigiana with gusto when I felt Mark's gaze on me.

"So, have you given any thought to how long you're planning on staying at Jeremy's house?"

I paused, taking a sip of wine and replacing my glass before answering. I hoped this wasn't about to turn into another argument, but his tone didn't sound upset, more like he was merely asking a question.

"I'm not sure," I answered truthfully. While I'd originally planned to go and stay with Carly before Jeremy returned, there seemed to be little point now. "Honestly, I've been renting for so long, I thought it might be time to think about buying a house. I'd like to find somewhere a little more permanent for Dylan and myself."

He nodded, spearing a piece of shrimp with his fork before saying, "You know, the housing market isn't great around here right now. Maybe it's the size of the town, but there don't seem to be a lot of options at the moment."

Oh, right. I'd nearly forgotten that he'd been searching for a house of his own.

"That's okay." I shrugged. "I'm not in a hurry. I can wait for the right place to open up."

He cleared his throat, glancing at me over the rim of his wineglass. "Perhaps it might be prudent to consider searching for a house...together."

Prudent? It took me a moment to grasp the meaning

behind his words, and I blinked in surprise. "Are you suggesting we should move in together?"

He met my eyes and cleared his throat again, his fingers drumming softly on the tabletop. "It just seems that if we're both looking for a new place to live, it makes sense to consider a place large enough for the three of us."

My heart warmed. It wasn't exactly romantic, but he was clearly nervous, and it was sweet. Honestly though, it wasn't something I'd even considered.

"I don't know," I hedged. "It's a bit early, isn't it? We've barely been dating for six months."

"True," he said. "But it'll save us the upheaval if we decide to move in together down the road after buying separate houses."

It was a valid point. I considered the idea.

"And besides," he went on, his voice growing gentle as he gazed at me, "It *feels* right." He reached out a hand and grasped mine across the table, giving my fingers a light squeeze. "Sometimes it doesn't take long to know the right thing to do."

My heart clenched in my chest, my insides turning soft and warm. I squeezed his hand in return, unable to stop the smile that spread across my face. "You might be right. I'll think it over, okay? I'll have to talk to Dylan."

He nodded, pulling my hand to his lips to press a sweet kiss to my knuckles before releasing it and returning to his food.

I watched as he took a bite of his shrimp, and I couldn't help but be struck by how completely different he was from Jeremy.

Jeremy had never formally suggested we move in together. Instead, we'd stumbled together back to the apartment he was living in at the time after an evening of drinks and dancing. Our heated night of passion had turned into two, then three, and I'd somehow never left. Eventually my stuff had made its way over to his place, and I'd let my own lease lapse, and we'd never looked back. It had been so typical of our relationship at the time—impulsive, passion-filled, impetuous. Immature.

Nothing at all like the man in front of me. Mark was everything Jeremy wasn't. He was a grown-up. He was responsible, and serious, and thoughtful. And if his offer to move in together was more practical than it was romantic, well at least I knew Mark well enough to know that when he made the offer, it was because he really meant it. He *wanted* us to live together, to share a space, a *life.* And that, I decided, was better than any impulsive decision, because it was made with his head, not just his heart. There was longevity in that, stability. And that was exactly what I needed.

"Oh my goodness, I can't believe I actually ate all of that," Mark groaned, pushing his plate away and breaking me out of my thoughts.

I scoffed. "Lightweight. Don't you know you have to prepare all day for a meal like this?"

He smiled. "Oh? And how do you do that?"

"It's simple. You eat a big breakfast to stretch your stomach out. But then skip lunch so you're super hungry by dinner time." I grinned as he laughed.

The waitress showed up then to take our plates, smiling between us. "Any room for dessert?" she asked.

Ah, the best part. And the tiramisu here was to die for. I opened my mouth to respond, but Mark beat me to it.

"Oh no, thank you though, it was delicious. We'll take the bill when you're ready."

She nodded and turned away before I could say anything.

"Mark," I exclaimed. "Call her back. Seriously, you have to try the tiramisu."

His blue eyes were wide and incredulous. "How can you possibly still have room?"

"Are you kidding? Dessert takes up a completely separate space inside you," I informed him. "There's *always* room for dessert."

He gave me an indulgent smile. "I thought you were a dentist. Don't you make your living telling other people to eat less sugar?"

I rolled my eyes. "Well sure, *other* people. But personally, I think I'd rather give up my teeth than tiramisu."

He laughed and the waitress returned with our bill. I waited for him to apologize and order the dessert, but he didn't, simply handed over his credit card.

I frowned, but he didn't seem to notice.

Once she'd left, he reached across the table and took my hand again. "I had a really good time tonight," he told me, and I relaxed. I'd had a good time, too. It'd been a nice break from the craziness following the fire, and I didn't need to ruin the mood with a silly complaint about dessert. Besides, he was probably right. It wasn't like I didn't *know* I ate too much sugar. And Mark probably just wanted the best for me. Maybe it was time to try to be a responsible adult.

"I did, too," I told him, rising to follow as he led the way out of the restaurant. We took the long way back to the car, window shopping along the storefronts lining Main Street and enjoying the warm summer evening before heading to where we were parked.

We were both quiet as we drove back to the house with the windows down, and I closed my eyes, enjoying the warm breeze as it mussed my hair. Mark left me at the door with a quick kiss and a promise to see me soon, and I smiled as I let myself in.

The lights were off in the foyer, so I followed the faint sounds and trickle of light down the stairs to the media room in the basement. The idyllic sight that greeted me brought the smile back to my face and caused a softness to swell in my chest.

Jeremy sat on one of the plush suede couches, his bare feet propped up on a footstool. Dylan was sprawled across his lap, snoring softly, a stuffed panda clutched in one hand as Jeremy smoothed his fingers through his son's dark rumpled curls. The lights were low, and a movie with cartoon sloths played quietly on the huge screen, which clearly Jeremy was invested in, since he could have easily turned it off and taken Dylan up to bed.

I hadn't said a word, but Jeremy must have sensed my presence, because he turned to glance at me in the doorway.

"Did you have a good time?" he asked.

I nodded. "Do you want me to take him up to bed?" I asked.

He shook his head. "It's okay. We'll hang out here a bit longer. Oh—I know you just ate, but we saved you a slice of cake from dinner. It's chocolate raspberry, from Geoff's. It's on the table."

I blinked. "Thank you."

"You're welcome to join us," he added, tipping his head toward the empty half of the couch. His eyes were pools of darkness in the dim light, and his voice was a warm caress, beckoning me in. It would be so easy, to curl up there on the couch with them. I'd done it a million times. He'd pull me in tight against his side, wrapping an arm around me to keep me close. If I closed my eyes, I could practically feel his breath stirring my hair, imagine the muscular band of his arm around my shoulders.

No.

I shook my head, and when I opened my mouth to speak I found my throat inexplicably tight, so I closed it again and cleared my throat. "Good night," I told him in a low voice.

I debated leaving the cake on the table when I passed the kitchen, but if I was honest with myself, there was never really any question there. Instead, I took it with me, waiting until I was up in my room with the door closed before I took a bite. The rich flavors of dark chocolate and raspberry sang on my tongue, and I savored the taste, trying not to think about why I suddenly felt like crying.

CHAPTER 8

JEREMY

My phone rang at some ungodly hour, and I groaned loudly, pulling my pillow over my head. Eventually it stopped, and I stretched, rolling to my other side and settling back in, but it immediately started ringing again. I poked my head out from under the pillow and blearily checked the clock. Eight forty-two. Ugh.

I fumbled on my nightstand for the phone, not even bothering to check the ID before swiping my thumb across the screen to accept the call.

Olivia didn't bother with pleasantries either.

"I just got off the phone with the Focus Gallery in New York. They're pulling you from the show in December."

Well, that woke me up. "*What?!*"

"Yeah," she said. "They said something about having to close a section of the space for renovations, and how now they don't have as much room as they'd expected, but we both knew it was bullshit."

I sat up, rubbing a hand over my face. "Well, at least I haven't started painting for that show yet. Fuck."

She sighed. "Yeah. Sorry, Jeremy. We hadn't signed a contract with them yet, so there's nothing I can do."

"God, this sucks," I groaned. "Scott needs to get his ass in gear so we can deal with this before it gets any worse."

There was a beat of silence on the other end of the line, and I caught my breath. "What?"

Another pause, and dread started to seep into my veins. "Liv, what don't I know?"

She gave another strained sigh. "It's not just social media anymore," she said softly. "Your story hit mainstream news this morning."

I cursed again. I knew that was coming, I just hadn't expected it to happen so fast. "You're gonna tell me not to read it, aren't you?"

She gave a muffled laugh. "Yep, and you're going to ignore me. But listen, it's not as bad as it looks, I promise. You still have the show in Toronto in the spring, and we've got contracts on that one. Plus, there's that other book deal in the works. We'll chase Scott out of whatever hole he's hiding in, and we'll get this fixed, okay?"

I collapsed back onto the pillows. "Okay, Liv," I grumbled. "You're the best."

"I know it," she told me. "Don't stress. It'll be okay."

We hung up and I tossed my phone onto the nightstand before I could give in and look up the article she'd mentioned. I'd find it later, and read it, and get even angrier, but I'd try to take her advice for the moment at least.

Well, some of her advice, anyway. Probably not the part about not stressing.

I'd never considered myself especially good at dealing with stress. I wasn't the most patient of people, and though my mouth got me into trouble sometimes, between Olivia's help and a certain amount of natural charm, I was pretty adept at getting out again.

But this meant my current level of stress wasn't one I really knew how to manage. The lawsuit was hanging heavy over my head, and Scott still wasn't returning anyone's calls. Olivia had promised she would try to get hold of one of the other partners at the law firm, but as it was Sunday there was nothing to do but wait. And every second we waited, the more nasty comments about me piled up online. Comments I still couldn't even defend myself against. Not to mention whatever was currently being printed about me in the news.

I rolled over and buried my face in the pillow, muffling my aggravated groan.

On top of all that was the stress of sharing the house with my ex-wife. I honestly hadn't expected that to be a big deal at all—after all, the place was huge, and she would be out of the house at work most of the time anyway. But hell, she'd only been there for three days, and I was already discovering how much I'd underestimated the impact of having her around.

It was all the little things I hadn't expected. Catching her walking from the bathroom down the hall to her bedroom in nothing but a towel, wet hair piled on top of her head and skin flushed from the heat. Droplets of water still clinging to her skin, her face bright and clear of makeup. A sight I'd seen a million times before but never remembered being quite so *affected* by. The unreadable expression on her face in the dark doorway of the media room when I'd told her there was cake waiting for her in the kitchen, that made me want to pull her down onto the couch next to me and make her tell me what she was thinking. The echoing sound of her laughter as she played with Dylan.

I could hear it then, the sound moving as she chased him through the rooms downstairs. It stirred up emotions in me that I couldn't quite identify, and that only added to my stress. I didn't *need* all this.

I threw back the covers and padded to the closet, where I

grabbed my swim trunks and pulled them on. I wasn't sure what Jeanne had planned for the day, but Dylan was going to be spending some time with his Uncle Sam and probably-soon-to-be-Aunt Ellen, so I planned to spend as much time as possible in the pool, swimming so hard I didn't have the energy to think.

I'd stop in the kitchen first for some coffee though. I could smell it wafting up the stairs. When Jeanne and I had been together, she'd always gotten up hours before me and the rich aroma of coffee permeating the air was always the first thing I'd smelled when I woke up. I hadn't even realized I'd missed it until it was gone, and I'd had to drag myself up to make my own damn coffee.

I definitely wasn't complaining about having that little ritual back, even if only temporarily. I threw a towel over my shoulder and stumbled down the stairs, following my nose toward the life-giving smell. The sounds of laughter had stopped, and when I reached the kitchen, I heard the muffled sound of soft voices instead, drifting around the corner into the open hallway.

"—meant to ask. What would you think about living with Mark?"

I stopped dead.

"Like…here?" That was Dylan, and I could picture the way his nose would be scrunched up and his brows drawn together in confusion.

"No, silly." Jeanne laughed. "I told you the other day we would need to find a new place to live, you and me, right?"

She paused, while I assumed he nodded.

"So, I was wondering what you would think if we found a new place to live, but instead it would be for you, and me, and Mark, too. All together."

I shouldn't have been standing there eavesdropping. I should've gone in, or at least coughed or something so they'd have known I was there, but I couldn't have made myself move if my life had depended on it. I was frozen in the hallway outside the kitchen, barely daring to breathe as I waited for my son's reply.

"He's...kinda *boring*," came Dylan's plaintive response, and I had to work hard to stifle my laugh. *That's my boy.*

Jeanne laughed too, but hers sounded a bit strained. "That's only because you don't know him too well yet. I think you'll like him a lot once you spend more time with him."

And just like that, all my irritation from minutes earlier crashed down around me. Because she was right. Dylan didn't know Mark. I didn't know Mark. Hell, how well did *she* even know Mark? They'd been together for like five minutes, and suddenly she was talking about moving in with him? Buying a house together, I could only assume, where Dylan would spend half his time, and she hadn't even mentioned it to me. My blood began to boil in my veins. And people called *me* impulsive. This was—

The sound of the doorbell broke me out of my spiraling thoughts, and I turned and stalked to the door, not even bothering to look back even though I knew Jeanne must have realized I'd been there.

I wrenched the door open with slightly more force than was strictly necessary, revealing my brother and his girlfriend standing on the front steps.

Ellen grinned at the sight of me and turned to Sam. "Okay, they're both alive. Pay up."

I raised an eyebrow as Jeanne came up beside me, Dylan's arms wrapped around her waist, though when they reached the door, he peeled himself off and flung himself at Sam instead, who was immediately lost in a wave of excited chatter.

I eyed Ellen. "You bet that we'd kill each other?"

She laughed, pushing past me into the foyer. "I bet that *she'd* kill *you* first."

Which I assumed meant Sam had bet I'd kill Jeanne first. I wasn't sure on whose behalf to be offended.

"Did you forget to put on clothes?" Ellen added, eying me with a smirk as she took Dylan's backpack from Jeanne.

Jeanne, for her part, snorted so hard I thought she might have dislodged something in her brain, and only when she turned her laughing eyes on me did I remember those were the same words she had spoken the previous day, when I'd greeted her and Mark at the door. My mood soured further.

"I was just heading out to the pool," I growled, ignoring the look the two women exchanged between them.

"Ohh," Ellen said. "I wasn't sure if this was normal attire for you." My jaw clenched tight, but she kept going before I could explode. "We'll bring Dylan back by six. Is everything in here?" She indicated the bag and Jeanne nodded before wrapping her arms around Dylan where he was still attached to Sam and giving them both a quick hug. I ruffled my hand through Dylan's hair, and they left amidst a flurry of good-byes and admonitions to be good.

When the door finally swung shut behind them, I turned to find Jeanne looking at me with a pleased smile.

"We sure showed them," she said to me.

I cocked an eyebrow in confusion, and she elaborated. "Placing bets to see who killed the other one first. They thought we couldn't live together and here we are, doing just fine."

I couldn't help it. I exploded.

"How could you think about buying a house with Mark without talking to me about it first?"

She blinked, and I could practically see her mind shifting gears, catching up to the fight we were clearly about to have.

Her eyes narrowed. "Talking to you about it...you mean asking your permission?"

"I *mean* even bothering to bring up this life-changing decision that will affect both me and Dylan. We agreed that any changes that affected his life would be made *together,* and you didn't even talk to me before deciding to move him in with...with some stranger."

"Look," she snapped, folding her arms across her chest, "first of all, Mark isn't 'some stranger.' And second of all, I didn't decide anything. Mark brought it up, and I told him I'd have to think about it. I was just feeling out Dylan to see what he thought of the idea."

I gritted my teeth, leaning against the door. The wood was cold against my bare back, and I had the vague thought that swim trunks and a towel was probably not the right attire for a discussion like this, but oh well.

"You still should have talked to me about it first," I insisted. "It's not Dylan's decision to make, it's ours."

"Fine," she gritted out. "Jeremy, dear, would it be alright with you if Mark and I looked for a new house together?"

"No!" I exclaimed.

Her glare was pure ice, but I refused to back down. "I don't like the guy."

Her gaze turned incredulous. "Of course you don't like him—he didn't suck up to you and stroke your ego like everyone else does."

I scoffed. "That's not it. There's something about him that rubs me the wrong way." It was true, I realized, and I wasn't sure what that something was.

Jeanne crossed her arms tightly across her chest. "How can you even say that? You only met the guy for like two minutes."

"And that's what—five minutes less than how long *you've* known him?" I shot back.

She turned on her heel, storming toward the kitchen, and I followed her, trying to force myself to calm down. Yelling at each other wouldn't accomplish anything.

"Look," I started, "you've only been dating him for a few months. I'm not saying don't move in with the guy someday. Marry him, I don't care." *Liar.* I squashed the voice ruthlessly. "But maybe don't rush into anything right now, when you already have so much else to deal with."

She had reached into the cabinet, pulling out a coffee mug, but at my words she turned and slammed it down on the counter so hard I winced. "What, don't rush into things, like I did with you? Don't make another stupid decision, you mean?"

I tried to ignore the fact that her words stung. "There wasn't a kid to consider then," I said coldly.

"And that's exactly why I asked Dylan what he thought about the idea," she exclaimed. "Besides, Dylan likes Mark just fine."

"I'm pretty sure I just heard Dylan call Mark 'boring.'"

She poured coffee into her mug, sloshing it over the side in her agitation. "I'd consider that a good thing," she snapped. "Boring means grown up. Mark is nice. He's stable. And maybe it'll be a nice change to live with someone who I don't have to fight with all the damn time." Her voice rose to a yell, ringing through the kitchen.

"Fine," I snapped. I'd had enough. "Do whatever you want; you're going to anyway. And I'll stay out of your way so you won't have to fight with me. You won't have to talk to me at all."

I stormed out of the kitchen, yanking the patio door open and slamming it behind me. Then I dove headfirst into the pool.

CHAPTER 9

JEANNE

I hated the way Jeremy got to me. The way I *let* him get to me. I was a calm person, a reasonable person. Everyone I worked with said I was easy to get along with. But that man got under my skin so easily, riling me up until it was all I could do not to punch him in his smug face.

It was even worse when he was *right*.

I should have talked to him first, I knew that. Regardless of his opinion of Mark, it was a decision he should have been involved in from the start. But I'd known how he was going to react, so I'd taken the coward's way out, trying to get Dylan on my side, and then when Jeremy had called me out on it, I'd gotten so flustered I couldn't even apologize like an adult, but had resorted to yelling at him like some spoiled teenager.

No, Jeremy had been right about talking to him first, and he'd been right about another thing—the two of us needed to avoid each other as much as possible. For everyone's sanity.

Fortunately, it wasn't all that hard to do. He spent the majority of the day in the pool, and when Dylan returned home the two of them watched a movie while I hid in my room. Then Jeremy disappeared while I fielded bedtime. I barely saw him for more than five minutes through the course of the evening, and the next morning I was out the door and on my way to work long before he was out of bed.

And thus began our awkward dance of avoidance. I had plenty to keep me busy—between work and dealing with the aftermath of the fire, I didn't need an excuse to stay away.

It turned out that the fire had been caused by some faulty wiring in the laundry room, and little in the house had been salvageable. I had insurance claims to deal with, a new car to buy, new clothing to shop for, toys and clothes of Dylan's to replace. At least by staying with Jeremy I didn't have to worry about replacing things like dishes and sheets and years of accumulated home goods. But I had plenty to mourn as well. Old photo albums, sentimental trinkets collected throughout my life. It wasn't hard to understand why Dylan still cried over the loss of his beloved stuffed Finley when some of my lost items hit me just as hard.

So, when I wasn't dealing with the fallout from the fire, I attempted to bury myself in my work, coming in early and staying late. But, in the end, my avoidance was short-lived. I just couldn't seem to stay away.

I told myself it was because I needed to spend time with Dylan, but if I was completely honest, it was also because the longer I stayed there, the harder it was to pretend that Jeremy was the same man I'd married six years ago.

Oh, his fundamental character hadn't changed—he was still infuriating, still cocky, his ego still grossly oversized. Still easily distracted by anything bright and shiny, and all the best things in life still seemed to fall easily into his lap with little effort on his part.

But I couldn't deny that he'd changed in ways I hadn't expected. He was impulsive, maybe, but no longer immature. No longer selfish and flighty. He had a gravity to him that hadn't been there before, and I wasn't sure if it was due to the lawsuit and having his reputation called into question, or maybe it was a product of being responsible for a child, or maybe it was something that had grown naturally over time and I'd simply not been around him enough to notice.

He was also thoughtful in a way he'd never been before. No matter how late I returned from work, I'd find dinner waiting for me, kept warm in the oven. He seemed able to sense when I missed Dylan and wanted extra time with him, or when I was overwhelmed and needed time to myself instead. He always had desserts stashed around the house to satisfy my sweet tooth, including things I knew he didn't even like.

Not to mention the fact that in the intervening years he'd somehow managed to teach himself to cook, and clean, and do his own laundry.

And oddly enough, his newfound responsibility made the quirks that remained less irritating than they initially had been. He was still incapable of getting up before the sun was high in the sky, and was barely functional before he'd had a cup of coffee. While at one point I'd found what I'd considered his laziness to be one of his most annoying qualities, these days I found myself leaving the coffeemaker on as I left for work so all he'd have to do is stumble down to the kitchen.

I was no longer irritated by his incurable need to sing at the top of his lungs in the shower, especially when Dylan joined along, humming off-key from another room to a song he probably shouldn't know the words to.

And on the rare occasions that we were able to spend more than five minutes in the same room without tearing each other's throats out, I had to admit I really enjoyed his company.

Unfortunately, those instances were few and far between.

To be fair, Jeremy was under a lot of stress as well. Despite spending countless hours on the phone with his assistant, he didn't seem to be having much luck dealing with the situation with his former model. I didn't press him for updates, but while I gathered he'd finally tracked down his lawyer, it seemed the man was in the middle of moving his office and had mislaid boxes of paperwork, including the release form Jeremy desperately needed to find. Either way it did nothing to improve his mood, and therefore he spent inordinate amounts of time in the pool working out his frustrations.

Which in turn did nothing to improve *my* mood, as I never knew when I might come around a corner to find him standing there in nothing but soaked swim trunks, fabric perfectly molded to his form and water droplets shining on his skin, which made me think things I should not be thinking and feel things I should *not* be feeling.

"Babe, you know, this office really is huge. We could easily fit another desk against the wall over there."

Mark's voice pulled me out of my thoughts and back to the present, and I turned to find him gesturing toward the far corner of my office, where filing cabinets filled the space under the window.

"I'm sorry?" I said, trying to force the gears in my mind into motion. It was after six in the evening, and Tris had just left for the day, closing the office and leaving me to lock up. I had planned to meet Mark for dinner, but since I was running late, he'd met me here instead, waiting patiently while I finished updating my patient files for the day. Or, that's what I was supposed to be doing anyway—not sitting there lost in my head as I recounted the last several weeks of my strange domestic situation with my ex-husband.

I shook my head and focused on Mark, who didn't seem to have noticed my lapse in attention and had instead crossed the room to stand by the window, measuring out the space with his hands.

"I was just saying, if we moved those filing cabinets, you'd have more than enough space in here for another desk. We could build a half wall or even a full wall for privacy."

I blinked, but then nodded and made a non-committal sound, turning back to my files as he wandered through the room. It wasn't that I was angry that he was basically redesigning my office space around me to make room for himself—it wasn't the first time, after all. He'd been in the week before talking about expanding the reception area to make room for additional patients, and over dinner the other night he'd suggested a few options for rearranging the hygienist's space.

It wasn't even that I thought it was a bad idea. We did have the space, after all, and adding another dentist to the practice was probably a sound business decision. No, it was the fact that he'd never really *asked* me.

I remembered his offhand comment the first time he'd visited, asking if I'd ever considered adding another dentist. Then when I'd teased him, asking if he'd meant himself, he'd smiled, asking why not. But other than that one exchange, it hadn't really come up again, and we'd definitely never actually discussed the idea with any level of seriousness.

No, he'd simply started making suggestions, taking measurements and making casual comments about the number of additional hygienists we could fit, and how long any renovations might take.

I had to admit, I'd been taken aback at first, but at this point it was easier to focus on my computer screen, letting him wander through the space and reorganize things in his mind. After all, this was how relationships worked, right? With compromise and sacrifice. Besides, if he did join me

413

here, I really did want him to be comfortable, and the space was more than big enough for two offices.

Besides, if this actually happened, there would be plenty of time to sit down and talk through all the details. For the time being, there was no harm in letting him brainstorm.

"You about ready, babe?" he asked, coming over to join me behind the desk, and I nodded, clicking out of the last file and shutting down the computer.

I was tired after a long day at work, so we ended up at a little chain restaurant on the outskirts of town, and the food was good, if not particularly memorable. The company was nice, the small-talk pleasant, and it wasn't until he was driving me back to the office so I could get my car and head home that the conversation turned serious.

"So," Mark started, glancing at me over the center console. "Have you given any more thought to what we talked about before? Moving in together?"

Honestly, after my talk with Jeremy, I'd kind of been avoiding the conversation. I hadn't brought it up, and I'd been dragging my feet on looking for a new place as well. I opened my mouth to respond, but he kept going before I had the chance.

"Because my realtor found a place that just opened up on the east side of town, a little three-bedroom ranch. It's a little older, but it's been fixed up; it's got a good-sized yard and it's off the road on a dead-end street. It overlooks the state park, so it has a good view." He gave a short laugh. "You should see the pictures—the previous owners painted every room a different color. We could fix that though. I figured if you had the time to come look at it tomorrow, maybe we could put in an offer this weekend."

Whoa, wait—what?

"Mark, I—"

He reached across the console and took my hand, wrapping his fingers around mine as he went on, his voice earnest. "My realtor thinks the asking price is a bit high, but it's not unreasonable, so if we went in a little under, we might have a shot. She's already drawn up an offer, so if you like it all we have to do is—"

"Mark, hold up."

He already had an *offer* ready to submit? I gently extricated my fingers from his and turned to face him. "I…I think it's too soon. I'm sorry, I *do* want to live with you, but it's just…with everything that's been going on, and this is all happening so fast…"

His face fell as I spoke, and he pulled the car up in front of my office and killed the engine.

"…I just want to wait," I finished lamely.

"Why didn't you say something earlier?" he asked, his brow creased. He looked like a small, hurt puppy dog and my stomach twisted with guilt.

"I would have, if we'd talked about it," I said. "I'm sorry. I guess…it just didn't come up again, and I didn't know you'd actually been looking."

"Of course I was looking," he said. "I'm living an hour away in a rental apartment. I need to find a place to live and get my practice set up. We aren't all living rent-free in a mansion."

I reared back, and he instantly backtracked. "Jeanne, I'm sorry. That was unfair and I didn't mean it. I'm just, surprised, I guess." He ran a hand through his hair. "I thought we were on the same page, that's all."

And we might have been, I thought, if we'd bothered to *talk* about it instead of making assumptions. But his words still stung. He'd said he didn't mean it, but at the same time, the words wouldn't have come out if he didn't feel them on some level, right?

"I'm sorry," he said again, and I softened at his look of

415

genuine remorse. "I just got excited at the idea of living with you." He gave a rueful smile. "But obviously I don't want to pressure you into anything you're not ready for." He leaned across the console and pressed a gentle kiss to my mouth. "You're worth waiting for."

I melted a little, pressing into the kiss, letting him know he was forgiven. See, this is how grown-up relationships worked. People made mistakes, and then apologized. We could move on together, as a team.

He pulled away, his eyes warm on me. "So, when do you think you might be ready?" he asked.

My heart sank again. "What?"

He leaned back. "Like, another few weeks? Should I wait on the house? Or do you think it'll take longer?"

My jaw dropped. "I don't know. I can't predict—"

"I just need to figure out if I should go look at this house or if you want me to wait and we can search together in the fall or—"

I blew out a breath. Why wasn't this working? Was it my fault for not bringing this up earlier?

"I think I'm going to look for a place to rent," I said, working to keep my voice even. "For me and Dylan. Maybe you could do the same? Look for a rental closer to town? And then we can revisit this later, when it's not so...time sensitive?"

He nodded, a little stiffly. And a few minutes later, when he kissed me goodnight, his kiss was brief and had an almost...obligatory feel to it. I sighed as I stepped out of the car, then circled around to the back of the building where my own car was parked. Why did everything have to be so hard?

* * *

Dylan was already tucked into bed when I arrived at the house, which only soured my mood further. I could have used a good hug. But I tiptoed into his dark room anyway and pressed a kiss to his soft cheek, smiling as he shifted and burrowed deeper beneath his blanket.

He was completely covered, blankets piled high, but his bare feet poked out the end, and I suddenly remembered that Jeremy had slept like that too. I hadn't thought about that in years, but I'd always made fun of him for it. He'd claimed his feet got hot but the rest of him was cold, and I smiled to myself as I backed out of the room, silently closing the door behind me.

I'd planned to go straight up to my room, maybe take a bath and try to relax before bed, but I stopped by the kitchen first. Jeremy had a habit of leaving desserts out for me on the nights I went out with Mark, as if he knew Mark disapproved of my sweet tooth.

Sure enough there was a loosely-wrapped plate sitting on the island, and when I uncovered it, a dish of Geoff's creme brûlée greeted me. I sighed, and my lingering bad mood began to ease.

I took the dish, along with a spoon from the drawer, and began to make my way up to my bedroom, but I paused when I heard excited voices. They were coming from the parlor, an unused decorative room at the front of the house that as far as I could tell served no purpose other than to look expensive.

I changed course, pausing to listen by the door. Not voices—only one voice, Jeremy's, and when I poked my head around the doorway, I saw he was gesturing animatedly as he spoke into his phone.

When he saw me, he beckoned me in with a wide grin, holding up a finger as he wrapped up the call.

"Yes, thank you. Thank you. Keep me posted." He ended

the call and tossed his phone onto a pristine white chair—far too fancy to actually sit in—before spinning toward me.

"Scott found all the paperwork. Emilia lied about her age —we have proof—and he's already talked to her lawyers. They're going to drop the lawsuit."

I caught my breath. "Oh my God. Jer, that's wonderful!"

He laughed, a big, deep, gleeful sound, happy and loud and completely unselfconscious, and opened his arms toward me. I ran to meet him. I don't know if it was his infectious happiness, or the heat of the moment, or just the fact that I really needed a hug after the day I'd had, but I didn't even pause to think before I was in his arms.

My creme brûlée was lost on a side table somewhere as he wrapped his arms around me and whooped with joy, and the feeling of his strong embrace was at once so familiar and yet so foreign it stole my breath away. But I locked my brain down tight, not allowing even a scrap of doubt, or worry, or guilt to worm its way though. Instead, I banded my own arms around his waist and squeezed, relishing the moment.

I looked up at his face. His dark eyes were sparkling, his cheek creased in a dimple, and I wanted to raise my hand and rub it over the hint of stubble that darkened his chin. I knew exactly what it would feel like, rough against my fingertips. The smell of cedar and linseed oil surrounded me, as comforting as his arms, and my hands tightened reflexively against the back of his shirt as I willed them not to move, not to touch his face.

His dimple disappeared as his expression turned serious, and I felt the exact moment he realized where we were, what we were doing. His attention shifted, his gaze dropping to my mouth as his expression turned serious, and my breath caught. His arms around me tightened a fraction, his lips parting on a sigh, and my heart ratcheted up to a frantic pace, blood thrumming through my veins in answer to the gleam in his bottomless eyes.

He bent his head toward me and the moment stretched, endless and filled with yearning as the space between us narrowed, until only a sliver of air separated our lips. I could feel the heat of his breath, the warmth of his skin, the tickle of a lock of his dark hair against my forehead.

He paused there, and I could have happily lived in that moment forever, my conflicting emotions buried under a tide of familiar desire. But then he pulled back. His arms released me, cool air filling the space where his solid warmth had been, and he stepped away, a mumbled apology on his lips.

And I just stood there, flustered and confused as the tide receded and let all my muted emotions bubble to the surface. I wasn't sure what bothered me more—the fact that the kiss had nearly happened in the first place, the fact that Jeremy'd had the wherewithal to stop it, or the thought that if he hadn't...I almost certainly wouldn't have stopped either.

CHAPTER 10

JEREMY

*W*hat the hell had I been *thinking?* I mean, I hadn't been thinking, that much was obvious. I'd been feeling, reacting on instinct, and it wasn't until Jeanne had already been in my arms, my lips a mere breath away from hers, that my brain had managed to catch up and kick on the alarm.

Crisis averted, I thought as I lie awake in my bed. I mean, honestly, Jeanne had a boyfriend, one that must be pretty serious if she was considering moving in with him, not to mention the fact that she was my *ex-wife*, and we'd already been down that road once before. No good could come from walking down it again.

But then why wasn't I filled with relief? I should be thrilled that nothing had happened, that I hadn't fucked everything up, instead of being fixated on the fact that she was lying in bed just down the hall. Was she wearing a tank top and yoga pants like she did to lounge around the house these days? Or one of those silk numbers she used to sleep in when we'd been married? Or nothing at all?

Stop it.

I shifted, punching my pillow into shape and turning to my side, away from the door, as if that would help block out the image of her face in my mind. Grey eyes wide, blond hair mussed, lips parted and begging for my kiss. The feel of her body in my arms.

Dammit.

Part of the problem, I knew, was that stopping the kiss before it started did nothing to stop my imagination from filling in the blanks. Because I didn't have to wonder. I *knew* what it would have felt like. I knew all the sounds she would make, the little sigh as she parted her lips for me, the way she would taste when I swept my tongue into her mouth. The way her eyes would drift closed, her hands fisting into my shirt as if she was holding on for dear life, the way she would surrender to me completely as I pushed my hands into her soft hair and made her moan—

Arrgh! Fucking pull yourself together.

We'd been doing such a good job of avoiding each other. We hadn't even fought in weeks. Looks like I would have to double down on that avoidance.

It'd been so good to have her there right at that moment, though, to celebrate this win with me. Because though I had no shortage of acquaintances, I wasn't sure I had anyone I could have called simply to bask in the relief of the moment. Olivia? Sure, but that was professional more than personal. Sam? Not a chance. He would have been happy for me, but in the strained, awkward way of our relationship. My mom? I snorted at the thought. And there were plenty of women I could call who would be happy to come 'celebrate' with me, but that wasn't what I needed. Honestly, I hadn't even thought about any of those women since my ex-wife had shown up in my bathtub.

I sighed.

Jeanne had been exactly what I'd needed.

I rolled over to my other side, then back again, before finally giving up and climbing out of bed. I was clearly too wired to fall asleep. Jeanne always said sugar helped her if she couldn't fall asleep, and while I knew that was as ridiculous as it sounded, at that moment I was open to trying just about anything.

I made my way down to the kitchen, where I remembered there was carrot cake in the fridge. I didn't bother to turn on the light, crossing the room in the dark before pulling open the door and rooting through until I found the cake leftover from my trip to Geoff's the day before.

"You too, huh?"

I nearly dropped the plate as I spun around, the fridge door slamming shut behind me. I hadn't even noticed the figure sitting at the island, Jeanne's dark form silhouetted against the night sky through the window behind her. She had the dish of creme brûlée I'd left out sitting on the counter in front of her, half empty with the spoon held lightly in one hand.

"Holy shit, you about gave me a heart attack," I accused her, pressing my hand against my chest to slow my racing heartbeat as I slid onto a stool across the island from her.

"Sorry," she said, not sounding sorry at all, and I was glad to see things were normal between us, or at least as normal as things got in our antagonistic relationship. There was no sign of awkwardness from our encounter a few hours earlier.

"I didn't know there was carrot cake," she said.

"Creme brûlée not good enough for you?" I teased.

She laughed. "Oh, don't pretend I wouldn't eat both. But I'm glad to see you're taking my sage advice about sugar helping you sleep."

I snorted. "Well, it can't make me more awake than I already am, at least." I took a bite of the carrot cake and sighed. "I can't stop replaying that phone call with Scott." It wasn't the only thing I couldn't stop replaying, but it was still true enough.

It was hard to tell in the dark, but I thought she smiled. "That really is wonderful news." She paused, then asked, "Do you know what happened? I mean, Emilia had to have known you had that release form. What did she think that lawsuit was going to accomplish?"

"Yeah," I said quietly. "It sounds like she just got in over her head. I didn't really know her well, but it seems she comes from a pretty conservative family, and when the painting got published in my book, her parents got pretty upset. Then when someone did the math and pointed out that she was underage, she freaked out, and blamed me so her parents wouldn't find out she'd lied."

"Huh," Jeanne said. "Did she think it would never come out?"

"Scott said the lawsuit was her parents' idea, not hers. I don't think she ever imagined it would blow up as much as it did." I gave a dark, unamused laugh. "I think she was hoping I was so rich and famous I would just let it go and pay her off or something."

"Damn." Jeanne was quiet for a moment as she ate the last of her creme brûlée, then set the spoon down in the dish with a clink. "So, is that the end of it then? Everything goes back to normal?"

I gave another short laugh. "Not hardly. So much damage has already been done. My book sales are way down, and I've already had a few galleries pull me from their shows." Not to mention the loss of income was hurting my finances in other ways, but I didn't need to bring that up right now.

"What?" Jeanne's voice was startled. "But that'll change now, right? Now that there's proof of your innocence?"

I shook my head slowly, swallowing a bite of cake. "I don't think it'll be that easy. So much in the art world is based on reputation, and that's a hard thing to recover. People remember the scandal, not the outcome." I shrugged, and Jeanne watched me in silence for a long moment.

"I'm really sorry, Jer," she finally said. "Isn't there anything you can do?"

I scraped up the last few crumbs from my plate. "Not really. Just fight it as much as we can and do damage control on social media. Scott says we could countersue for defamation and financial damages, but I don't think there's any point."

"Why not?"

"It won't help anything," I said, feeling tired. Maybe Jeanne's sugar solution really was helping. "The damage is done, after all, and dragging Emilia down with me doesn't benefit either of us."

I was surprised when her hand came out to cover mine where it rested on the countertop. Hers was soft and warm, the pads of her fingers light on the back of my hand.

"Is there anything I can do to help?" she asked in a quiet voice.

I flipped my hand over, giving hers a tight squeeze before releasing her grip, and there was a warmth in my chest as we sat together in the dark. "You already have."

* * *

The warm feeling persisted all through the following day. Scott gave us the okay to do damage control on social media, and I gratefully turned my accounts over to Olivia so she could start rebuilding my reputation.

In the meantime, I threw myself into painting, spending as much time as I could in my basement studio. I still had a couple of upcoming shows that hadn't cancelled on me, and though the landscapes I was working on weren't what anyone was expecting from me, they were all I was feeling inspired enough to work on.

Besides, aside from swimming laps, painting was one of the only things that could keep me from obsessively checking social media and stressing about the judgmental comments that continued to pour in. Not to mention the decline in book sales that still showed no sign of recovery a few weeks later. Or the lack of new gallery bookings or art sales that would generally be picking up around this time of year.

I tried not to stress. I knew these things took time.

And at least if nothing else, my home life was good. Jeanne and I had settled into some kind of a truce, where we were managing to keep our snarky arguments to a minimum and just commit to enjoying the last of Dylan's summer vacation.

Dylan, in particular, was adjusting very well to having both of his parents around most of the time, and I felt a pang of guilt at the thought that it was temporary. I hated the thought of uprooting him once again. Though I couldn't help but notice that Jeanne seemed to be dragging her feet on moving out. She had eventually admitted to me that she'd decided not to move in with Mark, grudgingly agreeing that it was too soon. I had tried not to gloat too hard.

But she hadn't told me what alternative plans she might have, and I hadn't asked, not wanting her to rush into anything. I knew it was only a matter of time before she was ready to move on, but I had to admit there was a large part of me that had gotten used to having her there.

No, not gotten used to. *Liked* having her there. Enjoyed her company. Wished things were simpler, wanted her to stay, wanted her...I shut down that line of thought.

Dylan, for his part, seemed to have forgotten entirely that

he would have to move again, and was completely focused on the idea of starting first grade.

On the weekend before school started, he spent the night at my parents' house, and when I went to pick him up on Sunday afternoon he was nearly bouncing off the walls with excitement.

"Gramma says she knows my teacher." He could barely keep still enough to get the words out, so I looked to my mom instead, where she was bent over the kitchen table, cleaning up paint from whatever mess she and Dylan had made that afternoon.

"That's right," she said with a smile. "Miss Hayes. She only lives a few blocks from here."

I wasn't surprised. My mom knew everyone, and everything about them.

"Dylan, stop touching things; you still have paint on your hands," she admonished. "Go wash them off and then start picking up your toys to get ready to go."

He flew out of the room with only a small whine of complaint, and I crossed to the table to help my mom clean up the mess.

"He sure is excited," she said, collecting brushes and setting them in the sink. "She's a very good teacher. You are going to keep him at that school, aren't you?"

I glanced up in surprise. "Of course, why wouldn't I?"

"Oh, I don't know," she said with a shrug and a sidelong glance. "What if Jeanne finds a house in a different school district?"

Ohhh. This was a fishing expedition, I realized. She was digging for information on Jeanne.

It was no secret that I was the favored child in this family, and both Sam and Jeanne took the brunt of my parents' disapproval. But while there were times I couldn't help but antagonize my brother over that fact, in reality I didn't find it nearly as amusing as Sam believed I did.

"He would still stay at his school," I told her, not rising to the bait.

"But she is still living with you, right?" my mom pressed.

I sighed inwardly. "Yes, she is."

"Well," she sniffed, gathering up the newspaper they'd been using as a drop cloth. "I hope she's at least paying you rent."

My jaw dropped and I glanced up sharply. "Of course she's not paying me rent."

"What? Why not?"

"Because I don't need it, for one thing." Though I wasn't entirely sure that was true at this point. "And for another thing, she lost everything she has in a *fire.* I'm not cruel."

My mother sniffed. "It's not like she can't afford it. Especially once that boyfriend of hers joins her dental practice. I just want to make sure she's not taking advantage of you."

"Wait—what?" *Mark was joining Jeanne's practice?*

My mother appeared not to hear the strain in my voice, because she continued cleaning, crossing to the sink to rinse out the brushes.

"Oh, yes, Sam told me last week. It makes sense though; she's always had more space than she needs in that place."

I was glad my mother's back was to me so she couldn't see me standing over the table, frozen in place as I tried to make sense of her words.

Mark was joining Jeanne's practice?

I wasn't sure why the knowledge was hitting me so hard. After all, I already knew she'd been thinking about moving in with him, but part of me had thought—hoped—that was just out of convenience, and besides, she hadn't brought that plan up again in weeks. But this…this seemed serious. And despite my best efforts, I couldn't seem to stop a single refrain from playing on repeat in my head.

But he's not right for her.

Which didn't give me pause nearly as much as the second thought, which crept up quietly on the heels of the first.

Not like I am.

CHAPTER 11

JEANNE

*T*he day my divorce from Jeremy had been finalized, I'd gone out drinking with my co-workers, and I'd celebrated so hard that Carly had been forced to drive me home and tuck me into bed. I only had vague recollections of the night by the time I'd woken the next morning, but I'd remembered her sitting by my bedside, forcing water down my throat as she'd humored me with placating agreements.

"Yes, Jeanne, he is the worst human on the face of the earth. You are a million times better off without him…That's right, his art sucks and he'll never amount to anything…Yes, sweetie, he'll never get through life without a woman to take care of him. Probably his mom," she'd added, and we'd both snickered at the thought.

When I looked back at that time, it was embarrassing, but with the distance of time and age, I also came to realize that Jeremy and I had really both suffered from the same thing—immaturity. Neither of us were the selfish, thoughtless people we'd been when we'd first gotten together, and while we both still had our faults, part of me couldn't help but wonder what might have happened if we'd found each other later in life. Or if we'd even just stuck it out together.

I supposed I'd never know, but I had to admit to a certain amount of nostalgia, coupled with grudging admiration for the man Jeremy had grown into.

The man I'd married years ago would never have been able to handle such a damaging scandal with such maturity. He would have been all over social media hurling insults right back. He never would have cared for another person the way I saw him care for Dylan, or even the way he took care of me.

It was like the worst of his negative traits had mellowed with age and maturity, allowing the positive traits to shine through—his upbeat, fun-loving personality, his fierce deter- mination and loyalty, even his teasing nature had become playful rather than hurtful.

I was finally starting to feel like things were at a good place between us—like we could hold an adult conversation without going for each other's throats. Like once I'd moved out and we'd resumed our own lives I wouldn't have to go out of my way to avoid him or dread seeing him on holidays and birthdays. Like maybe we could find our way back to friendship, at least.

But when a soft knock came at my bedroom door late in the evening on the night before Dylan's first day of school, I opened it to reveal a man who looked like he'd taken one more punch than he could handle.

He'd been very careful to give me my own space, and had never come to my room before, but my surprise at seeing him there was immediately wiped away by concern as I took in his posture and expression.

His dark eyes were ringed with worry and lack of sleep, his shoulders were slumped, and his hair was a wreck as if he'd been running his hands through it. In the months that

I'd been here, I'd seen Jeremy stressed, and angry, and tired, but I'd never seen him look so *defeated* as he did right then. I felt a chill run through me. "Are you okay?" I stepped aside, giving him space to enter, but he didn't, just leaned in the doorway as if he needed the support to keep him upright.

"What happened?" I prompted again when he didn't answer, and only then noticed that he was holding a letter in his hand. I recognized it as part of the stack of mail I'd left on the table in the foyer the day before.

"We need to talk," he said in a hoarse voice, holding out the letter. I took the envelope from him and pulled out the folded paper inside.

It was from the bank. I sank down on the edge of the bed, words jumping out at me as I skimmed the letter. I had to read it twice before I could make sense of the words there.

"Foreclosure?" My voice had turned hoarse as well, and I had to clear my throat to get the words out. I stared up at him. "What does it mean, foreclosure?" As if I didn't know what the word meant.

He hovered in the doorway, as if he really wasn't sure if he should enter, then when I beckoned him in, he folded right where he stood to sit cross-legged on the floor, his back propped against the door frame. He scrubbed a hand over his face, mussing his dark hair even more in the process, then seemed to gather himself to look at me directly.

"It's not a foreclosure, not yet. But I've been missing house payments."

"You've been missing house payments," I repeated. And I'd just been thinking about how much more responsible he'd become.

His expression was pleading. "I kept waiting for things to turn around—for book sales to pick up, for art to sell, for new gallery show bookings...but they're not coming."

"It hasn't been that long yet, though," I protested. "You said it was a long process."

"I know. And things will pick up; they will. But…" He gestured vaguely around himself, then took a deep breath. "This…it's unsustainable. I've been living beyond my means for years, and even if things do turn around and I can catch up on my payments, I don't think…" He looked queasy.

I narrowed my eyes. "What exactly are you saying?"

He took another deep breath, as if steeling himself to deliver the next words. "I think I should sell the house now, before it goes into foreclosure. I can make up the missed payments, and then it won't hurt my credit, and that way I can try to…get control of the situation before it gets worse."

My brow furrowed. "Sell the house? Now? But…what would that mean for us?"

His voice dropped to a whisper. "I…think you'll need to find somewhere else."

My voice came out shrill. "Find somewhere else?"

He glanced up. "I mean…that was the plan anyway, right?"

"Well, sure, but it's not that easy. I was going to buy a house, but the market is slow right now, and I want to stay close to work and…and Dylan's school, and…" My voice caught as I grew more flustered. "I didn't realize there was an expiration date here."

His mouth was pinched, his expression pained.

I glanced up at him sharply. "Look, I can pay rent. Let me help you pay your mortgage for a bit until we've both found new places to stay, and you can look into selling then."

"Jeanne, no." His face was gray. "It's really nice of you to offer, but it won't help. I need to sell it now."

My eyes widened. "Just how far behind *are* you?"

He shook his head, his face set in stubborn lines. "I can handle it, but I need to list the house."

"You obviously *can't* handle it," I shot back.

His eyes blazed and his spine straightened. "Look, I know it's inconvenient. The timing is terrible, and I don't want to do this anymore than you do. But I'm trying to be responsible here, and if—"

"Responsible?" I exclaimed. "Yes, because you've been so *responsible* so far, buying a house you couldn't afford, and didn't need, and then stopped paying on it, when it's the only place your *kid* has to live." I knew I was being mean and unfair, but I couldn't seem to stop myself. The expression on Jeremy's face had grown dark, the defeat in his eyes turning to a blaze of anger, and a part of me was relieved. He still had some fight in him—he hadn't given up, and it made me want to provoke him more.

"I mean, honestly," I went on, the glittering warning in his eyes feeding my own anger, "what the hell were you thinking with this house anyway? Thirty people could live here comfortably. Why would you waste your money on—"

"It's none of your damn business what I spend my money on," he cut in coldly.

"Obviously it is, if you can't afford it and you won't let me help," I snapped.

"I don't need your help. And it's not like you're homeless," he scoffed. "So, you won't get the perfect house in the perfect neighborhood right this second. There are plenty of apartments to rent while you look, and you know Carly or Sam would let you stay with them if you need more time. Honestly, I don't know why you didn't stay with Carly in the first place."

"Clearly, I should have," I retorted. "But I guess you'll get your wish. I'll be out of here tomorrow, and after you pick up Dylan from school, you can explain to him why he's getting uprooted yet again."

An expression I couldn't quite identify flashed across his face. "Jeanne, come on. It's not like it's going to sell immediately. You don't have to leave tomorrow. There's plenty of time—"

"No," I cut him off, rising to my feet and stepping toward him in the doorway. "It's fine. I shouldn't have stayed this long in the first place. Besides, it'll be easier for you to show the house if I'm not here. I'll be gone tomorrow."

I crossed the space and took hold of the open door, making it clear that I was going to close the door whether or not he moved out of it. "Good night."

He scrambled to his feet and moved back a step. "Jeanne, seriously—"

"Good night, Jeremy," I repeated, then shut the door in his face.

I didn't wait to calm down; I just grabbed my phone off the nightstand. But I didn't call Carly; I called Mark.

"Hey babe, I didn't expect to hear from you so late." Despite his words, Mark sounded pleased to hear from me, and I waited for the rush of warmth to hit me from the comforting sound of his voice, but it didn't come. I must have been too upset.

"Sorry, I hope I didn't wake you or anything." I gripped the phone tight to my ear.

"No, it's fine. What's up?"

"I…I was wondering if your offer for me to move in with you still stands?"

There was a rustle of fabric at the other end of the line, and I imagined he was sitting up in bed. "Of course," he said. "Why, what happened? Is everything okay?"

"I—" I should tell him what happened. If our relationship was serious, which it obviously was, I should be up front with him. But I didn't want to talk about it. Not yet, anyway. "Yes, everything is fine. I just think I've been staying here long enough."

"Okay," he said slowly. "But I thought you weren't ready to move in with me."

"I'm not ready to buy a house with you," I corrected him. "But this...this is a good first step, right? If we live together now, we can see if we're compatible. See if it's going to work out before we think about buying a house."

"Well, that's true." He sounded pleased. "That's a smart idea."

I felt a pulse of pleasure. That's right. Jeremy could do what he wanted, but *I* was going to be responsible and make smart, adult decisions.

"It's still pretty far for you, remember," he cautioned. "My place in Glassbury is about an hour away from Fairfield. Will that work for your job? And Dylan?"

"It'll be fine," I said firmly. To myself or him, I wasn't sure. "It's temporary."

"Great. When did you want to move? I can help move your things."

"Would tomorrow work?" I asked.

There was a beat of silence. "Tomorrow's...fine. Are you *sure* you're okay? Nothing happened there, did it?"

"No," I assured him. "Everything is fine. I'm just ready to move on."

"Okay," he said. "Call me in the morning when you're ready then, okay?"

We said our goodbyes and hung up, and I sat back against the headboard with satisfaction. See? That was what a grownup conversation was like. No yelling, no cursing, no emotions spiraling out of control. Just simple, easy, and calm. Why was it so hard to have that with Jeremy?

I tipped my head back and let out a long sigh. After the fact, with my emotions calming and the tide of pulsing anger ebbing from my blood, guilt was quickly washing in to take its place. How could I have been such a jerk? How could I have said those things?

He'd been clearly upset, faced with losing his house—which he obviously cared about no matter how ridiculous I thought it was—and trying his best to do the right thing, and all I'd been able to do was yell at him and make him feel worse. I knew it wasn't his fault. He was trying, and I had been so surprised I'd acted without thinking, saying things I didn't even mean.

For half a second I considered going down the hall and finding him to apologize. But no, we'd just end up yelling again. That was practically all we were capable of.

I sighed again and slid down the headboard to lie flat on top of the comforter.

Oh well, by tomorrow it would no longer matter. My life was moving onward and upward. I was taking a big step, moving in with Mark, finally moving my life in the right direction. I would no longer have to deal with Jeremy, wouldn't have to interact with him at all outside of Dylan.

I should have felt pleased.

CHAPTER 12

JEREMY

I called a realtor first thing the following morning. It was hours before I would normally be up, but it had been a long restless night of tossing and turning, mentally replaying my conversation with Jeanne—if you could call it a conversation—and vacillating between anger and guilt and frustration and sadness.

Should I have handled things differently? I wasn't sure. Maybe I should have seen the writing on the wall earlier. Maybe I shouldn't have relied on Olivia's promises that everything would bounce right back to normal. Maybe I should have accepted Jeanne's offer to pay rent.

But no. That would have done nothing but delay the inevitable. I was doing the right thing, no matter what Jeanne thought. The right thing for the future. I loved this house, but Jeanne was right—it was too big, and I wasn't the same person I'd been when I'd bought it. The money would come again, one way or another. I'd be okay, I knew that. But I'd be better off saving for Dylan's college education than falling into debt by trying to afford a house with a five-car garage. I only wished it hadn't all happened at the worst possible time, with Jeanne here, when everything had been going so well.

My realtor was a loud, boisterous woman I'd known for years. Her name was Paulette, and she had fire-engine red hair she teased to within an inch of its life and a personality equally as large.

"Sugar, I put you in that house, I'll get you out of it," she assured me. "I'll come by and take pictures later this morning and we'll get it listed by tonight. Have a little patience though," she cautioned. "There's not a huge market in Fairfield for houses of that, er, size. It might take a little time."

"That's okay," I said. "As long as we're making progress."

"I'll take care of you, sugar," she promised.

The silence after I hung up the phone had a sense of finality to it, and I blew out a long breath. I was doing the right thing. I *was*.

Dragging myself out of bed, I stretched, then padded down the hall to get Dylan ready for his first day of school. I found him up and dressed, practically bouncing off the walls, and my heart lightened considerably.

"You ready, buddy?"

His answering squeal nearly made me cover my ears, and I laughed as he barreled down the stairs to the kitchen. To my surprise—and a little bit of relief—Jeanne wasn't up, and I started the coffee maker as I got Dylan his breakfast. It was a bit of a scramble, finding his backpack, making sure he had all his school supplies, packing his lunch and getting him out to the street before the bus came, but his presence helped considerably to lighten my mood. Enough so that by the time the bus had come and gone I thought maybe I should find Jeanne. To apologize, or even just to talk it out more.

I didn't want her to leave this way. I didn't want to return to the way things had been, where we were basically strangers, passing Dylan back and forth with as little contact as possible.

I poured an extra mug of coffee as a peace offering and made my way up to her room where I knocked quietly on the door. There was no way she wasn't up; she was probably avoiding me.

There was a long pause before she opened the door, a wary expression on her face. Behind her, clothing stacked on the bed, and my heart sank to see she was packing.

I proffered the coffee and cut right to the chase. "I'm sorry. I didn't want to leave it like we did last night."

She sighed and her expression softened. "I'm sorry, too. I didn't mean…well, I didn't mean a lot of what I said. I know this is harder for you than it is for me. I was…unfair. And unkind." She took the mug out of my hand with a quiet murmur of thanks.

I scrubbed my hand through my hair. "Are you really leaving today then? You know you can stay as long as you want. My realtor said I should expect it'll take a while to sell."

"I am," she said gently. "I think it'll be for the best." She gave me a tremulous smile, her gray eyes sad.

"I don't want things to go back to the way they were before." The words came out in a rush, before I was sure I should say them.

She stared at me, and I hastened to explain. "I wish things hadn't happened the way they did between us. I miss having you around…as a friend. I don't want to go back to trying to avoid you at awkward holiday dinners with my parents, and hurried five second exchanges of Dylan."

Her eyebrow lifted as her slight smile solidified into a smirk. "So, you avoided me at family dinners, huh?"

I narrowed my eyes, though I couldn't keep my own

mouth from lifting in a smile as well. "Like you didn't do the same."

She laughed, and her expression warmed. "I don't want to go back to that either," she said softly, looking toward the window. "Sometimes I think...maybe we didn't really give ourselves a chance, all those years ago. To be friends, I mean. I miss you."

The words were simple, but they made my heart leap in my chest. She faced me again and smiled in a way that lightened her whole face, and my breath caught at how beautiful she was. Those bright, intelligent eyes and full pink lips. I found myself grinning back, unable to keep the foolish expression from my face.

Finally, she turned away from me, taking a long sip of her coffee before setting the mug on the bedside table and surveying the mess on her bed.

I pushed off of the door frame and stepped into the room. "Is there anything I can do to help?"

She shrugged. "I don't think so. I really don't have very much stuff. I just have to check the rest of the house to see what I've forgotten. Dylan can stay here until I'm all settled in at Mark's and we'll talk to him together, okay?"

My blood froze solid in my veins. "You're going to Mark's?"

She glanced up at me and I saw the wariness return to her eyes. "Yes," she said slowly. "Where did you think I was going to go?"

"I thought you told me you weren't ready to move in with him," I said, working hard to keep the accusing tone out of my voice and failing miserably. "I thought you were going to Carly's, or maybe Sam's."

She gave an exasperated sigh. "I told you I wasn't ready to *buy* a house with Mark. But he has plenty of space, and it makes the most sense to go there."

Warning bells were sounding in my mind. *Stop,* I told myself. *It's none of your business. Don't make things worse.* But it was too late. I couldn't stop the words as they blurted out.

"Do you love him?"

"What?" she exclaimed. "Of course I...I mean—"

Her stumbling response only goaded me further. "Do you even hear yourself?" I demanded, moving further into the room. "You don't move in with someone you love because he 'has plenty of space,' or because it 'makes the most sense.'"

"You do if you're an adult, making responsible decisions," she countered hotly.

I shook my head. "Is that what this is? Is that why you're with him? Because you think it's the responsible thing to do?"

"No, I—"

"You move in with someone you love because you *need* to be with them, as much as you can." I cut her off, taking another step forward. She backed away, her legs hitting the side of the bed.

"Because you can't imagine your life apart, because you want to wake up next to them every morning," I went on, ignoring my voice cracking on the words. I couldn't even make sense of these feelings bubbling up inside me, feelings that had been growing for weeks. I only knew I had to make her understand.

"And how do you know I don't feel that way about Mark?" she asked, her voice a little breathless.

I scoffed. "Mark isn't right for you."

"How can you say that? You don't even know him."

I stepped forward again, crowding further into her personal space. Her eyes were wide, but she didn't move away. She had nowhere to go.

"I know he doesn't treat you right," I breathed, my eyes locked on hers.

"How so?"

"He judges you for eating sweets."

"How do you know that?" Her voice was weak.

"Because every time you go out to dinner with him you come home and eat the dessert I leave out for you."

"I really need to eat less sugar anyway," she said, but her voice lacked any conviction.

"He's pushing his way into your dental practice."

"How do you know that?" she repeated.

"My mom told me, which means everyone must know. Was it a decision you made together? Has he even really asked you about it? How do Carly and Tris and the others feel about it? Has he asked them? Does he even know their names?"

She didn't answer any of my questions, which was all the answer I needed. I took one final step toward her, until we were so close I could feel the heat of her body all along the front of mine. She could have sat down on the bed to move away from me, could have pushed me back, but she didn't. She just stood there, her gray eyes locked on mine, her face flushed and filled with too many emotions to identify.

I pushed my luck, lifting my hand and taking a lock of her blond hair, letting the strands run gently through my fingers like silk. My voice was a whisper. "You think he's trying to be helpful and make things easy on you, but he's really just walking all over you, forcing you to do things his way, treating you like a child and making decisions for you. You may think you love him, but he doesn't love you, or he wouldn't treat you like that."

Her lips parted, her tongue darting out to moisten them, and my gaze followed the movement. "Where's your fight, Jeanne?" I asked quietly. "The woman I married had more backbone than anyone else I'd ever met. What happened?"

Her eyes lit with the spark I'd been looking for, and I hoped I hadn't pushed her too far.

"It's called compromise," she told me, her brows drawing down. "You wouldn't understand. All you understand is arguing, and fighting."

"At least I'm fighting *for* something," I said.

Her breath caught, and her voice dropped to the barest whisper. "What are you fighting for?"

"I'm fighting for *you*, Jeanne." The emotions swirled in my chest, making it hard to pull in air. I had to leave before I did something stupid, like kiss her. "We had our problems, you and I," I told her, "but I never tried to turn you into a different person. I love you for exactly who you are."

Her face drained of color, and I let the moment stretch as I traced my eyes over her, memorizing every inch, before I backed up a step, then another, then turned and left the room. Guess I hadn't been able to keep myself from being stupid after all.

* * *

"Sugar, I thought you'd be happy!"

"I am happy, I just…seriously, two offers? You listed it *yesterday*. I thought you said it would take a while."

It was too much, all so fast. Jeanne had left—she'd actually left, after I'd bared my soul to her—and then not even twenty-four hours and three showings later, the house was practically sold. I'd expected to have weeks, if not months.

Paulette was laughing on the other end of the line. "The market does what it wants to. One of the potential buyers is looking for a quick sale though. They want to close as soon as possible. How fast can you be out?"

I sighed. "I can put my stuff in storage and be out by the weekend."

"Perfect. I'll be in touch."

I hung up the phone and sat, staring blankly out of the huge picture window. The treetops were a bold, vivid green, like glinting emeralds with dappled shadows stretching down off the ridge toward the state park, but in less than a month they would be starting to change. It was my favorite time of year, when clusters of red and orange and yellow would start to peak through the canopy until the entire forest looked like it was on fire. I wouldn't get to see it this year. Wouldn't get to paint it. Not from this vantage, anyway.

I'd wanted to show the view to Jeanne. Wanted her to see my recent run of landscape paintings and get her opinion on the new direction of my artwork. Wanted her to see how beautiful this house could be in the autumn. Wanted to curl up with her and Dylan and watch movies with mugs of steaming hot chocolate. Wanted to fall asleep with her by my side, curled against me as we gazed out of the window at the perfect view. I *wanted...*

Everything I'd had once, and had let slip through my fingers. And here I was. I didn't have the view, and I didn't have Jeanne.

I turned away from the window, glad there was no one here to see the glimmer of tears in my eyes.

It was time to go.

CHAPTER 13

JEANNE

*W*hen I was in the hospital right after Dylan had been born, a kind nurse had taken pity on me and given me a lifesaving paper with a kind of flow chart on it. If your baby is crying, first check the diaper. If that's clean, is he hungry? Is he cold? And on down the list so a frantic new mother could be sure she hadn't forgotten anything important.

I wished some kind soul would give me a flow chart for life. If the guy buys you flowers before the third date, it's okay to sleep with him. Or, he needs to use the L-word ten times before you can consider moving in together. If there's a child involved, turn to page five. It sure would help stop me from second guessing every single decision I ever made.

Like I was second guessing this one.

In the wake of Jeremy's admission, I'd fled. Yep. Some combination of panic and cowardice had driven me straight out the door and into Mark's apartment, and on the way I'd managed to convince myself that I'd overinflated the entire situation in my mind.

Jeremy hadn't *really* meant what he'd said. He'd been so

445

caught up in disparaging Mark he'd gotten carried away. He certainly hadn't meant to tell me he *loved* me. And even if he had, it didn't change anything, right? It was too late for Jeremy and me. We'd had our chance, and we'd blown it. I was with Mark.

It didn't matter how Jeremy felt about me.

It didn't matter how I felt about him. I didn't even *know* how I felt.

God, what a mess.

I thought things would get better when I got to Mark's. I truly did. And they'd almost started off that way.

We hadn't figured out the details with Dylan yet, but since school had started and I was currently an hour from Fairfield, it'd made sense for him to stay with Jeremy during the week. It would give me time to settle in at Mark's without having a six-year-old under foot.

The second I walked through the door he swept me off my feet in a hug. "Babe, I'm so glad you're here." The kiss he pressed to my lips was quick, and I mercilessly tamped down any feelings of relief at that fact. "Let me show you around." He took my hand, pulling me into the apartment.

I forced a laugh. "I have been here before, you know."

He shot me a dazzling smile. "Sure, but now it's your home, too."

Home. My home. The words echoed in my head and I shifted my weight.

"I changed some things around for you," he went on. "And, I have a big surprise." His grin was excited, and I forced a smile in return as he led me through on a brief tour.

The apartment was nothing special, a generic three-bedroom place with white walls and laminate countertops, but it was in good repair and Mark had done his best to make it feel homey despite the fact that he hadn't planned to stay there long. He showed me through the master, where he'd emptied out a couple of drawers and half the closet for me, and into the bathroom where he'd put together a basket of lotions and soaps and scented candles for me.

"Because I know you like taking baths," he said proudly, and this time my smile was genuine.

"That's very sweet of you," I told him, looking through the basket. The memory of Jeremy's enormous jetted tub flashed through my mind, but I shut the thought down.

His grin widened. "That's not even the surprise. Come see."

He took my hand again, pulling me down the short hallway to the spare room.

"Voila." He opened the door with a flourish, and my mouth fell open.

The last time I'd been here the room had been storage, piled high with books and boxes. Since then, it had been transformed into a kid's room. No, not a kid's room—a baby's room. The bed was made up with a soft blue bedspread featuring cute cartoon owls and bears, suitable for a newborn. A light-up mobile hung over the pillow, and there was a tiny bookshelf in the corner, piled high with unopened toys. I crossed the room to look closer. Large play blocks, board books, a thirty-piece puzzle. Play-doh. A small wooden train set.

"What do you think? It's for Dylan," Mark announced, drawing my attention away from the toys.

That was good, at least. It seemed like an obvious statement, but part of me had been a little concerned Mark might think I was pregnant. I tried to relax my shoulders, pulling them down away from my ears. Oh God, how on earth was I going to deal with this?

"This was very thoughtful of you," I said, turning to face him. "He's…um, he's six, though, you know that, right?"

"Oh, sure," he said, waving dismissively. "I know some of

it is a little young, but there was a big sale, and you don't really ever outgrow your childhood toys."

I gave a shaky noncommittal laugh, unable to find it within myself to tell him that when you were six, you most definitely *did* outgrow your childhood toys. I didn't even want to hear Dylan's reaction to the room. It wouldn't be good.

Something on the bed caught my eye, and I stepped closer. My breath caught as I lifted a stuffed shark from the pillow.

Mark saw what I was holding and beamed. "It's a replacement for Finley. That's the one you said he lost in the fire, right?" He chuckled. "Maybe he won't even notice it's different."

I set the stuffed shark on the pillow, using the motion to hide my face. While the gesture was undeniably sweet, how could I tell him that not only would Dylan notice the difference, but he would likely burst into tears at the sight of it? Not to mention Mark hadn't *asked* me about any of this. Of course, it was obviously intended to be a surprise, but how could he be so off the mark?

"When did you even *do* all of this?" I ran a hand down the soft comforter. It really would have been lovely for a newborn. "I only told you I was moving in yesterday."

"I went to the store this morning," he said, the light in his eye undimmed by my lukewarm reaction. "I can't wait for him to see it. I hope it'll help him feel right at home here."

I swallowed hard, unsure what to say. He'd misread the situation, and once again made assumptions about what I would want, and it really should have been my first red flag. And in case I was still too dense to realize it, the universe saw fit to send me a second one later that evening when Mark celebrated our new cohabitation by cooking me a romantic dinner.

The food was delicious, the candlelight intimate and the wine just enough to take the edge off of the bad feeling I'd been carrying around with me all day. It was enough to make me overlook the fact that there was no dessert. But...

"What do you mean, you don't *allow* sugar in the house?"

His shrug seemed more perfunctory than apologetic. "I'd just really appreciate it if you didn't bring anything back here. It's easier that way."

I closed the door of the sugar-free fridge and turned to peer at him. "Easier how?"

"If there's sugar around, it's hard to avoid eating it. If we don't keep it in the house, then there's no temptation."

I eyed him. "So, because *you* can't control yourself, *I* can't eat anything sweet...like ever?"

"It's not that I can't control myself," he said, an edge creeping into his tone. "It's just—babe, we've talked about this. We're *dentists*, right? We know better."

His tone had a sense of finality to it, and while it immediately put my back up, it didn't make me want to argue the way I did with Jeremy. It seemed like that should be a good thing, but it wasn't. I simply felt...tired. Like it wasn't worth the effort.

I crossed the room and sat down at the table just in time for him to change the subject to red flag number three. "Speaking of dentists, I meant to ask you the other day. Are your hygienists trained to do laser treatments?"

Does he even know their names? Jeremy's voice echoed through my head, and I gave it a shake to block out the memory.

"No, we don't have a laser, why?"

He leaned back, folding his arms behind his head. "Well, it could be a potential new revenue stream. We'd probably have to consider looking for new hygienists, but there are—"

"New hygienists?" I cut him off. "As in, replace Carly,

Grace and Marisol?" My heart dropped to lodge somewhere in the vicinity of my stomach.

"I mean, we could pay for them to go through the training, but it'd probably be cheaper if we found someone fresh out of dental school who…"

He kept talking, but I stopped listening. Why? Why was I like this? Why was I so stubborn, so unable to admit when I was wrong? Why was it so hard for me to admit when Jeremy was right?

"I can't do this." I cut him off mid-sentence, pushing to my feet.

He blinked up at me. "That's okay, we don't have to find new hygienists. We don't even have to bring in a laser if you don't want; it was only—"

"No, not that." I swallowed, but my heart seemed to have risen up from my stomach and lodged in my throat instead. I could hear it beating throughout my whole body. "This." I waved a trembling hand between us, widening my gesture to take in the whole apartment. "I can't do *this*. I…want to break up. I don't think this is going to work."

His mouth opened and closed like a fish. "I…but you just got here," he said lamely, glancing around like he'd misplaced something and couldn't quite figure out what it was. A second later he turned to face me again. "What about Dylan's room…and our dental practice?"

My eyes burned, and once again Jeremy's words whispered in my head. *Where's your fight, Jeanne?*

I didn't let the tears spill over. "We never argue," I said quietly.

His brow creased in confusion. "Isn't that a good thing?"

"I thought it was," I said, placing a hand on the table for support. "I thought compatible people didn't argue, they compromised. But we're not compromising, are we? It's only me. *I'm* compromising. I'm giving in, and losing myself in the process. I'm sorry."

I swallowed, trying to keep up with my racing thoughts, trying not to let his wounded expression make me feel guilty. I wouldn't back down.

I met his eyes squarely. "I love sugar, and I don't care that it's bad for me. I don't want to change my dental practice, even if we have more room than we need. I don't want to live in Glassbury. I…" My voice dropped to a whisper, but I forced the words out anyway. "I don't want to choose responsibility over passion. I'm sorry, Mark."

Red flag number four: he didn't fight for me. He was very gentlemanly when he helped carry my bags back out to my car, and didn't argue, or raise his voice, or cry, or do anything that might have showed me he actually cared.

I should have been relieved.

Instead, I cried all the way to Carly's house.

* * *

"Girl, as your dental hygienist, but more importantly as your *friend*, I seriously can't let you eat any more ice cream."

I set the carton on the nightstand with a grunt. It was empty anyway.

"Seriously, it's been practically a week." Carly sat on the edge of the guest bed, pushing loose tendrils of chestnut hair off her forehead. "You know you can stay here as long as you want to, but you have to pull your shit together. When do you get Dylan back?"

"He's at his grandparents' right now," I said with a sigh. "I get him Sunday afternoon."

"Okay, it's Friday, so that gives you two days. Surely you can at least take a shower by then, right?" Her words were teasing, but her eyes were worried. She leaned down, smoothing my hair back, and I was suddenly reminded of the last time she'd taken care of me through an emotional meltdown, the night after my divorce was finalized.

"God," I mumbled. "Why don't *you* ever have embarrassing breakdowns so I can nurse *you* through them? Why's it always gotta be me?"

She laughed. "Because *I* am a responsible adult," she informed me.

I groaned, pulling the blanket up over my head. "Oh God, don't say that. I tried that; it didn't work for me."

She snorted. "Your relationship with Mark didn't make you a responsible adult. What makes you a responsible adult is the way you take care of Dylan. And the way you run your practice. The way you're there for your friends. What you had with Mark was just...hell, I don't know. I don't even know what you saw in him."

I gave a small laugh. "Me neither," I said quietly, and it was the truth.

She extracted the blanket from my fingers and gently pulled it away from my face. "Seriously though, Jeanne, I haven't seen you this torn up in years. I'm worried about you. Honestly, I didn't even realize you were that into Mark."

At that, all the suppressed emotions welled up and overflowed, tears leaking from my eyes no matter how hard I tried to hold them back. "I wasn't," I whispered, my voice cracking on the words.

"But—" she started.

I saw the second she understood, her eyes growing wide as she pulled in a sharp breath. "Fuck, Jeanne, you went and fell in love with Jeremy again, didn't you?"

"*W*hat the hell happened, man?" Sam's voice was soft, a little cautious, but with none of its usual animosity.

My feet dragged as I stumbled through his doorway, my bag falling heavily by my feet. I was exhausted. It had been a long, sleepless week, filled with careful conversations with Dylan, explaining in terms a six-year-old could understand why his life was changing yet again, then packing up my entire life and livelihood and cramming it all into a storage unit for the foreseeable future.

It helped me to understand a little bit better how Jeanne must have felt after the fire, showing up at my door with nothing but the clothes on her back. At least I had a suitcase with me.

Sam guided me into the living room of his small, cozy apartment. I collapsed with a sigh, unsure how to answer his question. He knew the gist; I'd explained the situation on the phone when I'd asked if he would take me in for a while.

"I'm surprised you didn't go stay with Mom and Dad," he said, levering himself down onto the leather sofa next to me.

I gave a short laugh. "Hah, and hear twenty-four hour live coverage on my mistakes? No thanks."

Sam didn't laugh. "Are you kidding? You'd be treated like royalty over there. Not to mention you'd have built-in babysitters."

I let out a breath. I knew my relationship with Sam had suffered because of my parents' favoritism. Since my relationship with my parents was also difficult, albeit in a different way, I had buried my head in the sand, selfishly not wanting to disrupt the golden bubble of my life.

But that bubble had burst, and it was time to grow up and deal with the fallout.

I steeled myself and met his eyes, the same dark brown as my own. "Sam, I'm sorry," I said quietly. He raised his brows, and I pushed on. "I'm sorry I've been a shitty brother. And I'm sorry Mom and Dad treat you as less, when you're quite obviously the only one of the two of us that has his head on straight."

Sam broke my gaze and looked down at the floor. His voice was gruff. "It's not your fault they treat me that way."

"No, but I should have stood up for you. I shouldn't have treated it like a joke, or like it didn't matter. I know it does. And if you don't want me here, I'll understand."

He blew out his breath and stood. "Nah, you know you're always welcome here. You want a beer?"

I knew that wasn't the end of it, and I would have to actually do the work to repair our relationship, not just say the words, but my chest still felt lighter with the words said and provisionally accepted.

We'd just settled into the sofa and had moved on to lighter topics when the front door opened and Ellen came in.

Sam's girlfriend was one of the best things that had ever happened to him, and they were very much in love, as was apparent by the sickening look the two exchanged as she set her purse down by the door. I tamped down my wave of envy.

"Marian's closing up downstairs," she told him, referring to the bookstore beneath the apartment that Sam owned. Honestly, how my parents could consider Sam's accomplishments any less than mine I couldn't fathom.

He laughed. "Were you painting down there again?"

Ellen was an artist too, and I was given to understand at the moment she was hard at work illustrating a series of children's books. I couldn't imagine getting anything done in such a noisy atmosphere, but Ellen smiled at him and shrugged. "I like the bustle. I get more done when there's chaos around me."

She took a seat on the ottoman near the couch, and turned her gaze on me. There was sympathy on her usually sunny face. She was close with Jeanne, and I wondered how much she'd heard about my situation from both my ex-wife and my brother.

"You okay, Jeremy?" she asked gently.

I gave a nod, though I wasn't sure how convincing it was. "I'm alright. Thanks for letting me stay here."

"So, what the hell happened?" she asked, and I smiled at her unintended repetition of my brother's words.

"I don't know. I fucked up, I guess," I said with a shrug.

"You mean because you lost the house?" Sam asked, but when I looked at Ellen, I could see she already knew what I meant, so I answered her silent question instead.

"I lost *Jeanne.*"

* * *

A few hours later, night was heavy through the window in Sam's living room. Only the dim lamp on the side table by the couch was lit, lending a quiet, gloomy feel to the room. It matched my mood exactly—the perfect atmosphere to throw a pity party.

But Ellen wasn't having any of it.

"Okay, let's hear it. I want the whole story."

Sam and Ellen had helped get me settled in their spare room and we'd had a quiet dinner together. Since the following morning was Saturday, an early day in the book-store for Sam, he'd already long since gone to bed, leaving his poor girlfriend to deal with me. Which she was apparently prepared to do.

I sighed and gave a half-hearted shrug. "There's not much to tell. Jeanne came back. Things have…changed. I've changed. I…" I shrugged again. "I *miss* her."

"You're in love with her," Ellen observed.

I nodded, not quite able to bring myself to meet her eyes. Considering my strained relationship with my brother, I didn't know Ellen all that well, and I could only assume she didn't have the best impression of me if all her info came from Sam. And Jeanne.

"Did you tell her?" Ellen asked.

I jerked my gaze up to meet hers. "Yes. I did. It didn't matter. She moved in with Mark anyway."

She grimaced. "Ugh. Mark."

My eyes widened. "Exactly. He's terrible."

She gave me a wry smile. "Oh, he's not *terrible*. But he's certainly not right for Jeanne. Of course, I'm not convinced you are either." Her gaze was sharp. "Convince me."

I slouched down further into the couch cushions. "What's the point? I couldn't convince *her*. She doesn't want me."

Ellen rolled her eyes to the ceiling. "Man, Sam and Jeanne paint a picture of you, but this sure wasn't what I'd expected."

I grunted, and she took it as an invitation to continue. "I figured you to be some smooth, suave, egomaniacal ladies' man who only cared about himself. But what I'm getting is more…woe-is-me angsty teen."

I snorted out a laugh despite myself. "Well, if you got that first part from Jeanne, I guess I'm not surprised. When we were together the first time, that's probably not too far off the mark."

"No, most of that I got from Sam, actually." Her gaze was direct. "What I got from Jeanne is that you're a great dad who cares about Dylan more than she thought you were capable of caring about anyone other than yourself."

I glanced up. "She said that?"

"Well, no," Ellen conceded. "But I can read between the lines." She folded her legs up beneath her, pulling a plaid blanket from the back of the chair to cover her lap. "I also got that you never make her feel bad for her flaws, whether it's eating a shit-ton of candy or her stubborn inability to admit when she's wrong."

I blinked, unsure how to respond, but she wasn't done. "I also got that you decided not to countersue the girl that pretty much ruined your name on social media and in all probability lost you your house, because you didn't want to ruin *her* life the way she had yours, even though legally, you probably would have won."

Jeanne told Ellen all of that? I wasn't sure what to think.

Ellen leaned forward, her gaze intent on mine in the dim light. "Obviously you've changed, Jeremy, but so has she. I know your divorce was something you both agreed on, but let me ask you this. What would you have done back then if she'd wanted to leave but you hadn't wanted her to go?"

"I would have gone after her," I said immediately. "I would have begged, and pleaded, and made sure she knew how I felt."

Ellen's brows lifted. "So, why the hell are you sitting here on my couch drowning in self-pity?"

I frowned. "That was then. This is now. Besides, like I said, I already told her I loved her, and she left anyway."

She leaned back, her auburn brows creasing as her eyes narrowed. "Tell me exactly what you said. Tell me everything."

I blew out an exasperated breath. "I don't know. We were arguing because she was going to move in with Mark, and I told her he was only taking advantage of her and trying to turn her into something she's not."

Ellen eyed me, her expression unreadable. "You were... arguing about Mark. And *that's* when you told her you loved her?"

I hesitated, and cleared my throat. "I, um...might have told her she had no backbone, too."

Ellen let out a guffaw. "Oh my God, I thought you were supposed to be charming."

My lips twisted into a smile, though I tried to fight it. "I also told her I was fighting for her, and that I loved her for exactly who she is," I said, crossing my arms.

Ellen snorted. "Well, that's better, I guess. But seriously, you sprung that on her in the middle of a fight, about Mark no less, and you're surprised she left?" She shook her head. "I was wrong. You two are perfect for each other. You're both stubborn idiots."

I glared at her, but there was no heat in it. Instead, all the heat in my body was concentrated in my chest, where my stuttering heart was coming back to life. Could she be right? Had I just gone about it all wrong, and maybe things weren't all hopeless? "So, you think I should..."

She rolled her eyes again. "You should *talk* to her. Like an adult. Tell her how you feel without arguing about it. Neither of you have to be right or wrong, you just have to *communicate*." Her wry smile turned soft. "And if she still shuts you down, then you can come back here, and I'll help you throw that pity party."

But I barely heard her words. The fire in my chest had turned into a raging inferno, and I was halfway into my shoes when I heard Ellen's voice from behind me.

"Jesus, Jeremy, I didn't mean *now*. It's after midnight."

I spun to face her, then crossed the room in a few large steps and bent, gripping her shoulders as I smacked a kiss to her cheek. "Thank you," I said, squeezing her shoulders tight before releasing her and striding to the door.

Her laughter followed me into the hallway and down the stairs.

By the time I was in my car and speeding down the highway toward Glassbury, my nerves were strung tight and my mind was racing. What was I going to say? How could I get her to listen? And *damn it*—why were there so many cars on the road in the middle of the night, slowing me down?

The hour long drive seemed to stretch on forever, until finally—*finally*—I pulled off the road into Mark's sleepy apartment complex.

The place was silent and dark. I knew it was a jerk move, approaching Mark's doorstep at—I glanced at my watch— one twenty-seven in the morning. But I couldn't quite bring myself to care. At least his apartment was an end unit with the door on the side, so I was unlikely to wake any neighbors.

I tried the doorbell, then knocked for good measure, grinning as I imagined myself throwing rocks at her window like a love-struck teenager.

I blinked in surprise at the sound of footsteps inside the apartment. I hadn't even needed to ring the bell a second time. The door swung open to reveal Mark, wearing pajamas but looking awake and unrumpled, like he hadn't been to bed yet. When his eyes met mine, the questioning look on his face flattened, his mouth twisting in distaste.

"Oh. You. I imagine this is all your fault somehow."

What was that supposed to mean?

I cleared my throat. "I know this is probably not the best time, and I'm sorry for coming by so late, but I really need to talk to Jeanne."

He let out a sigh that seemed to have been dredged up from the depths of his soul. "She's not here. Not that I'd let her talk to you if she were."

I almost laughed that he imagined he could *let* Jeanne do anything. But that was his whole problem, wasn't it? The man acted like all decisions were his to make. Well, if he wanted a subservient girlfriend, he'd sure picked the wrong woman. My train of thought derailed as his words suddenly registered. "What do you mean, she's not here?"

He let out another sigh, animosity nearly dripping in his tone. "I *mean* she's not here. She broke up with me. She's gone."

Alarm bells started ringing in my head. "She broke up with you?"

He sent me a last scathing look, then stepped back into the apartment, one hand on the doorknob.

"Wait—where is she? Where did she go?" I called as the door began to close.

The snap of his reply sounded the second before the door shut in my face. "I don't know. Go away."

I spun and jogged back to my car, emotions swirling in my chest. *She broke up with him!* But that didn't mean she wanted to see *me*. Excitement and nerves made my fingers tingle.

I cast a quick glance over my shoulder at the apartment building as I pulled out of the lot. All things considered, that had gone remarkably well. He hadn't yelled or punched me or anything. I couldn't say I would have behaved as well had our positions been reversed. But it only went to show I'd been right all along. He hadn't really loved her. Hell, he hadn't even known where she'd gone.

Fortunately, I had a pretty good guess. My heart pounded a rapid tattoo in my chest as I turned north and slammed my foot down on the gas.

Someone must have been smiling down on me, because thankfully the traffic on the highway had cleared out. The drive was still interminable though, my muscles tight and jumpy with adrenaline. If I'd been able to ditch the car and just fly back to Fairfield I would have.

Carly lived in a small, tidy house in a quiet neighborhood, and I was out of the car practically before the engine was off. She, too, answered the door faster than I'd expected.

"It's nearly three in the morning, Jeremy. I could have been sleeping."

"But you weren't. Is she here? Please, I need to talk to her."

Carly wasn't glaring, which was a good sign. In fact, she seemed more amused than irritated. If Jeanne had been upset with me, Carly definitely wouldn't be smirking. Besides, if anyone should be irritated, it was me. I'd just driven to Glassbury and back on a fool's errand.

"You can't talk to her right now," she said.

My heart stuttered. "Mark said she broke up with him. You can't tell me she didn't come here," I said.

She threw her head back and cackled. "You went to see Mark? Oh, that must have been priceless. And yes, she came here. But no, she's not here now."

Her eyes sparkled and I had to suppress a growl. Damn woman was enjoying this. She was going to make me work for it. "Can you possibly tell me where she is, please?" I ground out, forcing polite civility into my words, if not my voice.

She laughed again. "Oh, you two really are a pair, aren't

you? What a mess." She looked me up and down, then finally relented. "She's out looking for you, you idiot."

My heart stuttered again, then soared, hope igniting like a flame.

"I told her to wait until morning," Carly went on, "but she just picked up and left. She's probably already back to your fancy mansion by now, wondering where *you* are."

Oh shit.

"But I don't live there anymore," I blurted.

"What?" Carly's face twisted in confusion, but I just darted in and pressed a quick kiss to her cheek.

"Gotta go. Thanks, Carly, you're the best. I owe you forever."

I was halfway into my car when her words chased after me, all traces of laughter gone from her voice.

"Don't fuck it up this time!"

CHAPTER 15

JEANNE

"*O*h my God, shut up," I grumbled, crossing my arms in front of my chest and slouching down in my chair.

But Ellen ignored me, her peals of laughter forcing tears to collect in the corners of her eyes. "You guys are so hopeless. He left here *hours* ago to look for you. You couldn't just text each other like normal people? Or, you know, *wait for morning?*"

I sighed, my mouth pulling up a little despite myself. He was out looking for me. Even though I was an idiot who had moved in with a guy I barely knew, *he hadn't given up.*

"Should I text him now?" I asked.

"I already did," she informed me. "He went to Mark's, then to Carly's, then to the old house. He's on his way back here."

My heart sped up. How mad was he going to be that I'd led him on this wild goose chase? Though to be fair, it was hardly my fault.

"Seriously," Ellen said, snickering again to herself. She shifted, making room as Sam dropped a steaming mug of tea down in front of her. He set another one on the coffee table in front of me, and I murmured my thanks.

He grunted in acknowledgement, clearly fighting a yawn. He was up as well, chased from his bed by the noise of my arrival. After I'd left Carly's in a rush, I'd sped to the mansion only to find the place deserted and a giant 'sold' sign in the yard. Confused, I'd done the only thing I could think of—I'd called Sam. In the middle of the night. Whose phone had been answered by Ellen, who had managed to tell me through her laughter that yes, Jeremy was staying with them, but no, he wasn't there because he was apparently out looking for *me*.

Something I would know, she'd emphasized, if either one of us had bothered to contact the other one. It seemed communication still wasn't our strong suit. Something to work on in the future.

The thought chased all others from my mind. The future. Was I really already considering a future with Jeremy again? Especially after just getting out of another failed relationship?

Yes. I was.

"Ugh," Sam groaned, plopping down on the couch beside Ellen and rubbing his eyes before throwing an arm around her shoulders. "I'd never have told Jeremy he could stay here if I'd known there was going to be so much *drama*."

Ellen snickered. "Nah, it's worth it. Jeanne, tell him about the baby's room at Mark's."

Sam glanced curiously at me, so I repeated the story, which was getting more amusing with the retelling.

"Wait, he didn't *ask* you before he went out and bought… what, a nursery?" Sam's brows climbed to his hairline, sending Ellen and I both into gales of laughter.

I wasn't sure if it was the story, or the lack of sleep, or my nerves at the prospect of seeing Jeremy, but I was definitely feeling slap happy. We traded more stories, passing the time as my nerves wound tighter, until finally Sam reached across the space between us and put a hand on my knee, squeezing firmly and stopping my leg's nervous bouncing. "Jeanne, calm down. It's only Jeremy." He gave me a wry look.

That's right, I told myself. This isn't some stranger you don't know. It's only Jeremy, who I'd seen at his worst a million times. Hell, the man had been through *childbirth* with me. We could handle whatever was coming.

At that second, the echo of footsteps in the stairwell drifted through the door and we turned in unison to face the entry.

I hadn't realized I'd risen until my feet pulled me a step forward, and then the door opened, and Jeremy was there. His form filled the space, filled the room, until he was all I could see, blocking out anything that wasn't *him.*

He definitely looked a little worse for the wear. He was wearing torn pajama pants and a faded university hoodie, scuffed sneakers on his feet. His hair was a complete mess, as if he'd been running his hands through it for hours.

And though we'd been together not even a week ago, it was like I was really *seeing* him for the first time in forever. He looked...older. How had I not noticed? Thin smile lines crinkled at the corners of his bottomless brown eyes and his body was leaner than I remembered from all those years ago, more muscular. His features were so familiar, from the hint of a dimple creasing one cheek to the straight line of his nose to the thick, dark eyebrows the same shade as his unruly hair.

His face was a roiling mixture of emotions—I could see worry and excitement, nerves and exhaustion and hesitation and...hope.

I stood frozen, unsure what the right reaction was. We had a lot to talk about, a lot to overcome, and none of it was going to get resolved at four in the morning. But as I stared at him in the doorway, he looked so *unsure,* an expression that was so completely foreign and out of character for him, that I opened my mouth and let out the only words that really mattered.

"I love you."

My voice cracked on the words. I was so out of practice saying them. Had I really never spoken those words to Mark?

The worry disappeared from Jeremy's face as his lips spread in a smile, the huge, cocky grin so at home on his features, and I barely realized we were both moving until we collided in the middle of the room.

His arms came up around me as I burrowed into his chest, one hand moving immediately to cup my jaw, his fingertips skimming the soft skin there before he tilted my face up to meet his, and pressed his lips against mine.

The kiss was soft and slow, but bottomless, six years' worth of emotions threatening to overwhelm me, and I fisted my hands in his shirt as if I might collapse without him there to support me.

Even Sam's loudly cleared throat from behind me wasn't enough to pull me from Jeremy's spell, and I only dimly heard Ellen's laughter as they retreated from the room. My attention was all on the man in front of me, and I pushed closer into his warmth.

His tongue gently licked at the seam of my lips, and I parted them on a sigh. He tasted like the coffee he must have been using to stay awake, and the familiar smell of linseed oil clung faintly to his skin. I could get lost in him, in the feel of his muscular back under my hands, the sensation of his tongue against mine and the pads of his fingertips against my face.

His hand moved from my jaw to the nape of my neck, threading through my hair in such a familiar way that I had to choke back a sob, pushing the emotion into the kiss instead and surrendering myself to him completely.

I wanted this to never end. I wanted all of him, forever. My hand drifted to his cheek, scratching gently over the rough stubble there, before moving to tangle in his hair, and his groan rumbled through me, pulling an answering moan from somewhere deep inside me.

A month could have passed by the time he pulled back, a year even.

Jeremy didn't relax his hold on me though, his dark eyes sparkling as he gazed down at me, and I couldn't resist. I pasted on a mock frown. "I didn't break up with Mark just to fall into your arms, you know."

His arms tightened around me and his grin stretched further. "Of course you did," he said.

I snorted and opened my mouth to reply, but he leaned down again and cut off my words with his lips. I chuckled as I lifted my arms to twine them around his neck. Everything felt so familiar, so *right*, and there was nowhere in the world I would rather be.

EPILOGUE

JEREMY

FOUR MONTHS LATER

"*I* can't imagine why no one has jumped on this one yet, I mean, that view practically sells itself."

Paulette was in full form this morning, her red hair teased so high I was surprised it could hold its shape, her makeup so heavy you could barely see her face beneath it. But she wasn't wrong.

I stared out the sliding glass door that led from the kitchen onto the porch. The house backed up to the same ridge my old mansion had sat upon, albeit at a different angle, miles away, but the view was no less stunning for it. With winter in full force, the treetops were barren, but the wide blue expanse of sky over the scraggly limbs was still breathtaking, and I could only imagine how it would look come spring.

"Daddy, why are the walls orange?" Newly seven-year-old Dylan came skidding into the room, not bothering to wait for a reply before taking off toward the living room. "They're purple in here," he called back before disappearing completely.

"*That* is why no one has jumped on this one yet," I told Paulette with a laugh. It was true. The previous owners had painted every room in the house a different color, all of them garish. Just standing there was enough to give a person a headache.

Paulette clucked her tongue. "Pfft, you can paint over it. Honestly, homebuyers have no imagination." She turned her gaze to me and waggled her brows. "But I know *you* can see the potential in this place. What do you think?"

What did I think? I thought she was right—that view would have sold me even if the house had been a cardboard box. What really mattered was what *Jeanne* thought.

I left Paulette by the patio door and went to search. I found Jeanne in the bedroom, her eyes wide when they found mine.

"You know what I just realized?" she said.

"What's that?" I asked, crossing the room and looping my arms around her. She leaned against me.

"This house...I didn't realize it at first, but this is the house Mark wanted me to look at with him. He was all ready to put in an offer when I told him I didn't want to buy a house with him."

I spun her in my arms to face me and leaned in close. "Is he going to be mad at us for stealing his house?"

She grinned, and the sparkle in her gray eyes made my heart stutter. "He's had four months to buy it, so I think we're safe. Honestly, I'm not even sure he stayed in the area. Besides," she tilted her face up close to mine, "What makes you so sure *we're* going to buy this one?"

I tightened my arms around her, and she lifted up onto her toes, skimming her lips lightly against mine.

"Because," I whispered, reveling in the feel of her soft mouth against mine, the warm puff of her breath, "I know you've always wanted to sleep in a lime green bedroom."

She laughed and kissed me for real, her lips fitting perfectly against mine. I could still scarcely believe I could have this whenever I wanted.

"Also," she said, smiling against my lips, "Sam and Ellen might kill us both if we don't get out of their space."

While the time with my brother had done wonders to repair our relationship, I couldn't deny she was likely right. I chuckled as I pressed our lips more firmly together, loving the way she felt against me.

We only broke apart when Dylan came into the room, his face scrunched in disgust. "You guys are gross," he informed us, then proceeded to grab my hand in one of his and Jeanne's in the other, towing us out of the room and down the hallway toward the violent pink room that would be his.

"Can I get bunk beds?" he asked, depositing us in the center of the room. "'Cause they could go right here, against this wall, and then I could put my desk over *here*, and you have to promise me you'll paint this room first, but I can't decide between light green or dark green. Can Gramma and Grandpa come see it when I have it all set up?"

I shot a glance toward Jeanne as if to say *see? Even Dylan knows this is our house*, and she smiled, rolling her eyes at me before crouching down to talk to Dylan about the merits of different shades of green paint.

Watching them together, with their matching bright gray eyes, Dylan's hair the same dark shade of brown as my own, both of them talking animatedly, I couldn't begin to imagine how I'd given this up in the first place. It seemed like a lifetime ago, like a different person had lived that life, someone who didn't know how lucky he'd been.

I sure realized how lucky I was at that moment though.

How rare it was to get a second chance like this. And it wasn't just my relationship that was falling into place—all the pieces of my life were slowly coming together.

Only the day before Olivia had called to let me know that a gallery in New York had shown interest in my new series of landscapes, and was ready with a contract in hand for a show in the early spring. Book sales were picking up as well, slowly but surely, as the short attention span of social media moved on to other scandals, and I'd already started some loose planning for my second book.

I was sure there would be lingering effects from the events of the summer, but with Jeanne by my side, I was pretty sure I could take on anything the fickle art world wanted to throw at me.

"Have you checked out the back yard yet?" Paulette's voice came from the doorway, and Dylan, attention diverted, leaped to his feet and careened out of the room.

I turned to follow, but Jeanne caught my hand before I could leave. When I turned to face her, I found a serious expression on her face.

"I really like this place," she told me. "I could see us here —it's close to work, close to your parents, close to town. But…"

She hesitated and I squeezed her hand in mine. "But what?" I prompted.

"It's just…well, it's a lot smaller than what you're used to. I don't want you to have any…"

"Regrets?" I finished for her.

She nodded, and I pulled her close, forcing her to meet my gaze and willing her to see how serious I was. "If I get to spend my life with you, I won't have a single regret."

She blushed at my words.

"I love this house," I went on, tightening my hold on her. "And I love you."

"But it doesn't even have a pool," she protested, though her smile was wide, her eyes twinkling.

I brushed my lips against hers. "So, we'll put one in."

"It only has a two-car garage," she teased.

I kissed her again. "Good thing I only have one car."

"It's—"

"Perfect," I growled, cutting her off, then silencing her further with my lips slanted across hers. She sighed, parting her lips and I responded to the invitation, deepening the kiss.

"Mommy? Dad? Did you wanna see the—oh gross, not again. And not in my room!"

We were both laughing as we pulled apart and turned to see Dylan covering his face with his hands. Paulette leaned against the doorjamb of the garish pink room, her vividly painted lips stretched wide in a smile. "So, I'm guessing you like it then?"

Jeanne laced her fingers through mine, and I squeezed them tight. "Let's put in an offer."

* * *

Thank you for reading *A Fairfield Romance: Books 1-4*. If you'd like to receive an email when I release a new book, please sign up for my newsletter: http://www.lydia-reeves.com/newsletter, and if you enjoyed the book, I hope you'll consider leaving a review.

ALSO BY LYDIA REEVES

To view the complete catalogue of books by Lydia Reeves, please visit https://books2read.com/ap/nzDw1l/Lydia-Reeves

CONNECT WITH LYDIA REEVES

Sign up for my email reader group:
https://www.lydia-reeves.com/newsletter

Visit my website:
https://www.lydia-reeves.com

Visit my Facebook page:
https://www.facebook.com/lydiareevesauthor

Find me on Instagram:
https://www.instagram.com/lydiareevesauthor

Send me an email:
lydiareevesauthor@gmail.com

Copyright © 2020 by Lydia Reeves

Cover images by Wicked By Design

ISBN 978-1-7337827-7-7 (ebook)

ISBN 978-1-7337827-8-4 (paperback)